KING ARTHUR AND HER KNIGHTS: BOOKS 1, 2, AND 3

ENTHRONED, ENCHANTED, AND EMBITTERED

K. M. SHEA

ISBN-10: 0692979891

ISBN-13: 978-0692979891

❦ Created with Vellum

CHARACTERS

Adelind: Wife of King Pellinore—Queen of Anglesey

Agravain: The second son of King Lot and Queen Morgause of Orkney.

Ban: One of two kings who marched with Britt against Lot and his allies. He is from France, is well groomed, and is said to have a son who is an impressive knight.

Bedivere: A knight Britt met in London when she was crowned King. Britt chose him as her marshal on an impulse, without any input from Merlin.

Bodwain: Britt's constable and one of Merlin's Minions.

Bors: One of two kings who marched with Britt against Lot and his allies. He is from France, although he appears to be half bear. His two sons are said to be gallivanting around with King Ban's son.

Ector: The man who was selected to be Arthur's foster father. He has taken a similar role in Britt's life.

Gaheris: The third son of King Lot and Queen Morgause of Orkney.

Gareth: The youngest son of King Lot and Queen Morgause of Orkney.

Gawain: The eldest son of King Lot and Queen Morgause of Orkney.

Griflet: A young, ignorant knight who is related to Sir Bedivere and is close friends with Ywain.

Guinevere: The daughter of King Leodegrance whom Britt dislikes thanks to modern King Arthur stories and legends.

Igraine: Mother of the real Arthur. Uther Pendragon was her second husband.

Kay: Britt's seneschal and supposed foster brother. He takes Britt's safety seriously and is often seen writing in a log book.

Lancelot: The only son of King Bors whom Britt despises thanks to modern King Arthur stories and legends.

Leodegrance: King of Camelgrance, one of Britt's first allies.

Lot: King of Orkney and Britt's worst enemy. He rallied kings and knights and led them to battle before Britt and her allies overthrew him.

Maleagant: A duke and friend of King Ryence.

Merlin: Britt's chief counselor who is also responsible for yanking Britt back through time. He openly uses Britt to accomplish his dream of uniting Britain.

Morgause: Daughter of Igraine and Arthur's half-sister. She is married to King Lot of Orkney and has four sons: Gawain, Agravain, Gaheris, and Gareth.

Morgan le Fay: Daughter of Igraine, Arthur's half-sister and full sister to Queen Morgause and Queen Elaine. She is known to have magical powers.

Nymue: The beautiful Lady of the Lake who "gave" Excalibur to Britt.

Pellinore: A noble-looking king who attacked Britt with King Lot, King Urien, and King Ryence.

Percival: A Knight of the Round Table and the son of King Pellinore.

Ryence: A cowardly king who attacked Britt with King Lot, King Urien, and King Pellinore.

Tor: The son of a cowherd who is made a knight by Britt. He has a squire named Lem.

Ulfius: An older knight who once served Uther Pendragon and now serves Britt as her chamberlain. He is one of Merlin's Minions.

Urien: The brother-in-law of King Lot and a king in his own right, Urien fought with Lot, Pellinore, and Ryence against Britt but has since become Britt's vassal because he believes she holds his son, Ywain, hostage in Camelot.

Uther Pendragon: Considered to be one of the greatest kings of England. He is the real Arthur's father and died some years ago —leaving all of his lands and money to Arthur.

Ywain: The only son of King Urien. He swore loyalty to Britt after being captured by her men and has revered her ever since. Morgause is his aunt.

ENTHRONED:

KING ARTHUR AND HER KNIGHTS BOOK 1

SWORD IN THE STONE

*K*ing Arthur is a legendary British king and hero. His historical existence and role is widely debated, but he is said to have been crowned at age fifteen on the day of Pentecost. The day of his crowning ceremony, he selected Merlin as his counselor, Sir Ulfius as his chamberlain, Sir Bodwain as his constable, his foster brother Sir Kay as seneschal, and Sir Bedivere as marshal.

"Britt!"

Although the stories and events linked to Arthur vary widely, most Arthurian stories include: the wizard Merlin, Uther Pendragon as Arthur's father, the sword Excalibur, and Arthur's wife Guinevere.

"Britt, come on. Pose for a picture."

Britt ripped her eyes from the travel guidebook's blurb to address her friends. "No thanks. Commemorative graveyard photos aren't my thing."

Lyssa—Britt's long-time friend and currently one of her three traveling companions—placed her hands on her hips. "We're not taking photos of the cemetery. We're posing with this sword. It's very knightly, I'll have you know! Now stuff it and pose. You're the fencer; this shot was made for you."

Britt slapped the guidebook shut and threw it into her backpack. "I am *not* a fencer."

"Sorry, Britt. She meant that you're into Historical European Martial Arts," Amber, the peace-keeper of the bunch, said as she took a photo of Lyssa—who was pantomiming pulling a rust-covered sword from what looked like a mutated anvil.

"The point is you're the one that knows all about sword fighting. It's only right that you pose with the sword," Lyssa said, brushing her palms together to rid herself of the grit the sword left on her hand.

Britt—still not totally willing—twisted around to look at the cathedral behind which the lonesome cemetery was nestled. "Lyssa, why did you want to come here? I didn't think anything of importance in King Arthur lore happened in London. I thought we were supposed to go see the Sherlock Holmes museum at 221b Baker Street today."

"That's not true. Arthur was crowned in London before he founded Camelot. And stop worrying; we'll have plenty of time to see Holmes, my dear Watson," Lyssa said, patting Britt on the back. "Grace, you're up."

Grace—the last member of their English Book Sightseeing Extravaganza—stepped up to the sword and placed her foot on the stone before wrapping her hand around the hilt. "Cheese," she said with a big, toothy smile.

Amber took the photo before offering Britt an apologetic smile. "Tomorrow, we leave for Bath. That will be fun for you— Jane Austen novels galore. Which ones take place there, again?"

"*Northanger Abbey* starts there, yeah, and half of *Persuasion* is set there," Britt said before returning the smile. "But I can't wait to tour Beatrix Potter's farm."

"Hilltop, right?" Grace asked, zigzagging around a gravestone.

"Britt." Lyssa pulled her eyebrows together. "Stop stalling, and pose for a stinkin' picture. It's a sword in a freaking stone. The photo op is priceless! Way better than the fake one at Disneyworld."

Britt stabbed a finger at the corroded weapon. "I'm not touching that. It's rusted and gross. I bet it's infected with whatever gives you tetanus."

"*Britt!*"

"Fine, fine, fine," Britt grumbled. She hitched her backpack farther up her shoulders before approaching the weapon. "After this, can we eat?" she asked, turning to face Amber after stationing herself behind the sword. "How about some fish and chips?" She reached out to touch the sword. The moment Britt's fingertips brushed the rough rust, a pillar of light, almost like a spotlight, shot out of the cloudy London sky and enveloped Britt. There was harp music and sparkles that fell like snowflakes before Britt was shocked.

The sword felt like harnessed lightning, like a high voltage taser. It made Britt shake uncontrollably, but she couldn't let go. Her hand wouldn't release the sword. Her arm surged with electricity and pain; the world went white, and then all was black.

$\approx$

"YES, this is the future King we've been waiting for. Sir Ector, congratulations. You are the proud new father of a foundling."

Britt *ached*. Every particle of her being tingled, and her eyes were heavy and gritty. She tried to form words but was only able to utter garbled nonsense. "Gyuuu Lysssa, hwate juuuu."

"...*This* is our future King?"

"Yes. He sounds stupid, but it's best not to judge him yet. Time travel makes even the most eloquent minds slow, I would think."

Britt managed to roll her eyes open, which allowed her to discover that she was flat on her front, surrounded by shriveled weeds. Britt spat dead grass out of her mouth and rolled over. She was going to *kill* Lyssa. A priceless photo op? HAH!

When Britt rocked to a stop, she found herself blinking up at a man. He had pale blonde hair, but his eyes were a dazzling shade of blue. He was drowning in a watery gray robe topped with a cloak that reminded Britt of cold water. It was definitely a cloak, not a jacket. It was practically a dress, as it fell past his knees. The man caught Britt's gaze and smiled—a gesture so handsome, it momentarily made Britt forget about his ridiculous outfit. "Greetings, new ruler of Britain."

Britt fell out of her smile-stricken trance. "What?"

The man's brow momentarily wrinkled. "You are of the female persuasion," he said, staring at Britt's chest.

"Yeah? Are we rare in these parts or something?" Britt winced as she eased herself upright. Lyssa, Amber, and Grace were nowhere to be seen. "Have you seen three other girls around here?" She frowned as she fished a dead leaf out of her blonde hair and peered around the graveyard. It was much smaller and much newer than she remembered. Maybe getting shocked had affected her eyesight?

"A *woman* as our king?" said a man. He stood behind the cloaked hottie, next to a shorter, stocky man. Calling the speaker a man was perhaps stretching it—he was certainly younger than twenty. Both of the onlookers wore warm cloaks that almost completely obscured their knee-length tunics and the belts strapped around their waists.

Britt stared until the young man grew uncomfortable and looked away.

The cloaked hottie kneeled at Britt's side, studying her with great intensity. "The sword brought her here, which means she is meant to be our king."

Britt cautiously looked back and forth between the three men. The way they casually tossed around the word "king" had Britt's hackles raised. Had she been kidnapped by some bizarre renaissance fair cult?

The stout, older man shifted. "Very well. She's our King then.

Only a fool fights Merlin's word," he said to his young companion.

"Wait, Merlin?" Britt said. She cast her eyes at the cloaked hottie before glancing at the sword—which had not a speck of rust on it and actually glowed gold, although it was still stabbed into the anvil. "I see what's going on here. Very funny, Lyssa. It's cute, but you should have paid for this experience for yourself. I don't give two hoots for King Arthur and his knights," Britt said as she heaved herself into a standing position. She shivered and brushed her bare arms. The temperature must have dropped while she was out of it. Before the sword photo, Britt was comfortable in a t-shirt. Now she was growing jealous of the warm cloaks the renaissance actors had.

"Lyssa?" the young man in the tunic asked.

"Merlin" stood and shooed the gawkers away. "Allow me to enlighten her to our…herm…problem. It will be easier to explain without an audience."

The stout man nodded and started off through the graveyard, his gait stiff but strong. The younger man leaned back on his heels.

"Merlin" smiled and pushed his cloak aside to place an arm on the young man's shoulders. "If you would be so kind, Kay. I know this ordeal has been upsetting for you, but things will turn out. Perhaps even better than I estimated with the original Arthur. Why don't you go polish your armor? You want to look good for the glorious event, yes? Of course you do. Good day," Merlin said, escorting the young man—Kay—to the graveyard gate. He pushed him through the border of the cemetery and watched him leave before he spun on his heels and locked his searing eyes on Britt. "Now, then. What is your name, lass?"

"Britt Arthurs." Britt shivered as she peered behind a gravestone. "Lyssa, Grace? Come on, Amber, help me out here," she said as she walked through the cemetery.

"You have two names?" "Merlin" asked, strolling behind Britt.

"What? Oh. Britt is my first name; Arthurs is my last name," Britt said when she finished exploring the back area of the cemetery. "So, who put you up to this? Lyssa? It must have been Lyssa."

"I do not know this Lyssa of whom you speak. I assume she is a companion of yours, in which case, I can assure you she is neither here, nor is she aware of this dire situation in which you have found us."

"I'm sorry, what?"

"Britt Arthurs—the heavens must have selected you, for I cannot believe it is mere coincidence that you also bear the name Arthur—you placed your hand on the Sword in the Stone, and it recognized you as its master and brought you back through time —very far in time might I add, based on your irregular clothes— to be crowned King of Britain," "Merlin" said, twitching his shoulders back as he drizzled his words like honey.

Britt nodded very slowly. "Lyssa, I hate you!" She turned from "Merlin" to shout at the gravestones.

"Won't you at least listen to my story?" "Merlin" asked as he strolled up to the sword.

Britt exhaled to warm her chattering teeth. This wasn't getting her anywhere, and Grace was going to be ticked if they didn't make it to the Sherlock Holmes museum. "Okay, I'm listening."

"Some years ago, Uther Pendragon, son of Constantine II, King of Britannia, was crowned King after both of his brothers were killed. He fell in love with Igraine—the wife of his enemy, Gorlois. He sought my help in winning her over which I—ahh— did. A child was conceived between the two of them, a male who was to become his father's heir. In exchange for my help, I was given the child to raise. I took him from the palace and placed him under the care of Sir Ector, who became his foster father. He was raised as if he were Sir Ector's own son, along with Kay, Sir Ector's real son. The boy, whose name was Arthur, was never informed of his parentage, however—."

"I know how the story goes. Sir Ector and Kay didn't know either, but one day they were in London, and Arthur pulled the sword from the stone while searching for a replacement sword for his brother, and he was crowned King of Britain," Britt interrupted, tapping her nails on an icy headstone.

"No, actually. Sir Ector and Kay knew all along who Arthur was. I separated Arthur from his parents because Uther was a warmonger who was likely to die at a young age, and I wished to see all of Britain united under Arthur's ruling. I knew Sir Ector would be an excellent advisor, and Kay would be raised to be Arthur's seneschal. After all, who would make a better seneschal than your brother who won't inherit the throne if you are killed?"

Britt settled in, intrigued by the new aspect of the story. "I see, that does make sense. Please continue."

"I had plans for Arthur to learn his parentage and pull the sword from the stone when he was old enough. This year, Arthur turned fifteen, and I judged the time had arrived. But before I could inform the lad of his birthright..." Merlin the Young and Handsome looked to his feet and muttered.

"Yes?" Britt asked.

"Merlin" sighed, losing several inches of stature. "He ran off with a shepherdess over the summer months. We haven't received any word of him, and I don't think we will. Not in time, at least."

"What do you mean? In time for what?" Britt said.

"Britain will unite under Arthur's rule because it is finally ready for a true King. I have spent years gathering knights and powerful lords who agree with my thinking. Britain will not survive if our lands remain splintered with as many rulers as there are lakes or trees. We need one King, and my compatriots agree with me. But...if the King does not appear this winter— which is what we have been preparing for, for *years*—I am not certain the opportunity will arise again in this century. Simply put, this is our one chance, and Arthur has ruined it by running off. I crafted the spell that holds the sword in the stone for *him*. No one else alive can pull it."

"So, in your 'story,' where do I fit into this? I'm not Arthur. I can't help you," Britt said, stooping to reclaim her backpack, which had dropped in the same patch of weeds she had woken up in. It was time to find Lyssa and Amber and go.

"Merlin" watched her with calculating eyes. "That is where you are mistaken. After it became apparent that Arthur would not be returning, I cast a *second* spell on the sword. There is a law regarding this sword—which I tied into the spell," Merlin said, fondly resting a hand on the sparkling sword. "'Whoso pulls this sword from the stone shall be crowned King of Britain,'" Merlin quoted. "It never gives a deadline to the proclamation. My second spell was designed to withstand time and to bring the first person who touched the sword and would be able to pull it out back in time."

Britt stared at the actor, unimpressed.

"Time travel spells are very difficult. It took months to craft, but obviously it worked because you are here."

"That is a load of crap. *Time travel*? I'm sorry, even for the sake of our vacation, I'm not willing to buy that. Lyssa, Grace, come on. We weren't supposed to do anything King Arthur themed today. You promised! I'm cold, and I want to go to the Holmes museum." Britt's voice echoed in the quiet graveyard.

"Merlin" rustled his cloak like a ruffled bird fixing its feathers. "I'm sorry. I fail to see the cause of your hesitation."

"Hesitation? Buddy, you're looking at solid refusal. For starters, you have got to be the worst Merlin actor ever. You're like, wearing Gandalf's robe and cloak from *Lord of the Rings*— which works, I guess—but you can't be much older than I am. Are you even thirty? Everyone knows Merlin is as old as dirt."

Merlin narrowed his eyes. "It's not my fault Uther wouldn't listen to me without a fake white beard. I don't know what sort of brutish land you come from—who has ever heard of a woman wearing leggings?—but appearances are important here. No one is going to listen to a fourteen-year-old boy wizard. Magic is all about deceiving the eyes to reveal the truth, which is what I did."

Britt hitched her backpack over her shoulders. "You obviously have a complex. But this will not work anyway. There's no way I could be your King because I'm not British. I'm American, a *tourist*. Plus, I'm not a guy," Britt said before turning around. "Amber, I'm leaving. Do you want to come with?"

"Yes, well the law doesn't say 'whatever Anglo male pulls the sword from the stone' does it? Your gender and homeland mean nothing to me. The only thing that matters is that you can pull the sword from the stone!" Merlin snapped.

"There's no way I can pull it!"

"Prove it!"

"Fine!"

Britt stalked up to the gleaming weapon and wrapped her fingers around the hilt. She was elated when there was no shock of electricity, but irked as the grinding of metal against metal tickled her ears when she pulled the sword free from the anvil.

Britt stared at the sword, which was well made—historically accurate even. "This means nothing," Britt said, stabbing the sword back in the "stone" as Merlin smirked. "Clearly it's rigged. I'm outta here." Britt marched across the cemetery, heading for the gate.

Merlin stopped smiling and lurched after her. "Where are you going?" he hissed, grabbing her wrist. "Are you mad? If someone sees you dressed like this, they'll burn you as a witch."

"Now that's a likely story," Britt said as she stubbornly forged ahead.

"You're indecent," Merlin insisted, still holding Britt's wrist when they popped out of the cemetery.

Britt took two steps into the dirt street before she stopped. The scents of hay, sweaty men, and animal poop hit her in an overwhelming wave. There was a rhythmic, metallic clang from

11

down the street—a blacksmith nailing a horseshoe on a horse. A man dressed in a tunic walked past, his ancient nag pulling a cart full of chickens. Buildings did not stretch to the sky in cement structures but squatted low to the ground with thatched roofs and wooden walls. It was even colder outside the cemetery, and a few flakes of snow fell from the cloudy sky.

Britt turned on her heels and fled to the graveyard.

"Now do you understand what has happened?" Merlin asked as Britt yanked her arm from his grasp.

Britt cupped her hands around her eyes as she sank to the ground, her knees weakened. "I couldn't have been out for that long. There's no way Lyssa could have arranged for me to be dumped in a renaissance village after getting knocked out—unless they drugged me," Britt pushed up her sleeves and inspected her arms, looking for any injection marks.

She didn't see any, but terror and adrenaline clawed at her heart. The world started to tilt, and Britt couldn't seem to breathe enough air. "Oh, crap," Britt said before sinking back on her butt and putting her head between her knees. "*Crap*," Britt repeated with more feeling. "Am I dead? Did I die when I was shocked? It's the middle of July; why is it *snowing?*"

Merlin placed a cautious hand on Britt's shoulder. "Britt Arthurs, are you alright? I did not think there would be any ill effects of time travel, but I am sure this must come as a shock to you. It is acceptable to find yourself overwrought."

Britt jerked her head up, ready to shout hysterics at the handsome wizard. When she met Merlin's eyes, she paused. Merlin was too cute for his time. He was suspiciously cute, in fact. His hair wasn't long either, unlike his two companions. It was short and soft, *and* he had no facial hair.

Britt inhaled before she let her head sink between her knees again. "That's it, I must be dreaming. I subconsciously made up a hot Merlin. I bet I'm knocked out and stuck in a backwater British hospital because of that lightning strike. I'm just experiencing King Arthur in my dreams because Lyssa has been forcing her chivalry propaganda on me. I can deal with this. I'm just unconscious. This is all a dream."

Merlin produced a vial and handed it to Britt.

Britt hesitated. Was it wise to take a drink from a stranger? She stared up at the handsome figment of her imagination and shook her head. It didn't matter; she was dreaming anyway. Britt took a swig from the vial and almost choked. She had been expecting water; instead the suspicious wizard had fed her a bitter liquid.

"What was that?" she coughed as Merlin reclaimed the vial and tucked it up a sleeve.

"Water laced with hops." He said. "To calm you. It's used in beer."

"I can't imagine why. It tastes awful," Britt complained.

"It also had some Valerian extract in it, which would account for the taste," Merlin said as he watched Britt shakily stand. "That is it?" he asked as Britt made a small circuit around him. "No more panicking? You aren't going to shed a thousand tears?"

"Nope," Britt said, watching her feet as she walked. "No sense but to keep dreaming," she muttered under her breath as she adjusted the straps on her backpack.

Merlin hummed in approval. "Excellent. I think you will make a great king, Britt Arthurs. You handle unexpected situations quite well. I don't think you will face such a mind-boggling situation as King as you did right now. Well done."

Britt snorted but finally lifted her gaze and rolled her shoulders back. "Alright, what next?" If this was a dream, it was best to play along.

"We prepare you for pulling the sword from the stone. Officially, that is to say. Come. New clothes are in order—you must be positively chilled in that garb—and I must introduce you to your family." Merlin wove his way to the back of the cemetery before ducking into the church.

$\sim$

TWENTY MINUTES LATER, Britt uncomfortably shifted her weight as she stood for inspection under Merlin's critical gaze.

She was wearing a tunic. A blue tunic that matched the shade of her eyes and hit her knees. Beneath the tunic, she wore an inner tunic made of linen that stuck to her like a second skin. She also had on hose, or chausses, as Merlin called them. Britt almost laughed in his face when the man explained that instead of wearing pants, men wore drawers, the tunic, and the fitted socks/chausses. The final piece of her ensemble was a stuffed doublet, which was worn under her outer tunic in an attempt to flatten her chest. It worked. She was as flat as a board and more than a little grateful for the extra layer in the cold weather.

"When you are king, your curves will be easier to hide, as it will be acceptable for you to wear armor. But for now, you are nothing but a squire, so this will have to do," Merlin said, selecting a belt.

Britt cinched it around her waist. "You're going to hide my gender then?"

"Yes." Merlin picked up a comb and leather cord. "I understand that the sword found you worthy in spite of your sex. All of my cohorts will understand as well, so they will be informed of the situation. The people I want to hide you from are your enemies—the greedy, tyrant kings we seek to overthrow—and the general population. Peasants are a rather superstitious sort of folk."

"I don't see how this will work, then. My hair is long, and I've got a girly face."

"Your hair may be long for *your* time period, but here it is common practice for women to have hair to their lower back, or occasionally even their knees. Your hair is actually rather manly —if a bit better kept," Merlin said, handing Britt the comb and cord. "Tie the upper half of your hair back, yes like that."

"Gee, thanks," Britt said as she tied off her hair.

"As for your features, they are unfortunately delicate. But that can be easily explained. We will say you have some faerie blood in your family. Everyone knows faeries are fine and beautiful, and no one will think twice about the matter. Perfect. You look just like a strapping young boy of fifteen. You are tall for your age, but that will be advantageous. Arthur couldn't quite manage a beard yet, so I dare say no one will question your lack of facial hair between your age and the faerie blood."

"Fairies? Those aren't real."

Merlin flicked Britt in the forehead with his pointer finger. "Of course they are. Don't insult them, or they'll ruin your life. Now for your family. Sir Ector, Sir Kay, enter as you will," Merlin said, turning to shout the words into the hallway.

Merlin's graveyard minions trooped into the room and stood at attention.

"Sirs, this is our new King: Britt Arthurs. From henceforth, you are to refer to her as Arthur. And a him. The sword has judged her to be a worthy candidate, and she pulled the sword from the stone unaided," Merlin said, planting his hands on his hips.

"My King," the two men murmured, kneeling before Britt—who was unconvinced of the show of devotion.

"Britt Arthurs, I present to you Sir Ector and his son Sir Kay. Sir Ector took you in when you were but a babe and lovingly raised you as if you were his own son." Merlin gestured to the shorter, portly figure.

Sir Ector had a fierce beard and large ears. His eyes were kind and his stout belly jiggled as he smiled, but Britt found herself prejudice against the man.

Britt's father had left her mother when she was ten. As far as she was concerned, fathers were unnecessary cranks in the mechanics of life. It was unlikely this man would be of any help to her at all.

"If the sword finds you worthy, so do I. It will be an honor to serve under you," Sir Ector said before bending his considerable girth into a bow.

"And this is your foster brother, the churlish Sir Kay. Kay is twenty and a proper knight in his own right. Because of his great love for you—or because he wanted cheap labor—he made you his squire," Merlin said.

Although the wizard's words were mean, Merlin cast a mischievous look at Kay.

The young knight bore it well and ignored the wizard. He was taller than his father and built like an American football player— wide but muscled. Unlike his father, he sported a mustache, and —Britt noted with vexation—his hair was only a few inches shorter than Britt's.

"My King," Sir Kay stiffly said, kneeling once more.

"The introductions have been made, so let us move out. Arthur needs to meet the knights who will serve him before the tournament on Christmas Day when he pulls the sword," Merlin started.

"Christmas? No wonder it's freezing. I was visiting England in the middle of July," Britt muttered.

"We have two days, men. We must use them wisely," Merlin continued, speaking to the knights more as if they were his troops than his companions.

The father and son nodded—Sir Ector cast a smile at Britt— and left the church.

Britt moved to follow them, but Merlin caught her by the shoulder. "A moment of your time, Britt," Merlin said, adding her name when Britt raised an eyebrow at him.

Merlin waited until Sir Ector and Sir Kay were out of hearing distance before speaking. "You are going to be overwhelmed in the coming days, but it is important that you grasp this. Lean on these two men. Kay was raised to be the King's helper, and I handpicked Sir Ector out of all the knights in the realm as the one most suitable to advise and raise the future King. They are willing to serve you…and they are hurting. Arthur abandoning his responsibilities cut both of them deeply. They miss him terribly, and they regret much. It would be a kindness to them if you did choose to trust them."

Britt turned to watch the father and son disappear from view when they exited the graveyard. "I'll think about it."

2

ENEMIES OF THE CROWN

The morning of the tournament, Britt sat on a wooden bench, watching the jousts. The many knights and lords Merlin had collected for his monarchy vision over the years were scattered through the field. Britt saw one or two of them every few minutes as they attempted to blend in and act normal. The ringleaders of the movement, though, were holed up in Sir Kay's tent.

Two knights—one dressed in green and the other in red—ran at each other from opposite ends of the field, their horses snorting and prancing. They lowered their lances as they drew closer. *Crack!* The green knight was knocked from his horse.

The red knight raised his lance in victory, and the crowd roared.

Britt sighed, disgusted with the lack of realism in her dream.

A shadow fell over her. "Having second thoughts, Arthur?"

Britt bolted from the rough bench, only to plop back on it when she realized it was Merlin. "No. I just find this idea of yours unrealistic at best. This is clearly a patriarchal society. Women have no rights. I find it excessively hard to believe that your knights would rally behind a woman."

Merlin collected his robes around him before sitting next to Britt. "You are correct. Women do not rule here. But to be truthful, it is not likely you will rule much."

Britt nodded, picking three of Merlin's knights out of the crowd. "I thought as much. You have all my officials, advisors, even my top warriors picked out for me. Will I do anything but sit on the throne and give a face to your monarchy?"

"You judge too harshly. I did not mean to say you will have no power, Arthur. It takes more than a single man to change the course of history. That is why I gathered so many men. We aim to forge a new Britain. A better one. You won't rule much at first, but as you win over the men, I think you'll be surprised at the power you will find you have." Merlin fixed his eyes on her and kindly smiled.

Britt shivered. "These men follow you. *You* are the only reason they accept me as their King, woman or not. Why are *you* willing to give me a kingdom?"

Merlin looked back to the tournament. The red knight was facing off against a knight dressed in crimson. "I was taught magic by the fae. Some of the most powerful magic users are women, so I do not doubt your capabilities."

"And?"

"And...perhaps I see more than you think I do, Britt Arthurs." Merlin's smile was so slight it was barely a curl at the corners of his lips. "*I* forged the Sword in the Stone, and *I* made the spell that keeps it there. I know what is required to pull it free, and anyone who is able to do that deserves respect," Merlin said as the crimson knight went crashing off his horse. He abruptly stood. "Come now. It's almost time. You had best go speak with Sir Ector and Sir Kay before you run off."

Britt stood and fixed her warm cloak before she followed Merlin to the tent.

The past two days had been nothing but a parade of manly faces and endless drilling of names and titles. Sometime between memorizing names and choking down lamb stew, Britt had realized that her dream was not like the books. This wasn't the victorious crowning of the young Arthur where everyone knelt at his feet and adored him.

Merlin was too calculating for that.

Britt's crowning was going to be a political movement. As King, she could choose whom to empower and whom to weaken. Merlin had every knight, baron, and prince arranged in the manner he saw most fitting. It was Merlin who was pulling the strings. All of the choices were his; Britt was nothing but his puppet.

"Boy!" Sir Ector boomed when Britt entered the tent behind Merlin. (Sir Ector was trying exceedingly hard to befriend Britt. Britt didn't know if it was to make their supposed relationship believable or if it was because he was greedy for power.) "Did you get to see a joust? Are you well?"

Britt considered the question more deeply than Sir Ector meant for her to. *Was* she well? Britt didn't care if she was the beloved one true king or merely Merlin's mouthpiece. As long as the man didn't put her life in danger or compromise her values, she didn't care *what* happened. This was all just a dream anyway. Besides, how often did one get the chance to rule medieval England? "Yes, I am well."

Sir Kay slid a glove on his hand. "I will be grooming my horse. You know where to find me when you retrieve the sword, My Lord?"

"Yes," Britt said.

Sir Kay opened his mouth, as if to say more, but he shook his head and exited the tent.

Britt thoughtfully watched him go. Sir Kay had yet to call her by any name or title besides "My Lord."

"Alright Arthur, let us begin," Merlin said. He planted a hand on Britt's shoulder and propelled her outside the tent. Sir Ector followed them.

Knights, squires, spectators, and tournament officials swarmed the area like brightly colored bees. They would be the unknowing audience to the play Merlin had written.

"Sir Kay is grooming his horse, Arthur. You're his squire; why are *you* not grooming that beast?" Merlin asked. His voice was a little louder than necessary, but he acted natural enough.

Britt bit her lip in falsified worry. "I'm looking for his sword, sir. I can't seem to find it."

"What, what?" Sir Ector puffed. "Kay's sword is missing? Didn't you bring it with you when we left the inn this morning, boy?"

Britt made a show of freezing, her eyes pointed to the sky.

"You left it behind?" Merlin said.

"Maybe."

Merlin and Sir Ector shared a laugh. "He was probably distracted with all the finery and knights. Well, boy, you had best go and get it." Sir Ector patted Britt on the head—a funny gesture considering Britt was taller than him.

"I'll be quick," Britt promised before she slipped into the crowd. Merlin was rubbing his hands together with what looked like a desire to grab Britt and yank her out of the flow, but it was too late; she was already out of reach.

"Nosey wizard," Britt muttered as she traced her way to the dumpy inn she was staying at with her "family." (It was chosen for its ideal location: it was within eyesight of the graveyard where the sword in the stone was held.) "He hasn't left me alone since I arrived. Guarding his investment probably. It's not like he didn't make me walk back and forth from the tournament field to the inn a dozen times yesterday."

Britt glanced over her shoulder as she left the tournament field and entered the city boundaries. She didn't see him anywhere, but she was willing to bet Merlin was tailing her.

Britt avoided a flock of chickens and their keeper, meandered past a tailor and his apprentice closing their tiny store, and victoriously found her way to the inn. She made a show of knocking on the door—even though she already knew no one was there. The innkeeper and his wife had closed up the inn as Britt and her knightly escorts left the establishment for the tournament fields.

After a plausible amount of pounding and shouting, Britt trotted to the graveyard, uneasily skirting around snow-dusted graves to reach the sword in the stone. She plucked it out of the stone just as easily as she had two days ago and slid it into a scabbard Merlin had hidden behind the stone for the day's events.

Britt waved to the priest who was standing in the shadows of the church—the Archbishop, a great friend of Merlin's. "I bet I will wake up when it's confirmed that I am King. It's been…interesting, but I won't miss wearing chausses," Britt decided.

She left the graveyard with a spring in her step, whistling in time with the horns from the jousting tournament that bathed medieval London in noise. Britt carried the sword in her arms, her mind attentive as she found her way back to the tournament.

The tents that peppered the field were within eyesight when Britt was knocked to the ground. Someone in boots kicked her in the back of the knees before smashing her between the shoulder blades, sending her flying. The sword slipped from her grasp and fell on the dirt road with a clang.

Britt sat up and glared at two drunken men dressed in dirt-crusted chainmail. (The tournament's first losers, apparently.)

"WatCH where yAR goIN'," one drunkard laughed, his words accented with hiccups.

His companion had the high pitched laugh of a squealing Chihuahua. "Dunce," he said, spit flying from his mouth as he and the hiccuper stumbled away.

Britt started to boost herself off the ground, but she startled and jumped some feet away when someone placed a hand on her shoulder.

It was a knight, a different one. This one far more impressive and polished in his shining armor, which was adorned in white and blue. His mount, a dapple gray horse, snorted and pawed the ground behind him. "Steady there, boy. I mean you no harm," the knight said.

Britt dusted herself off as she eyed the stranger. He seemed more the kind of knight who fancied himself chivalrous than a recreant knight, but his helm completely obscured his face. "Sorry, sir," Britt said, discreetly straightening the doublet under her tunic.

The knight bent over and retrieved the sword that was previously in the stone, setting Britt's hackles up. The knight hefted it before offering it to Britt, hilt first. "That is a fine sword you have there."

"Thank you, sir. If you'll excuse me, sir," Britt said, taking the sword before backing away from him. She bobbed a bow once or twice for good measure—Merlin didn't have enough time to give her a medieval manners lessons before the tournament—before she ran, hoping to lose herself in the tournament crowd before the knight thought further of the quality of her sword. (Merlin would be *ticked* if someone stole the sword.)

Britt reached the safety of the jousting field with no further complications. She found Sir Kay with his horse, hiding behind his tent.

"Got it," Britt said, offering Sir Kay the sheathed sword.

Sir Kay leaned forward and inspected the hilt. "Well done, My Lord," he bowed.

Britt waited, but her "foster brother" did nothing more. "Aren't you supposed to take it to your father?" she asked.

Sir Kay twisted his mouth—making his mustache flatten like a unibrow. "We'll go together," he said, tying up his horse.

"That isn't what Merlin wanted, though. He thought we would catch more attention if you make a big scene and then Sir Ector makes an even bigger scene looking for me," Britt said.

"A pox on Merlin. I'm not taking the Sword in the Stone from my future King," Sir Kay grunted before he marched off.

Britt paused, deliberating on his words, before she shrugged and hurried after him, still carrying the sword.

Sir Ector was stationed just outside the tent, pulling on an ear. His forehead wrinkled when he saw both Sir Kay *and* Britt, but he took it in stride. "What's the matter, sons?" he asked.

"Arthur's gone and brought me a sword that isn't mine," Sir Kay said.

Britt looked questioningly at the tall man. That wasn't what Merlin had instructed him to say at all. Hissing captured Britt's attention, and she looked around. Merlin was some feet away, glaring at Sir Kay and twisting the sleeves of his robe in smoldering anger.

"Well, boy? What do you have to say for yourself?" Sir Ector asked, stroking his beard.

Britt snapped to attention, thrusting the sword in front of her. "The inn wasn't open. I took the first sword I could find, sir."

"Let me take a look at it...What, what? W-why, this is the sword in the stone!" Sir Ector said, his eyes popped with what Britt suspected was not completely faked awe. "Arthur, you pulled this?"

"I, the inn.... Kay needed a sword." Britt dug her foot in the slushy muck of the field in an attempt to look regretful.

"How did you get it? No one can pull the sword from the stone!" Sir Ector said.

"The sword in the stone?" boomed one of Merlin's carefully placed cohort knights—Sir Bodwain, if Britt remembered correctly. He had a distinctive, craggy nose, and his skin was leathery from the days he spent outside. "Impossible!"

"But it is." Sir Ector wagged a finger at Britt and the sword. "The boy pulled it!"

"He can't have," Sir Bodwain said.

"Enough," Merlin said, entering the fray with his hood pulled up, his hypnotizing eyes glowing in the shadows of his hood. "You there, send your squire ahead to St. Paul's cathedral and inform the archbishop. If this boy pulled the sword once, he can pull it again," Merlin ordered, sticking his nose in Sir Bodwain's direction.

"Very well," Sir Bodwain boomed.

The loud conversation had caught a few other knights' attention, and as Britt and her escort left the jousting tournament, knights and Londoners alike trailed after them. A small crowd of ten or twenty additional onlookers stormed the cemetery with them when they arrived.

The archbishop was already waiting for them, of course, being that he was in on the act.

"Merlin," the Archbishop—an older gentleman with a dignified air to him—said as they breeched the cemetery borders. "I should have known it was you. What have you stirred up now?"

Merlin propelled Britt to the front of the group. "This boy claims he has pulled the sword from the stone."

"If that is so, then you may put back the sword in its place and pull it forth again," the Archbishop said, indicating to the empty anvil, unruffled by the absence of a church artifact.

"Very well. Go ahead, Arthur," Merlin said.

Britt dutifully approached the anvil, pulled the sword out of the scabbard, and slid it back into place.

"Wait! Once it has been pulled, perhaps anyone can pull it. Someone else give it a try," another one of Merlin's knights shouted.

Knights rushed the stone, scrabbling for the sword. Britt would have been run over if Merlin had not whisked her out of the way.

Britt was mildly surprised as she watched the knights strain—their faces red with the effort—as they all tried to pull the sword at once. "Yeah, this is definitely a dream," Britt muttered.

"Did you say something?" Merlin asked.

"No."

"Ah. One moment," Merlin said before he cleared his throat

and cast his arms at the sky. "Everyone, step aside! Let Arthur try," Merlin declared.

The knights didn't listen and scurried around the sword like rats on garbage.

Merlin frowned and whacked the nearest knight on the helm with his walking stick. "Move, invalid," he snarled at the knight before he bulldozed his way to the sword. "If you don't want to be cursed—" Merlin roared over the shouting knights.

The knights threw themselves away from the sword, their plate mail ringing as they knocked into each other.

"Much better. Now, Arthur," Merlin said, turning to her. "Go ahead, lad. Give it a try."

Britt adjusted the fall of her warm cloak before she joined Merlin at the anvil. She gripped the hilt and tugged on the sword —which easily slid out.

Sir Kay kneeled in an instant. "My Lord," he murmured.

Sir Ector was next, although he was slower to move, and his eyes teared up as he knelt. "It is a miracle," he said, his chest heaving.

Sir Bodwain joined Sir Ector. "We have a King again."

Some of the onlookers copied the knights and knelt with wide eyes and hushed whispers.

Britt uneasily shifted, but remembered it was her turn to speak when Merlin jabbed a sharp elbow into her side. "Father, brother, do not kneel before me," she begged, moving to stand in front of the two knights and doing her best to feign a British accent.

"No, My Lord Arthur, I am not your Father, not by blood at least. I never knew your true parentage, but you pulled the sword from the stone. You must be the son of Uther Pendragon!"

"How can this be?" Britt said.

"When you were but a babe, a stranger brought you to my manor. He gave me a great sum of gold and instructed me to raise you as though you were my own son," Sir Ector said, wiping tears from his eyes.

(For the sake of appearing impartial, Merlin had instructed Sir Ector to leave out the part about Merlin being the stranger and of knowing all along exactly who Arthur was. "It did not work for our favor, so there is no point in telling it anyway," Merlin had said.)

Britt knew what was supposed to happen next. She was supposed to fall to the ground, weeping and crying that she had lost her father and brother. The trouble was Britt was still unimpressed with the occupation of fatherhood. Britt dropped to her knees, hoping the crowd would observe her unemotional response as shock. "What a wretched day, for in it I have lost my father and brother. And mother," Britt said, adding the unscripted mother bit. She knew her tone was wooden and unfeeling, but almost everyone was watching Sir Ector and Sir Kay anyway.

Merlin moved behind Britt. "Archbishop, what do you say to summoning all the knights and princes and barons from the tournament to come to this cemetery and see the will of God?"

Brice, the archbishop, tucked his hands in the sleeves of his priestly robes. "I say that sounds wise. Let us commence with the summoning in all speed."

"You will not leave me, even though I am not your son or brother?" Britt said, reciting the well-rehearsed line.

Sir Kay shook his head, but Sir Ector replied with a fierceness that surprised Britt. "Never, My Lord."

"As long as we can be of use to you, we will stay, My Lord," Sir Kay said.

Britt looked to Sir Kay, surprised. Merlin had told Sir Kay to keep his mouth shut during the cemetery interchange. Kay met Britt's gaze and nodded before lowering his eyes to the ground. The young knight meant every word.

"Stand, Arthur. This is not a time for weeping, it is a time of great joy. Finally, Britain will have a king again!" Merlin declared as he pulled Britt to her feet.

~

BRITT STOMPED her feet and flapped her cloak in an effort to warm herself as she watched lords and knights parade past the sword—which was once again stabbed in the anvil—and grapple with it.

It seemed everyone from the tournament had turned out, intent on giving the sword in the stone one last pull. The sword pulling had gone on for most of the afternoon, and the air grew increasing chilly as night loomed on the horizon.

Britt leaned forward and tried to catch Merlin's eye, but he was busy talking to the Archbishop, planning the next move probably.

"Are you cold, boy?" Sir Ector asked.

Britt leaned back against the church. "No, I'm fine, thank you."

Sir Ector held a rough wool blanket. "Are you certain? Winter has yet to truly bare its teeth, but it is still cold."

"I'm fine," Britt insisted. She almost shrieked when Sir Kay materialized next to her and shoved a hot mug in her hands.

"Warm cider," Sir Kay grunted. "Drink it."

"Thanks," Britt said awkwardly.

The father and son stood with Britt, blocking some of the noise and excited shouts of the crowd when yet another knight failed to pull the sword from the stone.

Britt hesitated before she brought the mug to her lips and sipped. The cider was stronger and sourer than what Britt was used to. It was not nearly as sugary either, but it was warm and tasted good.

"How much longer will this last?" Britt asked, once again watching the knights.

Sir Ector turned to study the interchange. "As long as it must. There can be no doubts that you are our true King."

Sir Kay eyed the crowd. "King Lot hasn't had his chance yet. He will be your biggest naysayer."

"King Lot?" Britt asked, taking another sip of the cider.

Sir Kay pointed out a tall man who wore a fur cape and a floor-length, purple-hued tunic. His face was craggy like cliffs, and a scowl seemed permanently etched on his lips. It was his eyes, though, that caused Britt to pull back. He had clear, grey eyes that judged every person who walked in his sight. They were cold, calculating, and hard, like chips of stone.

He stood with three other men, speaking to them as he glared at the crowd.

"Who is that with him?" Britt asked.

"Ah yes. That would be King Urien, King Pellinore, and King Ryence," Sir Ector said.

King Urien was unremarkable, resembling most males of the day in build and hair length. King Pellinore was more...*noble*. He stood like a warrior, his hand resting on his sword as he sifted through the crowd with narrowed eyes. King Ryence resembled a ferret.

"They are all Lot's allies?" Britt asked.

"Not usually, no. King Urien always sides with Lot, and Ryence follows whoever seems to have the winning side. King Pellinore is most often a lone man, though. It is unusual that he allies himself with anyone," Sir Ector said, thoughtfully stroking his beard.

"Looks like he's changed his ways," Sir Kay growled as King Lot approached the sword in the stone/anvil.

The tall man pulled on the sword, his face cracking with effort even though he didn't pull until he was red in the face like the other barons, knights, and kings before him. After pulling for a few moments, he took three sweeping steps backwards and scowled at the sword. He then tilted his head up and walked away, as though the competition was a child's game.

King Pellinore was next—pulling with everything he had—and King Urien and King Ryence were directly behind him. All three kings failed.

"Trying to figure out a way around the sword to claim the throne, he is," Sir Kay said, nodding in King Lot's direction.

"He'll fail. The common folk won't let that happen," Sir Ector promised.

Britt didn't get a chance to reply as Merlin stepped in front of the sword in the stone. "All afternoon, you mortal men have tried, and all afternoon, you have failed. There is only one in Britain who is worthy and able to pull this sword!"

"That's our cue, My Lord," Sir Ulfius said, appearing behind Sir Kay.

"Right. Thanks again, Sir Ector, Sir Kay," Britt said, passing the mug to Sir Kay before brushing off her cloak.

Sir Ulfius escorted Britt up to the sword in the stone as Merlin rattled more about the sword and worthiness. When Britt was an arm's length away he finished, "and behold, here is the rightful heir to the sword in the stone."

The Archbishop—who was probably the best actor out of everyone involved—pushed his eyebrows up towards his hairline. "Merlin, who is this youth with you? Certainly he is very fair and noble to look at, but he cannot possibly be the one who is to pull the sword from the stone."

"This is Arthur, the true son of Uther Pendragon and his Queen Igraine," Merlin said, placing a hand on Britt's shoulder.

The crowd murmured in astonishment, and the Archbishop slumped back in his chair before leaning forward in well-faked interest. "But how can that be? No one has ever heard that Uther had a son."

"You are indeed correct, for I made sure to bury that fact and keep it secret from all men. For I saw it in the stars that Uther

Pendragon would die before his son would be old enough to survive the onslaught of his father's enemies *and* the burden of ruling Britain. On the night he was born, with his parents' blessing of course, I took Arthur and entrusted him to Sir Ector of Bonmaison," Merlin said, gesturing with his free hand.

Britt had to admire Merlin. The crowd was putty in his hands as he spun his marvelous story. He had enough charisma to make any modern day politician green with envy. Perhaps that was why men called him an enchanter.

"Sir Ector did not know Arthur's true parentage and raised him as his own son. If anyone doubts the truth of my words, they can be verified by Sir Ulfius, one of Uther Pendragon's own knights," Merlin said, stepping aside so Sir Ulfius could salute the crowd.

The cemetery was breathlessly quiet as people leaned forward to listen to Sir Ulfius.

"The words Merlin speaks are true," Sir Ulfius said.

The crowd erupted in a wind of whispers, and Merlin sharply elbowed Britt when she mutely stared at the sword.

Britt rocketed forward and asked the Archbishop. "May I try my hand at pulling the sword?"

The Archbishop inclined his head. "Indeed, all may try. I pray that the grace of God will shine upon you."

Britt knew she could pull the sword from the stone, but as Britt approached the anvil, her heart pounded in her throat, and her ears buzzed. She could feel the weight of the stares.

What if she couldn't pull it?

"Of course I can pull it. This is *my* dream—even if it is an unfortunate setting," Britt muttered before she placed a hand on the sword. She could feel a sudden ray of sunlight cast upon her back as she pulled the sword out of the anvil. The ring of its metal blade pulling free from the anvil echoed in the graveyard.

Britt swung the sword once over her head—where it caught the sunlight and cast dazzling rays like small strikes of lightning

31

—before resting the tip on the ground. Britt settled into a relaxed stance and finally gathered the courage to look at the assembly.

Mostly people had slack, shocked faces. Jaws hung open, and more than a few men rubbed their eyes to clear them.

Britt glanced at Merlin, but he seemed unaffected by the silence and was grinning in triumph.

Britt opened her mouth to whisper to the self-professed wizard, but instead jumped and almost bolted when the crowd roared.

Most of those present—the knights, barons, princes, and kings—raised their voices and shouted together in an alarming cry that shook Britt's bones. It took her almost a minute before she realized it was not a war cry, but a statement of jubilation.

It was a good ten minutes before the assembly had finally quieted down enough for anyone to be heard. Unfortunately, the first audible words were not ones of encouragement.

"Surely you jest that this beardless youth would be set before us as our King," King Lot said. His voice was deep and fathomless, like the darkest and longest of caves. "This must be a plot crafted by Merlin and Sir Ulfius to further their power. I will have none of it, nor will I have this mere *boy* as my king!"

"Here, here!" King Urien shouted.

"He is no King. He is not even a warrior. What honor does he have?" King Pellinore demanded, sparkling in his black armor.

"He has pulled the sword from the stone. It is a sign from the heavens; we cannot go against it," another knight argued. (Britt was fairly certain he was one of Merlin's.)

"I believe Merlin!"

Merlin leaned closer to Britt and muttered over the loud argument. "Sheathe the sword back in the anvil, and pull it out again. Do it at least two more times. We must show them you are capable of pulling it."

Britt did as she was told, and when she plucked it out of the anvil for a fourth time, the Archbishop, who was watching, spoke. "Has Arthur not performed a great miracle? Each of you has tried your hand at pulling the sword from the stone—yes, even you, King Lot. It is known that whoso pulls the sword forth shall be King of Britain. Do you doubt the words of the sword? How then can you naysay Arthur as your ruler?"

"We are not satisfied. We would have a different sort of ruler than a beardless boy who knows nothing, and whose pedigree is attested to by one knight and a petty wizard," King Lot snarled. "We will not be satisfied until another trial is held that more men of Britain might have a chance to pull the sword," King Lot snarled before he left the graveyard, with King Pellinore, King Urien, and King Ryence at his heels.

3

CROWNING THE KING

Britt was stormed by knights and noblemen as Merlin slipped off to the Archbishop's side. Although many of the knights rallied around Britt, it was decided that there would be another trial to see if anyone else could pull the sword from the stone at Candlemas.

"Don't scowl so, Arthur. Those who attempt to pull the sword from the stone and fail—and they *will* fail—then have no rightful claim to the throne. This will make your crowning that much easier," Merlin insisted.

Britt was unconvinced that another trial would win her more supporters, but mostly she was surprised that she hadn't woken up from her dream yet. She supposed it probably was because she hadn't been crowned king yet, so she was relatively amiable to Merlin's wishes and agreed to another trial.

Candlemas was the second of February. The day was chosen for the sword trial to give men enough time to travel from all parts of Britain to London. Merlin used the time to make more allies and further educate Britt in the ways of medieval society. For hours each day, she was forced to study military campaigns, charts of nobility, and religion.

Britt was somewhat surprised, though, that it was Sir Kay and Sir Ector who thought of the more useful sorts of knowledge.

"Tell me, Arthur. Do you know how to ride a horse?" Sir Ector asked one day as he stood with Britt and Sir Kay in the stables. (The father and son were her assigned babysitters for the day as Merlin was meeting with King Leodegrance—one of the kings who was not opposed to her.)

"I do," Britt said as she watched Sir Kay clean his saddle. "I'm not on a knightly level, though. I can keep my seat, and I know the paces, but I can't even jump. My sister was the real horsewoman of the family. I only learned because of her."

Sir Kay grunted.

"It will be good enough. Your skills will increase when we leave London and begin riding again. London. Hmmph. No one rides in London. Everybody walks everywhere," Sir Ector said, shaking his head.

"But I don't even have a horse," Britt argued.

"Nonsense, Merlin and I picked out a sweet little bay mare for you not two nights ago when I reminded him you would need a mount. That wizard is so absorbed in the future, he sometimes forgets the simplest things. Ah, where was I? Oh, yes. Your mare." Sir Ector said, stopping in front of a stall that housed a small horse.

Britt slipped into the stall with the mare and set about introducing herself to her horse. The mare was plainly well broke and well trained. A child could have ridden her saddle-less without any trouble. Britt felt a little insulted—she wasn't *that* bad of a rider—but reasoned it was probably for the best. Britt had no desire to ride a stallion, like Sir Kay did.

"Sir Ulfius owes me a drink. He thought you wouldn't know how to ride," Sir Ector laughed.

"Well, normally he would have been right. People in the future don't typically ride horses," Britt said as she ran her hand down the mare's neck.

"They don't know how to ride? How do they get around then?" Sir Ector said, sounding dismayed.

"Ahh, we have horseless carriages," Britt said.

"Sounds like sorcery to me," Sir Ector snorted. "Kay, what's wrong boy?"

The knight had paused in the middle of buffing his saddle. "My Lord," he said, his voice almost strangled sounding. "Do you know how to handle a sword?"

"I do. I can fight loads better than I can ride," Britt said, hanging her arms over the stall door.

"How good are you?" Sir Kay asked.

Britt bit her lip. "I don't really know. I was good compared to the students I practiced with...but swordsmanship as a hobby is even more rare than horseback riding in my time."

"A *hobby?*" Sir Ector said, his voice trilling.

"Do you mind if we spar?" Sir Kay asked as he stood, abandoning his tack. He seemed strangely intense. "I would like to observe your skills."

"Sure," Britt shrugged, exiting the stall.

Sir Ector tried to talk Britt out of it as she and Sir Kay walked through the cold streets to a meadow outside of the city limits. He fell silent, however, when Britt and Sir Kay started fighting.

"That will do," Sir Kay declared after three matches. Britt had won all three, but she reasoned that the knight had to be holding back. How else could she beat him?

Sir Ector was speechless.

"Am I no good?" Britt worriedly asked, glancing at her "foster father."

"Britt you are..." Sir Ector trailed off before kneeling. "My Lord," he said.

"My Lord," Sir Kay echoed, joining his father on the ground.

THE CANDLEMAS TRIAL came and went. It was utterly unremarkable to Britt, perhaps even boring. Many knights, kings, and barons showed up. All of them tried pulling the sword, and all of them failed. Britt pulled the sword from the stone and stabbed it back in the stone multiple times, freezing because it had finally snowed and the wind cut through all but the warmest of cloaks. Lot and his allies were not moved.

A third trial was scheduled at Easter. Britt felt for sure she would wake up from her unusually long nap by then, but the trial came, men came, and no one could pull the sword but Britt. The days passed by in a haze. Britt almost felt as though she had been stuck in London for a few days instead of months. But that was how dreams worked, or so Britt supposed.

Since she first pulled the sword from the stone on the day of the Christmas tournament, Merlin had banned her from wandering around alone. Sir Kay was Britt's escort of choice as he usually left her alone or practiced riding and swordsmanship with her. If Britt was with any of the older knights—or even worse, Merlin—she was usually coerced into learning more about her allies and enemies. (And frankly Britt did not care that King Lot preferred red roan horses to chestnut-colored ones.)

"This isn't working. Your plan to unite Britain is going to fail, Merlin," Britt yawned. She was riding out the Easter trial in the comforts of a pub.

"It's working," Merlin said, running a hand through his light blonde hair. "I didn't think everyone would immediately accept you as King. I planned for it to take a season. What you have not noticed is that each and every time you pull the sword from the stone, more men join our cause," Merlin said, stabbing a finger at Britt.

"What do you mean?"

"The commoners. Peasants, they are deeply in love with you already. Knights respect those who are known for battle prowess, the will of God, royalty, and magic. You might appear to be green in the art of battle, but the sword proves the other three. Mark my words that many a knight thinks you are the true King."

"At this rate, I'm going to wake up before I am crowned king," Britt muttered.

"What did you say?" asked the sharp-eared Merlin.

"Nothing. If this doesn't work out, will you send me home?"

"It will work out. It must," Merlin said, suddenly involved in studying the pattern of the wooden table.

Britt frowned as she watched the enchanter avoid her gaze. "What aren't you telling me, Merlin?"

Merlin took a sip of his drink and muttered into his mug.

"Merlin," Britt repeated.

Merlin sighed. "I can't send you back to your time."

Alarm shot through Britt, and the world spun before she reminded herself that it didn't matter because it was just a dream anyway. "Oh?"

"It's easy to bring a person from the future to the past because to that person, it is history. It has already happened, and they could learn about it if they searched. Once in the past, though, it is very difficult to send a person to the future because no one knows the future," Merlin said.

"So you're saying you could keep sending me back through history, but I would never be able to come forward through time," Britt said, ice settling over her heart.

"That is correct. The faeries are more able to conduct time travel, but only a select few can manage it, and it is forbidden as it would wreak chaos on the fabric of time," Merlin said.

"I see. Good thing this is all just a dream then," Britt muttered to herself before she rubbed the back of her neck, unable to cast off the feeling unease.

A FOURTH TRIAL was scheduled for Pentecost.

"This could go on forever," Britt complained the morning of the Pentecost trial. She fed a carrot to Sir Kay's horse as the quiet knight brushed it.

"Merlin will end it soon, My Lord," Sir Kay said, running a hand down his horse's front left leg. He still had an aversion to calling her Britt or Arthur.

Britt picked up a brush and turned to her horse. "I'm starting to doubt he will. We've been at this for months," she said as the mare nuzzled her.

"Merlin will see it through. He is nothing if not determined and filled with perseverance. He planned for this when he was but a child himself. He will put you on the throne," Sir Kay said.

At that moment, Merlin banged into the stables, upsetting Britt and the horses.

"What are you doing out here? The trial starts at noon! You're filthy and wretched-looking," Merlin said, clearly aghast.

Britt dusted horse hair off her tunic. "Always the charmer, aren't you? But who cares when the trial starts? I'm only needed for the last few minutes, and it's just going to end with scheduling another."

"No, it will not. Brice—the Archbishop—has decided enough is enough. He is going to crown you today regardless of the dissatisfaction of King Lot and his conspirators. Come lad. You need to be properly dressed."

"*What?*"

"You need to be properly dressed! You look more like a pig keeper than a king."

"No, before that. I'm going to be crowned *King*? Today?"

"I do not understand your shock. That has been our goal all along! Now, stop yapping and start moving. Thank you, Sir Kay, for staying with Arthur," Merlin said as he dragged Britt out of the stables.

Sir Kay shrugged, and his horse neighed.

~

BRITT LEANED against a doorway as she watched man after man pull and yank on the sword in the anvil. More than one older baron had thrown out his back during his attempt, and watching the knights strain was an easier task than listening to Merlin and his cohorts battle it out behind her.

"We need to press Arthur's heritage. He's the son of Uther Pendragon. He's the rightful heir to the throne," Sir Ulfius said.

"A royal pedigree means very little to the general population. They will follow anyone who is charismatic and offers them protection. We should show our support of Arthur the instant he pulls the sword from the stone, and the people will follow our lead," Sir Bodwain argued.

"Pulling the sword from the stone is a miracle. No one besides Arthur can pull it; let us use the sword as our rallying cry," another knight said.

"That won't work. He is generally unimpressive to look at. Certainly he's tall enough, but he hasn't so much as a spot of fuzz on his chin. In spite of Merlin's best efforts, he still looks like a girl. Not to mention he hasn't a spine to speak of, he shows no ambition, and his leadership skills are woefully absent," another knight challenged.

Britt yawned—she had grown use to the arguments and abuse concerning her looks—but turned around, shocked, when she heard Sir Ector growl, "My Britt has plenty of pluck. It cannot be helped that *you* don't understand that, you great gaping fool!"

Merlin patted Sir Ector on the shoulder. "His name is Arthur," he reminded him as he passed them, his voice light in spite of the argument.

The knights spared Merlin a glance before they continued to argue the best strategy to rally people behind Britt during her crowning ceremony.

"Aren't you going to join in?" Britt asked Merlin when he joined her at the open door.

"And ruin their fun? Goodness, no," Merlin said, adjusting the fall of his storm-colored robe on his shoulders.

"You usually run these types of conversations with an iron fist, though. You become a bulldog over anything that has to do with my rule," Britt said.

"A bull-dog? What a hideous image. And no, I intend to leave the knights be for several reasons. The foremost being that it will keep them occupied."

"Oh? Aren't you worried about getting the peasants to like me?" Britt asked.

"No, not at all," Merlin shook his head.

"Why not?"

"We have no reason to court them because, as I have previously mentioned, they're already in love with you. Now, the moment is here. Come. It's your chance to pull the sword from the stone," Merlin said, stepping into the cemetery.

"But shouldn't we—?" Britt trailed off and pointed over her shoulder where all the knights (excluding Sir Kay) were still arguing.

"Nay. They'll merely get in our way. Come along, Arthur," Merlin said, pushing his way through the crowded cemetery.

Britt reluctantly followed, lingering at Merlin's elbow when he reached the sword in the stone, cutting in line. "Archbishop," Merlin boomed. "Today marks the fourth trial, the fourth day men have come from near and far to pull the sword from the stone. For the three trials before this, Arthur has been the only one to pull and sheathe the sword in the stone. Do we let him try again today?"

The peasants who were swarming in the streets, barely able to see the trial taking place in the cemetery but waiting nonetheless, clamored over each other.

"Yes, let Arthur try!"

"Give him a chance!"

"Arthur!"

"Let Arthur pull the sword!"

The Archbishop stood up—his chair had wisely been brought out of St. Paul's Cathedral for the day—and held up his hands, quieting the commoners. "Please, Arthur, do try," the Archbishop kindly said.

Britt exhaled as Merlin edged aside, clearing her way to the sword. The feeling of power and magic still oozed off the sword, but it no longer impressed Britt as it once had. She had been forced to watch too many trials and act like a performing monkey to be intimidated anymore.

Britt unceremoniously reached out and wrapped her hand around the sword's hilt before pulling it. The familiar sound of the sword sliding free was thunderous in the sudden quiet of the cemetery. Britt swung the sword once and held it above her head.

The people in the streets *roared*. They sounded angry, and their faces twisted as they shouted at the top of their lungs. Their words were indecipherable, and for a few moments, Britt was afraid they would storm the cemetery to rip her to pieces. Then those near the front of the crowd were finally heard.

"Hail, King Arthur!"

"The true son of Uther Pendragon!"

"Long live King Arthur!"

"The rightful King of Britain!"

Britt took a step back, her eyes wide as she stared at the crowd that stomped and roared for her.

Knights and barons began to join the vocal display of loyalty, some more easily than others. Surprisingly, even a number of the kings began to kneel. King Leodegrance was among the first of men to bow, sweeping his long tunic to the side so he could kneel before Britt.

King Lot and his buddies, however, glowered at Britt from the back of the cemetery.

Britt smirked at him and flexed her shoulders.

"What are you planning?" Merlin said—barely audible even though he spoke directly into her ear.

"Not much. I think it's high time I indulge myself a bit," Britt said.

"What? What are you—" Merlin broke off and lurched backwards when Britt again heaved the sword into the air, holding it above her head.

She completed a fancy twirl before stabbing the sword at the stone. It was a gutsy move—if the sword didn't slide easily in, Britt would very likely ruin the sword and break something in her hand. But the sword slid cleanly in. Britt released the hilt with her right hand and placed her left hand beneath the guard. She pushed up, popping the sword out of the stone, and balanced it for a second before fixing her grip on the hilt and performing a forward and then backwards twirl.

The little performance made the peasants cheer even louder—Britt could feel the ground beneath her feet hum—and Merlin turned white.

"What?" Britt asked, observing with great pleasure as King Lot turned red with fury.

"Good God, I never thought to ask if you could handle a sword," Merlin uttered.

"I can," Britt assured him. Obviously he didn't speak with Sir Kay and Sir Ector much.

"Is it a common trait in your time period?" Merlin asked, his eyes narrowed. Mostly he avoided asking Britt questions about the future—he was more concerned with the present than the future he claimed—so the inquiry surprised Britt.

"No. It's a lost art," Britt said.

Merlin started muttering under his breath, a strange mixture of prayers and curses based on the snatches Britt heard. Her attention was reclaimed by the masses, however, when the Archbishop approached Arthur.

"It appears, young Arthur, that the people have chosen," the Archbishop said. He opened his mouth to say more, but Merlin's knights had finally gotten themselves organized.

They—with the several dozen barons, kings, knights, and princes that had decided to join Britt—shouted in one voice. "Long live King Arthur! We will have no more delay, nor any other king, for so it is God's will; and we will slay whoso resists Him and Arthur!"

Merlin nodded in satisfaction, and the Archbishop smiled. "Come," he said, gesturing to St. Paul's Cathedral. "A graveyard is no place for a crowning."

Britt trooped inside with the kings, barons, and knights. The cathedral was not big enough to house the peasants as well, but the doors were left open, and those standing in the doorways shouted out details to the crowds in the streets.

"Put your sword on the altar, dedicating it to God," Merlin whispered to Britt as everyone settled into place.

"What? All this work for a sword I don't even get to keep?" Britt hissed.

"We will get you a better one. An enchanted one. Just do it."

Britt heaved her eyes to the ceiling and marched to the altar. She hesitated as the crowds grew quiet and dropped to her knee, holding the sword above her head. She stood, unnerved by the silence as she placed the sword on the altar.

She bounded back to Merlin, relieved as the crowd of men looked at the altar with great reverence. "Now I know how Frodo felt about the Ring," Britt sighed.

Merlin frowned. "What are you babbling about?"

"Nothing."

"Come, Arthur. It is time," the archbishop said as he swept past Britt, carrying a crown.

Britt glanced to Merlin, who nodded, before she followed the bishop. She shifted uncomfortably when they stopped in front of the altar.

"Arthur," the Archbishop started—for the first time since Britt met him, he did not wear a smile. His gaze was piercing, and his mouth was set as he spoke. "Do you vow to be a true king to all people, lords and commons alike, and to deal only in justice until your life ends?"

Britt hesitated, but she heard Merlin's soft whisper.

"Say you do, Arthur."

"I do," Britt said, forcing her voice to be strong and unwavering.

The Archbishop's face was transformed into its usual smile. "Then by the will of God and the ready agreement of man, I crown you King Arthur, King over all of Britain. Behold, your King!"

The outdoor crowds' roaring and celebrating made the indoor enthusiasm tame, but many of the knights and lords seemed resigned, if not content, with Britt as their King.

Britt idly wondered how different the ceremony would have gone if they knew she was a woman.

"My King."

Britt fixed her gaze on the speaker, a knight who was perhaps Britt's age—in his early twenties or so—who had pushed his way to the front of the cathedral to kneel.

"Too long have we delayed you from your crown. I beg for your grace and pardon on all of us, that you would forgive us for our transgression."

"What is your name, knight?" Britt asked.

"Sir Bedivere, my King."

Britt glanced to Merlin. The young sorcerer narrowed his eyes as he inspected the knight. When he met Britt's gaze he nodded almost imperceptibly.

Britt rolled her shoulders back and stood tall. "Rise, Sir Bedivere," she ordered.

The knight rocked to his feet, his posture straight as he faced her with unwavering courage.

Britt stared at him for a moment before she smiled. "Of course I will pardon you," she said as she looked across the cathedral, still smiling. "I offer my pardon to all who would join me in my new reign. Let the past remain behind us. Our future is bright, and I wish for all of you to stand with me, not only as subjects but as brothers in justice," Britt said. When she finished her speech, her smile widened—all of the speech lessons with Merlin were finally paying off.

Her smile faltered, though, in the stark silence that clouded the cathedral. Men stared at her with wide eyes. Britt saw more than one jaw drop open, and near the back of the room someone dropped a helm or a piece of armor judging by the magnificent clang.

Britt looked to Merlin, who was smiling like a devious cat that had eaten not just one bird, but a flock of them. Sir Kay stood next to him, and he appeared to be glaring at the crowd of men while his father wiped tears from his eyes.

A knight near the front of the crowd mutter, "Saints behold us, he is for *certain* of faerie blood."

～

THERE WAS a great feast held in Britt's honor that night. When Britt first ate in her coma-induced dreams, she was prepared to eat stew for every meal. She was pleasantly shocked at the great variety and amazing taste of the delicious food she had a chance to consume, but the feast overshadowed all of it.

There was pheasant, venison, geese, chicken, and (Britt was none too thrilled over) rabbit. It wasn't all meat, thankfully. There were also tarts and friend oranges, spiced wine that was served with toast, and fruits and nuts.

Britt sipped the wines and ales slowly. Her tolerance level of alcohol had gone up considerably since the start of her dream, but she was certain Merlin would not tolerate a toasted King.

Speaking of the wizard, Merlin had been Britt's shadow since the crowning ceremony. But, to make her look the king part rather than outright boss her around (as he had for the past few months), he was relatively closed mouthed and kept his advice to muttered statements.

Britt suspected the feast was trying for the bossy man, and she wasn't surprised when he shoved a piece of thick parchment at her from underneath the table. Britt took a discreet glance at the paper and recognized her own handwriting—if she wanted to be able to read anything, she had to write it; the writing style of Merlin and the knights was nearly unrecognizable as English.

It was a list Merlin had beaten into her brain: the names of his selected knights and the titles and positions he wanted her to give them.

Britt nodded to Merlin, who stood up and approached the minstrel that was wandering about, plucking an ancient version of a harp and singing about hard-to-pronounce places and people.

The minstrel stopped singing after Merlin spoke to him. The wizard nodded in thanks before cracking his "walking stick" on the ground. "We have feasted and celebrated the crowning of our new king. The time has come for King Arthur to bestow great boons, fiefs, titles, and positions on those whom he would."

Most of the banquet attendees murmured to each other in excitement as they turned their attention to Britt, but from her advantageous position at the head of the room, Britt saw King Lot and his three crony kings stand.

"We," King Lot said, his eyes cold and piercing, "will refuse any gifts this beardless boy offers us."

"What did you say?" Sir Ector roared, leaping to his feet.

"Is there a reason why he is so obsessed with my lack of a beard?" Britt sighed.

"This *boy* king you've found comes from low or unknown birth," King Urien, one of Lot's lackeys, sneered.

Sir Kay also stood and narrowed his dark eyes at the mocking kings.

"He's barely older than a babe. He can't rule yet," King Pellinore said. The ferret-y King Ryence nodded vigorously behind him.

"Indeed," King Lot agreed. "Instead, *we* shall give *him* gifts of good, hard blows on his back."

All of Britt's supporters/Merlin's Minions leaped to their feet, roaring in anger and fury.

"And that pretty much ends the party," Britt supposed as she sipped her goblet of sweet wine. She leaned back in her chair, adjusting for maximum comfort as she watched the shouting match.

"You seem relaxed for one whose right to rule is being questioned," Merlin said, popping up at Britt's shoulder.

Britt glanced at the wizard and shrugged. "Why should I be upset when I have dozens of men to be upset for me?" Britt asked, gesturing to the crowd. She frowned when she spotted Sir Ector barreling towards King Lot with an alarming amount of agility. Britt looked for Sir Kay, hoping he would stop his father, but the knight seemed to be making a beeline for King Urien.

"Perhaps it is just as well that you have become King, and not the real Arthur," Merlin supposed as he plopped down into a chair next to Britt. "He had a horrible temper and took offense to the least of things. A king of solid spirits is not a bad thing, so long as you don't appear to be a coward."

Britt half smiled as she took another sip of her wine and watched Sir Ector's progress across the banquet hall.

"I must admire Lot's perseverance," Merlin said, watching the furious king.

"He acts like a juvenile delinquent," Britt snorted as she watched her "adopted father" and the foreign king enter a shouting match.

"A what?"

"Oh, sorry. Umm, a naughty, spoiled child," Britt supplied.

Merlin shook his head. "You have such an odd way of speaking."

"Just wait until I bust out slang. I've been pretty nice to you so far," Britt said, watching King Urien move to slug Kay. The grave knight dodged the blow before knocking the king on his butt.

"So you know whom to appoint to what positions?" Merlin asked.

"YES," Britt said, watching the knight from her crowning ceremony, Sir Bedivere, shake a scrawny-looking baron who was siding with Lot.

"Excellent. In a few days, we shall set out to get you a new sword. It would be wisest to wait until Lot and his ilk leave London. The lake from which we will obtain your new sword is not far from the place I mean to fortify as your castle."

"Oh?" Britt asked, leaning forward as she watched Lot push Sir Ector, making the older man stumble backwards a few paces.

"Indeed. It is partially why I chose that particular location. The construction is almost finished, I believe. There is just a small length of the outer wall that has yet to be built. I thi—,"

"Merlin, how do we shut everyone up?" Britt asked, her throat tightening as she watched Sir Ector attempt to ram Lot. The king and knight collided.

"What?"

"I want to silence them, stop this," Britt said, stabbing her finger at Sir Ector, who was puffing as King Lot pulled a dagger.

"No harm will come out of this. There might be a brawl, but even if daggers are used, there will be no serious injuries," Merlin said, waving off Britt's concern.

"Merlin," Britt repeated.

"Very well," Merlin sighed. He got out of his chair and meandered over to a fireplace. Britt could see his mouth moving, but the hall was too loud to hear anything. When he gestured, the fireplace, the torches, and all flames in the hall burst to at least twice their original height, roaring in fathom-less hunger.

Men shouted and cowered before the sight, covering their heads with their arms and forgetting their quarrels for the moment.

"*SILENCE,*" Britt yelled, cupping her hands around her mouth.

The room obeyed—mostly, Britt suspected, because they were already half hoarse.

Britt studied King Lot for a moment before she once again took up a relaxed posture, planting her elbow on the armrest of her chair and leaning her head against her hand. She slightly narrowed her eyes and did her best to look unaffected and cold.

"King Lot, you are nothing but an old windbag. If you so dearly desire to face me in combat, it can be arranged," Britt said, her voice chilly as she stared down the king.

King Lot scowled and shrugged his shoulders to fix his cloak. "I will meet you on the fields of war," he vowed before he banged out of the room, the three other kings and their supporters on his heels.

The rest of the feast attendees spoke to one other as they reseated themselves and set the table right. Sir Ector and Sir Kay approached Britt's table.

"I'm sorry, Arthur," Sir Ector said.

"What for?" Britt asked, stretching her legs out in front of her.

"I didn't knock down that doghearted clotpole," Sir Ector declared.

"It's fine," Britt smiled. "There's always next time."

"The boons, Arthur," Merlin said as he reclaimed his chair.

"Of course," Britt said, pitching to her feet. "To start the festiv-ities, I wish to announce those whom I would have directly serve me. First of all, I bequeath on my foster brother, Sir Kay, the title of seneschal of the realm. Of Sir Ulfius—a steadfast knight belonging to my deceased father—I ask that he serve as my chamberlain. The great and wise Merlin, I do request to be my counselor, and Sir Bodwain of Britain I name as constable," Britt finished. She glanced at Merlin before she added in a rush. "Finally, I ask Sir Bedivere to serve as marshal."

Britt sat down in her chair as the people murmured and gossiped among each other. Merlin had never instructed Britt about assigning a marshal. She only knew it was a necessary job because she overheard Merlin quarreling with Sir Ulfius over who should be assigned to the position.

Merlin growled under his breath about pert lasses, but he did not seem to be as furious as Britt thought he would be.

Britt didn't know what possessed her to name Sir Bedivere as her marshal. It was an impulsive act, but she wanted to repay the knight for his loyalty.

Sir Kay stood only to kneel on the ground. "I thank you, my King, for your great generosity. It would be my honor to serve and protect you."

Sir Ulfius and Sir Bodwain—also fully expecting their positions—knelt as well.

"I will serve you for the rest of my life, my King," Sir Ulfius said.

"You are my lord and liege. Thank you, my King," Sir Bodwain said.

Sir Bedivere scrambled to his feet. "I-I thank you, my King," he said, clearly shaken in comparison to the other men.

"We will talk about this later," Merlin muttered to Britt.

"You don't like my choice?"

Merlin narrowed his eyes at her, making him look hawkish, before he stood and declared. "I will live to serve King Arthur!"

4

THE LADY OF THE LAKE

"**F**urthermore, I am your counselor. The very title implies you ask me for my opinion before you do anything at all."

"I don't think—" Britt started.

Merlin ignored her and continued. "In this case, God was merciful, and you assigned one of the best knights in the realm to an appropriate position, but don't think that will always happen! One must rely on good sense and logic, not luck," he said as he spread a bedroll on the ground.

"If he's one of the best knights in the realm, why didn't you try to recruit him earlier?" Britt kicked at a log that had rolled from the firewood stack.

Sir Kay had gathered enough wood to burn their fire for a week. They were only camping out for the night—on their way to a blasted lake to get another sword—but Britt had decided over the months that Sir Kay was the Boy Scout type. He was not merely prepared; he was set.

"Because he's young and green, and he hasn't a spot of land to his name. I went after men of influence, not legends that make maidens misty-eyed. But that is not the point," Merlin said.

"Look, Merlin, I get it. I'm not supposed to do anything

without your permission except breathe. I KNOW. You've been harping on about it since we set out two days ago. Can you give the topic a rest yet?"

"Have you learned your lesson? I think not."

Britt grumbled and looked to Sir Kay, who was busy scratching away in some sort of logbook. Britt wasn't sure exactly what he was doing, but whenever she tried to interrupt him, Merlin threw a hissy fit. Sir Ector was there as well. He was already passed out on the far side of the fire, softly snoring.

"I am not saying you are an imbecile incapable of making decisions—you handled Lot quite well. It is merely that you *still* do not understand all the ways and customs of this kingdom in spite of my efforts to educate you," Merlin said, settling down on his blanket. "Tomorrow, you *must* be respectful. The lady we are going to visit is not one of my allies; she is of the faerie. The faerie do as they please and side with no one."

"I'm going to sleep. Good night." Britt turned her back to the fire and pulled a thin blanket up to her shoulders.

Merlin poked around the fire for a bit longer, muttering the remaining chastisements he intended to give Britt, before he also turned in. Britt listened to Sir Kay rustle papers as she slowly drifted off to sleep.

Several hours later, Britt bolted upright. Fear grasped at her throat, and her heart pounded in her ears as she heaved gulps of air and stared at the fire.

It was a nightmare. Britt couldn't remember what about, but the terror that burned her heart and gnawed at her stomach felt too real to ignore.

After a few moments, Britt relaxed and glanced around the makeshift camp. Sir Kay—she was startled to see—was watching her. When he was satisfied she was well, he closed his eyes, propped up by horse packs.

Britt shifted, trying to make herself more comfortable, and

almost kicked her backpack—the one she had worn on the day she was struck by lightning and blasted into a coma.

As the days stretched into months and Britt hadn't woken up, she avoided looking at the backpack more and more. The sight of it brought a stab of homesickness and fear to her heart. Why hadn't she woken up yet? Was there something seriously wrong with her? Was this a medical-induced coma, or had she hit her head on something? Britt knew dreams often seemed to last longer than they were in actuality, but the length and clarity of this odd King Arthur dream was starting to frighten her.

Britt hesitated before she reached for the backpack and pulled it towards her. She opened it up and unearthed the British travel guidebook, flipping it open to the informational section on British mythology and legends.

"*King Arthur,*" she murmured, reading the section about the famed king, "*is a legendary British king and hero. His historical existence and role is widely debated, but he is said to have been crowned at age fifteen on the day of Pentecost. The day of his crowning ceremony, he selected Merlin as his counselor, Sir Ulfius as his chamberlain, Sir Bodwain as his constable, his foster brother Sir Kay as seneschal, and Sir Bedivere as marshal.*"

Britt went numb, and the book dropped from her hands.

How? How was it possible that Britt, knowing very little King Arthur lore, had dreamed of those particular men?

"Well, it is my dream. I can dream up information to fill a guidebook, too," Britt muttered, picking up the book again. She flipped through it, her desperation growing with each page she turned. City maps, historic notations, points of interest, it was all there, detailed, organized, and displayed.

Britt threw the book away from her. Her heart thundered painfully in her chest, and Britt started to feel light headed.

It was real. For months she had been in denial, but it was time to face the facts. This historical nightmare was real. Tears fell from Britt's eyes, and she gasped for air as she tried to face her new reality.

Her mother, her friends...would she ever see them again? Hadn't Merlin said he couldn't send her back? Could she even *survive* in this era? Britt knew very little about King Arthur, but she knew he died. And she knew he fought a lot.

"No, *no*," Britt whispered, shaking her head.

"...Britt?"

Britt looked up, wide-eyed and frightened, into the fatherly face of Sir Ector.

The older knight squatted down in front of her. "Lass, you're crying. What's wrong?"

Britt burst into tears at the kind question and babbled through her sobs. She was terrified; she was frightened; and she would never see anyone who knew her again.

"There, there," Sir Ector said, kneeling so he could reach out and hug Britt.

Britt slumped against the fatherly man and sobbed.

"What is her problem?" Merlin demanded as he sat up, his hair mussed.

"I-I want to go home," Britt spat out through snot and tears.

"Oh, Britt," Merlin sighed before he joined Sir Ector and placed a warm hand on Britt's head.

"When the night rolls back and dawn comes, things will be brighter," Sir Ector soothed, not at all bothered when Britt pounded on his shoulder with a fist.

All night Britt mourned the loss of her family, friends, and her life.

~

"THIS FOREST DOES NOT END," Britt sourly said the following day, perched on the back of her mare.

Merlin glanced over his shoulder. "It is called Arroy, the

Forest of Adventure, for good reason, Arthur," Merlin said, although he did not chastise Britt's terrible mood.

Britt glared at the trees. "That's a lame name," she said as the rest of her company moved around her in good cheer.

Sir Kay looked confused with Britt's use of modern language, but he kept silent and rode behind her, occasionally patting his mount in reassurance.

Britt's sorrow had left her shortly after dawn, only to be replaced by bitterness. Merlin and her foster family seemed to accept this and wisely said nothing. On a normal day, Britt would marvel that Merlin would willingly take her verbal abuse, but she was still too grief stricken to care.

"The lake at which I hope to obtain for you a new sword is enchanted. Although it lies close to your castle, Arthur, it is considered the property of the faeries," Merlin said.

"Fantastic. I always wanted magical neighbors."

"You never know, Britt. I have been told a time or two that faeries brew the best of ales. Perhaps you could trade with them." Sir Ector laughed and slapped his thigh in mirth. His horse seemed to share his amusement as it shook its head.

"A trade route with the faeries?" Britt repeated, cocking her head as she considered the idea. (Sir Ector was the only one out of the group to whom she was not hostile.)

"Here we are," Merlin said when they reached a break in the trees.

Before Britt stretched a large lake. It looked nothing like any of the lakes Britt had ever seen. For starters, there was no trash littering the ground, and the water was clear with not so much as a spot of algae floating on the surface. It seemed...clean. Fresh and untouched. Flowers bloomed on the shores, and further down the lakefront, a mother deer drank with her baby. Up the opposite shoreline was a wooden boat, and far out in the center of the lake, Britt could see a sword, held above the water by what looked like a human arm.

"Oh," Britt said, remembering what sword Arthur was famous for obtaining besides the sword in the stone.

"This is the home of the—" Merlin proudly started.

"Lady of the Lake, yeah, yeah. So where is she?" Britt asked as she dismounted.

Merlin pushed his eyebrows together as he studied Britt. "She will arrive shortly. No one visits the lake without her knowledge," he said as he also dismounted.

Sir Ector and Sir Kay slid off their horses and led them to the shoreline to drink.

Britt followed, exhaling stiffly as Sir Kay took Merlin's horse from him.

"What sword is that, held by the arm in white samite in the middle of the lake?" Sir Ector asked, shielding his eyes as he squinted across the lake.

Merlin nodded his head at the sword, as if to pay it homage. "It is a legendary weapon, far beyond the likes of what we seek."

Britt frowned at the wet ground as her mare shuffled into the lake to get a drink. "That's Excalibur. It must be," she muttered, making Sir Kay glance at her as he soothed his horse and Merlin's.

"Behold, here comes the fair Lady of the Lake. Allow me to do all of the talking," Merlin warned as he started down the lakefront.

Just past the deer, a woman appeared, walking in their direction.

She had pitch black eyes and ink black hair that fell almost to her feet. She was garbed in a green dress and wore a strand of emeralds set in gold. Her face was smooth and her expression was lofty. Besides the incredibly long hair, Britt didn't see anything particularly magical or faerie like about the petite lady.

"Lady," Merlin said, bowing before her. Sir Ector joined Merlin in his bow, tossing the reins of his horse to Sir Kay.

"Welcome, Merlin the enchanter," the lady said. "I have been told the new king, the true King of Britain, travels with you under your protection."

Kay juggled the three mounts, paying minimal attention to the faerie visitor.

"How do you think she gets her hair that long and beautiful?" Britt whispered to Sir Kay.

Sir Kay shrugged. "Servants?" he suggested. He paused for a moment before dumping all of the reins and digging his logbook out of his horse's pack, inscribing something unreadable on the pages.

"King Arthur does indeed ride with me," Merlin said, indicating to Britt.

Britt blinked but made no move to bow or play nice with the faerie lady, who studied her carefully.

"The rumors are true, then, that Britain's new king is not only young, but has some of the blood of my people. He has our elegance and beauty," the Lady of the Lake said.

Merlin coughed to hide his fright, and it occurred to Britt that the wizard never thought that particular lie would spread to the supposed faeries as well. "Yes, my esteemed lady. If you know that, then surely you must know why we have ridden here?"

The Lady of the Lake returned her attention to Merlin, playing her mystic role to the beat. "You have come to obtain a sword for King Arthur, an enchanted sword."

"Surprise," Britt dryly said.

Sir Kay coughed and avoided meeting Britt's eyes.

"We have," Merlin confirmed. "We would be forever in your debt if you would grant King Arthur this boon."

"I believe I have just the sword," the Lady of the Lake said, approaching the waters of her lake. She stepped into the lake until she was knee deep before she elegantly bent over and pulled a sword from the depths of the water.

"I present to you Hrunting," she said as she exited the lake waters, holding the sword in her arms. Britt noted that perhaps the faerie part was not a total sham as the lady's dress appeared to be dry.

"Hrunting," Merlin whispered, his eyes glowing as he stooped over the sword to inspect it. "The sword of Unferth, given to Beowulf at Unferth's death."

Britt looked to Sir Kay for an explanation, but the young knight shrugged in ignorance.

Sir Ector ahhed over the weapon, but judging by his lack of belly jiggling, Britt suspected he didn't know who Unferth was either.

"Hrunting, the sword which has never failed anyone who hefted it in battle," the lady said, a trace of a smile curling on her lips.

Britt frowned. Hrunting? Even though she wasn't an Arthur nerd, Britt knew Arthur's famous sword was called Excalibur. What the heck was Hrunting?

Merlin blinked. "I thought it failed Beowulf when he fought Grendel's Mother, and he abandoned it as a result. Its magic is still intact after such a failure?" Merlin carefully asked.

"Of course," the Lady of the Lake said.

Merlin smiled—the fake one he used when he knew he was about to force something on Britt that she would not like. "Thank you, kind lady. Arthur, come claim your sword."

Britt narrowed her eyes as she passed her reins to Kay—the poor knight—and stalked purposefully towards Merlin, Sir Ector, and the lady.

Merlin's eyes widened as he observed her countenance, and he shook his head slightly before hissing to her behind his clenched smile. "Remember your manners, *Arthur*."

Britt ignored the order and instead stared at the sword. It was rusted, brutish, and unadorned. "No," she said.

The Lady of the Lake blinked. "Pardon?"

"No. This isn't my sword. I want Excalibur," Britt said.

Sir Kay had to lean against his horse, he started coughing so

59

hard, and Merlin placed a hand at the back of Britt's neck and squeezed.

"I'm sorry. The lad doesn't know what he's saying," Merlin laughed.

"Yeah, I do. There's no way I'm walking out of here with a sword that doesn't work. I want Excalibur," Britt said as Sir Ector retreated—also coughing occasionally—to help his son with the horses.

"Arthur, we are guests in this enchanted place. Do not act rudely," Merlin said, his smile so tight Britt could almost hear his teeth cracking.

The Lady of the Lake sneered. "Excalibur is meant for greatness, boy. A beardless youth such as yourself is not even worthy to look upon it."

"Okay, cut the mystic crap," Britt said, shaking Merlin off her neck. "I want Excalibur, and I know you are going to give it to me."

"Am I? Are you a soothsayer *and* a king now? Did your foster father and brother teach you magic arts as well?" the Lady of the Lake drawled.

"Don't talk about my family like that," Britt growled. "And if you don't give me Excalibur, I am going to slap you back to Beowulf so fast your head will spin!"

"Brute! Is this how you treat a lady of great standing?" the Lady of the Lake demanded.

"It is when she is a stuck up snob who needs a haircut," Britt said, looming over the petite woman.

"You *rude beast!*"

"Petty wench."

Merlin was on his knees, in the throes of horror, but Britt heard Sir Ector quietly tell Sir Kay, "Perhaps we shouldn't have let the boy spend so much time in London taverns."

"You crash about this sacred sanctuary like a wild boar. You *ruin* the holiness of this place!" the Lady of the Lake declared.

"Like I care! My eyes are puffy; I have a headache; and I want to go home. Just give me the stupid sword."

"You will *never* win a maiden's heart!"

"Oh, no. Whatever will I do?" Britt asked, rolling her eyes.

The Lady of the Lake's mouth dropped. "You're a woman," she said on sudden insight.

"So are you," Britt snorted.

"Fine!" the Lady of the Lake snapped. "Take the sword—if you can. Many have tried, but no one can pull it. Good riddance!" she said turning on her heels and stalking away—still carrying Hrunting.

"How do you plan to get out there, Arthur?" Sir Ector asked as Britt marched past him.

"I'll use the boat," she said, glancing over her shoulder. She was anxious to push off the shore before Merlin recovered his mental abilities.

The wizard was still bent over, white faced and horrified.

Britt hopped in the boat, and Sir Kay handed the horses over to his father long enough to push the boat farther into the lake.

Britt eased the oars of the boat into the water and rowed out to the sword. She hadn't rowed much before, so she circled Excalibur a few times before she drew close enough to grab it.

Britt eyed the arm clasping the sword. The water at the center of the lake was deep blue, cloaking whatever the arm was attached to. Close up, Britt could see that the arm was wrapped in a sleeve made of some sort of cloth that looked like silk, and golden bracelets were fastened around the thin wrist. It was a woman's arm, for certain.

"This is weird beyond all belief. I always thought the legends about King Arthur were written by total stoners," Britt muttered as she reached for Excalibur's hilt. The second her fingers touched the sword, the arm holding onto the blade released it and disappeared into the water with lightning fast movement.

Britt barely had time to grab the sword before it disappeared into the lake. "Holy—you jerk!" Britt declared after successfully hefting Excalibur into the boat.

She took the time to admire it for a few moments, turning it over and weighing it in her hand. Aesthetically speaking, the sword was beautiful. It wasn't as ornamental as the sword Britt had pulled from the stone, but both Excalibur and its scabbard thrummed with a power that the sword from the stone did not have. Moreover, Excalibur was perfectly forged. It was smaller than Sir Kay's sword—an excellent match for Britt's height and strength—but it was beautifully balanced and wielded almost as if it were custom made for Britt.

Britt glanced over the side of the boat and shivered before rowing back to shore.

"You retrieved it?" Sir Kay asked as his father attempted to console Merlin.

Britt climbed ashore before she picked the sword off the bottom of the boat. "Yes," she said, hefting the weapon over her head.

"*What?*" the Lady of the Lake screeched from some distance down the shoreline. She gaped in utter disbelief, her eyes wide, her shoulders slack. Britt didn't think she was angered so much as she was shocked. "No man can pull Excalibur from the lake, and women are not meant to lead and wield weapons!"

"You know what I say to that? Crap. Utter crap," Britt said before she turned to face her escort. "Shall we go?"

"Yes, let's," Merlin said, having recovered to a certain extent, as he tottered over to his horse.

Britt hefted herself onto her mare's back after securing Excalibur. "Thank you, lady," Britt said before she rode after Merlin—who was leaving in great haste. Sir Kay and Sir Ector murmured their respects before following Britt.

"I am not certain it was wise to insult a faerie neighbor to her face," Sir Kay said.

"It was a great sight though. Well done, Arthur!" Sir Ector hooted.

"You called her a petty wench! Britt, whhhhhy?" Merlin moaned.

"Does it matter? I have Excalibur, and that's what we came here for, right?"

"Excalibur is more than I ever dreamed for you," Merlin admitted, slowing his horse until he rode next to Britt so he could observe the sword. "Those of us who deal in magic suspected no one would ever be able to remove it from the lake. I underestimated you, Britt."

"Thank you," Britt said with a smile.

"*However,* insulting the Lady of the Lake and demanding such a sword! Have you not listened to anything I have told you these past few days? Clearly you are in need of a reminder."

"Dang it."

5

ARRIVING AT CAMELOT

"Wait. I thought we were going back to London?" Britt said, late in the afternoon as they plodded along a dirt road, still riding in a forest.

"No. We must prepare for war, and to do that, your home base must be fortified. Sir Ulfius and the others set out shortly after we left. I suspect they arrived late this morning. As I mentioned, the castle is only a short ride from Arroy," Merlin said.

"So, it's an actual castle, with walls, and a tower, and everything?" Britt asked.

"Yes."

Britt twisted in her saddle to look at Sir Ector and Sir Kay. "Have you two seen it?"

Sir Kay shook his head, and Sir Ector said, "I have not, but I do not imagine Merlin would build you anything less than a fortress."

"What is it called?" Sir Kay asked.

Merlin shrugged. "Capital? Carduel?"

"What?" Britt said. "No, not either of those. Everyone knows Arthur's castle is called—"

"Ah, you can see it from here," Merlin said, gesturing to a break in the trees.

"...Camelot," Britt said with great longing as she stopped her horse and stared at her new home.

Britt had seen photographs of castles before; she was even supposed to tour several with her friends during her trip to England. In the photos, the castles were usually smaller than expected, crumbling or partially covered with moss, and worn and weathered.

Camelot was bright and shining. It was placed next to a river —part of the river was diverted to go directly into the castle, and was settled in a huge stretch of meadow. It was surrounded on three sides by forest, but the fourth side opened up into a stretch of green plains—perfect for grazing livestock and farming.

The walls were high, and the central structure—the castle keep—was not at all tower like, but squareish in shape, several stories tall, and, based on what peeked over the castle walls, decorated with impressive architecture.

"It's beautiful," Britt said, somewhat breathless.

"I am pleased to see that *something* has managed to impress you," Merlin said, his voice laced with sarcasm even though he wore a pleased smile.

"What did you call it?" Sir Kay asked.

"Camelot."

"Cam-elot. Camelot. It will do," Merlin said, rolling the new name across his tongue as if tasting it.

As Britt and her riding party approached Camelot, Britt could not shrug off a cloud of acceptance. The great castle before her and Excalibur strapped to her side seemed to settle around Britt like a familiar jacket or a favorite blanket.

It's not a mistake, Excalibur seemed to say.

It's not just a legend, Camelot quietly echoed.

Instead of calming Britt, the familiarity of it all made her increasingly more uneasy. "This isn't my life. This isn't me," Britt muttered as they rode through the great gates.

"Did you say something, Arthur?" Sir Ector asked.

"No," Britt said, raising her eyes to take in the bustling innards of Camelot. Soldiers and guards were posted on the walls, and commoners and servants clamored in the streets for a glimpse of their new king. "Merlin, exactly how are we paying for all of this?"

"With the treasury, of course. Before he died, Uther Pendragon named his son the next king, leaving all his property and assets as his inheritance. No one knew of the son, so I created the sword in the stone to prove Arthur's pedigree. Since you pulled it and became King of Britain, all that Uther owned is now yours," Merlin said, squinting at the sunlight. "Now, Arthur, if you would please?" he said, indicating to the crowds.

Britt exhaled and slumped in her saddle for a moment before she turned and faced the people with a white smile, set posture, and unshakeable confidence.

The onlookers went wild. Children tossed flowers at Britt and her horse, women waved ribbons in the air, and men clapped and stamped their feet.

"Hail, King Arthur!"

"Long live King Arthur!"

"Excellent work," Merlin said, barely audible over the roar of the crowd.

The shouts followed them to the castle keep, where the guards moved to block the stampede.

"Leave your horse; a stable lad will take care of it," Merlin said as they dismounted—he still had to shout to be heard over the cheering crowds that were held in check by the guards. "This way, lad."

"Sir Kay, aren't you coming with us?" Britt yelled when the tall knight headed in a separate direction.

Sir Kay shook his head. "I will meet up with you shortly, My Lord. I must check on some tasks first."

"Arthur, come along," Merlin said, pulling Britt by the neck of her tunic.

When they entered the keep, the shouts of celebration were muffled, and Britt was finally able to hear herself think.

"Are you paying off the citizens or something?" she asked.

"Paying off?" Merlin blinked. "You mean did I pay them to celebrate your arrival? No. However, everyone here at Camelot has waited for you for years. You are a rather suspicious human being. Does loyalty mean nothing to the people of the future?"

"No," Britt slowly said.

"Enough chatter. I am starving. Where can a man get something to sup on?" Sir Ector said.

"We will eat soon enough. We had best learn if Sir Ulfius and the rest arrived safely. That pet knight of yours, Sir Bedivere, was supposed to come with them," Merlin said.

Britt's head spun as Merlin led her up and down stone hallways before they arrived at what appeared to be some sort of study.

"This is your room, isn't it?" Britt asked, her eyes tracing the books and scrolls that lined the walls.

"It is. It is my study. I have quarters that are not far from yours, as well." Merlin stopped a servant in the hallway. "You there, lass. Go find Sir Ulfius, Sir Bodwain and the like. Tell them King Arthur and Merlin wish to speak to them," Merlin said.

"And send for some provisions!" Sir Ector boomed before Merlin shut the door.

Britt frowned when she found what appeared to be some sort of globe model of the Earth. "Do you think the earth is round?"

Merlin flattened his eyebrows. "Of course. Every scholar worth his salt knows that."

"Oh." Britt paged through Merlin's drawings of plant life as

Merlin and Sir Ector rearranged benches and chairs for an optimum sitting pattern.

Within minutes, someone knocked on the wooden door.

"I see you made the journey safely. Come in," Merlin said when he opened the door.

"Our ride was uneventful, but we've received some bad news from our sources in London," Sir Ulfius said, the first to enter the study. He paused and bowed in Britt's direction. "My Lord."

Sir Bodwain and Sir Bedivere were right behind him. "King Lot has gathered another five or six kings to his side," Sir Bodwain said, stroking his beard. "My Lord," he added with a bow.

"Which kings?" Merlin asked, plopping down in a chair.

"My Lord King Arthur," Sir Bedivere said, kneeling in front of Britt before he turned and addressed Merlin. Even though he was not one of Merlin's brood, he obviously knew who the real power was. "We do not know. We think them to be petty princes or dukes that are puffing themselves up. Individually, they will not add much to Lot's rebellion, but the clutch of them together might be a nasty blow to us."

"King Leodegrance stands with us, and many dukes and barons will send us provisions, but few can or will spare us any men," Sir Bodwain said. "Many knights pledged themselves to King Arthur, but I've heard reports that Lot has 50,000 men on horseback, and another 10,000 on foot. We cannot even begin to rally that number."

"So you believe we need more allies," Britt said.

Merlin and the knights turned and stared at her. Sir Ulfius and Sir Bodwain looked shocked. Sir Bedivere nodded—agreeable and not surprised. Merlin looked oddly contemplative.

"Exactly. Well said, Arthur," Sir Ector said.

Merlin rubbed his chin. "King Ban of Benwick and King Bors of Gaul might serve you well as allies. They both rule across the sea—too far away to be a worry to your kingdom, and both have grudges against King Claudas. We could offer to help them in return."

"Grudges? Of what sort?" Sir Ulfius frowned.

"I believe Claudas ran Ban out of his kingdom, and there were whispers of trouble with Bors' sons and Claudas' heir," Merlin said.

"Let us send word to them immediately, if that is the case. If we want to stand against King Lot, we will need their men as quickly as possible," Sir Bodwain said.

"Getting them across the ocean in a timely manner might be a puzzle," Sir Bedivere said.

"Leave that mess to me, but Sir Bodwain is right. Let us craft a letter for our potential allies," Merlin said, standing up. He was walking towards a workbench when someone knocked on the door.

"Is it our dinner?" Sir Ector hopefully asked.

"Come in," Merlin carelessly said, tossing scrolls aside as he found an inkwell and quill.

The door opened, and Sir Kay nodded to his fellow knights. "Is the King available for a time?"

"Of course. Take as long as you like, Arthur," Merlin said.

The knights stood and bowed when Britt pushed away from the bookshelf and joined Sir Kay at the door.

"Is something wrong?" Britt asked when the door closed behind them.

"No, I merely wished to present to you a…gift," Sir Kay said after a suspiciously long pause.

"Oh?"

Sir Kay turned and called down the hallway. "Cavall, here."

A *giant* dog trotted around a corner, up the hall, and stopped at Sir Kay's side. He was a charming apricot-fawn color with a black, wrinkled face and greatly resembled an English Mastiff.

"He's the size of a small pony," Britt said, her eyes huge as she stared at the gargantuan dog. "I bet he could take down a bear!"

"Not quite, but that is the idea," Sir Kay said, clearing his throat. "His name is Cavall. He is yours."

"I'm sorry, what?" Britt blinked.

"Cavall is to be your dog. He is a year old and well trained. He will be a suitable canine for you."

Britt scratched her ear as she stared at the dog—who hadn't so much as quivered since he sat at Sir Kay's side. "Wow. He's….He's big."

"So you have said several times."

"Will he stay at the…oh what would you call it, the kennels?"

"No. He is to remain with you. At all times," Sir Kay said, oddly firm.

"Oh. Ah, thank you. He seems well mannered, and he is very… handsome," Britt said.

"Are you afraid of dogs?" Sir Kay asked.

"No, not at all. I just haven't ever owned one, and I've never met any that are quite this big," Britt said before offering her hand to the dog.

Cavall sniffed the hand and thumped his tail several times as he lifted his soulful eyes to Britt's face.

"Good boy," Britt said, crouching in front of him to pat his shoulder.

"If you have any problems, please seek me out, or the kennel master. A boy from the kennels has been assigned to Cavall. He will see to his basic needs," Sir Kay said.

"Excellent. Thank you, Sir Kay," Britt smiled.

"It is my pleasure, my King. Would you like something to eat or drink? I could take you to a dining facility."

"That would be much appreciated, if you don't mind."

"Not at all. This way, I believe," Sir Kay said, going back down the hallway.

Britt started to follow him before she hesitated, looking back at the sitting mastiff. "Cavall, here," she called.

The obedient canine stood and padded to her side, keeping

pace with her. Britt briefly placed a hand on his head, and was surprised when Sir Kay smiled as he watched the exchange.

Catching Britt's eye, Sir Kay cleared his throat and wiped the smile from his face before speaking. "This way, My Lord."

~

"I HOPE you are pleased with your rooms, My Lord," Sir Ulfius said as he led Britt through the castle keep.

"I'm sure I will love them. You said all of my things were moved there?" Britt asked, glancing behind her to make sure Cavall was still following. He was.

"Yes. I placed Excalibur there myself this afternoon while you dined, and I brought that, that black *thing* you guarded so closely during our days in London."

"My backpack? Excellent. Thank you, Sir Ulfius," Britt said when the older knight paused outside a door.

"It is my pleasure and my duty as your chamberlain, Sire," Sir Ulfius said, sparing Britt a smile she could barely see behind his impressive facial hair before he opened the door. "The Great Chamber: your room, My Lord."

The room was big—almost embarrassingly so considering Britt would be the only occupant. She was going to *freeze* in the winter. There was a fireplace with a chimney to siphon the smoke away. A wooden stool was placed in front of the chimney, and the walls were decorated with tapestries of battle scenes. The only other furniture was the bed—which had a canopy suspended from the ceiling that cascaded over it—and a wooden bed stand.

Britt wasn't completely surprised by the room. She had roughed it out in the London inn long enough to know that bedrooms were not the personalized rooms she was used to. However, she was heartened by her backpack—which was carefully placed in the corner.

"Thank you, Sir Ulfius. It's wonderful," Britt said when she realized the knight was waiting in silence for her judgment.

The older knight nodded in satisfaction. "Do you need or require anything else, My Lord?"

"No, this is great. Thank you for bringing me here," Britt said as she—and Cavall—walked to her backpack.

"It is my honor, My Lord," Sir Ulfius said with a partial bow before he left, closing the door behind him.

Britt hesitated. Excalibur and her saddle bags were stacked carefully beside her bed frame. She sat down momentarily on her bed—pleasantly surprised by the feather mattress. She peeled up the mattress to glance at the medieval version of a mattress spring, which was formed by ropes woven and intertwined together—before digging through her bags.

After a minute, she found what she was looking for—her British travel guidebook—and got up to approach her backpack. She stopped when she reached it and nudged it with her foot. She started to crouch, intending to open it, before she shook her head and made a retreat to the bed.

"I can't look at it. Any of it. If I look at my stuff, I'll only remember what I've lost," Britt told Cavall as the dog lay down at the foot of her bed. Britt looked around her room again, cringing at the overwhelming masculinity of it, and sat down on her bed. "So, this is where I'll be living. This is my room," she said, the words tasted bitter in her mouth, and she closed her eyes against the stark reality.

Britt wanted to go home.

∿

"*THE ONLY STORY AS FAMOUS, or perhaps even more famous, than Arthur is the romantic relationship between Guinevere and Sir Lancelot —Arthur's best knight. It is said that Guinevere's affair with Lancelot destroyed Camelot and King Arthur's Court—*" Britt stopped reading and threw the guidebook, making her guards jump when it smacked against the stone ground of the wall walk.

Britt leaned against the crenellation—the wall of the walkway that was built in a saw-tooth pattern. "Why doesn't the guidebook have more information about Arthur? I don't care about Guinevere and Lancelot!" Britt spat, shivering in the chilly night air. "I've hated *them* since childhood!"

It had to be midnight or later. Time was relative to Britt since she arrived in medieval England. She knew it was three weeks since her arrival at Camelot. The days were interesting enough. Sir Kay took her riding and sparring; Merlin continued his usual/unwanted lessons; Sir Ector stood with her and made amusing comments when she held open court and listened to "her" knights argue back and forth about the best way to attack King Lot and his allies. It was the nights that were the worst. In the middle of the suffocating nights, Britt would wake up screaming for her mother, for her sister and friends, only to be hit with the realization that she would never see any of them again.

"I'm an orphan," Britt reflected. "An orphan with insomnia." She pushed herself to her feet and retrieved her British guidebook. She dusted it off, sparing a smile at Cavall when the giant mastiff slowly approached her, his nails clicking on the stone. "Gentlemen, we walk," Britt announced to the six guards strategically grouped around her—new protective measures compliments of "her" knights. (Although Britt suspected Sir Kay was the ringleader of this idea.)

As she had for the last two weeks, Britt walked up and down the walkways of Camelot's outer walls, occasionally stopping to stare out at the darkened countryside or to twist on her heels and watch the dimly lit innards of her castle.

The weather was cool—much cooler than Britt's home in America—but the endless walking would eventually push Britt into exhaustion, allowing her to sleep.

Britt placed her hand on Cavall's head and walked. The guards in front and behind her clinked in their chain mail—their matched steps beating a steady rhythm. The air was peppered with smoke from household fires. Britt couldn't smell anything yet, but she knew in a few short hours, the castle cook would be up, baking heavy, filling breads.

"So, it's true."

Britt whirled to face the speaker—who stood behind her. Cavall growled, and her guards raised their weapons.

It was Merlin. Of course. "The King of Britain paces the walls of Camelot at night like a prowling lion...or a tortured soul," he said as the guards lowered their weapon.

Britt half smiled. "You sound surprised."

"That is because I am," Merlin mildly said, his hands clasped behind his back.

"I didn't think anything could happen in this castle without your knowledge." Britt patted Cavall on the side to soothe the dog so he finally relaxed his stiff stance.

Merlin ignored the comment and nodded to the guards. "Move on to Arthur's rooms. I will return him to his quarters and back into your care when we are finished talking."

The guards saluted the wizard and left in an organized formation.

Britt watched them go, moving closer to Cavall when the wind blew across the river and straight up Camelot's walls.

"Arthur, what is wrong?"

"What do you mean?"

Merlin gestured into the night. "When Kay told me you walked the castle walls like a desperate man seeking redemption, I thought he was exaggerating. Alas, he was right, for you do look hopeless."

Britt dryly chuckled and turned to stare into Camelot. "You have such a way with words, Merlin."

"I am serious, Arthur."

"It's **BRITT**," Britt snapped. She placed a hand over her mouth to hold back additional words. "Merlin, you don't have a family, do you?" she finally managed.

"I have a mentor, an old hermit who raised me. But no, I have no parents nor siblings."

"I have a mom. She worked a lot when I was in school, but she made sure we did fun things on the weekend. She encouraged my passions, no matter how weird they seemed. Before I came here, I talked to her just about every day on the phone. I have an older sister, too. She was the one who first taught me how to ride horses. Even though I was just her kid-sister, she would let me play with her and her friends. She lives just an hour away from my apartment. We would meet up for coffee or a movie every few weeks so we could catch up. I have a goldfish and some awesome friends. One of them is my next door neighbor, Issie. She and I do our laundry together Tuesday evenings. Do you get what I'm saying?"

Merlin slowly nodded. "I do not recognize many of the activities you speak of, but I see that you mean you have a home and kin."

"All of them are dead to me."

"What?"

"All of them are lost. I will never see any of them again. Everything and everyone I have ever known is gone. Forever. I will never ride a horse with my sister again. I will never call my mom and laugh over my latest work fiasco. I can't even go by the name I was given at birth. All of that is gone. I have no one, and you are asking me *why* I seem like a desperate soul in the late hours?" Britt's voice was free of malice as she stared at Merlin with level eyes.

He was quiet. "I'm sorry, lass," he finally said. "I do not give you enough credit. You are strong. Your grieving is not unjustified. What would help you?"

Britt turned to look at the darkness lurking outside the castle walls. "I don't think anything can. Just time."

Merlin nodded before he gracefully seated himself on the ground, huddled against the parapet—the wall of the walkway. "Tell me about your sister. How did she teach you to ride a horse?"

"She taught me out of selfishness, really. When my dad left my mom, we moved away from the hall that was teaching me swordplay. Mom said between my sister and me, we could only have one extracurricular activity. Since I couldn't find any swordsmanship classes at the time, I was open for a new hobby. My sister wanted to keep riding, so she knew she had to win me over. She stuck me on this ridiculously fat pony named Chubby..."

"...My sister got into jumping and dressage. I thought dressage was dead boring, and jumping scared the pants off me..."

"...favorite horse ever was this beautiful black gelding named Orion. I rode him until his owner sold him, and then I finally found another place that taught historical swordplay..."

Britt talked long into the night. By the time Merlin helped Britt to her room, the eastern horizon was a lighter color, hinting at the sun that would soon rise. Britt collapsed on her bed and heard Cavall sigh when he lay down near her while she drifted off into sleep, remembering her days spent riding with her sister.

"DID YOU GET A NEW HORSE, Kay? He's gorgeous," Britt said, shading her eyes from the sun as she approached her foster brother outside the castle stables about a week later.

Kay held the reins of a gorgeous black horse—probably a gelding—who was kitted out in splendid tack and stood quietly behind the tall knight.

"No. This is your horse," Kay said.

Britt shook her head and flexed her fingers as she pulled a

riding glove on. "No, I have a little bay, remember? Merlin was afraid I was horse stupid and would fall and crack my head open so I got the half-dead mare."

"Yes. Merlin decided you are a competent rider and purchased this new mount for your exclusive use," Sir Kay said.

Britt grinned and folded her arm across her padded chest. "You would rather have me stick with the bay mare, wouldn't you?"

"As your seneschal and foster brother, I am always concerned with your safety, My Lord," Sir Kay diplomatically said.

Britt chuckled and squinted at the horse. "I don't get it. Why the sudden change?"

"I believe Merlin thought you might find this horse more favorable than your previous mount."

Britt slowly stroked the horse's sleek neck. His fur felt like silk beneath her fingertips. "He is a beauty. Is he—or she —spirited?"

"Not uncontrollably so. I believe he is within your abilities to control," Sir Kay admitted.

"Then what about him don't you like?"

"It is not that I dislike him, My Lord."

"Put a sock in it, Kay. If you were happy about him, you would twitch your mustache. What's up?"

"I do not at all understand what you are saying, but I will admit I am not altogether pleased with the fact that he is a courser, a horse trained for battle," Sir Kay said.

"Huh." Britt leaned back on her heels as she studied the horse. "In that case, I might agree with you. What's his name?"

"Hengroen."

"That's a mouthful. Can I rename him?" Britt asked.

"I'm not certain that is possible. He is trained—,"

"I'll shorten it to Roen. How is that boy? Do you like it, Roen?" She grinned at the horse.

To Britt's—and Kay's—shock, Roen lifted his head and nuzzled Britt's cheek with his velvet muzzle.

"Well, then," Britt swallowed, shock cooling her heart like ice. "Roen it is."

Sir Kay wordlessly handed her the reins and retreated to the stable, glancing over his shoulder at the pair and shaking his head.

Britt carefully examined her new horse to the best of her abilities—running her hands across his body and murmuring sweetly to him, glad she had thought to leave Cavall with the kennel boy for her daily ride with Kay.

When Kay exited the stable with his horse, tacked and prepped for their ride, Merlin pounced on them.

"Arthur, I see you have met your new steed," he said, tucking his hands inside his sleeves.

"Yeah. He's very impressive," Britt said. "Thank you for getting him for me."

"Indeed, I am glad you think so. I hope you enjoy him in the days to come. I'm afraid you won't be able to ride with Sir Kay just yet, though."

"Oh?"

"No. I have come to you bearing news. Wonderful news."

Britt took a step backward and warily eyed Merlin. "Somehow I doubt that. I don't often like your brand of news. What's up?"

"The heavens, of course. But that is not what is important; it is this: both King Bors and King Ban have agreed to be your allies! They are already in Britain. They are marching through London with 300 knights, and they have left an army of 10,000 horsemen across the sea."

"10,000? With our 20,000, we will have half the army Lot has," Britt said. "Didn't he have 50,000 mounted men and another 10,000 foot soldiers?

Sir Kay nodded.

"Yes, but we have a great deal more knights than Lot has. I believe if we employ stealth and other effective strategies, we will win," Merlin pronounced.

She squinted at the wizard. "You're going to go get the 10,000 horsemen, aren't you?"

"I am. You and the rest of our men from Camelot will march to our fortified camp and prepare for war."

"You're just going to let me prance off into a war? What about protecting your project?" Britt asked with a raised eyebrow.

"Sir Kay assures me you are a more than competent swordsman, and you will have Excalibur with you."

"So?"

"The scabbard of Excalibur is enchanted. Whoever bears Excalibur and the scabbard will not die from bleeding out."

"Blood loss is the only worry you have for me?" Britt said.

Merlin shrugged. "No, not at all. But you're far more valuable to Lot and his allies alive than you are dead. You will not die on this battlefield."

"How comforting."

"Sir Ector, Sir Kay, Sir Ulfius, Sir Bodwain, and Sir Bedivere will be with you. I will meet you at our camp."

"Alright. Good luck," Britt said.

"To you as well. And Britt," Merlin said, reaching out to place his hand on her cheek, forcing her to look at him. "Be safe. I have great confidence in you. You will do well while I am gone."

The wizard's usage of her real name was not lost on Britt. "I'll try," she smiled.

Merlin lightly cuffed her cheek. "That's a good lass. Right then, I'm off. Enjoy your ride," he called over his shoulder before he hurried to the stable.

Sir Kay and Britt watched Merlin mount up and ride off through Camelot before the tall knight turned to Britt. "If all is as Merlin says, we had better get you properly acquainted with Roen."

6

NEGOTIATING WITH HOSTAGES

During the preparations for war, Britt mostly felt…useless. Sir Kay was busy buying and arranging for provisions for the newly raised army and was unavailable for swordplay, jousting practice, or their regular afternoon ride. Sir Bodwain and Sir Bedivere organized the troops that poured into Camelot, and Sir Ector was almost always answering a correspondence sent by bird from Merlin, King Ban and King Bors, or any of the other army leaders.

Their departure from Camelot was rather sudden. Sir Ector received an urgent letter from one of the camp leaders, and within the day, they were out.

"Can someone please explain to me *why* we are hurrying like my grandparents when they're late for a fish fry?" Britt asked, briefly standing up in her stirrups to relieve the strain on her rear.

Roen was a much smoother ride than the bay mare, but she still wasn't accustomed to riding for hours.

Sir Bodwain rubbed his craggy nose. "It's military matters, Sire."

"Why don't we just tell the boy? He is King; he should be informed," Sir Ector argued.

"Arthur is King, but it is Merlin who must make the decisions," Sir Bodwain said.

Sir Bedivere frowned. "I do not think that is how it is supposed to work."

"Gentlemen, unless you want me to turn Roen around and ride back to Camelot, please inform me *what* has you all in a tizzy," Britt warned as her black horse arched his neck and neighed.

"Some of our men have captured Ywain, the heir of King Urien," Sir Ector said.

Britt briefly pinched the bridge of her nose. "King Urien, he's Lot's brother-in-law, yes?"

"Indeed. His wife and Lot's wife are sisters," Sir Ulfius carefully said.

"So we're hurrying to our camp to decide what to do about this Ywain guy?" Britt asked.

"Exactly," Sir Ector beamed.

"Right. And how many more days do you think we will have to travel to get there?" Britt said.

"It is not a matter of days, but a matter of hours. We will arrive shortly before the evening meal, My Lord," Sir Bodwain said.

She nodded to her escort. "Ah. Thank you."

The knights picked up their conversations of war, and Britt stewed over the unsteady future of young Ywain.

WHEN THEY ARRIVED, the army camp was in an uproar.

Sir Ector grabbed the shoulder of a knight who was running with a sheathed sword. "You there, what's going on here?" Sir Ector demanded.

"Ywain has gotten loose! We are searching the camp for him," the knight said before hustling off.

"He what?" Sir Bodwain bellowed, then followed Sir Bedivere into the thick of the swirling camp.

"Arthur, you had best stay here. This could go badly. Come along, Kay," Sir Ector said as he grabbed his sword from his horse. The father and son headed around the outskirts of the camp, disappearing from sight in the crush of knights.

Britt glanced at Sir Ulfius, who was frowning at the chaotic mess. "You can go as well, Sir Ulfius."

"My Lord, it would be irresponsible to leave you alone," Sir Ulfius gravely said.

Britt laughed. "Are you kidding? I'm at our fortified camp with a couple thousand babysitters at hand. And Ulfius, you know I'm not completely useless with a sword."

"My Lord," Sir Ulfius said, looking uncomfortable.

Britt sighed as she pulled her helm off her head—one always had to ride responsibly—and shook out her hair. "I won't tell Merlin if you won't. Good luck." She nudged Roen forward. "You can find me at the royal tents," she called over her shoulder, but Sir Ulfius was already gone.

"This Ywain guy must be a ninja. Or MacGyver," Britt said plunging into the fray. She could see the royal tents off in the distance—it was impossible to miss them. They were ornate and an all around eyesore decorated in gaudy colors and flags. "Say what you will about Merlin, but he spares no expense on my behalf. Uther must have been filthy rich."

Britt dismounted Roen when she reached her tent and removed her gloves before tightening the leather cord that held her hair back in a half ponytail. She strapped Excalibur to her side and was about to set out in search of water for Roen when she heard a hoarse cry.

"Help!"

Britt tied Roen to a hitching post and hurried to the source of the cry: a small grouping of about twenty or so men. She pushed her way to the front of the crowd—some of the knights from London recognized her and stepped aside, bowing as she approached.

At the center of the crowd was a spindly boy who looked no older than sixteen and a well-groomed man dressed in an expensive-looking suit of armor.

The boy had a dagger at the man's throat.

"Ywain?" Britt asked the knight closest to her.

"Yes, My Lord," the knight—one of the London ones —nodded.

"Why is no one approaching him?"

"He has a dagger at King Ban's throat, my Lord."

"So? Ban's wearing a full suit of armor. Spider-limbs doesn't exactly look like a seasoned warrior; he wouldn't be able to get through the mail." She thoughtfully tipped her head. "And that is King Ban, eh?"

"S-someone, do something," King Ban gurgled.

Britt looked up and down the circle before setting her shoulders. She wasn't sure how her sword skills measured to the average man of the time, but she knew that she could fight Kay, and Kay was no prancing lightweight. Unless this boy *was* a ninja —which was unlikely based on the fear she could see in his eyes —she would have no trouble against him.

Britt stepped past the boundary of bodies and into the cleared circle around Ywain and King Ban.

"C-come no closer!" the teenager warned, his voice cracking.

She held up her hands. "Easy there," she said, mimicking the voice her sister adopted when soothing a frightened horse. "I'm not going to hurt you."

Ywain's eyes were huge, and Britt could see that his hand holding the dagger to Ban's throat shook with fear. "Stay b-back!" he warned.

King Ban rolled his eyes like a nervous cow. "Someone kill the boy," he said.

A man holding a bow stirred, and Britt barked. "Don't move, *any* of you," she said. Everyone crowding around the altercation stilled.

Ywain licked his lips, his eyes darting from side to side as he looked for an exit.

"Let him go, Ywain," Britt said, her voice smooth and cool like iced coffee on a sweltering day. "I know you don't want to hurt him." She slowly approached the pair.

"Take me out of this camp, and I'll let him go!" Ywain shouted.

Britt shook her head. "No."

"What are you doing? Do what he says," King Ban hissed before gurgling when Ywain applied pressure to his neck.

"Silence!" Ywain said, his voice cracking again.

"You don't want to kill him, Ywain," Britt said, holding the boy's eyes as she drew closer. "You know you wouldn't leave this place alive if something happened to him," she said, within an arm's length of King Ban.

Ywain hesitated, and Britt struck. With her ungloved hand, she chopped at the muscles above his elbow, making his forearm pop up—removing the dagger from Ban's throat. She plucked the dagger from Ywain and tossed it away, but the boy reacted as well. He kneed King Ban in the back (making the man stumble into Britt) and grappled with the king's sword until he pulled it from its sheath.

"Oof," Britt said when the king knocked into her. She stepped back several paces to steady herself, and a knight caught Ban before he face planted.

"Stay back!" Ywain repeated, holding King Ban's sword in front of himself in a stance that was not so horrible that it made Britt grimace, but was not so good as to make her nod in approval.

Several knights unsheathed their swords before Britt shouted, "I said *not* to move!"

Again, everyone fell still—Ywain included—and she exhaled in satisfaction before she drew Excalibur from her scabbard. She twirled it once through the air in a fancy gesture she could not refuse herself before sinking into a low position, an emotionless expression fixed on her face.

Ywain slightly shifted his stance, sweat beading on his forehead as he still shook with fear.

Britt, following her training, struck like a snake. She lunged forward, landing blows on Ywain with the ferocity of a wild animal. Excalibur sang like crystal when its edge clashed against King Ban's sword.

She moved forward, pressing Ywain back on his heels as her cloak billowed behind her like wings. She struck so fast, she didn't give him time to counter strike or attempt to attack. She completely overwhelmed him.

She pushed her advantage, keeping up a seamless string of attacks to force an opening. She wrenched Excalibur, using it like a lever, and popped King Ban's sword from Ywain's hands. With the sword gone, Britt brought the fight closer to Ywain and grabbed him by the tunic. She flipped him over her knee, and he land on the ground with a painful thud.

The entire battle lasted mere seconds.

Ywain gasped, trying to get air again, and Britt stood over him, Excalibur pointed at his throat.

"W-who *are* you?" Ywain wheezed when he had enough air.

Britt gave him a business-like smile that did not reach her eyes. "Arthur, King of Britain," she said before looking up when she heard a strangled cry.

"My Lord!"

"Ah, Sir Bodwain. Perfect timing, could you take charge of our young prisoner? I need to find water for Roen."

"My Lord, you just—he—!" Sir Bodwain gaped.

Sir Bedivere, who was with him, looked curiously at Sir Bodwain. The knight still did not know the truth of her gender and identity, so he was not surprised and dazed like Sir Bodwain, but instead was approving. "I'll do it," he volunteered when Sir Bodwain did nothing but gawk at Britt.

"Escort him nowhere. I say we cut off his head right now and send it to his father. He attacked King Ban *and* King Arthur. He deserves death," a knight Britt recognized from the Pentecost feast darkly said.

"No," Britt said, glancing down at Ywain who was now ashen. "Killing him would only further enrage Urien. He lives."

"For now," Sir Bedivere muttered, kneeling next to Ywain. "One move, boy, and you will find yourself singing with angels," he said as Britt took several steps back, allowing the knight to haul Ywain to his feet. Sir Bedivere held a dagger to the boy's back. "Will someone show me where we've been holding him?"

"This way," a knight said as the crowd began to disperse.

"King Arthur?"

Britt turned when she heard herself addressed and came face-to-face with King Ban. "King Ban?" she said.

He nodded. "It is an honor to meet you. I must thank you for your interference." He gestured behind him to the location of the scene.

"No, it is I who must thank you," Britt said—speaking carefully. Merlin had warned her to curb her twenty-first century language around the kings, who were more likely to judge her than her knights. "Your willingness to be my ally has brought me great hope."

"You are skilled with the sword," King Ban said, shaking his head. "I have never seen a warrior strike quite like that. You completely overwhelmed your opponent."

Britt shrugged and slid Excalibur into its scabbard. "Not really. I am taller than Ywain, giving me a longer reach. Plus, he is little more than a boy, green and inexperienced."

"I was told you are fifteen?" King Ban asked.

Britt hesitatingly nodded. (The age thing was still a sore spot.) "I am."

"That *boy* is seventeen, two years older than you. You call him inexperienced?" King Ban asked with a raised brow.

Britt froze, caught in the trap for a moment before she shrugged. "I was born with a sword in my hand, I suppose. I'm not afraid to admit that while I excel at the sword, the remaining knightly arts elude me," she smiled.

King Ban chuckled. "I have a son who is a number of years older than you. I hope one day you meet. I am sure you would get along splendidly."

"He remained in your lands across the sea?"

"No. I believe he is somewhere here in Britain. He is something of a knight errant." King Ban smiled.

"I see. If that is the case, perhaps I will indeed make his acquaintance. Tell me, King Ban, do you know where I could procure some water for my mount and myself? We traveled hard today, and I'm dead th—and I am rather parched," Britt corrected herself.

The king smiled. "Of course, of course. This way. I would be honored to be your guide."

~

YWAIN'S FATE was not resolved until Merlin arrived at the camp a week later—gleeful and joyous that he had been able to smuggle 10,000 mounted soldiers through Britain without alerting King Lot.

Britt spent most of the week with King Ban and his brother-in-law, King Bors. (Once again a set of kings related by their wives. Britt had to wonder if all royal consorts traditionally came from one or two big families, or if coincidences were commonplace in the time of fairies and magical swords.)

King Bors was the opposite of the refined King Ban. He was a big, gruff man with enough hair to make a monkey green with envy. He laughed easily, was generally good tempered, and he swung his sword with purpose and great experience. He was the better fighter of the brother-in-law kings, but Britt swiftly learned that King Ban was usually the tactician as he had a streak of intelligence that he hid behind his careful manners and clothes.

Britt, Ban, and Bors frittered away most of the day inspecting troops—a tireless, endless process in Britt's estimation. Usually one of Britt's regular babysitters accompanied them. Most often it was Sir Bedivere, but Sir Bodwain and Sir Ector took a turn as well.

When Merlin finally did arrive, Ywain was not discussed at length until the following day.

"We should have him executed," King Ban stiffly said. (He still hadn't forgiven the kid for the hostage thing.)

Sir Ector frowned. "It would certainly send a message to our opponents, but I'm not sure if it is the kind of message we truly want to present."

"Ransom him. He is his father's heir. Urien would pay handsomely to see him returned to his care," Sir Ulfius suggested.

"Better yet, cripple 'im first, and *then* ransom him. A cripple king won't cause many skirmishes further down the road," King Bors said, his great mass perched on a stool as he poked a stick in the cooking fire.

Britt, sitting in an arm chair Merlin had summoned from goodness knows where, rested her left cheek on her left hand.

"King Urien is King Lot's strongest ally. It is doubtful that his son's death would cow him," Merlin said, his eyes fastened on Britt.

"I wasn't suggesting he be executed for Urien. It should be a natural result for attacking a king, much less two kings," Ban sniffed.

"You could banish him after you cripple him," King Bors said after a few moments of silence.

Sir Bodwain exhaled loudly. "King Arthur banishing Ywain will be of no consequence to Urien, who does not recognize King Arthur's right to rule. If he does not see Arthur as King, he will not recognize his decrees."

"Let's hear your idea then," King Bors snorted, stirring coals with his stick.

"Arthur," Merlin interrupted. "What do you think?"

Britt hesitated before she withdrew from her chair, restlessly pacing. "I think the greatest coup would be if we could convince Ywain to join our ranks."

King Bors dropped his flaming stick. "What?"

"Impossible," Sir Ulfius said.

"It's a grand idea, but it would never work," King Ban said with a magnanimous smile.

"I want to hear his reasoning. Why would that be the best outcome, Arthur?" Merlin asked, leaning forward in interest.

"What would horrify Urien more than his own son following the upstart king?" Britt asked.

"True, true," King Bors boomed.

"If one could do it, it would be the best path," Sir Kay said, finally speaking.

"It would take a kind of charm mortal men don't have," King Ban said, shaking his head.

Britt turned to face King Ban and smiled—not her polished politician/Arthur smile, but her usual smile. "Exactly," she said.

King Ban blushed and looked away, and King Bors whistled. "You're going to try and charm him with your faerie blood then? Good luck. If you can manage, won't Urien be a sight to see," he laughed.

"Do you think you can do it? Without exposing certain matters of State?" Merlin asked, his expression of interest hadn't changed.

"I would like to try," Britt said.

"Try, then," Merlin nodded. "I, too, am interested in the results —if there are any. Go on. What are you waiting for?"

"You mean start now?"

"Of course. We march on Lot in three days. You have that long to change young Ywain's mind. Good luck."

Britt was almost booted from the circle and was bodily escorted to Ywain—who was currently in Sir Bedivere's keeping.

"Ywain," Britt said, drawing near to the stake to which the boy was tied.

"Beardless upstart," Ywain spat.

Britt tipped her head and narrowed her eyes at Ywain—who sported not even a hint of a beard. "I'm not certain you should mock me based on my lack of facial hair or physical features. That might come back to bite you," she said. "After all, I could point out how you are also lacking in that department, or that in spite of you being older than I am, I am still a great deal taller than you."

"You aren't a great deal taller, just a little bit," Ywain grumbled.

Britt shook her head in amusement.

"What do you want?" Ywain sullenly asked, sinking his neck into his body.

Britt turned to look out at her camp and thought. What could she say to this stubborn boy to change his mind? What was it about King Arthur—the legend, the real one—that made knights rally behind him? "Tell me, Ywain. What is your greatest dream?"

"I will never share. That enchanter of yours will use it against me!" Ywain said.

"My greatest dream and hope is impossible. It can never be achieved," Britt said, hopelessness sinking into her voice. "That is why I have another dream."

"To rule over all of Britain?" Ywain snorted. "That is fair impossible."

"No," Britt said, turning on her heels. "I wish to make a court of knights that fight for what is right. I don't want to rule over a kingdom that is concerned with surviving; I want to forge one that flourishes and is peaceful, with knights who aren't at war all the time, but traveling and doing good deeds, protecting the innocent."

Ywain was quiet for a few moments. "That's foolish talk," he said, but his words had no bite to them.

"Perhaps, but it is still my goal," Britt said, turning to face him as she warmed up to the subject as she thought of Arthurian lore. "I want a place where all of my knights can come and be equals. A place where they can share the good they have done and be honored for it. I want people near and far to talk of Camelot, not because of its great military strength but because its courts are justly ruled."

Ywain shook his head. "It can't be done. No one can hold peace like that in the land. Not even Uther Pendragon."

"It has been my experience that no one can achieve a task unless they try first," Britt smiled. "Have many others tried?"

Ywain looked away briefly. "If that's your possible dream, what's your impossible one?" he asked eventually.

Britt lost her smile and looked down at Excalibur. "It's not worth dwelling on."

"What are you going to do with me? Try to get me to talk about my father's plans? I won't say a word. Not ever!" Ywain angrily said after a few moments of silence.

"I agree," Britt said. "And I don't really know what we're going to do with you, but we won't kill you."

"Not yet," Ywain bitterly said.

"Not at all," Britt corrected.

Ywain looked unconvinced and shuffled around the stake he was tied to until his back was to Britt.

Britt conversed frequently with Ywain over her three-day deadline. She gradually pulled and nudged a few details out of the young man, like the fact that his sister had a wonderful singing voice, and he had a beautiful hunting hawk. Britt learned to bring water and basic provisions, as Ywain was given undesirable food, if any. Suspicious that her men might be mistreating the young prisoner, Britt even visited Ywain during her nightly pacing.

"Have you come to kill me in my sleep?" Ywain said, spotting Britt's shape among the tents.

"Hardly," Britt chuckled as she slipped out of her hiding spot and approached the prisoner. "I thought you would be asleep."

Ywain looked sharply away from Britt, but not so fast Britt didn't see the fear in his eyes. He was afraid to fall asleep.

Britt sighed and sat on the ground. "At Camelot, my dog as well as my guards shadow me when I cannot sleep," she said, gesturing over her shoulder where the armor of three knights gleamed in the moonlight. "Tonight you'll have to pinch hit for Cavall."

"I'll what?" Ywain suspiciously asked.

"You will be a substitute for my dog," Britt said, pulling a wooden carving of Cavall that Sir Bodwain had given her. "He is a wonderful listener."

Ywain grumbled under his breath, but he fell still when Britt started talking. "He is as big as a lion."

"You've seen a lion?"

"I have. They're beautiful cats, the size of a bear hunting dog or more. A male lion's mane is beautiful. It flows around his head like, like a halo I suppose. Personally, I think the females are prettier—not to mention they do all the hunting. No one values the beauty of a female animal enough. Everyone always says the male is more beautiful," Britt complained. "Instead of worshipping animals like the peacock, society should follow the example of the male seahorse—which carries its young in a pouch before they hatch. Or something like that. It's been ages since I saw the Animal Planet special about them. Anyway, the male seahorse is the picture of fatherhood—none of this abandoning stuff that is all the rage in American culture. What do you think?"

Britt waited for a response, but there was only silence.

"Ywain?" Britt asked, rolling into a standing position before tip-toeing to the young man.

He was fast sleep.

Britt smiled and moved to leave the area, but Ywain snorted awake. "Arthur?"

Britt plopped down next to a fire some feet away from Ywain and returned to studying her carving of Cavall. "This society treats women like crap. That's the first thing my knights will have to right. Under my rule, a knight will have no right to hold a girl against her will."

"I thought you were talking about lions."

"We were, but then I was enraged by thinking about how no one admires the beauty of a female lion, which made me think about the girls of this age. How many of them are married against their will? I have no hope of forcing women's rights—this time period doesn't even have rights for the common man—but I will at least teach my men to treat women with respect!" Britt rattled as Ywain drifted off to sleep again.

BY THE MORNING of the last day Britt had to convince Ywain, she had no idea how she would persuade the prince to join her, and she told Merlin as much.

"What do you mean?" Merlin frowned. "You almost have him."

"I don't. I don't have a clue what I'm doing. I feel more like his mother caring for him than I feel like a king winning a subject," Britt sighed.

"Sometimes, Britt, the most difficult task in being a king is to know when your subject needs you to set the crown aside. He's a young boy, and he's a dreamer. He's not difficult to understand.

Test him today, and I think you'll be surprised with the results," Merlin said.

"Test?" Britt asked, tilting her head as she thought.

"Yes. Test. Now go away. King Ban and King Bors are coming to discuss tactics, and if they realize I'm not hiding you in the forest with them tomorrow, they're going to throw a fit."

Britt thoughtfully left Merlin's tent and approached Roen—who was tacked and waiting for her. Britt hefted herself onto his back, nodded to her babysitter of the day—Sir Bedivere—and headed off to Ywain.

"Stand up, Ywain." Britt said, momentarily sliding off Roen. Ywain curiously did so, his eyes growing wide when Britt pulled a dagger. "Relax," she chuckled, before cutting to the rope that connected him to the stake. "Come on," she ordered, again mounting Roen—towing Ywain with by his rope.

They walked through the camp, garnering a couple dozen bows and murmured, "My Lord"s.

Ywain looked increasingly nervous as they left the camp altogether and rode into the forest. When they were perhaps a mile from camp, Britt finally stopped.

"Here we go. You're free, Ywain," Britt said, dismounting Roen before she cut the rope binding Ywain's wrists.

"I'm what?" Ywain said, his jaw going slack.

"You're free to go. You are no longer my prisoner."

"W-what about King Ban?"

"He will be disappointed, but I'm sure he'll make it somehow," Britt wryly chuckled, glancing at Sir Bedivere.

The young knight was watching the exchange, but he did not seem disbelieving or angered, which surprised Britt.

"You can't just mean to let me go. I know where your camp is! I know strategic information," Ywain insisted.

Britt remounted Roen to hide her grimace. She hadn't thought of that. She figured if he ran back to his daddy, all she would lose out on was a prisoner. So much for that idea. "Perhaps," Britt agreed before wheeling Roen in the direction of camp. "But I genuinely like you, Ywain. I have no wish to see you muddled in this war between your father and myself. Take care. Maybe we'll meet again," Britt said, glancing at Sir Bedivere.

Sir Bedivere moved his horse like Britt. He did not seem inclined to turn around and snatch up Ywain. (Which was somewhat unfortunate.)

Ywain sputtered behind them for a few moments as Britt cued Roen into a walk. "My King!" Ywain finally shouted.

Britt halted her horse and twisted in her saddle. "Yes?"

"Did you really mean it?"

"Mean what?"

"Everything you said about your knights. How you want them to ride around and do good deeds, not fight in wars? How you want females to be protected?"

"Yes, I meant every last word," Britt said, some of her blond hair falling over her shoulder in a golden curtain.

"Why? You're a good swordsman. Maybe the best. You don't have to be nice to everyone. You could rule through sheer strength."

Britt scratched her ear. "I don't want a kingdom like that. I want chivalry and honor."

Ywain ran through the undergrowth, startling Roen and Sir Bedivere's mount when he skidded to a stop in front of them.

"Then please, let me serve you, My Lord!" Ywain said, kneeling before Britt, looking at the ground.

Britt's eyes almost popped out of her head. "Ywain, do you understand what you're saying?" she hesitantly asked.

"I know I am the son of Urien, and I still love my father, but please, King Arthur, please let me serve you!" Ywain cried, looking up at her.

Britt stared at the teenager in great perplexity. She turned to look at Sir Bedivere, hoping for direction or advice. Sir Bedivere nodded once in approval, as if this was the outcome he expected all along.

"He either has too much faith in my abilities, or he is startlingly smart like Merlin," Britt muttered to herself as Roen swished his tail. "I do not mean to doubt you, Ywain, but how can you possibly still love your father and support me?"

"I love my father because he raised me. He is my mentor and parent. But you, My Lord, I love as my King. My loyalty and body belong to you," Ywain said.

"You would see me spare your father?" Britt asked.

Ywain hesitated, clearly torn, and Britt smiled. "I will do it, if it is in my power."

"But…why? My King?" Ywain asked.

"I am not in the business of killing the fathers of my friends. Additionally, starting a kingdom such as the one I want on stains of blood is not a wise route," Britt said.

"My King, I do not deserve your grace, but I wish to be a part of your kingdom," Ywain said, again bowing his head.

Britt hesitated as she internally reviewed every book she had ever read that involved accepting fealty. Unfortunately her favorite authors, like Jane Austen, had very little to say on the matter. She would have to rely on Hollywood.

"A Jedi gains power through understanding, and a Sith gains understanding through power," she said.

Ywain blinked. "I beg your pardon?"

"Forget it. I'll wing it. Ywain, I am honored by your declaration of fealty. I will do my best to see that I do not fail in pursuit of a just and honorable kingdom. In return, I ask that you would ride with me and be my sword and my shield and strike when I cannot. I will be your king, your friend, and your brother if you will be my knight, my guard, and my justice."

Britt was surprised to see Ywain actually blink back tears. She whipped to face Sir Bedivere, who also looked touched. Britt frowned, more than a little confused, but Ywain said. "I will, my King, My Lord, and my liege. Thank you, thank you, thank you."

Britt opened her mouth but was unable to find anything to say. It was just as well, as Merlin sprouted out of the underbrush as if he were a plant. "Marvelous," he said, joyously clapping. "Well played! Welcome, young Ywain, to King Arthur's court!" he said, pounding the young man on the back.

Ywain coughed under the smack but grinned and sheepishly reached up to rub the top of his head as Merlin continued.

"You have won a staunch and passionate knight, Arthur. I have foreseen it! Ywain is destined for great things."

"Really?" Ywain asked, clearly delighted.

Merlin nodded gravely. "It is for certain. Now, let us return to camp and tell the great news to our comrades in arms!"

Sir Bedivere nodded and dismounted his horse so he could walk next to Ywain. "Welcome, Ywain," he said.

"Thank you," Ywain beamed before the smile fell off his face and he started talking. "I don't know many of my father's plans, but I *do* know their rough numbers. They intend to push Arthur's army all the way back to Camelot where they will lay siege on the castle, as they think Merlin will hide our King during the fighting," he said as a rush of words fell from his mouth in a mad waterfall, spilling every secret of King Lot's army that he knew.

Britt, still mounted on Roen, narrowed her eyes as she watched her knight and newest addition to her company walk back to the camp, exchanging intelligence. She looked down at Merlin. "You didn't foresee anything about him at all, did you?"

"Of course not. I'm a wizard, not a prophet. Hold your blasted beast still. I don't fancy walking through all those bushes again," Merlin said, trying to mount up behind her as Roen kept swiveling to avoid him.

Britt halted and allowed Merlin to climb up behind her. "If you can't see the future why say those kinds of things?"

"Ah-ah, but I *can* see the future. Pieces of it anyway. But I see grand pictures, the fates of nations and such. I honestly have no idea what the future is like for individuals, but one does not need to be a prophet to make an educated guess. Besides, words have power. Young Ywain *will* be your knight until his dying breath now, and he *will* go out and accomplish great deeds, merely because he has been told that he can."

"Is that why he chose to follow me? Because of mere words?" Britt asked.

"Don't underestimate your powers of persuasion, lass," Merlin warned in her ear. "You have several assets that no other man in this age has. You are educated and smart, and you are a female. Which, oddly enough, works to your advantage."

"You are surprised?"

"I am. I thought your gender would be a great disadvantage. Instead, it seems to be one of the things that draws your knights to you. I don't know any grown man that would be able to ask another man to fight for him without blushing. It's just as well you didn't smile at him. He might have gone straight to the heavens first."

"You lost me there."

"The point is your words have great impact on your fellow men. You treat them with respect and expect them to be chivalrous and honorable. You *expect* more of them, and they want to be better men because of it. Mark my words, more men will fall to your cause as they meet you and speak to you."

"Is there any hope Lot would give up to me if I talked to him?"

"Not a chance."

7

TO WAR

B ritt frowned as she looked out at her army. 20,000 mounted
men pooled in front of, behind, and around her in a mass of
glinting armor and tense warhorses. She raised her eyes and
looked across the plains where the 60,000 troops of Lot and his
allies stood. Hopefully they were cheering and growing careless
as they took survey of Britt's army—which is what Merlin
wanted them to do. Merlin had ordered King Ban and King Bors
and their 10,000 mounted soldiers to remain hidden in the forest
due north of the battlefield. They would ride out and surprise the
rebel kings when signaled.

Britt shifted in her saddle, making the leather creak, and
returned to watching her army.

"Are you fearful?" Merlin asked, popping up next to Britt on a
horse that was misleadingly gangly and skinny. (Knowing Merlin,
Britt suspected it could probably outrun most horses on the
battlefield.) "Worried for your life?"

"No, not at all," she said. "I know Arthur doesn't die here, so I
won't either."

Merlin shook his head. "I sometimes wonder if your vague

understanding of what you *claim* to be lore of King Arthur will one day ruin you."

"Maybe, but for now I'll trust what little I know," Britt shrugged.

"If you are not being overcome by fear, what is it that is placing that grave expression on your face?"

"I know that *I* won't die here, but I know that some of my men will," Britt said, gesturing to her army.

"And that frightens you?"

"It makes me regretful and sad. I don't like people dying for me."

"Then you will have to make sure that every drop of bloodshed is worth it, that every knight who goes to receive his heavenly reward today goes with satisfaction, boasting that he helped put the great King Arthur on the throne," Merlin said.

Britt adjusted her helm and nodded. "I will. And I will see to it that there is never again such a day as this in my kingdom."

Merlin shook his head. "Don't make vows you cannot keep, Arthur. After today, I doubt anyone will try to steal your throne again, but you have allies, and they have neither your artless feminine charisma nor my intelligence to secure their throne. They will need your help and your men. I applaud your determination for peace and prosperity, but I do not think it wise to count today as the last battle your kingdom will see."

Britt exhaled, her shoulders falling. "Do I have to give a speech or something before we fight?"

"What? A speech? To whom?"

"The men," Brit said.

"Whatever for?" Merlin asked, his eyebrows furrowing as he stared at Britt.

"I don't know...to hearten them or something?"

"They already know why they fight. There is no need to bolster their courage. I don't know what the people are like from your home, but when a man makes the decision to become a warrior or a knight, he accepts his death. The battle will commence when Sir Ulfius and Sir Brastias—you remember him from our war meeting last night, yes?—open the attack with their band of 3,000. They await our signal."

"Oh. So, in a few hours it will start?"

"Saints alive, no. I actually came to tell you that we are ready. Sir Ulfius and his men can depart," Merlin said, puttering around with his saddle bag.

"Already?" Britt asked, her voice cracking.

"Indeed."

"Oh. Okay. Um. All I need to do is ride over to the large rock and climb it, right."

"Correct. Come. Let us make haste. I do not want Lot to get the first strike in. He has King Pellinore on his side, and Pellinore is a smart warrior who might think up something nasty," Merlin said before heeling his mount.

Merlin and Britt rode their horses to a large boulder that was about the size of a draft horse. Britt climbed the rock and stood upright, shielding her eyes to watch the battle.

"Now remember, you stand back here with the rearguard," Merlin reminded Britt from the ground.

"I know," Britt said, squinting as she watched a large number of her knights rally for a moment before they peeled off from the army.

Britt swallowed the last bit of pride she had left as she watched the knights thunder across the space between the two armies. Maybe Lyssa was right about knights and chivalry.

The mounted knights were a beautifully cruel sight. Their horses, geared and covered in armor, moved like brightly colored flames galloping across the fields, burning everything in their path. The knights were polished—lances, swords, and maces drawn as they shouted.

Britt could barely make out their battle cry.

"For Arthur!"

The splendor of the image was twisted when the band of 3,000 descended on the front lines of the opposing army. Men were knocked from their mounts; horses screamed; and as far away as she was, Britt could still hear the metallic song of weapons hitting armor.

Britt crouched on the top of the bolder, the chain mail beneath her armor scraping her skin as she watched the battle.

Sir Ulfius and Sir Brastias lay waste to Lot's front lines, scattering the soldiers as if they were sheep. Men were slain and injured on both sides, but the winning side was clearly Sir Ulfius's men. They swept from the right side of the field to the left. Knights were unhorsed, but they fought fiercely, taking down their enemies with armor-crushing maces and dazing them with powerful, painful blows to the head.

Sir Ulfius's horse was cut down underneath him. Undeterred, the older knight scrambled to his feet and ran through the enemy, taking down man after man until he crossed swords with King Ryence and one of the petty barons siding with him.

The men—both horsed—circled Ulfius, striking him together.

"Oh, no," Britt said, about to slide off the boulder.

"Stay, lass," Merlin ordered. "Just watch."

Sir Brastias—the other commander of the 3,000—thundered onto the scene on his splendid horse and smashed King Ryence off his horse with his spear. The enemy baron rushed Sir Brastias. When they clashed, they slipped off their horses and hit the ground with such force, they both rolled.

Sir Brastias was dazed for a moment, and the baron tottered to his feet before staggering towards Sir Brastias, his sword drawn.

Sir Kay and six of the best knights of Camelot thundered across the plains, reaching Sir Brastias in time to pounce on the baron before he struck.

"That cheeky seneschal. I told him to stay with the main army.

He is up to something," Merlin muttered as Britt briefly closed her eyes against the slaughter.

Once recovered, Sir Brastias teamed up with Sir Ulfius on foot, dodging stampeding horses to dismount enemy soldiers.

Sir Kay and his six companions cut a path through the heart of Lot's army. Their horses trampled men as the knights leaned from their saddles and devastated mounted enemies. They stopped only when they reached King Lot.

Sir Kay's companions spread around the king in a smooth circle, moving in perfect synchronization as they attacked the king's guards.

Sir Kay thrust his spear at King Lot, piercing the king's side before unhorsing him. He was unable to finish the job, as King Pellinore—the strategic one—burst through the ranks of Kay's companions and started attacking him with great ferocity.

By now, layers of Britt's army separated from the main body, riding off to areas that were previously assigned to them or to locations where Britt's knights were in trouble.

Britt glanced north, to the woods.

"Nay. We have no need of the brother kings yet," Merlin said, guessing her thoughts.

Britt shut her eyes. The reek of blood and bile had finally reached her.

"You can move to the back of the army, Arthur. I do not intend for you to encounter combat today," Merlin said.

Britt forced her eyes open. "No," she said. "These men are dying for me. The least I can do is witness their courage with open eyes," she said, swallowing.

Reinforcements had reached Sir Kay and his companions—and just in the nick of time, as Kay was briefly dismounted. His horse fought off enemy soldiers until Kay recovered his wits and remounted. Britt breathed a sigh of relief.

Britt scanned the battlefield, noting the position and condition of her various knights. "You're certain Ywain is not mounted and in this battle?"

"I am. He was our scout earlier this morning, as nothing would happen to him if he were caught. He is waiting on the far side of the army and will meet with me before we decided to call in the brother kings," Merlin said.

Britt nodded, looking at the colors and emblems on her knights' horses and armor. She froze, every muscle in her body stiffening.

"Arthur? What's wrong?" Merlin asked, his horse pawing the ground. "Arthur? Arthur. Britt!" Merlin said, trying to get her attention.

Britt wordlessly slid off the rock and mounted Roen. The black gelding took off as if he were a black bolt of lightning. Britt clung to his back, Excalibur warm on her hip as her heart exploded in her ears.

"Arthur!" Merlin shouted somewhere behind her.

The image of King Urien striking Sir Ector, sending him careening from his horse, replayed in her mind again and again. Britt had to help him.

Determination wrought of iron kept Britt on Roen's back as they burst through the front lines of her army, galloping towards the left side of Lot's army.

In the weeks and months to come, men would describe Britt's charge as a thing of deadly majesty. Roen exploded forward, alone, across the plains. Britt's army swept behind her like a metallic veil, chasing after the dust of their king. The ground shook, and the flags held by Lot's standard bearers were almost ripped off their poles from the onslaught of a great wind that rolled across the plains with Britt.

Britt didn't shout. She was deadly quiet, her cloak twisted behind her like red wings. As she neared the front lines, she pulled Excalibur from its scabbard. The mystical sword sang as it was freed. When the sunlight struck the blade, it seemed to ignite like the hottest depths of a star, casting light across the field in a blinding wave.

Sir Kay, who was within sight of King Lot, heard the enemy monarch say, "It can't be."

Lot's soldiers shouted in fear at the sight of Britt.

"It's the red dragon!"

"Uther Pendragon is back!"

"We're doomed!"

"All is lost!"

At the last moment, Roen twisted, running parallel to the battle, away from Lot. Soldiers and knights on both sides shouted when Roen turned again and plowed through the ranks. All eyes followed the horse's progress, looking ahead to see Britt's target: King Urien and Sir Ector.

The king didn't notice Britt's deliberate journey. His back was to her as he jabbed his sword at Sir Ector.

The older knight was wounded, the armor on his left shoulder crushed from a mace blow, his helmet gone and trampled somewhere by a horse. He favored his left leg as he backed away from the gleeful king. Urien charged after Ector, his sword flashing, and slammed blow after blow upon Sir Ector.

Britt broke through the wall of soldiers separating her from the enemy king and her foster father. She kicked King Urien between the shoulders as she passed him, making the king stumble.

Britt dismounted Roen and turned to face Urien, her hair leaking out of her helmet to mark her like a shining blonde beacon.

King Urien snarled and lunged at Britt, his face twisted and angry.

Britt, on the other hand, was emotionless and silent. Her blue eyes were intense with anger so cold and smoldering her look alone pushed Urien's men back. She didn't raise Excalibur to block King Urien's swipe at her. Instead—in the prime of his arc

—Britt crouched and rammed her shoulder into the King's stomach like a defensive lineman on a football team.

King Urien was knocked backwards. His eyes popped open with shock as Britt abandoned her vision-limiting helm.

Britt twirled Excalibur. "Stand, Urien," she commanded, her eyes a blistering blue.

King Urien staggered to his feet, still shocked, before he shook his head and roared, charging at Britt like a mad animal.

As the king raised his sword, Britt burst forward, landing a blow on King Urien's open left side. She pushed King Urien back, striking with incredible speed rather than strength. Sir Ector later described the fight, quietly and without his usual exuberance, as a mortal man desperately fleeing an enraged Elvenking.

King Urien retreated from the onslaught but fell on a slaughtered horse. He scrambled to stand but froze when he felt the icy tip of Excalibur sliding past the chainmail on his neck, resting against his sweat-covered skin.

"Do not move," Britt said, her voice quiet but edged in burning fury, "or I will not hesitate to kill you."

"You're nothing but a boy," King Urien croaked.

"That may be, but right now my fondness for your son is the only thing that is keeping Excalibur from biting your throat," Britt said.

"What?" King Urien said, starting to wiggle until Britt leaned against her sword and placed a foot on Urien's chest.

"You will live, Urien, but be warned. Never let me see your face again. Leave me and those of mine alone, and never, *ever* strike Sir Ector again. If you do, not even Ywain will be able to save you," Britt said, her voice growling and guttural.

She abruptly pulled back from Urien—one of her knights leapt to take her place in holding the king prisoner—and made for Roen. "Sir Ector, are you well?" Britt asked as she mounted her horse, ignoring Urien's panicked inquires.

"But my son! Ywain, do you have him?" Urien cried.

Sir Ector slowly lifted his gaze from the king and nodded to Britt. "I'm fine, My Lord."

Britt smiled briefly, although the gesture did nothing to warm her face. "It's Arthur, father," she said, directing her black horse into the battle so quickly she did not see the smile bloom on Sir Ector's face.

Roen jumped a slain soldier, nearly tossing Britt from his back, but she grimly held on as the black horse plunged past fights and skirmishes. This time, they were not alone. A small company of knights desperately chased after Britt, protecting her flanks and occasionally zipping forward to strike down a stray knight or soldier.

Lot saw Britt and her knights coming. Rather than face the flint-faced "boy king," Lot grabbed a horse and fled.

He didn't get six feet before Britt popped him off his horse, nailing him square in the chest with Excalibur's scabbard. As the King fell and scrambled to right himself, Britt dismounted Roen, her long hair whipping in the wind.

Enraged, Lot raised his sword and shouted as he rushed at Britt.

Britt followed her previous tactics and struck before Lot was ready, using a combination of speed and cunningly placed blows to push Lot back and keep him on the defense. Rather than wait for an opening, she kept up a solid line of attacks and forged her own holes in the king's defense.

When she pushed Lot off balance, she grabbed him by his shoulder armor, peeled it back, and stabbed the king.

Lot shouted, and a small company of his soldiers rushed Britt. Her knights picked off most of them, but she was forced to abandon Lot to fight his men.

Lot dragged himself to a horse and mounted it, setting off to the deep depths of his ranks. "Kings, to me! We will circle around them and crush them!" Lot shouted.

No sooner than Lot had spoken than a horn sounded from

the woods in the north. Merlin, King Ban and King Bors charged out of the woods, 10,000 soldiers on horseback following them with deafening cries.

King Pellinore pulled his horse around Lot's. "Who is that who rides with Merlin and a great host?"

Lot cursed. "'Tis King Ban and King Bors of the south. They have brought reinforcements without our knowledge. Retreat!"

King Ban and King Bors swept across the battlefield, reinvigorating it as they chased after Lot and his remaining allies.

Britt, meanwhile, was plucked from the fray and deposited on her horse by Sir Bodwain, who managed to drive her from the fight.

He sat with her, watching the majority of Lot's army flee while other parts of Britt's army took captives.

"Well done. The battle has been won," Merlin pronounced, trotting up to Britt and Sir Bodwain on his spindly horse.

"How?" Britt asked. "They only retreated. We didn't catch King Lot, and he didn't surrender."

"It doesn't take a king to surrender to force him to admit defeat. We have seen the last of King Lot's army, although we may not have seen the last of him," Merlin said before frowning at Britt. "You should not have rushed into battle like that."

Britt shrugged.

"I must apologize, My Lord. I seem to have underestimated you in a multitude of ways. I did not think you would be such a good fighter given your...circumstances," Sir Bodwain said, bowing his head. "May I seek your forgiveness?"

"There is nothing to forgive, Sir Bodwain," Britt said, resting a hand on the pommel of the sheathed Excalibur. "But I am glad you have corrected your opinion of me."

"Indeed, I have."

"So. What do we tell Urien of his son?" Britt asked, turning her horse to watch her knights tie the captured King.

"Tell him we have his son, and if he dares to stand against you again, we shall not hesitate to slaughter him," Merlin said.

Roen snorted as Britt wheeled him to face the enchanter. "Merlin! I would *never* allow that! I'm shocked you're even suggesting it."

"I'm not saying that's what we would really do, lass. However, sometimes a lie is a kinder thing than the truth," Merlin said.

"You think if he knows Ywain has sided with me, it would kill him?" Britt asked.

"No, but he might do something stupid that he would later regret. For now, it is best if we keep the father and son apart. Speaking of which, there's the lad now," Merlin said, squinting in the sunlight as he pointed to the slight hill on which Britt's army was previously parked. "Arthur, would you go get him and carry him back to camp? Sir Bodwain will escort you."

"I don't need an escort. The battle is over," Britt said as Roen danced in place.

"Perhaps, but there are still enemy soldiers about. The fighting is not finished yet, there may be a stray soldier or two who escape capture and seek you out. You need protection," Merlin said, gesturing to the battlefield. Lot's army was fleeing, pouring out of the plains in a frenzy, but Britt could still hear the clang of swords and armor.

"Fine. You will tell Urien?"

"I will."

"Let's go, Sir Bodwain. Your babysitting duty commences."

"My what?"

"Never mind," Britt said before heeling Roen. The gelding lunged into a smooth canter, effortlessly carrying Britt up the sun-painted hill. Ywain was nothing but a silhouette at the top, his springy hair casting long shadows in front of him.

"You won, My Lord!" Ywain shouted, pumping his fist in the air.

"We won," Britt corrected him as Roen slowed to a trot. "I

could not have done it without King Ban and King Bors, or any of my men for that matter," Britt said as she drew close enough to Ywain to see a smile on his shadowy face.

"But now you are the rightful King of Britain, and no one can say otherwise!" Ywain said.

"Oh, I'm sure King Lot will still say no. He'll bellyache for months. But Merlin seems to think the worst is behind us. You don't have a horse?" Britt asked, stopping Roen near the young man.

"No. Merlin said it would be best if I went scouting on foot."

"Then mount up behind me. We're returning to camp," Britt said.

"Oh, I couldn't, My Lord," Ywain shook his head.

"Why not? Roen is a strong horse, and you don't weigh much more than I do. If we only walk and trot, he'll be fine," Britt said.

"But, my King…you're the King. It wouldn't be right for someone to ride with you," Ywain said.

Britt snorted. "That's kind of you to say, but it isn't like that. Merlin catches a ride as if I were a taxi service. Come on. I want to go ride past the army one last time to look nice and regal before we go back."

Ywain look unconvinced.

"Aren't you hungry? Wouldn't it be nice to return to camp quickly?" Britt coaxed.

Food was the last thing on Britt's mind. She was mostly working on not throwing up from the overwhelming, suffocating scent of blood. But she knew the sooner she got off the field, the better she would feel, and chances were Ywain—who had seen no combat—would be starving.

"As you wish, my King," Ywain said, finally convinced as he made for Britt's horse.

Roen side-stepped Ywain for several moments until Britt leaned over and offered her arm. Ywain eagerly climbed up, looking out from his post.

Britt directed Roen down the slight hill before trotting up and down the field in front of her army—which was reorganizing itself.

Britt's men took a few moments to shout and raise their swords in the air as Britt rode past.

"We had best head back to camp, sire, before you start some sort of battle," Sir Bodwain shouted above the roar of the troops.

"Very well," Britt said before turning Roen south, in the direction of their camp. As Britt rode past, she spotted Merlin in his Gandalf-look-alike robe, standing with King Urien. The king looked utterly dismayed; his eyes were fastened on Ywain.

The youth wasn't aware of his father, and he was grinning and whooping with the rest of Britt's men.

Merlin spoke to King Urien, who nodded as he watched Britt ride off with Ywain, disappearing behind a thicket of trees.

8

THE END OF THE BEGINNING

"Arthur, are you alright?" Merlin asked later that evening when he found Britt sitting in front of a crackling campfire.

"I can't sleep," Britt said with a weak smile.

"I'm not surprised at that, but that cannot be all that is wrong with you. You look terrible," Merlin said as he plopped down next to Britt.

Britt gazed past her fire. Most of her men were still awake, celebrating the victory with ale and songs. There were still guards on duty of course, but in general, the camp was lively and exuberant.

Merlin watched Britt for a moment. "Are you missing home, lass?"

Britt shook her head as Sir Bedivere and Ywain danced past, splashing drink and laughing loudly. "No."

"Then what is it?"

Britt pulled her knees to her chest and hid her face in her hands. "I feel awful. I bathed twice already, but I can't get the scent of blood off me, and whenever I close my eyes, I hear the cries of the dying and the scream of swords and weaponry. And the blood, too much blood."

"Oh, lass," Merlin said, his voice filled with pity as he placed a hand on her shoulder. "It was your first battle, and you are not a creature meant for combat."

"I can fight!" Britt shook her head.

"Yes," Merlin said, squeezing her shoulder to draw Britt's attention, "but you cannot kill."

"You mean because of what I am? Because I'm a…" she trailed off rather than admit her gender.

Merlin shook his head. "No. It's because you have eyes in your heart."

Britt stared at Merlin's deep blue eyes for a few moments before she bolted, running to the nearest bush, where she threw up. Merlin followed her, gently holding Britt as she wretched.

When she was finished, the enchanter gave her a wooden cup filled halfway with water. "Take just a sip," he advised after Britt rinsed out her mouth. "Do you feel better?"

"A little," Britt admitted. "Does it ever go away?"

"What?"

"The aftertaste of battles."

"Mostly, yes. But a small part of you will always remember the devastation you witnessed," Merlin said.

She groaned.

"It's a good thing, actually. If no one remembered wars, the majority of our nation's leaders would be warmongers, seeking out the destruction of everyone around them," Merlin said.

"What did King Urien say?" Britt asked, shakily standing.

Merlin threw an arm around her waist in support. "That he would keep clear of us. He begged us not to harm Ywain, although I suspect he knows that Ywain wants to be with us."

"Will Ywain ever be able to go home?" She asked, wincing when she sat down in front of her fire harder than she meant to.

"In due time, he will. Let him grow and become one of your knights. When he is a man Urien can respect, he will return home, and both father and son will be glad for it," Merlin said, sitting so close to Britt that part of his robe rested on her knee.

Britt closed her eyes and slumped momentarily against Merlin. "I want to go home."

"To your place in America?" Merlin asked, cautiously pronouncing the name of the country.

"Yes. No," Britt groaned.

"No?"

"Yes, I want to go back to America, but that's not what I was talking about. I want to go back to Camelot. To see Cavall and listen to peasants squabble," Britt said. "I want to smell the cook making that awful, heavy bread. I want to be with civilians."

"Then let's go."

"What?" She opened her eyes and sat upright.

"We'll have to leave Roen behind. He's had a long day and deserves his rest. But we can take a fresh horse from the stables. A large, sturdy one. Perhaps one of the draft horses that pulled the supplies here," Merlin said as he stood and brushed his robe off.

"Are you crazy?" Britt asked.

"Now what would cause you to ask such a question?"

"We can't just leave in the middle of the night! We'll fall and break our necks."

"Pish posh. The moon is near full—it is bright enough to cast a shadow on you. The two of us can safely make the journey. With luck, we'll be back to Camelot in time for late breakfast," Merlin said.

"Just the two of us? What about a guard?"

"When did you become such a worried baby chick? You don't need guards when you travel with me, lass. Fear not," Merlin smiled.

Britt stared at the enchanter. Her brain shouted at her that he was clearly insane, but breakfast at Camelot with Cavall and her surprisingly soft bed (at least softer than the ground) was tempting.

"Well?" Merlin asked.

Britt sighed. "Only if we get Sir Ulfius, Sir Kay, or Sir Bedivere to promise to bring Roen back. I think all the other knights are drunk beyond reason."

"Fantastic, we'll be home before you know it! Soon you'll be listening to peasants argue over land rights and chickens as you rest your feet on your beastly dog!"

∼

"LASS. LASS WAKE UP."

Britt groaned in her sleep and rolled her head to the left, twitching her nose when scratchy fabric tickled it.

The ground rolled beneath her, and Britt faintly remembered her late night ride upon a *gigantic* draft horse with Merlin.

"Britt, wake up. We're home."

Britt slowly opened her eyes with great effort and smiled. Camelot was splayed in front of her. The barest hints of the sunrise were left on the horizon as the sun glowed cheerfully in the meadow. Sound leaked out of the castle fortification. Even at this distance, Britt heard a cow moo and a rooster crow.

The draft horse sneezed as Merlin fussed. "Come on you great hunk of horse flesh. Get moving," he said.

"Merlin, is there really no way for you to send me home again?" Britt asked, staring at Camelot as the calm pack animal and enchanter fought.

Merlin fell still. "No, lass. I'm sorry."

She closed her eyes for a few moments and said good bye to her old life one last time. Tears leaked out of the corners of her eyes when she opened them, and she leaned forward, out of her slumped position against Merlin. "I'm home," she softly uttered.

"Aye. Welcome home, Britt," Merlin said.

THE END

RESEARCHING ARTHUR

Before researching my brains out for *Enthroned*, I thought that King Arthur ascended his throne the way the Disney movie, *Sword in the Stone*, shows it. I thought he pulled the sword from the stone, people wigged out, and BAM, he was king.

I thought wrong.

Britt's story follows the original timeline of Arthur's crowning. He did pull the sword on New Year's Eve, but many people refused to recognize him as king so there were a number of other contests in which knights, princes, barons, and so on could try pulling the sword out too. Britt's crowning on the day of Pentecost follows with typical Arthurian tradition, as does her war against King Lot, King Pellinore, King Urien, King Ryence, and the other unnamed kings and barons.

Additionally, before I started collecting King Arthur books and became an Arthur fanatic, I always assumed that King Arthur lived in the time of knights and castles and princesses.

Once again, I thought wrong.

There was a real Arthur. However, that Arthur was a great warrior and probably a general of some sort—not a king.

Knights, castles, and even plate armor didn't exist in his time yet as he was around when the Romans were still in Britain. When I started writing *Enthroned* I had a choice. My stories could follow history and the 500 words we know about the real Arthur, or they could be based off the legend that came about as a result of medieval writers who plunked Arthur down in a time that was relevant to their audience. I decided to go with the latter, mostly because it would give me more material to draw from.

There's so much material, in fact, that many of the different legends counter what other Arthur stories and legends have to say. (As a preface, the Lancelot-Grail Cycle and the Post-Vulgate Cycle are essentially prose cycles of King Arthur stories. The writers of each cycle focused on different themes and different characters.)

Let's take, for example, the Lady of the Lake. She was originally a villain of sorts. In the Lancelot-Grail Cycle the Lady of the Lake is called Viviane. She learns her magic from Merlin, who falls in love with her, and when she learns everything she can she gets sick of him and locks him in a tree, or beneath a stone depending on the story you're reading.

It isn't until the Post-Vulgate Cycle of King Arthur stories that writers started adding that she bestowed the legendary Excalibur on Arthur. In Le Morete d'Arthur the author, Thomas Malory, split the Lady of the Lake into two characters. Both are called the Lady of the Lake but the one who helps Arthur gets a name and is seen as a benefactor where as the one who traps Merlin remains more of a villain. Many writers followed in his footsteps by making the Lady of the Lake good.

In spite of her original character, I've never read a modern King Arthur story in which the Lady of the Lake was anything but good and beautiful. When I first started writing this series a few readers were upset with me because my Lady of the Lake is a bit of a bag, but she's like that because I wanted to pay homage to the original Lady of the Lake—the nag who traps Merlin in a tree. (Don't worry, I won't be doing that to Merlin in my series.)

What's the bottom line? There are more versions and legends of King Arthur lore than I could ever write about, but I do try to go the extra mile and include some of the earliest Arthurian lore in my stories. Hopefully you enjoy reading it.

ENCHANTED:

KING ARTHUR AND HER KNIGHTS BOOK 2

1

DEPARTURES AND ARRIVALS

T he door creaked when it opened. "Britt? Are you in here?"

Britt pushed aside a shield that was decorated with a goose egg-sized ruby. "Yeah."

"What are you doing in the treasury?"

It was Merlin, Britt could tell by the musical quality to his voice and by the flapping noise he made when he shook his Gandalf-rip-off robe. "Are you in need of gold, or are you seeking treasures to display in the castle keep?"

"Neither. I'm looking for something." She pushed aside a tray of gold goblets to inspect the square table on which they were arranged. She shook her head and edged farther into the treasury, hopping over a pile of ivory and skirting a silver statue.

"I see. Do you think you could dispatch a servant to search for your item? I left King Ban and King Bors with Sir Kay. They mean to leave Britain by the end of the week unless you ask otherwise," Merlin said.

"And you want me to ask otherwise?"

"I do," Merlin acknowledged. "King Urien has made peace with you, but that leaves King Pellinore, King Ryence, and—most worrisome—King Lot as your enemies."

"I thought you said you weren't expecting military campaigns from them again." Britt rolled up the edge of a tapestry to inspect the table it was thrown across.

"I don't. But I enjoy the extra confidence Ban and Bors' 10,000 mounted soldiers bring—even if Kay bellyaches over the cost of feeding them." Merlin watched Britt crouch down and crawl under the table.

"You don't *really* think the fighting is over, do you?" Britt sneezed and hit her head on the bottom of the table. "Ouch."

"No, quite the contrary actually. King Pellinore will return home to lick his wounds—he's a brilliant knight but he knows when to leave well enough alone. And I expect his wife will make him stay home and mind his lands for a while. King Lot will sulk for the time being. He will make another attack against us, but I suspect it will be more on the level of espionage—not military force," Merlin said.

"Then it's King Ryence you're worried about," Britt said, sliding out from her inspection point beneath the table.

Merlin frowned. "Yes," he admitted as Britt stood and fluffed her blonde hair to get dust out of it. "King Ryence has given up on *you*, but I fear he is turning his military strength to one of your allies, King Leodegrance."

"Ah." She grabbed a burning torch that was secured to the wall and raised it over her head. "Alright. I'll ask Ban and Bors' to stay another…three weeks?"

"That would be an acceptable time frame, thank you."

"You're welcome," Britt said, standing on her tiptoes as she looked around the room with a frown.

"Whatever are you looking for anyway?" Merlin asked.

"The Round Table."

"What?"

"You said I inherited all this stuff from Uther, right? I'm almost positive that he was the one who owned Arthur's Round Table before Arthur got it. It should be in here…but I can't seem to find it. Unless it's the size of a coffee table, but that's ridiculous. It's supposed to be big!"

"We are discussing the possibilities of warfare, and you are searching for a circular table," Merlin flatly said.

"Don't tell me you haven't heard of it!"

"As I recall, Uther had some dozens of round-shaped tables in his castle. I don't particularly remember any of them being of importance, although I will ask Sir Ulfius for you if it means that much to you."

"I would appreciate that, thanks," Britt said, brushing dust off her tunic. "I should go talk to Ban and Bors now?"

"Dressed like that? *No.* You look like a muddied street urchin. Faerie wings, you are odd."

"Yeah, yeah. I'll go get cleaned up. I need to find Cavall anyway."

"Keep that hairy mutt outside the great hall," Merlin ordered as they made their way to the treasury door.

"No."

"You are acting like a child."

"I am a twenty-first century woman masquerading as a fifteen-year-old boy king who makes no decisions about his own kingdom. The least you will allow me to do is to make decisions regarding my pets."

"Fine."

～

"So, Merlin thinks there may yet be trouble?" King Ban—a well-groomed, well-mannered man—said as he folded his hands behind his back, following Britt down a dirt path that circled the outer walls of Camelot.

"He does, and I agree with him. I find it unlikely that these men, who have been thorns in my side since the day I was crowned in London, are through with me after one battle," Britt said, placing a hand on Cavall. The fawn-colored dog kept pace with Britt, his wrinkled muzzle twitching.

"They certainly ran from you with their tails between their legs. You did not even need our soldiers during your victorious battle," King Bors said, brushing a bug out of his massive beard.

Britt was silent as she composed her thoughts—replying always took time for her as she had to not only think about her answer, but also come up with a flowery way to phrase it to suit her audience. "Perhaps." She turned to face Ban and Bors. "But I'm not certain I would call it a victory. We beat them off, but they did not surrender. As such, I would greatly appreciate the support your army and men symbolize for a little while longer. Surely your kingdoms can spare you a few weeks more?"

King Bors smiled. "Of course, friend," he said, his voice booming in the stillness of the surrounding fields.

King Ban nodded. "We are your staunch allies. We shall stay as long as you need us."

Britt gave the kings a benevolent smile. "Thank you. I hope some time in the future I will be able to repay your generosity."

King Bors waved a meaty hand. "It is what allies do," he said before turning to Ban. "We had best inform our men of the change in plans."

King Ban nodded. "If you will excuse us, Arthur?"

Britt slightly inclined her head. "Of course," she said, her hand still resting on Cavall.

The kings turned and walked back up the path, their tunics swishing as they moved.

As soon as they were out of sight, Britt turned to face the castle wall and discreetly fixed the fitted doublet that smashed her chest down, giving her tunic the appearance of lying on a flat chest.

"I'm lucky summers are cool here, or this would really be the pits," Britt muttered, hiking up her pantyhose. (Merlin still insisted they were called chausses. Britt knew better.)

"So that's why Merlin said you were one of faerie blood. He had to explain your elegance and calm."

Britt whirled around, grimacing when her eyes landed on the Lady of the Lake. The black-haired beauty had ~~unwillingly~~ allowed Britt to ~~steal~~ pull Excalibur from her magical lake after she had offered Britt a different sword. Britt suspected she only got away with Excalibur because the lady was dumbstruck over the revelation of Britt's real gender. If the Lady of the Lake knew Britt's entire story, she probably would have died from shock.

Britt had been yanked back through time to the era of King Arthur when she accidentally touched a sword—the famed Sword in the Stone—while vacationing in Britain with her friends. When she arrived, Merlin informed her that the real Arthur had run off with a shepherdess, and all of his plans to unite Britain under one King were hinged on finding someone who could pull the Sword from the Stone.

After a brief period of believing it was an elaborate prank set up by her friends (or that maybe she was in a coma, dreaming), Britt pulled the Sword from the Stone even though she was a woman, an American, and from the twenty-first century.

Merlin grumbled a little over Britt's unusual time-traveling heritage, but he had no other option. Adapting and clever as ever, Merlin plowed forward with his plans—using Britt as his symbolic king.

Only a few knights of Camelot knew of Britt's gender, and even fewer knew she came from the future. All of the knowledge-able knights were Merlin's men, and all of them were in seats of power, working with Merlin—and supposedly Britt—to unite Britain under one king for the good of all peoples.

The Lady of the Lake was the only other being to know Britt's real gender.

"What do you mean?" Britt asked.

The Lady of the Lake shrugged, sending ripples down her pretty, green dress. "No fifteen-year-old *boy* could hold himself with the stately poise you possess, nor could a boy be as wise and careful in their replies as you are. Those with faerie blood are known to possess not only incredible beauty, but wisdom and knowledge beyond their years. Why, Merlin is said to have some faerie blood in him."

Britt carefully nodded as she turned around. She could see her guards yards away, alert and watchful. They did not seem overly worried about the magical lady standing with Britt.

Britt wished they would be. She hadn't parted on good terms with the Lady of the Lake when she took Excalibur. "I see," Britt said, sparing Cavall a glance. The large, wrinkly faced dog was still. "May I be so bold as to inquire what brings you to Camelot?"

"I see how it is. Now, you're all politeness and sweet words since you've got your sword. Shrew," the lady said.

Britt shrugged, unapologetic. "That's not a bad thing. Most people would act the reverse, Tinker Bell."

The Lady of the Lake frowned. "Tinker Bell?"

"It has not escaped my attention that you have yet to explain what you're doing here."

The Lady of the Lake twitched her skirts aside. "I decided a visit was in order. Rumors of your victory against King Lot, King Urien, King Pellinore, King Ryence and the others have reached my lake. You have become quite the king," she said, turning her nose up in the air.

Britt kept her stance relaxed. As far as she remembered, the only legends about the Lady in the Lake involved Excalibur. It was unlikely she had a larger role to play, so there was no need to be defensive with her. "As I told King Ban and King Bors—which I am certain you overheard—it was not a true victory."

"At least you don't still have an enlarged ego," the Lady of the Lake said.

There was silence for a few moments. Britt shifted and glanced over her shoulder at her guards. They were still on alert, their eyes endlessly scanning their surroundings.

"So, you're really ruling, even though you're a woman?" the Lady of the Lake said. Her voice was barely above a whisper, but it dripped with disdain.

"I am. Most of them don't know of it. But a few do," Britt admitted.

"Merlin and his minions?"

"Yes."

The Lady of the Lake frowned and inspected Britt from the top of her head to her shoes. "Rumor has it you want a court ruled by honor, justice, and chivalry?"

Britt wryly smiled. Young Ywain—a young man who had defected to Britt's side even though he was the son of King Urien —was the only person to whom she had told her plans. Apparently he couldn't keep his mouth shut. "I do," Britt said. "I can't make laws or rules about women. I can't give them rights, and I can't feed all the poor. My lords and knights would rebel. But if I have a code of conduct and reward those who act in chivalry, I think I will be successful."

The Lady of the Lake lowered her snotty gaze long enough to stare at Britt. "You really mean to change Britain?"

"Yes."

There was more silence again, and Britt considering trying to sneak off. The Lady of the Lake abruptly broke the silence, her words spilling over themselves like a frantic river. "A lady of great magic is traveling from the north. Her goal is Camelot. She means to ensnare you and the men of your court. I do not believe you will fall for her magic. You have Excalibur after all, and she will not expect you to be a woman. There. You've had a warning. You're a complete fool if you still fall for it."

Britt blinked at the faerie lady before smiling. "I see. I didn't think things would be peaceful quite yet. Thank you for the warning…"

"Nymue."

"Nymue," Britt said, carefully pronouncing the name.

The Lady of the Lake, Nymue, twitched her skirts again. "I'll be going then. Wouldn't want to stick around this place too long," she scoffed, pushing some of her long, black hair over her shoulder.

"Safe travels home, Nymue," Britt said.

"Of course, I'm not some sort of second rate nymph," Nymue sniffed before adding, "Good luck."

Britt glanced over her shoulder to spy out her guards. By the time she looked forward again, Nymue was gone.

~

A WEEK later Britt was throwing a pouch stuffed with dried beans for Cavall when a messenger threw open the doors to the throne room. "My Lord, I bear ill news!"

"W-what, what?" Sir Ector snorted, rocketing out of the chair he was dozing in.

"Come in and give your message to the King," Merlin invited the messenger, never removing his intense blue eyes from the abacus he was using.

Britt swept down the stairs that led up to her throne, tossing the beanbag one last time before wiping her drool-moistened hands on her tunic. "Pray do tell us, what terrible news do you have?" Britt asked as Cavall dutifully retrieved the beanbag, his nails clicking on the stone floor.

The man—a soldier—stumbled into the room, losing his balance twice before Sir Kay shut his logbook and steadied him.

"I bear news from King Leodegrance," the messenger said, slumping on a bench Sir Ector pulled out for him.

"Well? Spit it out man!" Sir Ector boomed.

"Wait, our guest looks parched and hungry. Bring something for this man to quench his thirst and end his hunger," Britt called to a young page hovering in the shadows of a wall.

"Working on your local tongue?" Merlin muttered to Britt.

"Am I over doing it?"

"A bit, unless you were aiming for the position of court bard or all around…pansy, I believe you call it?"

Britt winced as Cavall spit out the beanbag in her hand. "I'll tone it down," she said.

In no time, the page returned with a tray of bread, fruit, dried meat, and a tankard of ale.

The soldier/messenger gulped down the ale, splashing it on himself before he shoved food in his mouth. "King Ryence has retreated from your great victory and instead has hastened to plague King Leodegrance of Camelgrance," he said around a mass of unchewed bread.

"You there, lad. Go summon King Ban and King Bors," Merlin called to the young page.

The soldier took another swig of ale. "King Leodegrance does not know the exact count of soldiers King Ryence has with him, but he estimates over 10,000."

"10,000? How did he muster that? He didn't bring that many soldiers to our battle against him," Britt frowned.

"We should have seen this coming. The kings of the failed plot might be through fighting Arthur, but it doesn't mean their quest for power is over," Sir Ector said.

Merlin moved a few beads on his abacus. "Indeed. I thought Ryence might try something, but I calculated that he would at least return home first to lick his wounds. Apparently he is a bigger fool than I imagined."

"Should we summon Sir Bodwain? As Constable, he should know of this," Sir Kay said.

"Sir Bedivere, too," Britt said before gesturing to another page standing along the wall. The boy nodded and trotted off, almost running into King Ban and Bors when they swept through the entryway.

"Well there, what's the trouble Arthur? What great, ruddy king has his nose out of joint now?" Bors boomed.

"Ryence," Britt said.

"He's taken 10,000 men and is marching against King Leodegrance," Merlin said.

A frown marred King Ban's handsome face. "The scoundrel," he said as Bors whistled.

"I believe a joint force would be the best plan, if you are up to it?" Merlin asked the kings.

"Of course!" Bors snapped.

King Ban nodded. "I am not of mind to abandon King Leodegrance. You shall have my aid."

"We should muster an army of 20,000. That will leave a fair amount of soldiers in Camelot to guard it," Merlin said. "Arthur and I will—"

A second soldier ran into the room, his chain mail jingling and swaying. His face was red with exertion. "Trouble, Your Highness!"

Merlin sighed and Sir Ector said, "What now?"

"Q-Queen M-m-Morgause, King Lot's wife!" the soldier said, panting.

"Yes, what of her?" Britt asked.

"She's here!"

"*WHAT?*" Merlin shouted.

Sir Bodwain and Sir Bedivere, who were entering the room at that exact moment, paused.

"What is wrong, Merlin?" Sir Bodwain asked, approaching the circle of knights and kings.

"What *isn't* wrong?" Merlin muttered before abandoning his abacus on the table. "Morgause, the wife of that stupid dolt Lot is here—"

"With all f-four of her sons," the soldier meekly added.

Merlin looked murderous and flexed his hands, as if in a desire to latch them around something. "Morgause and her brats are here, and King Ryence marches on King Leodegrance with over 10,000 soldiers. With Morgause's arrival, Arthur and I cannot ride off to defend King Leodegrance with King Ban and King Bors. You'll have to go in Arthur's stead, Sir Bodwain. Sir Bedivere will remain behind to act as constable and marshal."

Sir Bedivere bowed his head in acceptance, but Sir Bodwain frowned. "I have no doubts of our victory against King Ryence. He is a coward and will likely retreat as soon as he gains wind of our march...but what will you do with Morgause, Merlin?"

Merlin rubbed his temple. "I do not know, yet. We will have to officially receive her of course. Arthur, ready yourself to meet with Queen Morgause. King Ban, King Bors, I would like you to leave as swiftly as possible. The less information Morgause receives on you, the better. You as well, Sir Bodwain."

"There is wisdom in your words. Bors and I shall return to our rooms and set out to our men as soon as our horses are ready," King Ban said.

King Bors nodded, and Sir Bodwain bowed before turning on his heels and retreating.

Britt climbed the stairs to her throne—an immense wooden chair smoothed with age and cushioned with three pillows at Britt's request—brushing Cavall hair off her clothes as she climbed. "Cavall, sit," she said, pointing to the fur rug nestled next to her throne. (Kay had acquired it for Cavall when Britt complained that the mastiff was getting stiff from sitting on the stone floor.)

When Merlin finished bossing around his minions, he tarried near Britt's stairs. "If only you would agree to wear armor. It would do wonders for your image. It would let you appear older, so you wouldn't have to worry about looking like a fifteen-year-old."

"No," Britt said, seating herself on the throne after adjusting her cushions.

"I promise it won't be uncomfortable. We have the best armor smiths," Merlin coaxed.

"No," Britt said, setting Cavall's beanbag on his rug.

"Ingrate," Merlin muttered before scuttling to his position at the left of Britt's throne.

Britt refused to wear armor or chain mail, not because it was uncomfortable or too heavy but because she was afraid. When she was brought back through time, her old life was essentially ripped from her. She lost her mother, her sister, her friends, her home... Britt didn't want to remove all traces of her old life, but that was happening whether she wanted it to or not.

Before being summoned to Medieval England, Britt was almost considered a master of Renaissance Mixed Martial Arts and was the best swordsman of her practice hall. But since her arrival, Britt had grown more tan thanks to the vast hours she spent outdoors; her hair—a dark blonde—bleached out in the sun so it was more golden.

Britt feared that if she wore armor, the last little pieces of her old life would disappear entirely. Sure, she looked flat and boyish when wearing tunics with her under doublet, but armor transformed her into an entirely different person—a person Britt didn't want to give herself over to be quite yet.

Britt was stuck on the throne for over an hour while the castle was a mad house of activity. As soldiers escorted Queen Morgause and her children into the castle (taking the maximum amount of time, under Merlin's instruction), guest bedrooms were aired out; Britt's throne room was decorated with banners, flags, and fresh flowers; and the most polished, impressive, and well-bred knights in Britt's kingdom were assembled.

Britt's butt started cramping up when a musician blew a horn and announced, "Queen Morgause, wife of King Lot, ruler of Orkney, and Prince Gawain, Prince Agravain, Prince Gaheris, and Prince Gareth."

Everyone held their breath. All of the knights and noblemen in the throne room stood at attention as the doors were opened.

Queen Morgause was roughly what Britt expected. She was beautiful and poised in a red wine-colored gown. Her beetle black hair was coiled in an elaborate braid; her lips were tilted in a slight smile, and she moved like silk in water.

Her sons, however, were not what Britt would expect as spawns of Lot and Morgause.

The oldest boy was dark haired like his mother, but he did not have a shred of her confidence. His eyes were fastened on the floor; his shoulders were slumped, and he moved like a mouse. He looked, Britt estimated, about eighteen or nineteen.

The next oldest boy was still in the gawky, skinny stage of the early teenage years. His face seemed to be fixed with a permanent scowl, but Britt could see the damp marks on his tunic where he wiped his sweaty hands.

The youngest boys couldn't have been older than nine or ten. They stuck together, resembling baby possums with their big eyes and necks sucked into their shoulders.

When Morgause reached the base of the stairs to Britt's throne, she curtseyed. "My Lord, King Arthur," she said in a voice that was just as husky as Britt's.

"Queen Morgause, welcome to Camelot," Britt said.

Morgause bowed her head. "I apologize, for we have arrived uninvited and unannounced...but I wanted to see you, My Lord."

"Mm," Britt said, glancing at Merlin.

"Please allow me to introduce my sons. This is Gawain, my eldest and the heir to the throne," Morgause said, placing her hand on the shoulder of the oldest boy.

Britt briefly held a hand to her forehead. Gawain, it was a name Britt remembered from Lyssa's—the King Arthur-crazy friend she had left behind in the twenty-first century—tirades. He was supposed to be one of Arthur's best knights. Was it possible that such a knight could be the offspring of her worst enemy? Not to mention the boy looked about as knightly as a rabbit.

"And this is Agravain, Gaheris, and Gareth," Morgause said, going down the line.

Britt inclined her head before she stood and trooped down the stairs, snapping her fingers to call Cavall after her.

"Well met," Britt said, Merlin joining her at the last stair. She discreetly rubbed her nose; Morgause was heavily perfumed. The scent, lilies, would have been delightful, but Morgause was wearing an overwhelming amount. It made Britt's nose itch and her head throb. "This is Merlin, my counselor and close friend," Britt said.

"Oh, we have met," Morgause said, a hint of a frown passing over her lips.

"Indeed, we unfortunately have," Merlin agreed.

Britt shifted her attention away from the glowering enchanter and queen and smiled at Gawain. If he was to be one of her court, it would be smart to start working on him immediately. "Welcome, Gawain."

The young man lifted his gaze to meet Britt's eyes and spoke. Britt saw his mouth move, and heard his voice, but instead of speaking English, it was like he uttered another language.

"I'm sorry, could you repeat your words?" Britt asked.

Gawain spoke again, and again Britt heard nothing but a garbled rush. Britt opened and closed her mouth a few times, her eyebrows furrowing slightly.

The snotty preteen boy, Agravain, said something. He was incomprehensible, although Britt felt the puffed up pride that was smoothed over his words to hide his fear.

"Um...Merlin," Britt said, taking a step back when one of the younger boys peeked out from behind his mother.

"Yes?" Merlin said, removing the glare from his features as he turned to face Britt.

Britt indicated to Gawain. "Can you..."

Merlin blinked. "Can I what?"

Britt stepped closer and muttered in Merlin's ear. "Can you understand them?"

"You mean you can't?"

"No."

A look of worry flashed over Merlin's face before he beamed at Morgause. "I apologize for the interruption. What brings you to Camelot, Morgause?"

"I am here as an extension of goodwill," Morgause said, smiling at a few of the nearest knights.

The knights blushed and elbowed one another when Morgause looked away.

Merlin snorted. "Extension of goodwill you say? Most people would label it correctly and call it spying. Or are you here to mourn the loss of a kingdom that will never be yours?"

Morgause smiled widely, but Britt could hear the queen's teeth grind. "Oh, Merlin, how silly you've become in your old age."

Britt frowned as she studied her knights while Merlin and Morgause bickered. A few of the men closest to the royal huddle watched Morgause with bright eyes and enamored smiles. "Boys," Britt muttered in disgust. If she got Nymue in the throne room, she could probably make her knights—the majority of them being young and unmarried—roll over and bark like dogs.

"—plan to welcome you to Camelot tonight with a grand feast, isn't that right, Arthur?" Merlin said.

"Of course," Britt automatically replied, smiling as she returned her attention to Morgause and Merlin.

"That is so kind of you," Morgause gushed, "to try and match the splendor of Orkney to make me feel welcome."

Merlin's smile was so big his eyes were mere slits. "Of course," he said. "Although the feast is not until this evening I would assume you and the young princes would like to retire to your rooms to freshen up? You are not as young as you used to be; it will take you longer to prepare for such an occasion."

"Old age has treated you well, Merlin. You have become so thoughtful! I can see how you secured the position of court magician," Morgause laughed.

"Chief counselor."

"Come now, we both know it is the same role."

Merlin and Morgause the frenemies beamed at each other as Morgause's sons spoke in their lilting, breathless language.

Britt sighed. "This is going to be a long feast."

2

PAYING A SOCIAL CALL

Britt observed her tablemates over the rim of her goblet of spiced wine. The only real friends seated at the royal table with her on the dais were Merlin and Cavall—and Cavall was stealthily hidden at Britt's feet. The rest of the places were taken by Morgause and her sons.

Gawain, who was sitting just past his mother, tilted his head and caught Britt's eye. Britt nodded to him and slightly raised her goblet in acknowledgement, immediately wishing she hadn't.

The Orkney prince spoke, still talking in the lilting gibberish Britt couldn't understand. Britt nervously laughed and chugged her wine to avoid having to answer the prince. When she looked up, he was still watching her, obviously expecting an answer of some sort.

Britt glanced to Merlin—who was wrapped up in talking/exchanging insults with Morgause—but the enchanter purposely ignored her. He seemed to think the best way to cover up the fact that Britt couldn't understand a word Morgause's sons spoke was to refrain from acknowledging it.

Britt, feeling lost, looked back at Gawain. He repeated his question and this time gestured below the table.

"That is Cavall. He was a gift given to me by my foster brother, Sir Kay," Britt said.

Gawain's shoulders slumped, and he returned his gaze to his pewter plate.

"I guess that isn't what he asked," Britt muttered before sipping her wine again. She lacked the appetite to eat.

"I am glad to see you conversing with my sons, My Lord," Morgause smiled. Her lips were the deep red of a waxed, red delicious apple.

"Yes," Britt said, glancing at Agravain, Gaheris, and Gareth. "They seem to be capable boys," Britt said before sipping her wine.

"I hope they find favor with you. They are, after all, your nephews," Morgause said.

Britt choked on her drink and coughed until she could manage another sip. "Pardon?"

Morgause took a bite of stag swimming in a plum sauce Britt normally avoided. "They are your nephews, and naturally your heirs, as you are my half-brother—if Merlin's story of your true parentage can be trusted."

Britt snapped her head to look at Merlin so quickly she almost gave herself whiplash. "Half-brother? My heirs?" she carefully repeated.

Merlin was no help as he had also been taken by a fit of coughing at Morgause's proclamation.

"You mean he didn't tell you?" Morgause said, her voice false and coy. "We share the same mother, Igraine. She birthed myself and my two sisters years before she met Uther, had you, and became Uther's wife."

Merlin finally found his voice. "What are you getting at, Morgause?"

"Nothing, I am merely explaining our family connections to my dear half-brother," Morgause said.

Britt thought for a moment before carefully replying. "I am

overjoyed to learn this. I greatly treasure my relationship with my foster parents and brother. I hope we can reach the same level of affection as I have for them."

Merlin muttered under his breath, but Morgause laughed. "How quaint. Yes, I hope so as well."

"Gawain is *not* Arthur's heir," Merlin said.

"Nonsense. Arthur is but a boy himself. Gawain is older than he is! As Arthur has no wife, much less children, Gawain must be his heir."

Britt covered a grimace by drinking more wine. She was greatly relieved when she saw Sir Bedivere climb the few stairs to the dais and bow. She opened her mouth to acknowledge the knight, but she was shocked when he addressed not Britt, but Morgause.

"Queen Morgause, it is a pleasure to receive you here in Camelot. Your presence adds to the beauty of the place," Sir Bedivere bowed.

"How charming you are. What is your name, good sir knight?" Morgause gaily laughed.

"Bedivere. I am Arthur's marshal," Sir Bedivere said.

Bedivere's statement made Britt sit up straight and pay closer attention. Never before had Sir Bedivere referred to Britt without some sort of honorific.

"Sir Bedivere, I am pleased to make your acquaintance," Morgause said.

"If I may ask, My Lady, how long do you mean to stay in Camelot?" Sir Bedivere said.

"As long as my dear brother allows me, I suppose," Morgause said, smiling beautifully at Britt before she leaned closer.

Britt held her breath to keep from coughing in Morgause's cloying lily perfume. "An extended stay, then?" Britt asked, briefly rubbing her nose. "I would have thought Lot would summon you home as swiftly as possible," she said with a sliver of a smile.

Morgause frowned as Sir Bedivere said, "Oh please, My Lady,

do stay. All of Camelot would morn if you were to suddenly leave."

Britt blinked. *What?* The whole castle was filled with panic and dread the moment it was announced Morgause had arrived! What was Sir Bedivere talking about? She chugged the last few sips of her wine and turned to Merlin to make sure he was hearing this. The wizard had his arms crossed and was studying Morgause with narrowed eyes.

Morgause laughed. "And I say again that you are charming and sweet. It is a shame we do not have more knights like you, Sir Bedivere, in Orkney," Morgause said, leaning forward to draw closer to the knight.

Sir Bedivere smiled in spite of the sudden onslaught of the lady's perfume. He was silent for a few moments before saying, "It is a bigger shame that Lot was not able to pull the sword from the stone, for then you would be Camelot's queen."

Britt dropped her goblet, which hit the wooden dais with a metallic clang before rolling for some paces. She held her hand out, as if she was still gripping her dropped cup, and stared at Sir Bedivere.

Somewhere behind Britt, an attendant scrambled for another cup as Morgause pulled back from Sir Bedivere, her smile not nearly as brilliant as she glanced at Britt. "Sir Bedivere, I fear you are speaking unfairly. Arthur is a fine king," she said, touching Britt's shoulder.

Britt continued to stare at Sir Bedivere, shaking her head slightly. She was barely aware of the attendant pushing a new goblet filled with wine into her hand before she knocked half of it back in one gulp.

Merlin had abandoned all pretenses of welcoming Morgause and was writing something in a small logbook, looking very much like Sir Kay.

"I suppose, but the realm would greatly benefit if you ruled, My Lady," Sir Bedivere said.

Morgause again leaned towards Britt. "Perhaps it is a shame that I am married and Arthur is my brother, in that case," she said, her voice teasing as she leaned into Britt.

Britt stared Morgause down with furrowed eyebrows and a frown creased on her face. The older woman quickly caught on to her bad mood and pulled back, clearing her throat.

Sir Bedivere blundered further as Britt sipped her wine. "You would make a splendid Empress of Britain, My Lady," he said, his eyes hooked on Morgause.

Britt pushed aside her herring pie and set her goblet—which was empty again—down on the table with a clack. "That is enough, Sir Bedivere," she said, her voice void of emotion and inflection.

Sir Bedivere took a step back at Britt's voice. His eyes were wide with horror, and he briefly placed a fist in front of his mouth. "My Lord, I-I don't know what came over me. My Lord," he stammered before bowing to Britt and leaving as abruptly as he came.

Britt eyed the knight as he left before she shooed the wine attendant away from her cup.

"Are you displeased, Arthur?" Morgause asked.

"I know you are not an idiot, My Lady, but you sound like one when you ask questions to which you already know the answer," Britt said, staring across the table.

Gareth and Gaheris seemed oblivious to the table's tension, but Agravain had sunk until he was almost entirely beneath the table. Only his head was visible over his plate. Gawain was staring at his lap, no longer touching his food.

Rather than snarling, as she would with Merlin, Morgause held her hands to her heart. "I apologize. Men can be such silly things. I take their words as compliments, but please be assured that I think you are a marvelous king," she said, placing her hand on Britt's bicep before she leaned closer again.

Britt stood, brushing Morgause off. "If you'll excuse me, I

believe I need a few moments of fresh air," she said, doing her best to smile at her table guests. "Cavall, come," she said, snapping her fingers as she trotted down the dais.

The mastiff snuffled as he edged out from under the table and followed Britt, leaving her astonished tablemates behind.

Ywain stood near the base of the dais with a new friend of his —Griflet, if Britt remembered correctly. Griflet was watching Morgause with calf eyes, but Ywain stared at Britt, worry creasing his lips.

Britt spared the young man a smile, and Ywain performed an elaborate bow. By the time he was upright, Britt had disappeared from the room.

~

LATER THAT EVENING, Britt stormed Merlin's study, throwing the door open without knocking. "What was *that*?" she asked without preamble before kicking the door shut behind her.

"*That* was Morgause, petty witch and temptress extraordinaire," Merlin wryly said, tucking a book into a bookshelf.

"Petty? Bedivere insulted me to my *face*, Merlin. That isn't petty magic," Britt said, pacing the width of the room.

Merlin blinked. "You are upset," he said, sounding surprised.

"Of course I'm upset! Why *wouldn't* I be upset?"

"Normally, you have a placid temperament that cannot be stirred. Why do Morgause's mind games upset you so?" Merlin asked.

Britt briefly leaned against one of Merlin's worktables. Her eyes were dark as she stared at the wall and hissed, "Because before this, I had not been insulted by one of my own men—to whom *I* bequeathed a title—in my own castle."

"Ah. When you say it like that…" Merlin trailed off, rubbing his chin.

"What does she mean to accomplish by swaying my men like this? Does she want me to throw them out of Camelot or toss them in the dungeon? She's trying to achieve something," Britt said.

"She's trying to win their favor, and yours, too. Fortunately for us, you aren't a calf-eyed boy who fancies older women. Morgause's magic will never work on you, but she doesn't know that, so she'll keep trying," Merlin said.

"Why?"

"She wants to win you over and lower your guard."

"She means to kill me."

"Morgause? No. She is too subtle for that. This trip of hers is for no purpose other than to parade Gawain around and win over the men of your castle so when Lot sends a warrior to kill you in stealth, Camelot will be besotted and will surrender peacefully," Merlin said, spinning a glass model of the sun.

"Oh, fantastic. That is *so* much better," Britt said.

Merlin shrugged. "It's better than attempting to kill you outright."

"Not really." Britt sat down in a wooden chair, stretching her legs in front of her. "So how are you going to break Morgause's enchantment?"

Merlin rubbed his chin and studied Britt. "I am not."

"*What?*"

"I am not going to break the enchantment Morgause has over the knights of Camelot. If I do, those stupid goats who are falling for it will become her pawns again the moment they set eyes on her."

"But we can't let her wander around loose, wreaking havoc! How do you propose we survive in a castle full of Morgause lovers?" Britt asked.

Merlin took a stuffed owl off his desk and put it on a high shelf. "It will be fine. The men who really matter haven't fallen for her tricks. Yet. Kay and Sir Ector are normal."

"What about Bedivere? He's not fine, and he's important," Britt said.

"If you're so worried, maybe *you* should do something about it," Merlin said.

"What are you talking about? I can't do anything. I don't know any magic."

"Yes, but if your men were undyingly loyal to you, not even Morgause's magic could entice them."

"So how do I make them undyingly loyal?" she asked.

Merlin didn't answer and brushed dust off a sorry-looking plant.

Britt sighed and massaged her forehead. "I don't understand you. You yell at me for doing anything without your permission, and then you refuse to help me when I ask for it."

"No one ever said being King would be easy," Merlin said.

"It's not like you gave me a choice! I'm not Arthur. I didn't get to run off with a shepherdess. I'm Britt Arthurs. *You* dragged me from my home and life so I could be your king. The least you could do is explain what is happening," Britt snapped.

Merlin didn't defend himself and dusted a second plant before changing the conversation topic. "It is troubling that you cannot understand Morgause's offspring."

"Yeah, but it's not surprising. Are they speaking Gaelic? They're from the north, right? Wait, isn't that Scotland? Maybe I just don't understand the Scotch." Britt wondered.

"No, they are speaking English, admittedly with a very thick accent. I wonder…" Merlin plucked a book from his bookshelf. He paged through it for a few minutes, his eyes tracing letters as Britt closed her eyes and tried to relax in the warm room.

"Ah-hah. Here is the problem," Merlin finally declared, pointing to a passage in his book. "It is the spell I used to bring you back through time. I knew there was a good possibility we may end up with a foreigner king, and it would do no good to have a worthy king if he couldn't understand what we were saying. Keeping this in mind, I added a portion to the spell which I borrowed from an ancient faerie magic which would enlighten whomever I brought back to understand my language. I never thought to include any provision for accents. Gawain and his brothers are speaking English, but their pronunciation is horrible. It is likely that their accents have kept the spell from working."

"If it's just a matter of accents, why can I understand Morgause perfectly?" Britt asked.

"Morgause was born in central Britain. She does not have an accent," Merlin said.

"I suppose that makes sense. This is good, right? It should be easy to fix," Britt said.

Merlin grimly shook his head. "I don't know. Faerie magic is difficult to translate, and I don't think I've ever seen a spell of theirs that refers to human accents. With time, it is possible I will be able to come up with something, but it will likely be months before I will have anything to cast on you."

Britt bit her lip. "Is there someone else who knows more about this sort of thing? Someone who could fix it faster?"

"No," Merlin sourly said. "The Fae teach very few humans the ways of magic. I do not doubt they would have a way to fix this, but as the only faerie people near us all live with the Lady of the Lake, I would rather not ask them. To begin with, she is not likely to help us, and it is very likely she would do something in retaliation for your heist of Excalibur."

Britt bit the inside of her cheek. Nymue might know? "Of course *she* would know." She sighed. "She's going to complain that I am hitting her up for a favor again if I ask for help."

"What?" Merlin suspiciously asked.

"Nothing." She stood. "You know, Merlin, I'm starting to think your magic might be all talk."

"What?" Merlin squawked.

"You can't break Morgause's enchantment, and you can't help

me understand Gawain. It seems like there isn't much you *can* do," Britt said.

"You ungrateful pig-child. Of course I can do magic. Lots of magic! I brought you here didn't I?" Merlin said.

Britt retreated to the door. "Whatever you say."

"Britt," Merlin said. "What are you going to do about Morgause?"

"Try to live with it, I guess."

"I told you, you could break her enchantment if you wish."

"I highly doubt that. Good night, Merlin."

Merlin sighed. "Good night."

THE FOLLOWING DAY found Britt in a very poor mood. After spending her nightly insomnia pacing hours pondering her available options, Britt concluded that if she ever wanted to understand young Gawain—whom history foretold as being one of her greatest knights—she would *have* to talk to Nymue.

"She's going to have kittens when I tell her I need something after our pleasant discussion outside the castle." Britt sighed, reaching down to pat Roen, her black horse.

"Did you say something, Milord?"

Britt groaned before twisting in the saddle. "No, I didn't say anything of importance," she reported to the six guards that followed her on horseback. "And I told you all, I was only going to the forest of Arroy. As I'll be back to Camelot before dinner, your presence is entirely unnecessary."

The captain of the guards shook his head. "Wouldn't be right, Milord."

Britt sighed and faced forward again. "It was worth a shot," she muttered. She wasn't looking forward to her guards observing what would predictably be Nymue's absolute refusal.

The frightened sobs of a child jerked Britt from her musing.

"What's that?" she asked, turning in her saddle as she tried to discern from which direction the cries were coming.

"What is what, Milord?" the guard captain asked.

"That crying. Someone is crying, this way I think." She directed Roen off the path.

"My Lord," the guards protested as they followed her into the thick woods.

"Milord, these woods are charmed. It might not be a child you hear—it could be a goblin or spirit," the guard captain said.

"I highly doubt that. If it is not a human, it is probably the wind," Britt said, ducking a branch.

Britt and her guards chased the sobs until they came to a small break in the trees. Sitting on a rock, crying her eyes out, was a ragged-looking child. Snot was smeared across her face, and she was covered in a layer of dirt. A basket of mushrooms rested near her bare feet, and she immediately silenced herself when she saw Britt and her guards.

"Hello," Britt said, swinging off Roen. "What's wrong? Are you lost?"

The little girl pulled her legs close to her body. "A-Are you a faerie that's come to take me?"

Britt smiled, holding back a grimace when she drew closer to the girl. The dirty child smelled overwhelmingly of sweat and pig. "No. I'm a...soldier," Britt said, crouching in front of the girl. (Britt had a feeling that a king finding this poor girl would be even worse in her mind than a faerie.) "I live in the big castle that's just past the edge of the forest."

"Camelot!" the little girl said.

"Yes, that's the one."

"I'm from Camelot, too," the girl said, wiping her dirty face on her dirty sleeve.

"Really? What are you doing all the way out here? We are a fair distance from Camelot."

"Mother sent me to the forest to pick mushrooms. I'm the

only one in our family that's good at finding them. I always pick lots."

"She told you to come this far into the forest to pick mushrooms?" Britt asked.

The little girl blinked back tears and miserably shook her head. "No. But I saw mushrooms, lots of 'em. So I went deeper 'n deeper in the forest, 'n I think a faerie bewitched me 'cause I lost my way, and I *never* get lost 'n I," the little girl didn't finish and instead broke off into a sob.

"There, there," Britt said, placing a gentle hand on the girl's head. "You happen to be in great luck. As I said, we're from Camelot. We're running an errand right now, but we'll be riding back home after that. Would you like to come with us?"

The little girl hesitated. "Do you swear by the cross you're from Camelot?"

"I do," Britt said.

"Say it."

Britt raised her hand and solemnly said, "I swear by the cross that my companions and I are from Camelot, and we will have you home by supper."

The little girl flung herself at Britt, almost knocking her backwards.

Britt coughed at the force with which the girl hit her, and the little girl's odor. Maybe she could dunk her in Nymue's lake before riding back to Camelot.

Britt stood, carrying the girl—who meekly said, "My mushrooms."

"Right, we mustn't forget the mushrooms. I'll have one of my men place them in a pack so they safely make the journey," Britt said, carefully stooping over to pick up the basket as the girl clung to her like a leech.

Britt passed the mushrooms off to the captain of the guards and idly eyed her protectors. "I don't suppose one of you would be willing to break off and take this girl home right now?"

"Not for your life, Milord."

"That's what I thought," Britt grumbled, turning to Roen. As Britt slid the little girl on Roen's back, she noticed three knights in full armor riding war steeds further in the trees.

Britt pointed to the girl and shouted to the knights, "Is she yours?"

Two of the knights ignored the shout and rode off into the forest. The remaining knight—who was dressed in blue and white—shook his head.

Britt mounted up behind the girl, blinking at the girl's sour scent. "Are you in need of assistance?" Britt asked the knight.

"You are Arthur," the knight said, his voice muffled by his helm.

"Yes," Britt said to the horror of her guards—who immediately spread around Britt in a defensive pattern.

"You mean to return her to her home?" the knight asked.

Britt tilted her head, "Yes."

"Why not have your men care for her?"

Britt wryly looked to her guards. "I don't think they would," she dryly said. "Any more questions?"

The knight shook his head. "You are a just man, My Lord," he said before riding off into the forest.

"That was odd. Right, who can lead the way back to the road?" Britt asked, turning to her guards.

The rest of the ride to Nymue's lake was uneventful. The forest was peaceful, and the lake was just as Britt remembered it. There was a boat near the beach where Britt and her men arrived; there was *still* a mother and baby deer eating lush grass near the shoreline, and the lake was clear and untouched.

"Nymue has a good eye for real estate." Britt dismounted Roen before lifting the little girl off the horse's back. "Stay close to my men," Britt told her, pointing to her guards. "I'm going to speak to someone. I will most likely be back right away."

The little girl bobbed in a wobbly curtsy—apparently having

picked up on the titles Britt's men and the knight used to address her.

Britt smiled at the girl before she walked to the edge of the lake. "Nymue will be here shortly. I need to speak with her alone. Remain at this beach, and I will stay within eyesight," Britt said when the guard captain joined her.

"Yes, Milord."

Britt smiled and slapped the man on his back before she turned towards the deer.

As expected, Nymue was just past them, dressed in her green outfit with her hair long and draping over her body. What was unexpected, though, was the big smile on her lips and the two women who were with her. They also looked vaguely "faerie" with long, unbraided hair and shimmery clothes—one wore blue; the other wore pale red.

Nymue raised her hand and nodded to Britt as she approached them but conversed with her companions. "— Cannot believe our good fortune that they finally left. The Slobs were on the brink of drinking us dry, and the Debaucher broke the hearts of all the water nymphs," Nymue said, her smile almost greedy.

The red faerie lady frowned, making fine lines crease around her mouth. "I do not understand why you detest them so. All three of them are very kind and honorable."

Nymue snorted like a wild boar. "They are not kind in any way of the expression. They do nothing but eat us out of the lake and cause a ruckus. Next time they wander back, do *not* let them back in our realm, I forbid it! If I hear that either of you approved their entrance, there will be repercussions."

"But they say the nicest things," the lady in blue insisted. "And all three are so handsome. They said I must make the moon envious with the glow of my skin."

"Pretty words drip off their tongue like the poison of a serpent. Do not let them back in, and that is final!" Nymue said, her eyes narrowed and her voice thunderous. She settled her shoulders and adopted her joyous-beyond-all-belief smile again. "They are gone now, so there is no sense in meditating over what is done. We can only rejoice that they have finally left."

Britt cleared her throat.

"Ahh, yes, King Arthur. I was getting to you. What brings you to my humble abode?" the Lady of the Lake said as she finally greeted Britt.

"A wish to return your visit," Britt said, mustering her courage. "I didn't know you already had company."

"They have just left," Nymue said.

The faerie lady in red smiled and fluttered her eyes. "Nymue, won't you introduce us to your guest?"

"Certainly—although I wouldn't bother with the beauty routine; the King isn't the type to dally in romance. Ladies, may I present to you King Arthur of Camelot. Arthur, these are my ladies in waiting, Aislin and Keela."

Britt performed her most elaborate bow. "It is a pleasure to meet you, ladies," she smiled.

Aislin and Keela giggled, and Nymue rolled her eyes. "If you will excuse me, girls. I wish to speak to the King alone."

Aislin and Keela coyly waved to Britt as they retreated down the shoreline, swishing their skirts.

Britt awkwardly itched the back of her neck. "Wow, are they ever barking up the wrong tree."

"I am not familiar with the words you use, but I agree with your implied meaning," Nymue said, settling her hands in front of her. "Now, what can I do for you?"

"Pardon?"

"You obviously came here to ask for another boon. Normally, I would send you home with your tail between your legs, but as I have just experienced a stroke of good fortune, I am inclined to be generous," Nymue said. "How may I help you?"

"I am in need of faerie magic. I am not from...Britain. The

only way I am able to understand what people say is through the use of a spell Merlin cast on me," Britt said.

"Intriguing. Continue."

"As useful as the spell is, I have hit an area in which its helpfulness is limited."

"I'm not one of your knights in court who needs to be petted and doted upon to grasp a basic concept, Sire. Spit it out."

"Queen Morgause of Orkney is visiting and has brought her four sons with her. I can't understand a single thing her sons say. It sounds like another language, but Merlin insists it is merely that they speak with a thick accent. The magic seems unable to translate it for me. Merlin said adjusting the spell to translate accents is beyond his abilities."

"Amateur," Nymue said, shooing a butterfly away. "You are in luck. I know of the spell, and I know how to spin it so you may understand Morgause's spawn. It will only take a few minutes—although we will have to stand in the lake. It makes my magic stronger—which I will need to finish this particular spell."

"I cannot thank you enough, Nymue."

"So now you say thank you with that pretty mouth of yours? I cannot say I am happy to help you, but I would rather have you on the throne than some idiot like the Debaucher, so I guess I will aid you."

MERLIN JUMPED Britt the moment she returned from her lake-visiting excursion.

"Where have you been? You said you were going for a ride, not a sightseeing tour." He paused and took a step back. "Why do you smell so horrible?"

Britt grimaced. "I'm making a new decree: we're building public bath houses."

"Like the one Romans built?"

"I have no idea. As long as it has fresh water people can use to wash, I don't care. I am going to single-handedly improve the hygiene of this castle if it kills me," Britt said, handing Roen off to a stable boy. "What have I missed?"

"The harpy squawked furiously when she realized you'd ridden off without her. She's in her den right now preparing for our dinner feast. Her spawn are seeing to their horses."

"Perfect, I can test them without Morgause hovering over my shoulder," Britt said, making for the stables.

"Test what?" Merlin asked. "Wait—you didn't."

"I did."

"And she actually *helped* you? By the bells of Heaven, if I knew that's where you were going, I would have tied you up and kept you here. The Lady of the Lake could have turned you into a frog, you know."

"I caught her in a good mood. Apparently she had just ridden herself of some unwanted lake-guests."

"Fortune favors the foolish, I suppose."

"So you claim, but we'll see if the spell actually works," Britt said as they entered the threshold of the stable.

Morgause's sons were clustered around two stalls. Gawain was in one seeing to a fine chestnut horse. Agravain was in the stall next to him, brushing a red roan. Gaheris and Gareth stood on their tip toes outside the stalls, straining to see their brothers.

Britt stopped just behind the two youngest boys. "Good afternoon to you, Gawain, Agravain, Gaheris, and Gareth. I trust you slept well last night and enjoyed your morning?"

All four boys bowed to Britt. "We did, my King," Gawain said.

Britt shot Merlin a triumphant grin.

The enchanter shrugged. "It's faerie magic. Of course it would work. I'm off—don't go disappearing again, or I shall send Sir Kay to sniff you out. Blast!" Merlin said when he almost collided with Cavall.

The giant mastiff dragged one of the kennel boys behind him without remorse as he approached Britt, his tail wagging.

Britt chuckled and crouched to rub the dog's shoulders. "It's fine. You may return to the kennels. Thank you for watching him," Britt told the boy.

"Yes, My Lord," the boy said, rubbing his arms as he made his retreat.

"Did you miss me, Cavall?" Britt asked the giant dog, laughing when he pressed his wet nose to her temple.

Gawain and his brothers stared at the exchange, reminding Britt that she was supposed to be winning Gawain over. "Do you have dogs back in Orkney?" she asked.

"Of course we do, My Lord," Agravain scoffed.

"I didn't mean if you had a kennel. Do you, hm...do you personally own any dogs?" Britt asked.

"No, My Lord," Gawain said. "I once had a small hunting hound, but since then, Father has taught us that affection for an animal is useless."

"That's a downright silly thing to say," Britt said, biting her tongue to hold back a laugh when Gaheris and Gareth stared at her with googlie eyes. "Where's your beanbag?" Britt asked her dog.

Cavall trotted down the aisle, disappearing from sight.

"Affection weakens a man," Agravain said. His voice sounded canned, like a parrot repeating words without knowing the meaning.

"And *that* is a *stupid* thing to say," Britt said, ignoring the collective gasps from King Lot and Queen Morgause's sons. "If you're an idiot with your affections and act melodramatic about it, then yes, it weakens you. But there are very few men here in Camelot of whom I am fonder than Sir Kay, my foster brother, and there are even fewer men I would trust more with my life than Kay. So, you see, affection does not weaken us, but makes us stronger."

The four brothers were quiet as they reflected on Britt's words.

"Good boy," Britt said when Cavall returned with his beanbag, which she threw for him.

When Cavall brought it back, Britt took the beanbag and scratched Cavall under his chin. "Good boy, Cavall."

"Can, can I pet him?" one of the younger boys, Gareth, asked.

"Certainly. Let him sniff your hand first so he knows you're a friend," Britt said, delighted she was able to share the odd bits of dog wisdom she had picked up since acquiring Cavall.

Gareth held a hand out to the giant mastiff. He swallowed hard when the dog snuffled him, but ran his hand down Cavall's massive shoulders.

Cavall sat patiently, looking a Britt with a loyalty that made her throat tighten.

"He's soft," Gareth said as Gaheris joined him.

Gawain leaned out of the stall to watch his younger brothers. "He's a fine looking animal. He was bred in your kennels, My Lord?"

"I believe so. Kay gave him to me when we first came to Camelot. He's more well trained than I could ever teach a dog to be," Britt said, passing the beanbag to Gaheris, who threw it.

Cavall watched the beanbag sail and looked back at Britt. She nodded, and Cavall got up to track down the makeshift toy.

"These are your horses?" Britt said, looking at the horses Gawain and Agravain stood with.

"They are, My Lord," Gawain said.

"They're some of the finest horses in Britain, My Lord," Agravain said, daring Britt to say otherwise.

"You should see Merlin's horse. It's as skinny as a deer but it runs like the wind. The thing is half bones, and the other half is spite. I'm sure it got its sweet temperament from its rider," Britt said.

"The black horse the stable boy led here before you arrived, was that your horse, My Lord?" Gawain asked.

"Probably. His name is Roen."

Agravain started brushing his horse again. "He seemed poorly muscled for a stallion. Ow!" he said when Gawain reached over the stall wall and smacked his brother on the head.

"He's not a stallion. He's a gelding," Britt said.

"Not a stallion? He can't be your war steed then, My Lord?" Gawain asked.

"He is my mount of choice for battles. He's trained for them, but as a bonus, I don't have to half kill him to keep him under control when a mare prances past. It's a wonder more soldiers don't ride mares just to make knights lose control of their horses," Britt said.

Outside the church bells rang. Britt counted the tolls before grimacing. "As entertaining as this has been, I must leave. We will dine soon, and Merlin will never forgive me if I arrive smelling like a pig. I will see you all this evening, I suppose—thank you, Gareth. Cavall, come," Britt said, taking the beanbag when Gareth handed it to her before leaving the stable, Cavall on her heels.

3

FAMILY LOYALTIES

"**Y**ou have done magnificent things even though you have been on the throne for but a short time," Morgause said.

Britt muffled a yawn as she strolled with Morgause. The evening feast was still in full swing, but when Britt expressed a desire to walk around the great hall, the queen insisted on coming with her. Unable to politely refuse her company, even though Morgause was the very reason Britt wanted to leave the table, Britt reluctantly accepted.

"Even the fae accept you, else they never would have given you a sword even half as grand as Excalibur," Morgause said with a meaningful look at Excalibur, which hung from Britt's belt. "Your men are so loyal to you. I heard how bravely they fought for you against my husband and his allies. They sounded so fearsome, but now that I have come I can see they fought out of love for you."

After a few moments of silence Britt realized Morgause was finally expecting a reply. "You are too kind, My Lady."

Morgause's smile did not glitter as it usually did. Instead, she pursed her lips and looked around, removing her attention from Britt.

Wherever Britt and Morgause walked, knights watched them like lovesick puppies. Morgause seemed to gain more admirers by the moment, or more realistically, her magic was able to reach deeper and deeper into the hearts of Britt's men every hour she spent at Camelot.

Britt stopped and turned around. Griflet and Ywain were still there. The pair had shadowed Britt and Morgause since they first stepped off the dais. Griflet watched Morgause with calf eyes, but Ywain kept his attention on Britt, which was starting to make her uneasy.

Britt twitched her fingers at the teenagers in a "come here" gesture. Griflet happily complied, claiming Morgause's attention as soon as he drew near.

"My Lady, you are simply beautiful this night," he said, bowing so low he had to adjust his tunic when he came upright. He completely ignored Britt. "You are more graceful than a swan."

Morgause laughed, and the sparkle returned to her smile. "Thank you, young knight."

"Oh, I am no knight. Not yet anyway. I am just a man who is happy to bask in your beauty."

"Are you sure you are not a knight? You speak and hold yourself like one," Morgause flirted.

"My Lady, I cannot say how glad your words make me."

Britt rolled her eyes at the nauseating display—Griflet was younger than Gawain and was making quite the spectacle of himself, although the other lovesick puppies probably didn't notice anyway—before she turned to Ywain.

The young man was intensely quiet, something unusual for him as he was prone to dramatic displays.

"Everything alright, Ywain?" Britt asked.

"I was thinking of asking you the same thing, My Lord," Ywain said.

"The food is delicious, and everyone is more or less behaving themselves. What more could I ask for?"

Ywain hesitated. "If I may be so bold, My Lord?"

"You are my defender, Ywain. If you have something on your mind, please share it."

Ywain glanced at Griflet and Morgause—who were still carrying on over each other—and leaned closer. "My Lord is not…amorous of Queen Morgause?"

Britt blinked. "The Queen is twice my age, married, and my half-sister. No, I cannot say I am at all amorous of her."

Ywain's shoulders heaved in relief. "I am glad to hear it. She is an enchantress, My Lord. She knows magic. She has powers over most men. She may seem nice, but she has the cunning of a viper, if you will pardon my frankness, My Lord."

Britt stared at Ywain for a moment.

The young man uneasily shifted. "Did I speak out of turn, My Lord?"

Britt smiled and set her hand on his shoulders. "You did not. I was merely thinking that I have underestimated you, and I should prize your loyalty more highly than I already do."

Ywain blushed with pleasure. "I am honored to hear that, My Lord. I shall do my best to keep Griflet away from her."

Britt chuckled. "You have my thanks."

Ywain bowed before he reached out and yanked Griflet by the arm, hauling his protesting friend away.

Morgause watched their abrupt exit with narrowed eyes. "Who was that young man?"

"The one complimenting you? That would be young Griflet," Britt said.

"No, the other one."

"Ah," Britt said, oddly unwilling to share Ywain's name. "He is not a knight, yet, although I expect I will be knighting him soon. I met him when I fought your husband and his allies."

"He is very loyal to you, isn't he?"

"He is," Britt said, unable to keep a chord of pride out of her voice. She had a feeling that Ywain was one boy Morgause would never be able to sink her claws into.

Morgause snapped out of her close observation of Ywain. "It is right for him to be so dedicated to you, My Lord. You are a good commander and a generous king."

Britt set her shoulders, preparing herself for more of Morgause's poisonous compliments.

"If you'll pardon the intrusion, My Lord?" Sir Kay stood at Britt's elbow, the corners of his mouth twitching under his mustache.

"Of course, what is it, Sir Kay?" Britt said.

"Merlin would like to speak to you alone. He says it is a kingly matter that we need not bore our guest with," Sir Kay said.

"I agree whole heartedly with him," Britt said. "I would not want you to go without entertainment for a single moment, and I'm sure any number of my knights would gladly take my place. If you will excuse us, My Lady?"

"Of course," Morgause said, unable to reply any other way.

As Britt and Sir Kay walked back to the dais, Britt briefly slung her arm around Sir Kay. "I cannot thank you enough, Sir Kay. I think she meant to suffocate me with her complimentary prattle."

"She's trying to win you over, My Lord. I think it has become a thing of pride for her," Sir Kay said.

"In any case, you still saved me."

"I cannot take the credit. It was Merlin who sent me."

"You are determined not to take a single compliment, aren't you?"

"Perhaps, My Lord."

"Very well then, as much as you dislike it, you still have my thanks," Britt said, nodding good-bye to her foster brother before joining Merlin on the dais. "I hear I have you to thank for my rescue."

Merlin shrugged. "It was no trouble. I do not wish to see you miserable, no matter how you may think otherwise," he said, looking out at the feasting crowd. "Him," Merlin said, indicating to Ywain.

"What?"

"Young Ywain, what did he say to you?"

"That Morgause is a poisonous snake."

"His loyalty to you knows no bounds. You have won him over for life."

"What makes you say that?"

Merlin tucked his hands inside the sleeves of his robe. "Do you not remember how Urien—Ywain's father—and Lot are related?"

"They are brothers-in-law, related through their wives, right?"

"Yes. Think on that for a moment."

Britt looked around the room before it hit her. "Morgause is Ywain's aunt?"

"She is his mother's sister, yes."

"That means he is supposed to be my nephew...does he know?"

"Of your supposed parentage? Yes."

"Then why hasn't he said anything?"

"Sometimes men want to believe in a cause bigger than themselves. That is how Ywain thinks."

Britt stared at Morgause, who was surrounded by knights clamoring for her attention. Kay stood at the base of the dais watching with a scowl. "Why didn't Morgause recognize him? She wanted to know who he was."

"Just because she is his aunt doesn't mean she has seen him more than a handful of times in his life. I'm not entirely sure if she has ever seen him, to be honest," Merlin said. "Regardless, he still would have heard of her from his mother."

"You don't think he'll be pulled in by Morgause?" Britt asked.

"No. There are a few that are loyal to you, and they will not be moved," Merlin said. "Ywain is one of them."

"And Sir Kay and Sir Ector?" Britt timidly asked.

Merlin nodded. "Them, too."

"I'm glad."

"If you're so glad, then you should work to win over more of your men."

"Yes, Merlin."

"Don't you 'yes, Merlin' me!"

"Of course, Merlin."

"That's hardly any better."

"You don't think I know that?"

"Harridan."

"I find it amusing that you resort to name calling when you can't think of anything better to say."

"Only to those who deserve it."

"Yes, Merlin."

EARLY SUNDAY MORNING, Britt dozed in the comfort of her bed. As usual, the previous night gave her only snatches of sleep. Britt still enjoyed the luxury of sitting in her warm bed with no one pestering her, though. The room was quiet and smelled faintly of flowers—a new bunch were placed in her room every afternoon, a custom Britt had grown to love.

Britt was taking her time in bed to mull through the bits of Arthurian lore she remembered. "Gawain is here, now. If I can get him to stay, that probably means Lancelot and Guinevere aren't far behind." Britt moaned. "I *hate* Lancelot and Guinevere. As soon as I find out who Lancelot is, I'm going to slug him in the nose."

If Britt remembered right, almost everyone portrayed the love between Lancelot and Guinevere as a beautiful but tragic thing. No one held them accountable for single-handedly ruining Arthur's life, and no one ever commented on what a sucky best friend Lancelot was, or what a faithless wife Guinevere was. Instead, they focused on how much they loved each other but how *Arthur* tore them apart.

The only person who ever thought differently was one of the instructors at Britt's first sword hall. Britt didn't remember much about the man besides his dislike of Lancelot and his mustache, as she was barely five when she first started her lessons. However, she did remember that her instructor was the first person to point out what a playboy Lancelot was.

Britt yawned. "Yeah, I don't care about the legends. As soon as Lancelot comes prancing into Camelot, I'm sending him prancing right out of here."

Someone knocked on the door. "May I come in?"

Britt stretched in her bed. "Sure, Merlin," she said.

Only Merlin and her guards ever woke her in the mornings, and her guards only shouted to her through the doors.

The door opened. "What are you doing? Did you not hear the first bell? You—."

The door shut soundly.

Britt picked her head off her pillow. "Merlin?"

Merlin, once again standing out in the hallway, hissed through the door. "You're still in bed."

"Yeah, so?"

"It is *indecent* for you to allow a man into your bedchambers when you are still in bed!"

Britt peeled back a blanket and laughed. "What? Why? I'm fully clothed. It might be warm outside, but it's freezing in here so it's not like I'm showing any skin."

"Indecent!" Merlin repeated through the door.

Britt rolled her eyes and sat up. "What did you want?"

"Get up. We're going to Mass."

"No, *we're* not. You might be, but I'm not."

"Oh, yes you are, you little heathen."

"It's boring. The pastor only talks in Greek or Hebrew or whatever that language is."

"He's the archbishop, and he conducts the service in Latin."

"Mmm, yeah that," Britt said, falling back into her bed with a thump.

"Do not lie back down, you unschooled foundling!"

"Too late," Britt said. "If you want me to go to Mass, you're going to have to drag me out of here. How *indecent* would that be?"

The door opened, and Merlin stormed in. "Drag you, you say? Fine! You were complaining I never use my magic, so I shall," he said, staring at the wall and *not* Britt in her bed.

Merlin pointed a finger at Britt and said something that seemed to boom in the room. The next thing Britt knew, she was drenched in icy water.

Britt launched out her bed, spitting like a cat—narrowly avoiding stepping on Cavall. "You jerk!"

"Get dressed. We're going and that's final," Merlin said, already out of the room, closing the door behind him.

Britt squeezed water from her hair. "I'll remember this!"

"See that you do."

BRITT WAS SEATED on her throne, absent-mindedly petting Cavall as she stared at the ceiling when Sir Kay arrived.

"I was told you wanted to see me, My Lord?"

"Ah, perfect timing. Kay—sorry—Sir Kay, I need your help," Britt said, heaving herself out of her throne. She picked up a few sheets of paper that were tucked against the side of her throne before trotting down the stairs. "I have decided I need a riding helmet."

"A what?"

"A riding helmet. Where I come from, people wear thick,

padded helms that encircle the top half of the head to prevent injury when riding. You know, in case the horse throws you or something. I was willing to go prancing around without one when I thought this was all a dream, but I've grown increasingly apprehensive with the idea of riding without one."

"Wouldn't a normal helm suffice?" Kay asked.

"No, the insides of a riding helmet are more cushioned. Also, the helmet rings across the forehead, then goes down behind the ears and encases the back of the head," Britt said, tracing out the trail with her fingertip on her skull. "Nothing covers the eyes so the rider maintains optimum vision. A strap is fastened to the helmet and cinches at the chin to keep the helmet on the wearer."

"I see. I could try talking to our armor smiths. I am sure we can come up with something for you, although it may take some time," Sir Kay said.

"I drew up a couple of rough sketches to give you a better idea of what I'm looking for," Britt said, handing Sir Kay the papers she held.

Sir Kay briefly looked over the sketches. "This will be a help. Thank you, My Lord. I will keep you informed."

"It's not too bothersome?"

Sir Kay spared Britt a rare smile. "Anything that further protects you and your welfare is *never* too bothersome, My Lord."

Sir Kay bowed and took his leave. Britt stretched and considered her options. "I could sit up on the throne, where even Morgause dare not bother me, or I could chance walking around —but she'll dog my every step, and I'll have to listen to my knights swoon over her," Britt groaned.

Across the room, Morgause, ringed by young knights, started walking in Britt's direction.

"I need to decide quickly," Britt said. Merlin happened to walk by the throne room doors at that moment, carrying a bundle of flowers.

"Cavall, come," Britt called to her dog before hurrying after her counselor. "Merlin," Britt called as she bolted into the hallway.

Merlin turned, barely visible over the pile of flowers. "What? Oh, it's you, Arthur. Looking to escape the harpy?"

"You don't need to say it so loudly," Britt said, catching up to him.

"I'll say it as loud as I please," Merlin snorted before starting off again.

"Actually, I did have something I wanted to ask you."

"Oh?"

"Yes, did you talk to Sir Ulfius about the Round Table?"

"Are you still going on about that? No, I haven't. I've been quite occupied since Morgause arrived, if you haven't noticed," Merlin said as they started climbing stairs.

"Could you ask him? It's important," Britt said, slightly out of breath by the time they reached the floor Merlin was looking for.

"It means that much to you, does it? Very well, I shall speak to him."

"Where has he been anyway? I haven't seen him at all since Morgause arrived."

"I've been closeting him away. He's loyal to me, but I'm not sure how loyal he is to you. It would be a dicey thing to have your chamberlain in love with Morgause."

"Ahhh," Britt said, blinking when they stopped outside a set of doors. "This is my room."

"It is," Merlin confirmed before he struggled to open the door. He entered it and kicked Cavall's blanket aside as he stomped over to the vase of flowers. He took the old flowers out and struggled to arrange the flowers he carried into the vase.

"*You're* the one who has been putting flowers in my room?" Britt asked. "I thought it was a maid."

"Nonsense. Do you think I let many people prance through your rooms? It would be dangerous indeed," Merlin said, cutting a flower stem shorter with a belt knife.

"*Why* have you been bringing me flowers? I mean, I love them. They're the only part of the whole room that I like besides my bed, but you didn't strike me as the flower type," Britt said.

"I am most assuredly *not* a flower man," Merlin said, "but you said you love flowers."

"What? When?"

"The night we spent on the castle walls. You said you and your sister visited a specific flower shop whenever she came into town, and you always wanted a house with a garden so you could grow your own flowers."

"You actually paid attention?" Britt blinked.

Merlin paused in his flower arranging and turned to face Britt with a furrowed brow. "Do you really have such a nasty image of me? Of course I paid attention. You are important, Britt, and I would like for you to be comfortable, if not happy," he said, reaching out to briefly rest his hand on Britt's shoulder. He leaned close to study her face. "Are you alright?"

"I'm, I'm fine. I'm just, surprised," Britt said, biting her tongue to keep from crying.

Merlin tilted his head and squeezed her shoulder. The deep blue of his eyes turned warm—like a tropical ocean.

Britt shook her head to clear her thoughts, then smiled ruefully. "You are forever catching me off guard."

He looked at her a moment longer with the unusual warmth before he pulled back. "Good," Merlin said, turning back to the flowers with satisfaction. "As an enchanter, it is my duty to push people off their guard," he said, gathering up the old flowers.

Britt and Cavall followed Merlin back into the hallway. "What are you going to do now?" Britt asked as they started walking.

"Throw these into the rubbish and find Sir Ulfius to ask him about your blasted circular table. What will you do?"

"It's the Round Table, and I'm not sure," Brit said when they started down the stairs. "Any news from King Ban, King Bors, or Sir Bodwain?"

"The company has arrived in Leodegrance's lands. King Ryence was starting to shift his troops, but nothing beyond that."

"Perhaps he will leave now that extra soldiers have arrived."

"It's possible. He is a spineless mouse of a man," Merlin said as they exited the staircase.

"He can't be that spineless if he rallied against Leodegrance," Britt said. She paused and took several steps backward. Gawain, Agravain, Gaheris, and Gareth were all seated on stone benches in front of a window.

"Not necessarily. Are you coming?" Merlin called from farther down the hallway.

"No…I think I'll go outside to check on Roen," Britt said.

"Don't ride off for a day again," Merlin warned before he started walking away.

"I won't," Britt said before turning to face Morgause's sons. "Aren't you all a cheery bunch?"

The four boys looked up at Britt.

Gawain shrugged. "We do our best to stay out of the way," he said.

"That must be dead boring. Come on."

Gareth and Gaheris shot off the bench and attached themselves to Cavall. The mastiff sighed but let them hug his shoulders.

"Where are we going?" Gawain asked.

"To the practice fields. I need to do a bit of stretching, and Excalibur is hurting for a fight," Britt said.

Agravain frowned. "You just told Merlin you were going to see your horse."

"I lied," Britt cheerfully said.

The four brothers grinned to each other as Britt led the way outside.

4

THE "SABLE" KNIGHT

B ritt smiled as the sun warmed her face. She snuggled farther into her couch—Merlin insisted it was a couch, but as it was nothing but a large pile of rushes with a fancy blanket thrown over it, Britt doubted this—and reveled in the silence and peace.

"We should make it back to Camelot by tomorrow afternoon," Merlin said, walking past Britt's napping couch.

"That'll make Arthur sorely disappointed," Sir Ector said, his voice hushed.

"Arthur is lucky he had a Morgause-free holiday at all. He'll be fine," Merlin briskly said.

"It was a good thing you did for Arthur, Merlin. Finagling lords and such so Arthur could leave Camelot for a bit. Well done," Sir Ector said, smacking Merlin on the back.

It took all of Britt's will to keep her eyes closed and breathe deeply as if she were still dozing.

Several days ago, Merlin had announced that Britt had to leave Camelot to settle a dangerous dispute between two barons in the south. The barons were a two- to three-day ride away, and they would be adopting a grueling pace to travel, so naturally

Morgause could not come. They left Sir Kay in charge and traveled south with a large band of knights (those that were the most susceptible to Morgause's charms), more at a care-free pace than a grueling one.

Britt *thought* it odd that the urgent dispute—a squabble over land rights—took only a day to right, and that they were taking their sweet time returning to Camelot.

"When you say it like that, it sounds like I'm going soft. It was for purely selfish reasons that I arranged for our travels south," Merlin insisted.

Sir Ector belly laughed. "Of course, Merlin. Whatever you say. Lo, what's this?"

"I'm not sure, but he looks badly hurt," Merlin said, marching off.

When Britt opened her eyes, Merlin and Sir Ector were halfway across the meadow in which they were camped. At the edge of the forest was a mounted knight and his squire. The knight was tipping in the saddle, and blood dripped from a nasty wound on his leg.

Britt's guards rushed to aid and apprehend the knight, and Merlin started questioning the squire.

Britt rolled off her couch and stood, brushing at her clothes and fixing her hair. She took a drink of water and ate a hunk of squashed bread before she judged enough time had passed that Merlin had very likely gotten most of the story out of the squire —no sense listening to the entire dramatic and traumatic tale when she could get the *Reader's Digest* version—and started meandering towards them.

"Arthur, this young esquire has been telling me of his master, Sir Myles. He just came from fighting the Sable Knight. The Sable Knight speared him and took his shield before hanging it on the branches of an apple tree—which is covered with hanging shields—and rode away without inquiring to Sir Myles if he was in need of aid," Merlin said.

Britt did not have to fake the sorrow and anger she felt. "That is horrible. It is dishonorable and black hearted to leave a fallen knight on the ground."

"It is even more dishonorable to take away the shield of a fallen knight who fought well," Merlin added, making the squire nod vigorously.

"You people have wonky priorities," Britt grumbled. "Are we properly aiding the knight?" Britt asked, peering over the swarm of her men that moved around Sir Myles in an organized fashion.

"To the best of our abilities, yes. The problem is that he has lost a great deal of blood," Merlin said.

"My Lord, if I may approach you?"

Young Griflet nervously rubbed his hands as he stood before Britt. Ywain stood some feet behind him, cheering his friend on.

"What is it, Griflet?" Britt asked.

Griflet squared his shoulders. "I ask that you would knight me, My Lord, so I may ride off and meet this Sable Knight and thrash him."

"No," Britt said before turning back to the squire.

"My Lord," Griflet protested.

Merlin elbowed Britt and shook his head.

"You've got to be jok—jesting. Griflet, you are young and untried. Approaching a knight like this sable guy is no small matter. If his apple tree is heavily laden with shields, it implies he is an excellent fighter. You haven't even beaten Ywain yet. You are not ready," Britt said to both Merlin and Griflet.

"If you have any affection for me at all, you will grant me this boon," Griflet said.

"Then it is certainly a good thing for you that at this moment I *don't* have any affection for you. Ow!" Britt said when Merlin elbowed her again. "What is it?" she hissed to the enchanter.

"Have you forgotten that young Griflet is the cousin of your dear Sir Bedivere?" Merlin said, dragging Britt aside.

"Bother, everyone is related to everyone in Camelot! And that doesn't change my decision."

"Then why won't you knight him?"

"Because he's going to get himself killed."

"First of all, that doesn't matter. His death won't be on your hands. He's responsible for his own fool head. The greater issue here is that he is related to Sir Bedivere. If Sir Bedivere discovers you refused to knight his young cousin, he will feel personally slighted."

"Sir Bedivere is sitting in Morgause's pocket right now. He's not going to react at all."

"Not now, but when Morgause leaves—because she *will* leave —he will hear about it."

Britt pinched the bridge of her nose. "Why is it a bigger deal if someone feels slighted or offended than if they *die*?"

"Griflet won't die. You are right—he's too green and inexperienced to be knighted if it weren't for his family relations. However, this sable chap won't kill him. He's only interested in collecting shields. Disarming Griflet will be child's play for him; he won't even have to hurt him," Merlin said.

"I'm still against this," Britt said.

"I know, but I'm not giving you a choice."

Britt turned back to Griflet. "Very well. I shall knight you, but know that in my heart, I still have misgivings, and I think you are ill-equipped for this adventure," Britt said, wagging a finger at Griflet.

"Thank you, My Lord," Griflet said, throwing himself at Britt's feet.

The young man kept vigil all night in a tiny chapel they found in the woods before receiving the Sacrament from the priest that kept the chapel. He was then reluctantly knighted by Britt.

Just as Griflet mounted his charge and rode off, singing like a loon and completely oblivious of the danger of combat, Sir Myles died.

The royal party stayed in the meadow—with Merlin's permission of course—instead of making the journey home.

Britt nervously paced as Merlin plotted for the future with a less-jolly-than-usual Sir Ector. Ywain lurked in Britt's shadow, watching her with wide eyes.

They didn't hear from Griflet until it was late in the evening and the sky was dusty pink.

Griflet rode into the meadow, slumping across his horse to keep himself seated. His shield was gone; his new armor was dusty and dented, and based on the red smears on some of his armor, Britt had a sinking suspicion he was wounded.

"Get him off that horse and start seeing to his wounds," Britt shouted before glowering at Merlin. "I believe your words were 'he won't even have to hurt Griflet.' If he dies, I will never listen to your advice pertaining to my knights again," she spat. Her anger was so fierce, it seemed to crackle in the air, and everyone kept a wide berth from her as she paced in the meadow.

In the middle of the night, Sir Ector came and put a hand on Britt's shoulders. "He'll live. He wasn't badly wounded—although I'm not certain his pride will ever recover. He wishes to speak to you, but he's sleeping now, so it would be best if you didn't approach him until morning."

Britt nodded.

"Try to get some sleep, son," Sir Ector advised before he waddled away.

When the sun first cast its morning light in the sky, Britt was at Griflet's bedside. The young knight had woken early, grimacing with pain.

After swallowing a mouthful of water, Griflet waved away a soldier who was trying to change his bandages. "I should have listened to you, My Lord. I will not doubt your judgment again."

Britt, who had been looking very stormy and flint faced, softened and spared Griflet a sliver of a smile. "I am glad the battle did not cost you your life. What happened?" Britt asked as Merlin joined her at Griflet's bedside.

"I found the three beautiful damsels Sir Myles' squire described," Griflet started. "With great reluctance, they told me in what direction I should ride in to find the Sable Knight. I found the apple tree filled with shields, and I smote the hanging shield that did indeed read 'whoso smiteth this shield doth so at his peril.' When I hit it, the Sable Knight came riding out of a nearby castle. We charged each other with spears. Mine shattered, but the Sable Knight's hit true and swung me from my charger. After the Sable Knight took my shield and hung it on the apple tree, I managed to ride back here."

Britt frowned—she didn't recall any mention of three ladies or a shield-sign, but as she had only heard the summary of the story it wasn't surprising—before she looked to Merlin.

The enchanter lifted his eyebrows and said to Britt, "The spear is not your weapon."

"It doesn't matter. Roen will keep me out of harm's reach until I can hit him with my sword. Roen did that in the battle against Lot and his allies; he will do it again. Besides, I would like to speak with this knight."

Merlin reached for a saddle bag resting on his feet. "I expected as much. As long as I accompany you, I see no reason not to. Let us depart."

"My Lord?" Griflet said.

Britt nodded to Griflet before she raised her voice so most of those in the camp could hear her. "This Sable Knight must be confronted. I will ride with Merlin to seek him out and punish him for his unjust actions."

The men cheered, and Griflet blushed bright red. "Um, My Lord, about his unjust actions..."

"Quiet ye wee lad," one of the more burly guards who usually attended to Britt said as he squatted down next to Griflet's pallet. "It's time ye change yer bandages. Don't ye be batting at me," the guard said before placing his hand on Griflet's chest and pushing the knight back in the bed.

Britt dressed in chain mail—ignoring the snide remarks Merlin made about her lack of armor—and buckled some spare supplies to Roen before mounting up. The black gelding pawed as the sun crept high enough in the sky to cast rays of light in the meadow.

"Take care, and God go with you," Sir Ector said.

Britt smiled and took up Roen's reins in one hand before she waved with the other. "Be safe," she wished before she and Merlin—astride his leggy, twiggy horse—cantered out of the meadow.

Griflet watched Britt go—her chain mail and the gold flourishes on Roen's tack sparkling in the morning light. She was unaware of it, but she was an inspiring image with her gleaming blonde hair and her genteel faerie features set in a look of determination.

Griflet glanced at Ywain, who sat by him. "I see now why you love him so," he said, his voice choked.

Ywain nodded. "He makes you want to be a better person and to see the world the way he does. Our King, he's a great man."

Griflet blinked back tears. "He is."

MERLIN FILLED Britt in on the finer details of the account Sir Myles' squire gave as they rode through the forest.

"So, we're looking for three damsels who can direct us to the Sable Knight?" Britt asked at mid-morning.

"We are, and I believe we may be near."

"What makes you say that?"

Merlin held a finger up in the air. "Listen."

Through the forest echoed the faint pluck of music, laughter, and chattering. The air was flavored with the smell of smoked meat, and if Britt squinted, she could see pieces of colorful tents through the trees.

"I thought we were looking for three girls, not a party in the middle of the forest," Britt said as she fixed the way her helm sat on her head.

"Think, why would three helpless ladies be alone in the woods? They obviously were a part of a bigger party. Come, someone in this procession likely knows the location of the Sable Knight."

They were so close to the grand party that Britt could make out a few of the tents and pitched pavilions when Merlin and Britt were accosted by a crowd of ladies.

There were five or six of them, all gaily dressed with braided hair and crowns of flowers on their heads. They whispered and giggled to each other as they watched Merlin and Britt.

Britt sighed at the attention and was glad her helm hid her face.

"Ladies," Merlin said, managing a half bow from his saddle. "We seek out news of the Sable Knight. It was told to us that a party of damsels whose beauty outshone the stars could set us in the right direction. Now that we have finally found you, would you be so kind as to share the desired information?"

Britt rolled her eyes as Roen itched his kneecap with his muzzle.

The girls giggled louder than ever.

"The Sable Knight? Isn't that—"

"Oh, yes, it is!"

"We passed his castle not a week ago before we camped here, didn't we?"

"We did. I've already told two knights where to find him."

A girl with reddish-blonde hair cleared her throat and smiled her prettiest smile at Merlin. The rest of her companions fell silent as she spoke. "The Sable Knight can be found south east from here, in that direction," she said, thrusting her finger in front of her. "Be careful, sir. He is a splendid warrior. I have never heard of his defeat," she said fluttering her lashes at Merlin.

Merlin handled her with a charm that was less than the choking kind he used with Nymue. "We thank you, fair maiden. Your beauty *and* your intelligence cannot be described," he said before turning his horse to catch up with Britt—who was already riding off in the direction the girl had indicated.

The girls squealed and ran in a ring around the reddish-blonde haired girl, laughing and complimenting her as Britt and Merlin disappeared in the trees.

"I didn't peg you as an amorous lover of women. It appears I am wrong," Britt said.

Merlin scoffed. "Hardly. Do you really think I would be so reverential to such an empty headed-girl without reason? That was Lady Guinevere of Camelgrance, daughter of King Leodegrance."

"*What?*" Britt halted Roen.

"The red head. She's Leodegrance's daughter."

"What did you say her name was?"

"Guinevere. Arthur, are you alright?" Merlin asked as Britt almost toppled from her saddle.

Guinevere. The unfaithful queen of England, the love of Arthur's life who ruined him by committing adultery with his best friend, Lancelot.

"She must be touring the countryside while her father is at war. Perhaps we should ask her to come to Camelot," Merlin said.

Britt wheeled Roen in front of Merlin's horse with an expertise even Merlin didn't know she possessed. The black gelding snorted and bumped Merlin's mount before throwing his head. His rider was scarcely more controlled. "Over my dead body," she said before she started off again.

"Well," Merlin blinked, cueing his horse to follow.

"How do you know she is Guinevere?" Britt asked.

"The tents were Leodegrance's colors, and some of his flags

flew from the top poles. Guinevere was wearing the finest dress, and her sash had her father's symbol stitched to it," Merlin explained. "Is something wrong?"

"No."

"You're acting rather oddly—even more so than usual."

"It's fine. Let's find this Sable Knight."

Britt and Merlin rode in the direction Guinevere had indicated for an hour. Just as Britt's butt was starting to hurt, they found the well-described apple tree whose branches groaned under the weight of countless shields.

Beyond the apple tree was a green, trimmed lawn above which loomed a great castle with a large tower and impressive walls.

Britt tried to snap her fingers with her leather gloves on. "This guy. This guy must be the cursed individual who declared people have to have perfectly mowed yards and lawns."

Merlin frowned. "What are you talking about? That's a jousting field."

"Whatever," Britt said as Roen picked his way through a stream before striding up to a shield posted by the apple tree. Britt studied the writing on the shield for a moment. "Merlin, I can't read a word of this. What does it say?"

"Whoso smiteth this shield doeth so at his peril," Merlin quoted. "We have come to the right place."

"May I?" Britt asked, reaching for a hammer that was chained to the sign-shield.

"At your leisure," Merlin said.

Britt took the mallet and pounded the shield a few times before she dropped the hammer and nudged Roen away from it. "Talk about ridiculous. He has a convenient hammer hanging from the warning shield? This guy is looking for fights."

The sound echoed across the hateful lawn/jousting field, and in no time at all, the castle gates opened. Out rode a giant knight covered in pitch-black armor. His horse was black, and the horse's tack was black as well.

Britt scratched her neck as she watched the knight and his charger approach in a controlled, confident prance.

"Hail, Sir Knight," the black knight said when he drew near. "Was it you smiteth my shield—though the warning says not to?"

"Wait, you're the Sable Knight?" Britt asked.

"I have been called that," the knight acknowledged. His voice was the deep thrum of thunder muffled by his metal helm.

"But your armor is black," Britt said.

"Yes," the knight said.

"But everyone calls you the Sable Knight," Britt said.

"Yes," the knight said, sounding as though he thought Britt was rather stupid.

"What were you expecting?" Merlin asked.

"Well, sable, right? Doesn't that usually mean fur? Or like, Sable collies are brown and white. You don't have a scrap of fur *or* brown on you," Britt said.

"Sable also means black in terms of heraldry," Merlin dryly said.

"What? How is that—never mind. So why don't you go by the name the Black Knight?" Britt asked.

The large knight turned his snorting horse in a circle. "The Black Knight sounds like a rogue name."

"And attacking people with spears and stealing their shields is *not* a rogue activity?"

The Sable Knight grumbled. "My name matters not! You have struck my shield, which does me a grave discourtesy. In return, I shall take your shield and hang it upon yon apple tree. If you refuse, I will fight you until I can rip it from your feeble fingers."

Britt rolled her eyes and plucked her shield off Roen's rump and tossed it on the ground. "Fine, there you go. So, Sable Knight. That's misleading. I really think you ought to change it."

The Sable Knight stared at Britt's shield on the ground.

Merlin covered his mouth with the inside of his elbow to stifle his laughter.

"For that matter, you should stop stealing knight's shields. Your apple tree looks like it's going to break from all the weight, and pretty soon the shields are going to get rusty. Not to mention, it looks gaudy," Britt continued.

"Don't you want to fight to defend your shield?" the Sable Knight asked.

"My shield? No, not really. That one clangs loudly when someone hits it; that's why I brought it with me," Britt said.

"Oh," the Sable Knight drooped.

"But I *will* fight you for another reason. You killed Sir Myles, and I never look kindly on slaying a fellow man for no reason, and you roughed up one of my knights."

"What was his name?" the Sable Knight asked, sounding almost conversational.

"Sir Griflet."

"I can't say I've heard of him."

"He's a young knight with an appalling sword stance and is untried in almost all forms of combat," Britt said.

"He has a flea-bitten gray horse," Merlin piped in.

"Oh, that young greenhorn," the Sable Knight said. "The one I tossed from his horse yesterday. I tried to talk him out of it. Anyone could see the lad barely had the basics of combat down. He refused for some time, so I saw no other way but to thrash him. I set him back on his horse when it was all over, though."

Britt blinked. "He didn't mention that part of the story."

"I do not care what others say of me. What matters is that you said you will fight me. Let us cross arms!" the Sable Knight said before wheeling his horse in a circle and charging at Britt.

Britt whipped Excalibur from its scabbard, her heart pounding in her throat as Roen tensed beneath her.

Merlin swooped in and swung his staff at the Sable Knight's

head like a baseball player. The large knight fell off his horse like a chopped tree and lay stunned for a moment.

"Merlin!" Britt said.

"He's fine," Merlin insisted. "You are not skilled at mounted combat, and I'm not going to let you risk your foolish neck for an equally foolish young knight. He's dismounted, so *now* you can fight him properly. I won't step in, I promise," Merlin said as Britt dismounted Roen and slowly approached the Sable Knight, who was lumbering to his feet.

"That was hardly fair," the Sable Knight said.

"I apologize. Do you still find yourself smarting for a fight?" Britt asked, elegantly twirling Excalibur.

The Sable Knight tossed his spear away and unsheathed his sword. "If the fellow on the spindly horse stays out of it."

"He will," Britt said, her eyes glittering as she watched the knight shift his stance.

"Then the answer is yes," the Sable Knight said before he ran at Britt, roaring like a fierce animal. He swung his sword at Britt in a horizontal chop. Britt ducked under the blow and rammed her shoulder into the knight's belly, her feet firmly planted.

The knight sent her skidding back a foot, but she had used his own charge against him when he hit her—a smaller, braced target —with the force of a car ramming into a tree. He bounced backwards, thrown off balance.

Britt lunged forward with Excalibur extended. She hit the Sable Knight in the chest at the prime of her swing.

The Sable knight managed to raise his sword in an attempt to block a second swipe Britt aimed at his chest, but Britt was only feinting. Instead, she whirled in a circle and caught the Sable Knight in his unguarded side, throwing him to the ground.

As quick as a snake, Britt wedged the tip of Excalibur under the knight's helm so it rested against the chain mail at his throat. Britt's shoulders heaved as she stared the knight down and leaned into her sword, applying pressure at his throat.

"I surrender," the Sable Knight said. "Surely I have not met a man more skilled at the sword than you," he said when Britt backed off.

Britt slid Excalibur into its scabbard. "I thank you, but I'm sure there are men a great deal more skilled than I," she ruefully said.

The Sable Knight shook his head. "If you are as skilled with the lance and spear as you are with the sword, you must be the greatest knight in all of England."

"I'm not," Britt said as she removed her helm from her head to wipe sweat off her forehead. "I can't use a spear at all, and Kay almost falls off his horse laughing whenever we practice jousting," Britt smiled.

The Sable Knight, who was in the process of boosting himself off the ground, froze.

"Is something wrong?" Britt asked, exchanging looks with Merlin.

"You are Arthur, *King* Arthur," the Sable Knight said.

"Yes," Britt said with great hesitation. (It seemed random knights in all parts of Britain were asking her that.)

The Sable Knight sunk to his knees and struggled to remove his helm. "I must beg your pardon, My Lord," he said when he finally wrenched it from his head, revealing a man who was approximately Sir Ector's age. His face looked noble but worn by the weather, and Britt vaguely recognized him.

When Merlin sharply inhaled, Britt retreated to her horse. "Yes?"

"My name is Pellinore. King Pellinore," the Sable Knight said.

Britt rummaged through her memories. "King Pellinore, King Pellinore. Sorry I—*oh*," she said, suddenly recalling King Pellinore as one of Lot's closest allies.

The Sable Knight/King Pellinore bowed his head. "Please, do not take further revenge on me."

"What?"

"I imagine you must plan to bring your army here and march against me. But I beg you, My Lord, please spare me," King Pellinore said.

"Why would I attack you?" Britt asked looking to Merlin.

"Because I have hurt one of your knights, and I fought you," King Pellinore said.

"Griflet got hurt because he's a young idiot who wouldn't listen to me. If you tried to talk him out of it as you say you did, I can hardly hold you responsible for attacking him—although perhaps you could have been a little less brutal."

"Singing a different tune now that you've met him, eh?" Merlin asked.

Britt glared at her counselor. "I *thought* the Sable Knight was going to be a blood-thirsty brute of a man. As asinine as your shield-stealing-apple-tree-plan is, I'm not going to go to war over it. Why on Earth are you doing it in the first place?"

"Furthermore, why are you *here*? You rule Anglesey; that's far west and north of here," Merlin said.

King Pellinore rolled his eyes to the side. "After I left King Lot with my troops, I picked up the trail of the Questing Beast and followed him south. When I lost the trail and thought to return home, I received a message from my wife."

"And?" Merlin prodded.

"She was not pleased. She told me I had been absent from my kingdom for so long I may as well stay lost."

"Ah."

"I made up my mind to return home anyway, but Camelot stands between myself and Anglesey…"

"Yes?" Britt said in the silence.

"You thought Arthur would attack you and your remaining guards when he heard of your crossing, didn't you?" Merlin shrewdly said.

King Pellinore sighed. "I did. I wronged my men by involving them in a war against a man who was clearly God's chosen King. I wouldn't get them slaughtered by crossing Camelot."

Britt looked around at the apple tree and the gloomy castle. "So you've holed yourself up here, challenging random knights who are smart enough to read and foolish enough to ignore petty warnings?"

King Pellinore was a stately man, but some of the majesty in his bearings left him when he hung his head.

Britt turned to Merlin, who considered King Pellinore. The wizard nodded after a moment, and Britt blankly stared at him before giving him a thumbs up and a thumbs down. Merlin rolled his eyes and ungraciously performed a thumbs up—a gesture Britt had forced him to learn for the sake of offering advice without using words.

"Stay here no longer then. Unless you pillage and plunder your way home, you're far more likely to be an irritation if you remain here, picking fights, than you are if you travel through my lands," Britt said, settling her helm back on her head.

King Pellinore stood, and the nobility returned to his being as he fixed his gaze on Britt. "You would offer mercy to one who was once your enemy?"

"Of course. Ywain is the son of my one-time enemy King Urien, and he's one of my favorites in my courts," Britt said. "As long as you keep peace with me, I have no quarrel with you. Unless you send your pretty female relatives to plague me," she added dryly.

"Queen Morgause is staying at Camelot," Merlin said at King Pellinore's inquisitive look.

"Oh. My sympathies," King Pellinore said, crossing himself.

"Indeed. We had best be off, Merlin. I would like to have some dinner and ask Griflet what he meant by leaving out the part of his story where King Pellinore advised him to leave," Britt said, mounting Roen.

"I thank you for your mercy, King Arthur," King Pellinore said.

Merlin gave her a meaningful look, spurring Britt to speak. "I hope we can be peaceful neighbors, if not friends, King Pellinore," she said.

"It would be my honor," King Pellinore said.

"Safe travels home. Goodbye," Britt called over her shoulder as she and Merlin started the journey back to camp.

5

DEFINED LOYALTIES

"**I**t is good to be home," Britt said, stretching her hands above her head as Roen walked through the inner gates of Camelot, heading for the royal stable. Servants streamed out of the castle to take saddle-packs, camping gear, and leftover provisions. Knights and courtiers weren't far behind them.

"Welcome home, King Arthur."

"I am glad to see you have safely returned, My Lord."

"God bless King Arthur!"

Britt flashed a quick smile at her greeters before she slid off Roen. "Wow, my butt hurts."

"I am glad to see your short holiday has not drastically changed your personality, My Lord," Sir Kay said, appearing at Britt's elbow.

"Sir Kay, it's good to see you. How did Camelot manage in Merlin's absence?" Britt asked.

"Are you not concerned with how it managed in your absence, My Lord?"

Britt chuckled. "We both know who the real leader is, Kay. Let's not bother to pretend otherwise."

"I wanted to warn you, My Lord. Queen Morgause means to make a request of you."

"Oh?"

"Yes. She wants to go—" Kay cut himself off when across the courtyard Morgause appeared.

"Arthur, you've finally returned home!" Morgause called, extending her arms as she walked towards Britt.

Britt hastily filled her arms with saddle-packs to avoid the embrace and coughed when Morgause's perfume hit her like a wall. "Morgause, you look lovely as usual."

"My Lord, how you exaggerate," Morgause said.

"Hah!" Merlin said as he passed behind Morgause with his horse.

Morgause shot him a glare before she smiled at Britt again. "I have been wasting away without you around to entertain me."

Britt looked past Morgause at the crowd of knights who trailed her like bees. "Somehow, I very much doubt that you were without company in my absence."

Sir Bedivere, who stood a few paces from Morgause, stared at the Orkney queen with calf eyes. He didn't appear to register that Britt stood in front of him, much less that she had returned.

All of the knights with Morgause were much the same. The commoners of Camelot had gathered in the streets and cheered for Britt; the servants had warmly welcomed her home. But her knights? They were too enamored with Morgause to notice Britt.

Morgause smiled playfully. "Jealous?"

Britt thoughtfully stared at Morgause until the queen's smile fell from her face and the stately lady looked away.

Britt turned to face the knights of her procession, still holding saddlebags.

"My Lord, allow me to lighten your burden," Griflet said, approaching Britt with the intent to take some of the packs.

Britt shook her head. "I appreciate the thought, Griflet, but you haven't recovered from your injuries yet."

"My Lord," Griflet protested.

"Ah, see? It turned out fine anyway," Britt said when a servant lunged to take the packs from her.

Griflet sighed and grumbled under his breath. Britt grinned and affectionately ruffled his hair. "I thank you all the same," she seriously told him.

"Young Griflet, you were hurt?" Morgause said, placing a hand over her heart, her face filling with horror.

Griflet sketched a bow. "T'was nothing, My Lady," Griflet said before swiveling back to Britt. "I am better now," he insisted.

"Your courage is impressive, Griflet, but I'm sure you must be sore from riding with your bruises and scrapes. Will you go see a healer—for my mind's ease, if not for your sake?" The way she said it, it wasn't really a question.

"As you wish, My Lord," Griflet sighed.

"Griflet," Morgause called, but the young knight was already gone, limping his way to the castle keep.

Britt wanted to shout and do a victory dance around Morgause. For once, she had won, and Morgause had lost the battle for favor. Britt couldn't help the wide, smug smile that curled across her lips. "Shall we go inside? I must admit I could use some refreshments," Britt said, planning to slip away with the excuse of needing to wash up when she got inside.

Morgause narrowed her eyes as she watched Griflet limp out of sight. "My Lord," she said suddenly. "I have a request to make."

Britt hesitated. "Yes?"

"In celebration of your return home, I ask that a hunting party would be thrown."

Britt froze and rolled her eyes until she could see Sir Kay. Her foster brother grimly shook his head. She scanned the crowd for Merlin, but he was nowhere to be seen.

"As honored as I am by your request, I doubt this is the best time to host such a party. I have been gone from Camelot for some time, I'm sure quite a bit of work has piled up."

"It has, My Lord," Sir Kay helpfully added.

"I foresee that I will not have much spare time in the next week. I don't believe I could leave Camelot for an afternoon, much less a day," Britt said, making her excuse as believable as possible.

Britt wasn't entirely certain what a hunting party entailed. She knew it meant men rode out on horses with hounds and hunted for game, using bows or spears depending on the quarry. Women occasionally went with to serve as spectators, or they had hunting parties of their own with trained hawks and other birds of prey.

King Bors and King Ban had tried to organize such an event before. Merlin, Kay, and Britt had all agreed it was not wise for Britt to join the festivities. She had never picked up a bow in her life, much less fired one while riding a horse. She would be a laughing stock if this deficiency was discovered, and Kay ominously predicted that the party would be a dangerous place for her.

Britt had to focus on training with the lance and spear—as inept with them as she was—so she could be mistaken as a passable knight. She didn't have enough time to train with the bow as well.

"Then let us schedule a hunting party for a fortnight from now," Morgause said, her beetle eyes glittering.

Britt tried to swallow, but her mouth felt as dry and chalky. "You will have to speak to Merlin, first," she said. "I'm not sure how he would feel about hosting festivities."

"Do you do anything without his permission?" Morgause challenged.

Sir Kay shifted until his hand rested on his sword, but Britt shook her head at him, her gaze momentarily flickering to the knights of Camelot who stared at Morgause with devotion. How could they stand there like that?

Britt took a step towards Morgause, ignoring her desire to

sneeze when Morgause's cloying lily perfume swamped her senses. She was taller than Morgause; the height difference was highlighted as Britt drew closer to her. "I don't often do. What of it?"

Morgause took a step back under the intensity of Britt's gaze, and Britt shifted her lips until she was tightly smiling. "Ask Merlin," she advised before stalking towards the castle keep, barely aware of Morgause's four sons who watched her leave.

~

"THIS IS HOPELESS," Britt said as she leaned on her bow and gloomily stared at the target at which she was supposed to be aiming.

Sir Kay smoothed the corners of his mustache as he thoughtfully stared at Britt's arrows. All of them were ringed around the outside of the target, a feat that would normally be praised if it weren't for the fact that they were less than a stone's throw from it.

Britt itched her right eyebrow. "Why did Merlin want me to even *try* archery? I thought our goal was to make me into a passable knight so I could joust should there be a demand for it?"

"That is the goal, but Merlin was hoping you would prove to be as natural with a bow as you are with a sword," Sir Kay said, retrieving the arrows.

"I'm not a natural with the sword. I worked hard to get to this level, and I started when I was appallingly young," Britt said, crouching down to pet Cavall.

Sir Kay grunted in approval as he placed the arrows in a quiver. "Try again," he advised.

"I'm getting worse the longer we practice. Why doesn't Merlin just tell Morgause to stuff it and go home if she wants a hunting party?"

Sir Kay thoughtfully looked at the sky. "I think he's hoping to use her."

"For what purpose? A hostage?"

Sir Kay shook his head. "Character development."

"Character development? What, are we in some time-period romance now? Forget character development; the woman is a cougar in all meanings of the word."

"My Lord?" someone shouted.

Britt whipped around and watched Gawain and Agravain ride up on their horses. Gaheris and Gareth followed in their wake on ponies.

"Hello, men. Enjoying an afternoon ride?" Britt asked, smiling for the boys' sake.

Gawain pulled his horse to a halt near Britt and Sir Kay. "Yes, My Lord," he said.

"We were looking for you!" Gaheris excitedly said, bouncing in the saddle as his pony trotted towards Britt.

"Gaheris," Agravain groaned.

"What?" Gaheris asked.

"Merlin told us where you went," Gareth said, clambering off his pony's back.

Both Gawain and Agravain blushed as Gareth and Gaheris threw themselves at Britt and then at Cavall.

"I apologize, My Lord. Their manners aren't what they should be," Gawain said, the tips of his ears turned red as he dismounted and bowed to Britt.

Britt laughed. "They're children. It's a joy to see their enthusiasm," she said, watching the boys cuddle her long-suffering mastiff.

"Merlin said you were practicing archery," Agravain said.

"We were," Britt confirmed, turning to Sir Kay.

Sir Kay gravely bowed. "We have since finished."

Britt smiled in thanks to her seneschal and retrieved Roen

from the patch of clover where he was grazing. "Would you like to ride together for a bit?"

"Yes!" Gaheris and Gareth shouted as they hurried back to their ponies.

"If it would please you, My Lord," Gawain said.

"Sir Kay, will you join us?" Britt asked as she swung onto Roen's back.

Sir Kay was frowning. "I have work to complete, and your guards should accompany you."

"We'll stay in sight of the castle. Besides, if you come, I have no need for guards. Please?" Britt asked.

Sir Kay sighed, his shoulders heaving. "Very well."

Britt shot Sir Kay her brightest smile. "Thank you, Sir Kay," she said before whistling. "Cavall come. Who would like to lead the way? Agravain?"

BRITT LEANED against the battlements in Camelot's walls as she stared at the night sky. An owl hooted, and Britt could hear the crickets chirp in the fields outside the castle. All the lights were out in the commoners' area of Camelot and in the farm houses built just outside the walls, but the moon was bright, and Britt could see quite clearly in the darkness.

"Milord."

Britt turned to face the guard that spoke.

He stood with another guard, with Gawain wedged between them. They had their spears crossed in front of him as the guard spoke. "We found him on the stairwell, watching you."

"It's fine. You may release him," Britt said. "Gawain, what has you up at this late hour?" she asked, beckoning to the young man.

"Someone said you hardly get any sleep at night since you stand on the walls of Camelot most of the time. I was wondering if it was true," the young man said.

Britt kept an acidic smile off her face—she was willing to bet money it was his mother who said that after one of Britt's knight's squealed about it.

"It is," Britt said, turning to look at the countryside.

"Why do you stand watch?"

"I'm not standing watch so much as I am…remembering."

"Remembering what, My Lord?" Gawain curiously asked as he rested his weight on the castle wall.

"Those whom I loved and will never see again. Everyone I lost and so desperately wish I could see just one more time," Britt said, unable to keep the wistfulness out of her voice as she recalled her mother, sister, and friends. When she turned to look at Gawain, the young man held a look of such distress that Britt changed the topic. "Or sometimes I dwell on the past week's activities. Like tonight."

"What activity?"

"Mmm, my meeting with King Pellinore. Now there is a man who looks like a true king," Britt dryly said with a touch of jealousy. "He stands like a mountain and nobility and respect practically drip off him. I was wondering how he does it."

"You very much look like a true king as well, My Lord."

When Britt turned her disbelieving eyes on the Orkney prince, he protested. "It's true!"

Britt chuckled. "While I appreciate the sentiments, I must disagree with you. I might be tall and a good swordsmen, but physically speaking, I am not impressive. I don't have that air around me most nobility of this time has, and I don't seem to command respect. If I did…" she trailed off. She could hardly tell Gawain that if she did his mother wouldn't be able to sink her claws into the knights of Camelot.

"You're wrong," Gawain said with a fierceness that surprised Britt. "You look and act more like a true king than even my father. That air you're talking about is nothing but snobbery—thinking everyone is beneath you and that you are of higher worth. You listen carefully to everyone, and you treat people with respect—even if they don't deserve it. You make simple tasks seem grand, and no one is too high or low to escape your notice. If it's looks you're concerned about, you needn't worry. Mother's half jealous because everyone as far as Orkney says King Arthur is the most beautiful being in all of Britain. Besides, you, you can make the world shake with your smile," Gawain finished, his last sentence was little more than an embarrassed squeak.

Britt was touched by the prince's outbreak, although he was clearly flustered with himself and stared at the ground. Britt reached out and placed a hand on his shoulder. "Gawain," she said, waiting until she held his gaze. "Thank you."

Gawain slumped to the ground in a kneel, as if Britt had shot him.

"My Lord, I have a boon to ask."

"Yes?"

"*Please* let me stay here in Camelot and serve you. I will abdicate my claim to my father's throne—I will cut all ties with my family and consider myself an orphan. I can serve as your shield bearer or, or a kennel master. *Please* let me stay with you."

Britt stared at Gawain, trying to keep her shock from showing. She thought it would take years to win Gawain over and see him become one of Camelot's knights. She wasn't expecting a declaration of loyalty and a plea to remain at her side. Besides, it seemed unlikely that Morgause—the ultimate home-wrecker in terms of demanding loyalty—was unable to keep her own children's loyalty.

"Why do you want to stay?" Britt asked. "You could be a king, Gawain. There is no need for you to serve me when you have your own kingdom."

"Because I have eyes in my head, My Lord," Gawain fiercely said. "Even if your knights are blind fools, I see who you are, and I would give my life to follow you," he said, flushing so deep the color was apparent in the moonlight and crawled all the way down his neck before disappearing in the collar of his cloak.

Gawain looked up imploringly at Britt, like he thought he might have gone too far. Britt flashed him a smile. "I would gladly receive you in my courts, Gawain."

"Thank you, My Lord!" Gawain reached for her hands and kissed them.

It took a lot of control to keep Britt from wiping her hands off on her tunic. "But," she said. "I think you should wait to make your decision to stay with me until your mother is ready to leave. Much can happen in a few days, and something might change your mind."

"Mother isn't going to change my mind," Gawain bluntly said. "Her *arts* don't work on me."

Britt laughed before she gave Gawain a hand up. "You are such fun. Thank you for seeking me out tonight, Gawain."

Gawain offered Britt a steep bow. "Thank *you*, My Lord."

∾

"I HAVE NOTICED that your banquet diet consists mostly of wine and that you appear to hold your cup with the intention of crushing it," Merlin said, awkwardly standing behind Britt as he whispered in her ear. His breath tickled her neck, and it felt uncomfortably intimate.

"That's because if I keep a stranglehold on my cup, I won't be able to *throttle* a certain woman," Britt said behind a smile. "Back up, will you?"

Once again, Britt was a prisoner to her table on the dais, and once again it was Britt, Merlin, Morgause, and her children. Normally, Britt would not mind the dinner so much. The past few had been quite passable as Britt was able to converse with Gawain, Agravain, Gareth, and Gaheris when Morgause was not fawning over her.

Tonight, however, the shape of the table had changed, and Britt found herself separated from Morgause's sons. Merlin was next to her, but he was a useless tablemate as usual.

Britt frowned when Merlin briefly rested his warm hands on her shoulders and gave her an encouraging squeeze before he left the dais.

Britt watched him go before she heaved a sigh and pinched the bridge of her nose.

"Tired, My Lord?" Morgause asked, placing a hand on Britt's arm.

Britt held her irritation in check before she offered Morgause a brisk smile and shrugged her hand away by lifting her wine goblet into the air. "You seem to ask that question often."

"The work of a king is very difficult," Morgause said. "Men have it so hard. We women couldn't possibly understand." The queen's voice unexpectedly hardened as she spoke.

Britt thought Morgause was almost boiling with anger, but she blinked, and the queen was back to simpering smiles and crinkled eyes.

Britt considered Morgause as she drank her wine, but her thoughts were interrupted by a clutch of knights that trooped up the stairs.

Britt looked long enough to see that it was Sir Bedivere and two other lapdog knights that, for all practical purposes, belonged to Morgause. Britt sighed and studied her wine goblet with great intensity. Her thoughts returned to King Pellinore, and she wondered if he had started home yet, how he came to have such an expectation of power, and what was a Questing Beast?

In spite of herself, she still heard pieces and bits of the conversation Morgause was having with the knights.

"A harper could not describe your beauty and fragile femininity, for he would lack the skill and the words to give you due credit."

"I thank you, sir knight. You are generous in your praise."

"....stand as an example for all women with your soft spoken words and the meekness of your temper."

"Please, kind sirs. I hardly think I am meek—"

"But you are, My Lady. It is such a pleasing trait to behold!"

"Your eyes are surely the fairest in the land. Truly, I do wish you were *my* lady."

Britt snorted in her wine cup before she set it down and pushed food around her plate when she felt the rebuking gaze of the serving page some feet away. The young boy had taken an unfortunate interest in her calorie intake.

When Britt looked up again, she found Sir Bedivere's eyes on her. Even though he was speaking nonsense to Morgause—something about her hair being as black as a crow's wing—his attention was distinctly on Britt. His entire body faced Morgause, and he was forced to uncomfortably roll his eyes to keep them trained on Britt.

Britt wondered why he adopted such a painful stance before she met his eyes and froze.

Sir Bedivere's eyes were *pleading*. Although the muscles of his face were relaxed and open, his eyes were saturated with despair and screamed for help. It was almost as if he was a prisoner, bound and gagged, and was wordlessly pleading with Britt to set him free.

In a heartbeat, the moment was gone. Morgause leaned across the table, drawing closer to Sir Bedivere and reclaiming his attention. The despair left his eyes, and he was once again reduced to a lovesick puppy.

The damage, though, was done. Sitting in her chair, looking out over the feasting hall, Britt realized all she had done was despair over the effect of Morgause's enchantment on *her*. She felt antagonized because Morgause had reduced her knights to salivating dogs, making Britt look like a fool.

Never had Britt thought how the enchantment affected her

men. It hadn't even occurred to her that they didn't *want* to be enslaved. She just assumed they were weak-minded or fools for a pretty face. But Sir Bedivere's silent plea...that wasn't from a fool. That was a knight, asking his King to save him.

Britt abruptly stood, her chair loudly scraping on the dais.

"My Lord?" Morgause said, looking inquiringly at Britt.

Britt tipped her head back on her neck, as though she were considering the heavens. "If you'll excuse me," she said, dazed sounding as she turned to sweep down the dais.

"Of course," Morgause said, although Britt barely heard her.

The enchantment was no longer a question of honor, but a movement of slavery. Something had to be done; she would see to that.

FOR THREE DAYS, Britt paced in the privacy of her chambers. A mirror hung on the wall across from her—or at least what passed as a mirror in the medieval ages. It was little more than a large, slightly curved disk of highly polished metal, but it still produced a clear reflection when one drew close enough.

Britt shied from it like a deer fleeing fire, although she occasionally stopped in front of it.

She knew a regular parade of men had stopped outside her doors: Sir Ector, Sir Kay, Sir Ulfius, Sir Griflet, and Ywain. Only Merlin had dared to enter her chambers, and all he did was wordlessly watch her for a few minutes before he went back in the hallway with Cavall and ordered everyone to leave her alone.

Britt had spent all three days pondering and thinking of the ways her men could be saved from Morgause—it could be done. Griflet seemed to have shaken off all traces of his admiration for Morgause, but Britt didn't really understand how that happened.

As the third day came to a close, Britt's tired mind grasped two concepts. First of all, Merlin would not save her knights.

Either he was a total hack of an enchanter, or he had decided for some inexplicable reason that Britt needed to sort out the enchantment herself.

Secondly, Britt knew in her gut that *she* would have to be the one to rip the enchantment from her men's eyes. For a time, she had entertained the idea of asking Nymue, the Lady of the Lake, to step in. But the memory of young Griflet lurked in the back of her mind.

"Unless it took getting his brains bashed out by King Pellinore, I think clearing the enchantment had something to do with me—as selfish as it sounds." She slowly moved to her mirror as if it were dragging her forward.

Britt studied her reflection in the metal mirror. There were traces of her old self there—the Britt from America. It was the way the tunic seemed foreign on her, as if she were donning a disguise.

She reached out and placed a hand on the mirror. "I wonder, if I become the king Merlin wants, the king Gawain thinks I am...will there be any of me left at all? Or will it all be King Arthur?"

She closed her eyes against the thought and was assaulted with the image of Sir Bedivere's pleading eyes.

"I owe it to him. I swore it in my vows that I would be a true King when they crowned me. But I don't want to give up all of me and be the Arthur of legends!" she moaned, briefly sinking to her knees.

There came at the back of her mind a nagging thought. What if she *didn't* become the Arthur of legends? What if she gave in and finally acted the part of king? That didn't mean she had to wear the ridiculous shoes and chausses when she could order boots and breeches to be made. Hadn't she already done as much by asking Kay to have a riding helmet made for her?

Britt grasped this mad idea and fanned the flames. "Even if I went back home, I could never be plain Britt from America again.

Change is not a bad thing, and who says I have to give up everything and adopt all details of life here?"

She stood and smiled at her reflection in the mirror. "Forget King Arthur. I'm King Arthur*s*. And *no one* enslaves my men and gets away with it."

6

THE BATTLE FOR KNIGHTS

The throne room was in an uproar. Britt could hear it through the door hidden behind a tapestry on the back wall of the throne dais.

A week had passed, an entire precious week. But it was necessary for Britt to set her plan into motion. She backed off more than usual, letting Morgause think she had won, and even did her best to occasionally give the queen a calf-eyed look.

Kay and a few others had taken Britt aside and asked her to do something—to kick Morgause out of the castle—but Britt refused, and Merlin surprisingly agreed with her. Merlin had even agreed to the queen's request of scheduling a hunting party.

Left completely unchecked, the theatrics and dramatics regarding Morgause had reached new heights. Based on the bits Britt could hear through the door, four of her knights were challenging each other to duels at the top of their lungs over a flower from Morgause's hair. Two men were quarreling over who should read Morgause their sonnet first, and the rest was lost in the mindless roar of lovesick knights.

It reminded Britt of the fanatical antics of the paparazzi chasing a celebrity.

"I believe you are ready, My Lord," Ywain said, bringing Britt out of her thoughts.

"So soon?" Britt asked as Griflet polished her left gauntlet one more time.

Ywain's smile was small, but it went deep. "You make quite the picture, My Lord."

Griflet shook his head in wonder as he backed up to stand with Ywain. "You look like an ElfKing."

Britt shifted and moved in her new armor—which the best blacksmiths of Camelot had scrambled to forge for her. "Someone said something similar about me in the battle against King Lot. What on earth does it mean?"

"It means you are a king too fair, just, and brilliant to be human. That you look holy enough to rule over the elves and the faerie folk themselves," Ywain said with hushed reverence.

"Ywain, Griflet, thank you for your help," Britt said. Neither of the boys had asked why Britt could not put on the armor herself when she approached them that morning. Their silence was the biggest blessing Britt could ask for.

"It is our honor," they said, bowing to Britt.

Britt smiled to them before she turned to the door and opened it. She listened to the men roar for a few minutes behind the veil of the tapestry and shut her eyes.

What if this didn't work? What if her knights remained within Morgause's grasp after this?

Britt felt the reassuring weight of Excalibur on her hip. "Then I'll take care of her," Britt whispered to the air. "Then I will chase her to the end of Britain, and I will make her wish she had never set foot in Camelot until she gives them up."

Britt turned around one last time to look at Ywain and Griflet.

Ywain bowed with an unfathomably deep smile, and Griflet's eyes filled with tears as he smiled broadly.

"You make me proud to be your knight, My Lord, even if I'm not any good at it," Griflet said on an impulse.

"You make me proud to serve you, My Lord. And as I agreed when I took my vows to you, you have my loyalty for all my life," Ywain said.

Their words gave Britt the last bit of courage she needed to step past the tapestry and onto the dais.

Britt confidentially crossed the dais, pausing at the top stair to slide Excalibur out of its scabbard. She picked up a shield next to her throne that she had planted the night before and adjusted her grip on it before taking a deep breath.

Already a few of the knights at the base of the dais were staring up at her, but silence was what she needed. Stiffened with resolve, Britt extended Excalibur and swung it against the shield. The rattling jar from the shield made her teeth shake, but the sound was unmistakable in the din of the room, and Excalibur flashed like harnessed lightning.

"*SILENCE*," Britt thundered.

A dropping hair pin could have been heard in the quiet that followed as all the knights looked up at Britt.

Britt set the shield down and sheathed Excalibur, unaware of the figure she struck.

Griflet had been close when he called her an ElfKing. As Britain had never had a warrior maiden king before, it had never beheld a figure like Britt.

She was tall, for both her time period and the one she was now in, but her narrow shoulders and lack of hulking muscle was made clear from the cut of her armor. Instead of making her appear weak, it highlighted the strength in her posture. Her high cheek bones, dazzling golden hair, and her blazing blue eyes spoke of beauty set on fire when matched with the confidence with which she held herself and her beautiful sword form.

Britt took the knight's silence for surprise, but in truth, it was closer to reverence. Had they *always* served such a splendid looking king? They had. They knew they had. They remembered the way Arthur flew at Lot and the usurp kings like a vengeful dragon when Sir Ector had been unhorsed. How could they forget that?

Britt inhaled deeply before speaking. "I must apologize, because I have wronged you. All of you."

The silence was choking. Britt had hoped for some kind of reaction, but there was none.

"I did not trust you when you have given me nothing but your confidence and devotion. I forgot so quickly the terrible battle we lived through together. I forgot how you fearlessly rode out and killed for me, how you were injured and even slain for me—a beardless youth," she said, cracking a slight smile.

No one laughed.

"I forgot that in London it was you who wanted me as your King, and it was because of you that I was crowned. It is altogether too easy to take personal credit for standing up here on this dais, reigning as king, but..." She paused and walked down the steps, her new armor gleaming in the light of the throne room. "The only reason I can stand is because of you."

Britt looked into the eyes of the knights closest to her. She had their attention.

"I have withheld my respect from you, and it is my wrongdoing. So I ask you today, forgive me and please follow me anew. I will not treat your devotion daintily, but with the roughest courage. For your loyalty is not some fragile thing, like glass, but the most solid thing I know. It is blood and it is blades and armor. It is roars in the battlefield and shouts of celebration. It is the very foundation of Camelot, and it is what makes this kingdom great. I thank you, and I beg for your forgiveness," Britt said before performing a formal bow, bending low at the waist.

Britt closed her eyes to shut herself against reality for a moment as she remained bent. No one said a word, and it was silent...until it wasn't.

In a glittering wave of chainmail and tunics, the knights of Camelot knelt. They planted themselves lower than Britt and watched her with grave intensity. The air sang with the shings of countless swords being pulled free from scabbards as the knights planted their blades in front of them.

Sir Bedivere was the first to speak. "Hail, King Arthur. Long live the King!" he said, his voice booming like a mountain giant. He repeated it again and again, like a chant. Each time more knights joined in until the mantra was the loudest of shouts, and Britt feared they would bring the castle down.

Britt's eyes burned as she straightened and looked at her sea of knights. It was a beautiful sight, and it made Britt's heart ache. She *had* failed them. She was too easily persuaded into thinking that her knights were fickle when she should have fought for them.

Never again, Britt vowed as a shy smile crept across her lips.

When she lifted her chin and flashed a white smile at her knights, they lost it. The shouting and roaring was louder than it had ever been for Morgause as the knights of Camelot celebrated their lord.

Britt looked down the aisle of the throne room, and pinned Morgause in place.

The beautiful queen was rolling her eyes from one side of the throne room to the other. Her expression was unreadable, but her lips tightened. The Orkney queen turned to speak to her sons, but Gawain and Agravain had knelt with Britt's knights and were shouting with them. Gaheris and Gareth were jumping up and down in boyish glee, yelling at the top of their lungs.

Britt made her move and swept up to Morgause while her back was to Britt. "Please, walk with me, Morgause," Britt said, forcefully tucking the queen's arm in hers before pulling her out of the clamorous throne room.

The queen's face was pale and drawn as Britt walked her out of the castle keep and in the direction of the stables. They walked past them, heading for a tiny herb garden Britt knew the cook kept.

It was abandoned at this time of the day, but it was tucked out of the way and—more importantly—out of sight.

Britt pushed Morgause into the small garden ahead of her and unsheathed Excalibur. The faerie sword flashed in the dim light as Britt held it at her side.

"Give me three good reasons why I shouldn't be done with you and kill you right now," Britt said.

While Britt acknowledged she had wrongly judged her men, she was more furious with Morgause than ever before. Morgause's trip was nothing but an act of war, and she had tried to enchain Britt's knights *and* Britt. While she would never go so far as to kill Morgause, the Orkney queen didn't need to know that. Besides, Britt didn't think Morgause would think highly of the other option—bondage in Camelot's dungeons as a hostage until her husband paid up.

Morgause widened her eyes and moved to step closer to Britt. "My Lord, why would you—"

"Not another step," Britt said, placing the tip of Excalibur's blade near Morgause's throat. "I know you have some kind of enchantment up your sleeve, so you had best stop pretending and start talking unless you want me to skewer you."

"How dishonorable, to lay hands upon a lady with the intent—"

"You are no lady," Britt interrupted.

"But a man should never attack a woman, it's, it's barbaric," Morgause said, retreating several steps.

"Oh? But it's perfectly acceptable for you to attack a man, is it?" Britt asked, her smile was frosty like cracking ice.

"I don't know what you're talking about," Morgause said. "Why are you so suddenly thinking ill of me, My Lord?" she asked, her countenance dripping with sorrow.

Britt narrowed her eyes at Morgause. If she wanted to get

anywhere, she would have to provoke the queen into revealing her true persona. "Did you try to take my knight's loyalty away from them in retribution for your husband's pitiful loss? Or," Britt purposely paused, "was it because it became apparent that your sons revere me and would leave you and your kingdom in a second to stand with me?"

Morgause froze, her posture taut and stiff.

Britt strolled around Morgause. "After all, what kind of love is more sacred than that between a mother and her sons? And to lose not one, but four of them? And the eldest being the heir to your kingdom? Now *that* is not only the illustration of shame, but also of irony. How deep their love for you must go," Britt chuckled.

"What do you know?" Morgause spat, her hands clenched in fists. "You think you're better than me? All you do is spout pretty words and deceive everyone around you into thinking you're a great king when you're *not*. You're nothing more than Merlin's puppet!"

"It's true," Britt said before leaning across the distance between her and Morgause. "But it doesn't change the fact that it only took pretty words to lure your sons away, where as *you* had to use magic."

Morgause screamed in fury, but Britt wasn't done.

"And your magic didn't even work on me—though heaven knows you tried. How pathetic you looked, fluttering your eyes at a man—your *brother* no less—who wouldn't even glance your way."

"You are no brother of mine!" Morgause snarled. "You are some sort of fae creature Merlin dug up from God knows where! Only faeries and women can resist the charms and enchantments I was given by the fae of the north!"

"Be reasonable, Morgause. If I was a faerie, I would have no desire to rule over a *human* kingdom," Britt said.

"You cannot deceive me. What other kind of male can be as beautiful as you?" Morgause snarled.

Britt laughed as she tugged on a lock of her hair. When she looked up, Morgause was staring at her.

All anger was gone. Instead, she studied Britt with intensity.

"You-you're a, a woman," Morgause said, her eyes widening.

Britt's smugness left her. "What? Now you're grasping at straws."

Morgause shook her head. "You wouldn't fall victim to my ensnarement, nor did you fight back with magic of your own. If you were a faerie, there would be more enchanters than just Merlin behind you, and you wouldn't have ridden into battle. You're a *woman*."

"Are you mad?" Britt demanded. "Not only is that a great insult, but—" Britt was cut off when Morgause took Britt's free hand in her hands and stared at Britt with something that looked like...*hope*.

Britt swallowed uncomfortably as the Orkney queen stared into Britt's eyes. "It's true. It's true—you *are* a woman!" she said, throwing her arms around Britt in an embrace. Ten years seemed to fall off the queen as her voice grew joyous and her smile bubbled with happiness rather than smug temptation.

"All these years trying—and here you accomplish it! Does Merlin know? He must know. If he threatens to usurp you, tell him I will see him turned into a rat," Morgause said.

"I'm sorry, what?" Britt said.

"For *years* my sister Elaine—wife of King Urien—and I have tried to see a queen rule in Britain," Morgause said. "It was the only reason I came to this blasted castle. If Arthur died and Gawain was his heir, naturally he would need some sort of regent until he inherited his Father's throne as well. I planned to be that regent."

"Um," Britt started, but Morgause was on a roll.

"Men are stupid and daft creatures, and they think us women

to be even less intelligent than they. If a woman was placed on the throne, think of the good she could do! But it has never happened because men *refuse* to believe we have an equal right to rule…until now." Morgause returned her lit up eyes to Britt.

"I'm not telling everyone I'm a girl," Britt finally said.

"No, I suppose you can't. But even if you aren't publically a female ruler, you can improve Britain! You can make life better for women," Morgause said with the devotion of a zealot.

Britt studied the beautiful queen for a moment. "Is it a hard thing? Being married to Lot, I mean."

The smile fell from Morgause's lips, and she looked at the ground. "It is easier for me than most, I believe, being that he is gone much of the time, and I have never had to fear him. But it is difficult. When one is treated like a mindless barn animal most of the time, it is difficult not to *be* a mindless animal. I cannot imagine how women who are only half as lucky as Elaine and I are treated."

Britt considered the problem as she stared at rows of herbs.

"But the treatment of women is only part of it. Some things you are already changing. I heard you have used crown funds to begin constructing a public bath house. Most nobility would see that as sprinkling pearls before pigs, but it is a fantastic idea, My Lord," Morgause said.

"I don't understand. I ordered construction before you knew I was a girl. Why didn't you think it was a fantastic idea then?" Britt suspiciously asked.

"I did think it was. But I was never going to say so because I thought it was Merlin's idea," Morgause said. "Merlin was always such a chauvinistic pig. I thought he would be worse as the King's counselor, but you've changed him. He's softer now…and kinder, too."

Britt laughed. "I highly doubt that. He's just happy that his vision for Britain is finally coming true. But, Morgause, there is no way I can trust you. For all I know, you're saying this to get on my good side since I have reclaimed my knight's loyalties and can freely kick you out of Camelot."

Morgause thought for a moment. "Fine, then I have news for you. In the hunting party four days hence, there will be men who will attempt to kill you."

"*What?*"

"It was my husband's plan. I have a letter if you wish to see it. He sent it to me through a courier while you were gone."

Britt clamped a hand over her eyes. "I'm getting a headache."

"Stay home from the hunting party, and you will be safe. I suggest you find yourself ill the morning it is due to set out," Morgause said.

Britt peeked at the queen from under her hand. "I still don't understand. Why are you telling me this? Why are you helping me?"

"It is true that there is something glorious about a rightful male sovereign. He makes orders and is instantly obeyed; he is the best and brightest of all his peers, and he rules with that distinction. But a female ruler…she inspires. She makes her men feel like they can be better men; she makes them feel trusted and warm. Although you wear the disguise of a man, Arthur, you rule like a woman. I think that is something Britain needs right now, and it is a goal I have long worked towards. I do not care who achieves it as long as it *is* achieved. And if I can help you reach that goal, it will be my greatest pleasure," Morgause said.

The sharp angles and slick, oily quality to Morgause was gone. Instead, she looked at Britt with tired eyes and a tattered smile, more motherly and womanly than Britt had ever seen her.

"Thank you," Britt said.

Morgause's smile widened briefly. "Sadly, as much as I long to stay and watch and advise you, I feel it would be best for you if I left. If I leave before the hunting party, I can tell my husband I thought my actions would make me avoid suspicion over your death. However, I will leave my sons with you."

"Pardon?"

"Gawain would never leave you, and I think Agravain is only slightly less devoted. Gaheris and Gareth do not love you as the older boys do, they adore instead. I suspect they will not be much saddened to stay at Camelot."

Britt balked. "I-I know what I said before was inexcusably rude, but—"

"You spoke the truth," Morgause plainly said. "Lot and I were never the type to shower affection on our sons, and because of my husband, I have had to spend much of their lives trying to teach them the things *I* would like to see changed. I must admit I find their great love of you painful but…perhaps it is for the best. As long as they remain here in Camelot, you can use them as hostages."

"I could never kill a man, much less your sons," Britt said objected.

"Who said you would actually have to kill them? Just threaten to as you did with Ywain and King Urien. Lot may not appear to love his sons like Urien dotes on Ywain, but he does have some feelings for them, and he is not a stupid man."

"You saw Ywain?"

"So, he is here then? No. I only heard of it from my sister, and when Griflet was enamored with me, he mentioned he and Ywain were great favorites of yours."

"Oh."

"My nephew aside, with my sons in your grasp, I doubt my husband will move against you again. Or at least for some time."

Britt stared at Morgause. "You are sacrificing much to see me stay on my throne."

"If I am right about you, it will be well worth it. And my trust is not completely unfounded. I witnessed firsthand how you rule and treat your enemies," Morgause's mouth trembled for a moment. "But I am giving you my greatest treasures, Arthur. I know you have a kingdom to rule, but please, be kind to them."

"Britt. My real name is Britt," Britt said before smiling at Morgause.

Morgause pulled Britt into another embrace. "Be kind but clever. You are meant for great things, Britt," she said before stepping back. "If you'll excuse me, I must start packing."

Britt nodded and watched the noblewoman hurry out of the herb garden. She waited a minute before following, ambling back to the castle keep.

As she rounded a corner, she spied Merlin—coming from inside the keep—and Sir Ulfius—coming from the opposite direction and wiping stable dust from his tunic.

"My Lord," Sir Ulfius said.

"*You*," Merlin said, thrusting a finger at Britt.

"Call a meeting in one of your studies immediately, Merlin," Britt said.

Merlin ignored the order. "I've been looking all over for you. Half the guards are combing the castle for your body, and Sir Kay is a wreck. Where did you run off to?"

"It doesn't matter, but I must speak to you privately. Both of you, and Sir Kay and Sir Ector as well," Britt said.

"Oh, no, you don't. You owe me an explanation. I demand it. You never told *me* you ordered armor for yourself before you popped up by the throne with a rousing speech! You should have told me. I could have helped you," Merlin said.

"No, you couldn't have. You have been as useful as a pigeon in matters concerning Morgause," Britt scoffed. "You said so yourself you couldn't break the enchantment."

"My Lord," Sir Ulfius tried again.

"I was lying! There would be more meaning if you were able to break the hold it had on your men. It turned out for the best."

"That's a fine thing to say now that the need for magic is over with. You're nothing but a roadside magician."

"*What?*"

"My Lord."

"Yes, Sir Ulfius?" Britt asked, turning to face the older knight before Merlin could recover from the blow to his pride.

"Merlin tells me you are looking for the Round Table?"

"I am."

"I know the table to which you refer."

"You do?"

"Yes, My Lord. I do not know its current location, but I am searching for it."

Merlin draped an arm across Britt's shoulders, clamping down on her like he thought she might run. "While that is marvelous news, we had best return to the castle, lest Kay rips his mustache off his face."

"When we see him, we should talk about the assassination attempt," Britt said.

"The what?"

"Someone is going to try to kill me."

"WHAT?"

~

"THEY WILL STRIKE against you in the middle of the hunting party?" Sir Ector said as he drummed his fat fingers on the table.

It had taken Britt a short while to explain the finer details of the assassination attempt Morgause had told her about. The most difficult part was explaining it without using the word assassin—apparently it didn't exist yet, as neither Merlin nor any of the knights knew what it meant.

"Strategically speaking, it's the best opportunity Lot would have. The party will undoubtedly go into the forest, where it would be easy to hide any number of warriors. All members of the party will be armed, but that would provide a cover for the killers if they tried to portray Arthur's death as a member of the party misfiring an arrow," Sir Kay said.

"So, Arthur remains at the castle, and the attempt is thwarted," Sir Ulfius said.

Merlin narrowed his eyes. "No."

Sir Kay's grip on the pommel of his sword tightened, and Sir Ector roared. It was Sir Ulfius who calmly said, "Are you mad?"

"If we catch Lot's men in the act, we can make them talk. We can then publically denounce the plot against Arthur's life—which will help us control Lot."

"Morgause is all but giving Arthur her sons. We have no need to try and control him," Sir Ulfius said.

"But if we make the plot public, Lot's allies will back away from him," Britt predicted.

Merlin affectionately patted Britt on the head. "Well thought," he praised. "Everyone is at peace right now because they can't afford another war. King Pellinore is indebted to us for letting him cross near Camelot to return home. He freely admitted he won't attack again, and I believe him. I've heard of his wife; she's a strong lass from the north, and she'll skin him alive if he rides off to war again. Ryence is backing out of his war with King Leodegrance as fast as he can now that King Bors and King Ban have come out to play. King Urien won't lift a toe to help Lot—brother-in-law or not—as long as we have Ywain. Without the support of his three closest allies, you can be certain no one else will step in to help Lot."

"In other words, you will have isolated him and broken his political power," Sir Ulfius said.

Sir Ector shook his head. "I still don't like it."

"You are gambling with My Lord's life to make a political move. If My Lord is injured, it will not bode well," Sir Kay said, his words filled with unspoken promises.

"You forget something important," Merlin delicately said. "If we don't catch this first plot, and Arthur plays invalid and misses the party, it doesn't mean that Lot's attempts to kill Arthur are over. It means the only one we know about has been canceled.

Lot may very well make any number of attempts, which will be far harder to fend off as we will not know when and where they will take place."

Sir Ector and Sir Kay were quiet as they mulled over Merlin's words.

"We are postulating all of this based off the words of a foreign queen with witch powers. Britt, are you certain of this?" Sir Ulfius asked.

"It's Arthur," Merlin hissed. Even in closed rooms, using Britt's real name was forbidden.

"No," the older knight said. "I don't want your play puppet answering. I want her honest opinion. Britt, what do *you* think?"

Britt swallowed as the knights stared at her. "I think Morgause can be trusted," she admitted. "And I think Merlin is right. Based on what Morgause has told me, Lot won't give up trying to off me—regardless of whether I have his sons or not—unless we publically humiliate him and break his political hold on northern Britain."

Sir Ulfius nodded, satisfied.

"Then we make plans for a guard," Sir Kay said, switching gears.

"We need to be careful not to plant too many, or we'll scare off Lot's men," Sir Ulfius said.

"Perhaps we could have extra guards dressed as servants. No one looks twice at servants, even servants carrying weapons." Sir Ector suggested.

Britt stretched when she stood. "I'm going out for a breath of fresh air," she said.

"Very well, but be safe. Merlin, do you have maps of the surrounding forest areas?" Sir Ector asked as he dragged his girth over to a bookshelf of maps and globes.

"Take guards with you, My Lord," Sir Kay ordered as he opened his logbook.

"Good evening, My Lord," Sir Ulfius said, sparing her a smile before he turned his attention to Kay. "Do we have any spies of our own that we could place in the trees?"

"None trained for combat, no," Sir Kay said as Britt slipped out the door. She started up the hallway, heading for her room.

"Going to get that blasted dog of yours?" Merlin asked.

Britt jumped; she hadn't heard the enchanter sneak out after her. "Yes, I left him in my room when I went to have Ywain and Griflet heft me into this armor. I doubt he's happy with being left behind."

"Do you need help getting out of that?"

"The armor? It would be appreciated," Britt said, stopping a few paces down the hallway to open the door to her room.

Cavall sat just beyond the door, his massive tail thumping on the ground as he gave Britt a look of mild chastisement.

"I'm sorry, boy, I had to leave you," Britt said, holding her arms out. The mastiff got up and padded to her, briefly snuffling her before taking up his customary post at her side.

"You won't need to wear full armor all the time, you know," Merlin said, shutting the door before he got to work unbuckling buckles and sliding pieces of armor off.

Britt slipped her hands from her gauntlets. "Really? You've been nagging me about it for weeks. I didn't know if you would let me take it off to sleep."

"Well, you *did* need a set of full armor—although I was thinking white or gold might be a better color for you," Merlin admitted. "But what I specifically wanted you to wear was a cuirass reinforced with a plackart, faulds, and maybe a gorget."

"I have no idea what any of those things are," Britt said as Merlin finished taking armor off her right arm.

"A cuirass is the chestplate. It covers your chest. The plackart reinforces it around your belly—and yours would most certainly cover your back as well. Faulds are bands—or flaps really—that rest on the front of your thighs. They wouldn't be necessary, but they—like a gorget which covers your throat—would help disguise your lack of male muscle development. I suppose you could always wear a hauberk—you'll love it, as it is all chainmail," Merlin sourly said as he removed the shoulder pieces of the armor.

"They would be decorated in your emblem, your symbol, of course. But we still have yet to decide what your symbol should be," Merlin continued.

Britt rubbed her wrists before stepping out of the chest piece Merlin pulled off her. "I'm sorry; I should have told you about the armor. But I wanted to confront Morgause on my own."

"I understand your personality well enough to know why you did it," Merlin dryly said as he heaped the armor in the corner. "And while I wish you had told me, I must admit you did well."

Britt's eyebrows rose. "Are you giving me a sincere compliment?"

"I've done it before from time to time."

"Yes, but it still is rare."

"If you want compliments more often, you should try behaving yourself," Merlin said, dusting off his robe.

Britt laughed and bent over to pet Cavall. When she looked up, Merlin was giving her the oddest look.

"What?" Britt asked, standing up.

Merlin was quiet for a moment before he approached Britt and placed both of his hands on her shoulders. "Be careful with this hunting party. Don't take any chances. As badly as I would love to beard Lot and silence him forever, you are more important. Do you understand?"

Britt uncomfortably shifted. Merlin's hands on her shoulders felt hot. "Yes."

A smile melted the hardness of Merlin's intensity. "That's a good lass. Enjoy your walk. Mind Kay, and take your guards with you," Merlin said, briefly brushing her cheek with his hand before he bustled out of Britt's bedroom, making a beeline to the study where Sir Ector, Sir Ulfius, and Sir Kay were closeted.

Britt waited until Merlin's footsteps disappeared from the hallway before she shook her head and briskly slapped her cheeks. "I am too old to be acting like a lovesick teenager. He shows zero interest in me anyway. It's just been too long since I've been on a date. And I don't know why I'm explaining myself to a dog," Britt grumbled, avoiding looking at her metal plate mirror so she wouldn't have to see her blush.

Cavall's tail happily wagged as Britt scowled at the ground. Her self-disgust was interrupted by a tapping noise on her door.

"My Lord?"

"Yes?"

"It's Bedivere, My Lord. May I come in?"

Britt did a quick inspection of her room—nothing particularly feminine or revealing was out on display—before she answered. "Enter."

The door opened, and Sir Bedivere slipped inside, throwing himself into a kneeling position before even looking at Britt.

"Bedivere?"

"My Lord, I beg of you to forgive me."

"For what?"

"I have been capricious and disloyal to you. I took a vow as your marshal to serve and protect you, and I have failed pitifully."

"Bedivere—"

"I followed the Orkney queen like a mindless animal, acted inexcusably, and cast your favor aside."

"Bedivere—"

"I do not deserve your mercy or forgiveness, and I am prepared for whatever punishment you give me."

"*Bedivere*," Britt said. She crouched in front of the kneeling knight, placed her hands on his shoulders, and shook him.

The startled knight met her gaze, and Britt sadly smiled. "I am sorry I took so long to rescue you," she said.

Sir Bedivere blinked several times before he closed his eyes.

"You are too good for us, My King. Certainly we do not deserve you."

Britt chuckled. "That's hardly true. Mostly I think it is I who does not deserve you," she said before standing, tugging on Sir Bedivere's arm. "I am glad you are back, Bedivere."

"As am I, My Lord," he said as he stood.

"Was it bad?"

"Yes," Bedivere frowned, his face growing stormy. "Most of the time, I was muddled and did not know what I was saying. But the few times I would remember, and wouldn't be able to control my own mouth? Those were the worst," he glumly said.

"It's over now. You are once again my faithful marshal," Britt smiled.

"And you are always my beloved sovereign, My Lord," Sir Bedivere said, placing a fist over his heart before tilting forward in a bow.

Britt could not help the rush of warmth and affection she felt at Sir Bedivere's heartfelt words. She reached out and embraced him, doing her best to heartily smack him on the back to make the gesture a "man hug." It wasn't until Sir Bedivere embraced her back that Britt remembered her situation (supposedly a male) and her state of clothing (armor-less) and started calling herself seven different kinds of an idiot in her head.

Thankfully, she was still wearing her fitted under-doublet—which was making her sweaty—but even so, Britt had a feeling Merlin would scalp her if he knew she was going around, hugging knights.

Britt ended the "man hug" as swiftly as possible, smiling at Sir Bedivere before slapping him on the back again to reaffirm her manliness. "I was about to step outside for a breath of fresh air with Cavall. Care to join me?"

"It would be my honor, My Lord."

~

THE ORKNEY QUEEN left the following day in a swift, unceremonious exit at dawn.

While Britt had forgiven the queen for her enchantment, few —if any—of Britt's knights had. As such, only Britt, her guards, Cavall, Merlin, Sir Kay—who probably came only to make sure that Morgause really left—and Morgause's sons went to see her off.

"I apologize, My Lady, that your departure is less…glorious than one would usually throw for a departing queen," Britt said.

Morgause laughed. "Don't be cross with your men, Arthur. I took the power of their will from them. They are bound to hold a grudge. Stay safe and take care," she bid before reaching out to hug Britt, making Merlin squawk. "Make us women proud. I am sending my youngest sister to you, Morgan. She feels as Elaine and I do pertaining to women on thrones, and she will do everything in her power to help you."

"Thank you," Britt reluctantly said before she realized that for the first time she was in close quarters with Morgause, and her nose wasn't burning. "Your perfume was part of the enchantment, wasn't it?"

"It was," Morgause admitted. "And I am fairly sick of its wretchedly powerful scent. It is a fae charm. Any man who smells it is supposed to fall hopelessly in love with the wearer. I had to wear at least twice the usual amount to get a concoction strong enough."

Merlin snorted. "Childish tricks, something one would expect of you."

Morgause eyed Merlin with the friendliness of a viper. "So says a petty, ancient magician who couldn't break the childish trick."

"I could have if I wanted to. Arthur, I *told* you it was more meaningful that you broke the enchantment yourself," Merlin said, almost whining.

Britt purposely turned away from Morgause as the queen

went to say goodbye to her sons. "I think Morgause might be right. I've seen you perform some magic, which I'll give you is pretty cool. But all of this big stuff you claim you're capable of? I haven't seen the slightest proof."

"You are the most ungrateful brat to ever be crowned king," Merlin said as Britt crouched in front of Cavall to pet him.

Sir Kay stirred. "Historically speaking, I don't believe that is an accurate statement."

Merlin eyed Sir Kay. "Of course *you* would say that."

"Can you do anything tomorrow, during the hunting party?" Britt asked, her voice quiet, so quiet only Merlin and Sir Kay could hear her.

"Aye," Merlin said, thoughtfully rubbing his chin. "I'll be following you, but in secret and out of sight. A hunt isn't a place for an enchanter, but I will go for your safety."

"Why wouldn't you normally come with us?" Britt asked, making the gesture for Cavall to give her his paw. It was the most useless trick ever, but it greatly cheered Britt to be able to teach her faithful dog something.

Merlin shook his head. "Most love the thrill of the chase but I, I can't stomach the kill. Not of stags anyway. I suppose boar hunting in the winter months might be different. But it was Blaise, my mentor, who first advised me to skip hunting parties. Hunting to live is one thing. Even war is sometimes a necessity. But hunting for socialization is far different."

Britt uneasily stood. "Great, I wasn't looking forward to it already."

"Do not worry, My Lord," Sir Kay assured Britt. "Merlin is an oddity."

"*What* did you just call me?" Merlin asked.

"My Lord," Morgause interrupted with her husky voice. "I thank you for your hospitality. You have been a generous host, and I hope you and your house are blessed for it," Morgause said as she stood with her mare. Her Orkney escort was already mounted and waiting.

Britt bowed slightly. "You have honored us with your visit."

"Don't come again," Merlin said, waving farewell.

"*Merlin*," Britt hissed.

Morgause laughed as she mounted her horse with some help from a footman. "I see through your protests, Merlin. You are quite amorous of me, I know it."

Merlin looked like he swallowed a frog. "Lady," he said, "wise, *old* lady. Please depart lest I be forced to help you depart."

Morgause turned her delicate mare and laughed over her shoulder. "Very well, I admit saying you are amorous of me is a bit much, but you have become softer towards my gender in your old age, Merlin. I know it! It can be seen in all aspects of your life. Farewell, you false magician, farewell my sons, farewell Arthur— true King of Britain."

Merlin growled, but the queen was out of hearing distance, disappearing through the gate that led out of the keep area and into the public/commoner area of Camelot.

"I like her," Britt decided.

"Great. Exchange letters with her, but *never* invite her back," Merlin said.

"That would be very rude, Merlin," Sir Kay said, startling both Britt and Merlin. "We are hosting her sons. How could we separate their mother from them?"

Merlin eyed Sir Kay again. "I think I liked you more when you had less of a cause and talked rarely."

Sir Kay inclined his head. "In that case, I must thank you for delivering my foster-brother to me," he said as Morgause's sons drew closer to Britt and her companions.

Britt crouched down. "Gaheris, Gareth," she called, extending her arms. The young boys ran to her, pushing their wet cheeks against her shoulders.

Sir Kay and Merlin shifted uncomfortably as Britt hugged the crying boys. After a few moments, they backed off, noses sniffling. Britt stood and moved away from Cavall, who was promptly tackled by the youngest Orkney princes.

"I didn't think the old hag was at all affectionate with them," Merlin said as he watched Gawain sling an arm across Agravain's shoulders. "It appears I was wrong."

"It's a hard thing, saying goodbye to a parent," Britt said, unseeingly staring out across the keep yard. She startled when Merlin placed a warm hand on the top of her head.

"I'm sorry, lass," he whispered. "I'm sorry."

7

A HUNTING PARTY

"We found a second trail going northwest. An assistant huntsman picked it up here."

Britt chewed her bread as she appeared to listen to the master huntsman. Britt and the knights and nobles who were riding in the hunt had gathered for breakfast outside for the specific purpose of hearing the master huntsman discuss the various trails his assistants had found and deciding which quarry they should pursue. Merlin had informed her this meeting was called an assembly.

Merlin had also told her that hunting parties used highly technical terminology and she was to stay silent at all times and let her closest knights—Sir Kay, Sir Ector, Sir Ulfius, and Sir Bedivere—answer for her.

"It is better for people to think you to be thoughtful than for you to open your mouth and prove yourself a fool," Merlin told her when hauling her from her rooms early that morning to hear Mass.

Britt fixed an appropriately thoughtful expression on her face, nodding slowly whenever someone looked at her.

Mostly, Britt was internally awed at her men's ability to drink soup for breakfast. The practice was apparently common, but the only thing Britt could stomach was the hearty bread she was supposed to dip in the soup.

Britt's gaze flickered to the carefully selected party of six soldiers that were to guard her. "Servants" scurried through the keep yard, carrying things from the keep to the horses that were tacked and waiting. No one noticed they carried swords and extra daggers, or that they oddly carried themselves like soldiers in spite of their station.

The kennel boys were organizing their dogs: chase-hounds, a few greyhounds, and some mastiffs. Cavall sat with a kennel boy, although his attention was mostly on Britt. Britt smiled and waved at her dog—Kay had been oddly insistent that one of the kennel boys take Cavall with the second group of chase-hounds and the pack of mastiffs that would be planted halfway through the trail to provide fresh dogs for the hunt. Britt doubted that Cavall would be able to keep up, but Kay said there would be plenty of huntsmen along to take charge of him if he tired.

Britt shifted in her chair and studied the assembly. Gawain and Agravain had been invited to come along. They were enthralled, clinging to the master huntsman's words. Gareth and Gaheris were too young to come, but Ywain, Griflet, and a number of other knights were present.

Merlin had limited the number of knights, telling everyone it was unreasonable to have a huge party when one was hunting. Britt's knights were satisfied only because Merlin promised the hunting excursions would be implemented on a weekly basis. Eventually.

"My Lord," Sir Ulfius jarred Britt from her observations. "I believe we should pursue the large stag that is traveling north-east. What do you think?"

Britt glanced at Sir Kay, who was nodding in support. "I

agree," Britt said as other members of the party murmured in agreement.

"Very well, My Lord," the master huntsman said. "In that case, we should set the dog relays along this path…"

∾

BRITT CAREFULLY SHIFTED in the saddle, making her horse's white ears flick. "Kay, you're sure I can't ride Roen?" Britt uncomfortably asked.

"Roen is trained for war, My Lord. Llamrei is trained for… preservation," Kay explained, his eyes ceaselessly sweeping through the party. Behind him, Britt's guards did the same thing. "Besides, no knight rides his warhorse on a hunt."

"I would feel more assured if I had Roen, or my riding helm," Britt said.

She, Kay, and her guards stood apart from the rest of the hunting party. They were waiting in the fields surrounding Camelot for the last of the hound relay to settle in along the path before they started pursuing the stag through the woods. They were starting south of Camelot and would swing up around it in an arc, traveling northwest.

"It's not yet finished, My Lord," Sir Kay said.

"I know," Britt sighed. "Is Merlin in place?"

Sir Kay adjusted his bow. "I informed him of our path before we mounted up. He was dressed most…uniquely. I would assume he is in a location that satisfies him. I believe the hunt is about to begin."

A huntsman blew a horn, and the hounds bayed as they were released and snuffled their way down the scent path.

"Be careful, My Lord," Sir Kay said as he cued his mount into a trot.

"I will," Britt said, swallowing the lump in her throat. She hated to admit it, but she was afraid.

Llamrei, the white mare Britt rode, seemed to pick up on her unease as she trotted after the rest of the hunting party. The mare was impressively large, but her gaits were deceptively smooth. She did not prance like the other horses, and she was almost as watchful as Sir Kay.

Britt held her breath when the hunting party entered the woods. She rode on the edge of the party, with her knights but on the outskirts of the group.

When Sir Kay explained the situation to the guards, they asked Britt if she would ride on the perimeter of the party. "It would be best to guard you when we are not completely surrounded. It makes it easier to recognize friend from foe," one guard said.

Britt was glad she had agreed. The hunting party seemed like a mad scramble. "It would be easy to get trampled if you fell off your horse," Britt muttered as she ducked a tree branch.

The bay of the hounds was a howling chorus, and the stamp of horse hooves was a drum beat as they followed the scent path and tracks of the stag. The huntsmen were grim men popping in and out of view in their green clothes compared with Britt's merry and lighthearted knights.

Britt had a hard time keeping a smile on her face as every shout of joy and dog's howl seemed like a beacon to her would-be assassins. Merlin had told her time and time again the previous day that she *had* to act normal. She couldn't appear to be nervous.

That order seemed especially hard as the biggest thing Britt wanted to do at the moment was throw up what little bread she managed to eat, turn on her heels, and run back to Camelot.

Facing down an enemy on the battlefield was one thing. There, she stood a chance with her sword skills. Riding through a forest where she was utterly defenseless against a sniper assassin? That was enough to set Britt's sense of fear on fire.

Britt forced herself to sit deeper in the saddle as she straightened her spine and flashed a smile at Gawain and Ywain as they rode past. *I won't let Lot win*, she decided.

The first hour of the hunt passed. They stopped to water horses and gather new dogs.

"How are you fairing, My Lord?" Sir Kay asked.

"As well as could be expected," Britt said, patting Llamrei's neck as she stretched her legs.

Sir Kay ducked closer for the merest moment. "You hide your fear well, My Lord," he said before mounting up when the horn sounded again.

Britt followed his example and slipped onto Llamrei's back, turning around to nod at her soldiers.

"If we don't bag the stag in another hour, you'll need to switch mounts. I hoped to keep you on Llamrei," Sir Kay said as they trotted along.

"I imagine it will be soon," Britt said.

Sir Kay shook his head. "There's no telling," he said grimly.

Fear curled around Britt's neck like an animal as the hunt continued. She smiled and joked with her knights, but her heart beat erratically in her chest. Her guards remained clustered around her, watchful and dedicated.

"Maybe it won't be today. Maybe Lot changed his mind," Britt muttered.

Something in the forest roared.

"My Lord," the guards said, crowding around Britt.

A huge boar charged through the forest, streaking past the hunting party. The hounds went *wild*, abandoning the stag's trail to give chase to the boar.

A second boar—this one enraged and snorting—plunged through the heart of the hunting party.

Some knights hauled their horses out of the way—for a boar could kill a dog, horse, or even a man—while others crowded forward to get a shot at the animal.

"Did anyone hit it?"

"Which one?"

"Either!"

"After the dogs! The boar will kill them all if it stops!"

"Blast those servants. Where are the spears?"

"We haven't any! We were stag hunting, not boar hunting."

"We can't disassemble now. We must finish the hunt!"

The party was in mass chaos as Britt's guards managed to pull her away from the mess without attracting attention. "It is best if they settle down before we rejoin them, Milord," the guard captain said as Britt watched some of the huntsmen chase after the hounds.

Sir Kay was briefly visible in the mad scramble of noble hunters, and Britt waved at him to show she was fine. She then pulled Llamrei in a circle—a decision that saved her life.

A short-shafted, black arrow pierced the ground where Britt and Llamrei had just stood.

"Protect the King," a guard bellowed.

The soldier closest to Britt ripped a shield off his horse's rump and tossed it to Britt. Britt caught it, slipped her arm through the arm bands, and held it above her head. The shield thumped and vibrated. Britt almost clocked herself in the head with it when arrows hit the metal surface with a great deal of force, but nothing hit her or Llamrei.

One of Britt's guards fired off an arrow, and a man screamed as he dropped from a tree.

"Take prisoners!"

"To the King!"

A guard flung himself from his horse, attacking a man who was dashing for Britt. Another guard shot a second assassin out of the trees.

The hunting party—those who hadn't run off after either of the boars—finally realized what was going on. Men roared and drew their swords.

"To King Arthur!" one knight yelled, his sword raised in the air.

"Stop!" Sir Kay shouted. "If you rush him in a mad group—" His words were lost in the clamor as the knights rode to protect their sovereign.

"Halt!" the guards around Britt roared at the oncoming rush. They were grim as they set themselves between Britt and the assassins and the hunting party.

At that moment, Britt understood their desire to keep her separated. Britt *knew* the knights that were in the hunting party. She was friends with them, but at that moment the hunting party was a swirl of chaos, and it would be easy for a covert assassin to sneak in and bum rush her with her would-be protectors.

Llamrei bolted.

It was not the scared, witless bolt of a horse that has been spooked and frightened. Llamrei didn't scream or toss her head. She didn't crow-hop or try to throw Britt from the saddle. The mare snorted as another assassin sprinted in Britt's direction—he was stopped by one of Britt's guards—before she turned to look at the yelling knights. There was an opening directly in front of Britt, and the mare took it.

Llamrei full-out galloped in the woods, a white streak in the blurs of browns and greens. It was a terrifying experience Britt never wished to repeat. Branches and bushes clawed at her face, arms, and legs. Britt crouched low against the mare who safely navigated her way through the woods with an almost human-like intelligence.

Britt had no idea in what direction they were going, much less where they were. All she knew was that the roar of fighting was muted, and then gone all together as Llamrei ran like saddled wind.

Britt peered ahead and saw a fallen tree in the path. It was big for all that it was half rotted. "Llamrei," Britt shouted as she tugged on the reins, still clinging to the mare's neck. The mare ran at the tree with determination, and Britt realized she was going to jump it.

Britt cursed colorfully and with great imagination as she set herself in the saddle and recalled the few jumping lessons she took with her sister.

As Llamrei launched herself into the air, Britt rose up out of the saddle—holding her butt aloft and body close to Llamrei. Her thigh muscles strained as she tried to hold herself balanced with the reins tight but not hauling on the mare's mouth.

The world froze as Llamrei soared over the tree. She landed front legs first. Britt shifted her center of balance so she leaned back and wouldn't crash into the mare's neck. Landing was a bit rough, but Llamrei crow-hopped to push Britt back into the saddle.

Britt was so elated she hadn't fallen off, she almost missed it when Llamrei streaked out of the forest and into grassland. Camelot loomed on the horizon. If Britt could reach it without falling off, she would be safe.

As if renewed by the sight of the castle, Llamrei increased her speed. She galloped at a pace Britt had never seen much less experienced. But above the wind that whistled in her ears and the pounding of her throat, Britt heard someone shout.

"Arthur!"

Hurtling across the field was Merlin—clothed in a green tunic —riding his lean horse. Charging out from behind him was a pack of giant mastiff dogs. Their kennel master released them, and they raced across the field. Britt risked a look over her shoulder—two men on horseback and three archers were behind her. By the set of their faces, Britt didn't think they belonged to Camelot.

Britt tried to redirect Llamrei to Merlin, but the mare ignored her pulling. A man shouted, and Llamrei abruptly planted her hind legs, swerving to avoid a spear launched by one of the horsemen.

Britt tumbled off the side, hitting the ground with an *oomph*. Llamrei screamed and skid and swiveled, planting herself between Britt and the oncoming horsemen.

As Britt tried to regain the breath that was knocked from her, something dragged the oncoming assassins off their horses. One fell with a shout, but another sprang from his horse rather than fell off it, and he ran at Britt.

He was intercepted by a huge, snarling mastiff who took him down by latching onto the man's arm and pulling.

"Cavall," Britt whispered as she watched the apricot-colored dog attack the assassin.

"ARTHUR!" Merlin shouted, his voice edged in panic.

Britt scrambled to her feet and saw more men dressed in muted colors join the assassins. Britt took up swearing again as she sprinted to Merlin's side, Llamrei trotting beside her. "This isn't an assassin or two; it's a freakin' army!" Britt hollered.

"I know. Llamrei, stand *down*," Merlin tightly said before he called to the kennel master with him. "Call the dogs in."

The mastiffs were laying waste to the armed men, but when the kennel master called on a horn, they returned to him at a lope, Cavall among them.

As soon as the dogs were back, Merlin said something and struck the kennel master in the head. The man collapsed and slumped to the ground. The dogs growled but stayed put.

"What did you just do?" Britt yelped, hysteria setting in.

"Never tell anyone what you're about to see. Do you swear it?" Merlin spat.

"What?"

"I mean it, Britt. *Never* repeat this part of the afternoon to anyone, even Kay. Swear that you won't!"

"I won't. I won't tell anyone!" Britt said as the men marched towards her and Merlin. There had to be over a hundred of them. Where was the hunting party? Why wasn't anyone coming from Camelot?

"Stay behind me; take hold of my cloak, and *don't* let go," Merlin said.

The young enchanter thrust his hand into the air. He shouted words in a foreign language Britt couldn't understand as the armed men marched against them. He slowly lowered his hand—still talking—until it was level with his shoulder. He clenched it in a fist and brought it back before he shouted one last word and punched forward.

The air around Britt and Merlin seemed to bend and bow in a circle. It shoved Britt to the ground with the force of a tornado as it rushed past them. Halfway across the field, it burst into flames. When the fire hit the enemy lines, it split like an opening fan, spreading up and down the line with a hungry roar.

Britt stared at the massacre. She could smell fire, ash, and burnt flesh. She raised her eyes to Merlin. He was standing protectively in front of her, his face devoid of emotion as he watched his magic kill.

Britt thought Merlin's magic was fake. Or perhaps not fake, but certainly not powerful. Of course she had seen him do little things—light fires without any kind of tinder or flint, make wet things dry—but she thought those were just flashy bits of magic he learned to impress people, and that his real power was the cunning of his mind.

As Britt stared at the scorched field, she realized she had no idea just how powerful Merlin was. And he wasn't through yet.

Merlin took one step forward, speaking under his breath. He reached out with a hand and pulled back. The closest line of trees fell, crushing enemies like ants.

Piece by piece, Merlin massacred the enemy using fire, wind, and trees. Men ran for their lives, but Merlin grimly caught them and held them in place with magic for the fire to finish them off.

Britt stared at the violated field as the last of the enemy were consumed. "I won't have to tell *anyone*," she muttered. The meadow was a mash of burnt ground, bodies, and fallen trees.

Merlin unsteadily sat, putting his head between his legs. "That was hard," he muttered. "I'm out of practice."

Britt slowly pushed herself into a standing position. "What will we say?"

Merlin raised a hand and carelessly waved it in the air. "I'll take care of it before they arrive."

The dogs growled, and Britt spun around. Two men had crept out of the woods behind Britt and Merlin. They had already edged past three of the dogs.

"Why aren't the dogs attacking?" Britt said, unsheathing Excalibur.

"They haven't been told to!"

"So, tell them to!"

"I can't," Merlin said. "They'll only follow the orders of the kennel master!"

"Sit," Britt ordered Merlin before she ran at the ambushers, wishing she wore armor—even though it would have been an odd clothing choice for a hunting party.

Britt studied both men for bows or quivers as she charged. They only had swords and daggers on them, which would considerably level the playing field.

Britt descended on the first soldier, mute and deadly as she pushed him back on his heels with the speed of her swings and jabs.

The second ambusher stepped in to stab at her with a dagger. There was a fearsome growl, and the ambusher screamed as Cavall dragged him to the ground.

Sweat dripped off Britt as she attacked. The enemy wasn't buckling.

She wasn't fighting a knight who knew the sword, lance, and spear. She wasn't fighting a common soldier. She was fighting a hardened assassin who lived by killing. He fell back under Britt's onslaught, but he wasn't leaving any openings, and he wasn't letting Britt force any openings either.

Britt knew she had to end it soon. Fighting with the constant push as she did sapped her of her strength and energy fast.

The assassin dodged one of Britt's swings and swooped forward, slashing at her thigh muscles. Britt redirected her swing into a downward cut, following through so she swung her sword up and behind her as she twisted in spite of the fire that bloomed on her thigh.

Cavall snarled; Llamrei screamed.

"Britt!" Merlin shouted.

Britt and the assassin swirled, eyeing each other. Britt had opened a nasty slice on the assassin's back, and the assassin had given Britt a deep wound on her thigh. Britt dared not look at it, but she felt it burn as she crouched in one of her attack forms.

The assassin stared at her thigh and cursed, and Britt's gaze dropped for a brief second. The laceration was deep. Not to the bone, but deep into the muscle. However...not a drop of blood fell from the wound.

Excalibur.

Britt rolled her shoulders as she recalled Merlin's lectures of the sword's scabbard. As long as she had it, she wouldn't die of blood loss. The thought heartened her, and Britt smiled. It wasn't a nice smile.

The assassin took a step back, but Britt was already lunging forward. She aimed her strike at the assassin's right arm. He blocked, but the maneuver brought her in close, allowing Britt to plant herself and knee him in the side.

The assassin lurched to recover his balance, and Britt pulled Excalibur away from his sword before jabbing its pommel into his neck.

He fell like a rock.

"I *love* this sword," Britt said, raising Excalibur to look at it.

"You idiot," Merlin wheezed, cracking the assassin on the head with his staff, making him fall unconscious. "Battle makes you mad."

Britt grinned brashly enough to put a pirate to shame. "Maybe, but I *love* this sword."

"We're going to die young, both of us. And it's going to be your fault," Merlin said.

Britt didn't answer and victoriously swung Excalibur through the air, her smile wild, her hair glittering in the sunlight.

"That's it," Merlin said, leaning heavily against his horse. "Your emblem has been decided. It will be a red dragon. It's the same as Uther Pendragon, but that's fine. He's supposedly your father anyway. And you're more of a dragon than he ever was."

Britt laughed again as she swung her sword in the air one last time.

～

MERLIN MENDED the worst parts of the field before he and Britt mounted their horses and limped back to Camelot. Merlin was grouchy and on the verge of passing out, but Britt was giddy with the pain from her wound.

Sir Kay, Gawain, and Sir Bedivere arrived at Camelot minutes after Britt. They clattered into the keep yard, calling for troops and scent hounds. Sir Kay collapsed to his knees when he saw Britt and openly wept in relief.

The expression of emotion finally made Britt lose the madness of battle, and she sat at his side, her hand resting on the normally stoic young man's back.

Britt's guards and the rest of the hunting party returned an hour later after Gawain streaked back out to the woods on a fresh horse to give the good news. They brought with the assassins—bound and gagged—that attacked the group. The assassins were taken for questioning, and it was revealed that they were Lot's men—surprise, surprise.

After living through Morgause's enchantment and topped with the bodily damage of their sovereign, Britt's knights all but demanded war. Britt was able to sweetly talk it out of them only because a pigeon with a correspondence from King Ban, King Bors, and Sir Bodwain returned to say King Ryence had been run off King Leodegrance's lands, and they were coming home.

Still, everyone from Sir Griflet to the head cook worried and fretted over Britt.

She didn't get a moment to herself until nearly midnight when she settled on the castle walls with Cavall and her guards as usual.

She stroked Cavall's head as she stared out at the grassy fields around the castle. She could barely see them in the moonlight, but she knew they looked untouched and green. Somehow Merlin had repaired all the damage he had wrought with his attack.

Britt heard her soldiers approaching before they spoke. "Let him through," she said, knowing who it was that approached her in the darkness.

Gawain joined Britt at the walkway, his eyes fastened on her face. Britt turned to smile at him in the sputtering light of the torches posted on the walkway.

Gawain fell to his knees. "My Lord, I'm sorry," he said, his voice broken with emotion. "I, I didn't know. None of us did. Our father is a treacherous, traitorous—"

Britt slipped her hand under Gawain's chin. "Your father is your father. You are not responsible for his actions, nor do you need to scorn him for my sake."

"But, My Lord, he ordered your death," Gawain whispered.

"When you become a knight, Gawain, one of the hardest lessons you will learn will be choosing when to fight. If we were to battle against your father, men would die because I was stabbed on the thigh. That is a foolish reason to go to war," Britt hesitated, shutting her eyes for a moment. "I remember what my battle with your father was like. Everything reeked of spilled blood. The ground was torn up like a graveyard, and there were bodies slumped everywhere. Sometimes I have nightmares of it, and I relive the worst of it."

"He has caused you such pain, My Lord," Gawain said. "If you still remember it…" he trailed off, hanging his head.

Britt once more tilted Gawain's chin with her hand. "It's a good thing, Gawain," she said. "If we forgot the pain of war, we would fight more than we already do. I'm not ready to rain a second battle like that upon my men, whom I treasure deeply."

"You will not put my brothers and me in the dungeons?" Gawain asked.

Britt raised an eyebrow. "Do you think I am the type to do that?"

Gawain furiously shook his head. "No, My Lord, but it would be within your rights!"

"Gawain—please stand. I can't crouch with you on the ground with this wound, and I'm starting to get a crick in my neck. Much better," Britt said when the young man stood. "I don't care about what is within my rights. You will be a great knight, I can tell. I want you to be a victorious hero and triumphant warrior. I want you to go on and do great things so everyone knows how wonderful the princes of Orkney are. I trust you, and I trust your brothers. You have my faith and love for life, Gawain."

Gawain blinked rapidly in the flickering light. "Thank you, My lord," he said, sounding choked. He knelt again briefly and kissed Britt's hands before standing. "If you'll excuse me," he said, his voice cracking before he fled.

Britt watched him go, feeling bemused.

"Yet another young man you've won for life. I'm impressed: you wield words as effectively as you wield your sword," Merlin said before gesturing at Britt's guards. "Shoo, all of you, scat. I shall deliver your dear king to his rooms when he is done pacing like a maniac. Go on, get. Yes, all of you. Shoo!" Merlin said, herding the guards down the stairs.

Britt grinned at the enchanter as he ruffled his robe—which he had donned once again—and joined Britt.

"I don't think it's so much pretty words as it is that they are starving for someone to tell them how great they can be," Britt said.

"It could be," Merlin nodded. "All the same, the fact is I have never seen anyone use respect and affection like a weapon. Well done."

Britt glanced down at Cavall, who seemed as calm and tranquil as ever. "Cavall...he, he's trained to attack, isn't he?"

"He was trained as a guard dog by the kennel master, yes. Kay had him specially trained to attack when anyone threatens his owner," Merlin admitted.

Britt shook her head. "All this time, I thought he gave Cavall to me because I needed a friend, but he's just another guard," she said, her eyes burning.

"Use your head for a moment, lass, and *think*," Merlin said. "The beast fetches an over-glorified *rag* for you. He does all matter of strange requests and bears the ungracious children you inflict upon him. As much as I am loathe to admit it, he is more than a guard, Britt. He is your dog, just as faithful and adoring of you as Ywain or Gawain. If he attacks, it is because of his love for you and not because he is trained to do it."

Tears fell from Britt's eyes as she placed her hand on Cavall's head. The mastiff panted as he looked up at her with teddy bear eyes. "Thank you," she said to both Cavall and Merlin.

Merlin smiled for a moment—it was soft, almost like a caress —and then leaned on the wall and looked out. "It's calm and peaceful up here."

"It is," Britt said. "Thank you, Merlin, for saving me today."

Merlin nodded and said nothing.

"Why don't you want people to know what you're really capable of? All this time, I've been mocking you and..." Britt trailed off.

Merlin thoughtfully stared at the stars. "If people knew what I was capable of, they would be terrified of me. I must admit, I thought you would be frightened. Few and far between are the mortals who can do what I can do. I would rather accomplish my goals by the use of wits and intelligence than by inflicting Britain with my powers and making all tremble at the thought of me."

It was Britt's turn to nod and say nothing.

Merlin suddenly turned to her. "Don't misunderstand me, lass. I can't pull off that kind of flashy show very often. I'm exhausted for now and probably won't be able to perform even a scrap of magic for a few days, so don't you go thinking you can call on me to roast your enemies whenever you need me to."

Britt shook her head. "No, never! I. I agree with you. Instead of wars or massacring people, I would rather accomplish my goals with pretty words and the gaining of loyalties."

Merlin laughed. "That's just a fancy way of saying wits and intelligence," he grinned.

"Maybe," Britt said.

Merlin plopped down so his back was against a battlement. "I should introduce you to Blaise."

"He's the hermit who raised you, right?"

"Correct. He would *love* you. He likes clever things even more than I do," Merlin chuckled, patting the ground beside him.

Britt slowly lowered herself to the ground with several painful winces. "Tell me more about him, please," she said, shifting into position.

"He's a regular fiend with words, and he quotes Holy Scriptures nonstop," Merlin dryly said, pulling another laugh out of Britt.

They sat together, shoulders and legs brushing, swapping stories late into the night, laughing over Merlin's recollections of his childhood. Britt let the clever enchanter speak. Recalling Blaise and some of his less-than-stellar moments seemed to ease the tension in his shoulders, and it was warm and wonderful to sit next to him like she was someone he cared about—*really* cared about—instead of being his hand-puppet he tried to control.

"Britt," Merlin said shortly before dawn.

"Hm?"

"Thank you."

"You're welcome."

THE END

THE CREATION OF QUEEN MORGAUSE

Enchanted was inspired by a paragraph I read in *King Arthur and His Knights* by Sir James Knowles. The paragraph described the visitation of King Lot's wife to Camelot after Arthur beat back Lot and his allies. King Lot's wife was sent to spy on Arthur, but after she meets him she confesses that her husband sent her as a spy and purposely leaves Gawain, her eldest son, with Arthur so Arthur can use him as a hostage against Lot. And yes, all of this happens in a single paragraph.

Several other legends, most famously Le Morte d'Arthur, have similar themes, although sometimes Lot's wife leaves all their children with Arthur instead of just Gawain. However, in the more modern versions of King Arthur legends, Morgause is typically an enchantress or witch of some sort who tries to seduce Arthur in order to help her husband. While both of these characters are married to Lot, the mother of Gawain, and always meet Arthur at some point in the king's life, these women are practically different characters. The wife who is sorry for her part in Lot's schemes was, in some of the oldest stories, named Anna. In Le Morte d'Arthur the character's name is Morgause, even though she does the same actions as Anna, and it is Morgause's name that most modern authors use when writing about King Lot's horrible wife.

(As a side note, no matter what King Arthur legend you look at, Anna/Morgause is always the sister of Morgan le Fay. They aren't the same characters, but the similar names can mess with you. King Artie and his cohorts are very good at that. Don't even get me started on the Bors'.)

I wanted to reconcile Morgause with her original character, Anna, so I morphed the modern with the ancient, and my version of Morgause was born. My Morgause is a mix of the two characters. She has the magic and cunning of the modern Morgause, but the sincerity and courage of the ancient Anna. With that kind of character it would be extremely tricky getting her to let go of her loyalty to her family and support Britt, which is why I made her something of a feminist.

I actually got the idea because of some research I was doing on Gawain at the time. Because of some quests he both failed and passed, Gawain was blessed and cursed to be the ladies knight—meaning he had to help any maiden he came across who needed assistance. Compared to the rest of the knights—Lancelot included—Gawain is considered to be the most sensitive to the plight of females in Arthur's kingdom. I decided that in order to mold that type of character into him, especially given that his father was something of a power-hungry/cut-throat king, he would need a mother who was not only equally as strong as King Lot, but extremely verbal about the fact that females are not lesser beings.

Morgause was a lot of fun. I enjoyed her bold personality, and I hope to have just as much fun with her sister, the infamous Morgan le Fay. On a final thought, all of Britt's pets—Llamrei, Roen, and Cavall—are all animals that are attributed to Arthur in THE oldest records of the legendary king.

EMBITTERED:

KING ARTHUR AND HER KNIGHTS BOOK 3

1

THE ARRIVAL OF LANCELOT

"*The sword he pulled, the crown he wore, and he just a fair-faced youth*, hah! Fair-faced youth, my horse's rear end," Britt said as she gnawed on a hunk of crusty bread and recited a line from the newest ballad echoing through Camelot.

Llamrei, Britt's white mare, looked up from grazing.

"No offense," Britt said.

The mare went back to eating.

"I've been here a year and a half. How old am I supposed to be now? Sixteen or seventeen? This ploy won't last much longer," Britt said. "Bedivere and his ilk have hinted since Christmas that I need to find a wife. Merlin won't be able to distract that faction much longer, and even I have heard some of the disparaging rumors about my unwillingness to grow facial hair."

It was, in fact, Bedivere's hinting that drove Britt from her courts that fine afternoon. Bedivere had set his young cousin Griflet after Britt to sing songs about a rich king who did great deeds on behalf of his beautiful wife. Of course, whenever Griflet started a game of Badger Britt, Ywain—Sir Ywain now, Britt had knighted him at the New Year—was sure to join in as well.

Favorable things could not be reported of Ywain's singing voice, so avoiding the duo became Britt's greatest ambition.

Britt rolled onto her stomach so she could look at Camelot. The immense castle was well within eyesight, perhaps even within shouting range. Britt was splayed near the edge of the forest that impeded on Camelot's land, surrounding about half of the castle.

She waved, certain Sir Kay was watching her through a spyglass as he hadn't sent a squad of guards after her...yet.

Britt finished her bread and smashed her face in the clover-covered ground. "I am pathetic. I'm a college graduate living off the taxes of others. I never thought my future career path would involve impersonating a teenage boy-king."

She would never be able to forgive the real Arthur for running off with a shepherdess. Since Arthur eloped and disappeared, Merlin was forced to cast a spell on the Sword in the Stone so that the next person who touched the sword and would be able to pull it out—meaning they had the qualities the sword was looking for—would be brought back through time to be crowned King of England.

Britt was the unfortunate candidate the sword chose.

She arrived, American, female, and older than Sir Kay—Arthur's older foster brother—but Merlin had faith in his spell and decided to use Britt anyway. It worked at first; Britt could pass off as a tall but slender fifteen-year-old boy, and to Merlin's delight, Britt was extremely skilled in the art of swordsmanship thanks to her interest in Renaissance Mixed Martial Arts.

However, even with the rumor that Arthur/Britt had faerie blood—making her more elegant and beautiful than the average male—sooner or later, Britt's cover would be blown. (After all, it was only a matter of time before Britt's knights demanded that she marry and produce an heir for the good of the kingdom.)

"I hate tradition," Britt said.

"My Lord?"

Britt pushed herself off the ground and had Excalibur unsheathed in the blink of an eye.

A knight stood a stone's throw away. He wasn't one of her knights—Britt didn't recognize the coat of arms painted on his shield. He wore a helm, obscuring his face, but he had the kind of armor most knights who fancied themselves chivalrous preferred —serviceable but elaborately decorated.

"Can I help you?" Britt asked. A glance at Camelot confirmed her suspicions of Sir Kay and the spyglass: the gates were opening to let out a squad of mounted guards.

"I was only wondering if you were well," the knight said. "You seem burdened."

"I'm fine, thank you." She relaxed her stance but didn't sheathe Excalibur. "I'm no more burdened than any other man."

"That's hardly accurate, My Lord. As King, you have a great many more burdens," the knight objected.

Britt walked to Llamrei and patted the mare's neck. "And how do you know me to be a king?"

"I have seen you before, My Lord. We met once in the woods when you found a lost girl, and I saw you when you first pulled the Sword from the Stone in London," the knight said.

"I remember the girl," Britt said. "She was the one who inspired me to build public bath houses in Camelot."

"That is so, My Lord," the knight said, bowing slightly at the waist.

"From whose courts do you hail?" Britt asked, glancing at the incoming soldiers. They set their pace at a canter and would be on Britt soon. She raised an arm and signaled that all was well. The soldiers slowed their mounts to a walk but kept coming.

"My father's, I suppose, but I have pledged my allegiance to none yet. Do you desire to run me off your lands?" the knight said.

"You aren't stirring up trouble? Badgering my subjects, stealing food and such?" Britt asked, confident he would answer no. Her people would have let her know if recreant knights were terrorizing them. During the past fall, the first, and only, knight who ever plagued her people refused to let anyone pass over a bridge. Britt arrived with an escort of knights two days after he set up camp. Sir Bedivere trounced the man in a joust before Britt beat the snot out of him in a swordfight. The knight repented and now worked as a guard under Sir Kay's watchful eye, but all heard of the tale, and Britt's lands stayed curiously clear of rebel-rousers.

"No, My Lord. I travel with my cousins, performing deeds for the wellness of mankind," the strange knight said.

"In that case, I don't care," Britt said, nodding to her guards as they spread around her in a fan formation, not intruding on the conversation but drawing close enough to spring into action should the need arise.

"I thank you for your generosity, My Lord," the knight said, pulling off his helm.

Britt was amused to see that he was handsome and young, falling somewhere between Gawain's age of eighteen and Kay's age of twenty-one. His black, curly hair was just a little shorter than Britt's, falling almost to his shoulders. He had dreamy green eyes and thick lashes most women would kill for. His jaw line was curved and his facial features angular. Had he been American and from the twenty-first century, Britt could have mistaken him for a celebrity.

She was delighted to see his face—and not because he was handsome, as he was too young for her taste—but because of one very important fact.

He was beardless.

The young knight shaved, unlike the majority of Britt's court. Even Griflet and Ywain were trying to grow scrawny beards with ill success. Britt and Merlin were the only clean-shaven officials in the whole castle.

Britt chuckled and sheathed Excalibur before she gathered Llamrei's reins.

"Is something the matter, My Lord?" the knight asked, puzzled.

Britt boosted herself onto her mare's back. "No. Nothing at all. I have suddenly been struck by a capital idea. It was good to talk to you, sir. As long as you remain on the path of the chivalrous, should you find yourself in need of anything, please come to Camelot."

"I thank you for your kindness and generosity. May all be well with you, King Arthur," the handsome knight said.

Llamrei chomped on the bit as Britt swung her in Camelot's direction. "Thank you, and you as well," Britt said, cuing Llamrei into a swift trot.

Britt's guards surrounded her in an instant. "Where to, Milord?" the guard captain asked.

"Back to Camelot. I must speak with Merlin and our associates immediately. I have the most brilliant plan!"

~

WHEN BRITT ENTERED Merlin's study, the attractive wizard was sitting in a comfortable armchair, yawning. Sir Ulfius was with him, looking at the ceiling with a great amount of dread. Sir Ector nursed a glass of wine and avoided Britt's eyes as she slammed her open hand on one of Merlin's wooden tables, making a loud crack.

"I have it."

"You have what?" Merlin asked, gesturing for Sir Kay to close the door behind him when he slipped in after Britt.

"A way to make my knights accept the notion that I shave," Britt said.

Merlin frowned. "You are King. You do not need a reason."

Britt shook her head. "As long as you and I are the only

supposed males in this castle with beardless faces, there is going to be suspicion," she paused. "Where is Sir Bodwain?"

"Keeping Sir Bedivere busy so he doesn't poke his head in the study just as we're discussing your feminine nature," Sir Ulfius said.

Merlin crossed his legs at the ankles and sighed. "Alright, let's hear your idea, My Lord," he said without any expectations.

"Rather than attempting to explain it, why don't we make it a court fashion for men to be clean-shaven?" Britt asked.

Sir Ector choked on his wine.

"My Lord," the normally well spoken Sir Ulfius started. "Facial hair is, well, custom. Once a boy becomes an adult—like a squire getting knighted or an apprentice becoming a master—it is a sign of manhood to grow facial hair and it aids with…um…heat retention and…"

"What Ulfius is trying to ask is do we have to?" Sir Ector said, his face turning the same fetching shade as a crimson tomato.

"Oh, no. I didn't mean the older knights. Heavens, no. Some things should not be seen by the light of day. No, I meant the younger knights. Perhaps all knights who are unmarried," Britt said.

Sir Kay shifted, the thick mustache on his upper lip twitching.

"With some exceptions of course," Britt amended.

Merlin rubbed his chin. "It is an interesting proposal, and it certainly holds promise. But how do we make it a court fashion?"

"The church could make a proclamation that all unmarried knights must shave," Sir Ector suggested.

"Yes, they could, and they would be willing to, but what would they tell the people when asked why they're making the proclamation?"

"It is an, erm, idea from God?" Sir Ector said.

"One would have more luck making it common if the knights adopted the practice in their own will," Sir Ulfius said.

"To make it fashionable, it would take a man everyone loves,"

Merlin said. "Right now, there are no such knights in your court. You are the favorite of all."

"It can't be me," Britt said. "I'm already beardless, and no one is following my example. Our fashion icon must be a man that knights imitate out of admiration or jealousy," Britt said.

"A fashion icon?" Sir Ulfius asked.

"The court favorite," Merlin supplied.

"I see. We must have a beloved knight take the first step and shave, is that it?" Sir Ector asked.

Merlin looked to Sir Kay.

Sir Kay raised his brows and shook his head no.

"Agreed," Merlin said to Sir Kay's silent refusal. "No one much likes you anyway since you keep a tight guard around Arthur."

Britt sighed and sank into an open chair. "The knight who gave me the idea would have been perfect. He was clean-shaven and as handsome as they come."

"Who was it?" Merlin asked in interest.

"I didn't ask," Britt said.

"Britt, you should know better. Names and relations are important," Merlin scolded.

"I didn't ask on purpose. As soon as I knew who he was, I would have to worry about offending whatever second or fifth cousin of his lives in my courts," Britt said.

Sir Ector muffled a crow of laughter as Merlin scowled.

"If I might venture to change the subject," Sir Ulfius said.

"I suppose—as long as we have no model knight, my idea isn't much good. What's on your mind, Sir Ulfius?" Britt asked.

Sir Ulfius pressed his fingers together. "I have located the Round Table you so greatly desire."

"Really? That's fantastic!" She flashed the older knight a brilliant smile.

Britt had always disliked stories about King Arthur—she hated Lancelot the back-stabbing best friend with a vengeance and found the courtly romances to be trite—but as one of her close friends in future America was an avid fan, Britt wasn't able to entirely escape stories about the famous king. As such, she knew vaguely of some of the more famous parts of Arthurian lore, like the Round Table.

"I suppose so," Sir Ulfius reluctantly said.

"You don't give yourself enough credit, Sir Ulfius. The Round Table is a big deal. Thank you for finding it. Where is it?"

Sir Ulfius shifted and avoided looking at Britt. "I have discovered that it was given to King Leodegrance by Uther Pendragon. He still has it."

"Leodegrance? That's even better news. He's been our ally since I was crowned king, and he owes us after Sir Bodwain and King Ban and King Bors saved him from that weasel King Ryence," Britt said. "He'll let us buy it off him. Have you asked what he wants for it?"

"I know you have your heart set on the table, so I had one of my comrades from Uther's court make an inquiry on your behalf," Sir Ulfius said.

"And?"

Sir Ulfius sighed. "His requirement is that you would take his daughter, Guinevere, as your wife."

"Not an option. Ask him how much gold he would like," Britt said.

Sir Ulfius shook his head. "He informed my comrade marriage was the only way he would see the Round Table removed from his halls."

"Doubtless he's figured out how important the Round Table is to you," Merlin said, finally chiming in. "He is an unimportant ally compared to King Ban and King Bors, and having you as a son-in-law would be the greatest boon he could ever ask for. If you marry his daughter, he'll be able to lean upon you even more. We will tell the prig to bugger off, and that will be the end of it."

Britt frowned. "I want the Round Table, Merlin."

Merlin threw his hands in the air. "Why? We'll make you your own blasted round table!"

"It wouldn't be the same."

"No, it would be better. It wouldn't be stained and scratched up like this cumbersome thing Leodegrance has," Merlin insisted.

"Do we know for certain that it is the Round Table?" Sir Kay asked, smoothing his mustache.

"No," Sir Ulfius said. "My comrade never saw the table; it is in storage. King Leodegrance only brings it out for great feasts and such."

"Good riddance," Merlin said. "It's probably a nasty, half-destroyed piece of furniture. Uther was a rough man. I can't imagine any table of his has fared well."

"Merlin...I really want that table," Britt said.

The young wizard met her gaze, and the two stared at each other for several moments. "Blast. Fine," Merlin said, mussing his blonde hair as he scratched the top of his head. "Have it your way. Kay, send an official courier to Leodegrance from Arthur inquiring about the price of the table. Make it absolutely clear that desires for marriage are intolerable."

Sir Kay bowed and left the room as Merlin planted his chin on his hand.

"Happy?" Merlin snarked.

"Abundantly so," Britt smiled. "Thank you, Merlin!"

Merlin rolled his eyes. "I still do not understand your fascination with circular tables," he said as Britt seated herself in the chair next to him.

"It's part of the legend," Britt said.

"You *are* the legend. You can make up your own legends," Merlin complained, raising his hand to acknowledge Sir Ulfius and Sir Ector as they rose and left the room.

"Maybe, but some things have to happen," Britt said.

"Like owning the Round Table?" Merlin asked.

"Like owning the Round Table," Britt echoed.

~

TWO WEEKS PASSED without any new revelations. Couriers were sent back and forth between Merlin and King Leodegrance without any successful bargains being struck. The usually affable king was quite stubborn in his demands.

"I'll go without the Round Table before I see Guinevere in Camelot," Britt said. Her intense hatred of Lancelot was matched by her disdain for Guinevere, King Arthur's unfaithful wife.

Cavall, Britt's giant apricot-colored mastiff, a guard dog given to her by Sir Kay, whined at her feet.

Britt leaned over the armrest of her wooden throne and affectionately scratched her dog's side. "It's nothing, my fine boy. Don't worry."

Cavall set his head on the ground and sighed.

Britt patted him once more and raised her gaze to her courts. It was mid-afternoon on a cool spring day. As most of her knights had little to do since they were, surprisingly, at peace with not even a hint of war on the horizon, most of them chose to sit in Britt's throne room and chatter as Merlin's Minions ran the kingdom.

Britt considered her knights. "We need to make things more efficient. We have all these knights with no work to do. Talk about a waste of manpower," Britt said, sitting taller when Sir Kay approached her throne.

"There is a foreign knight who wishes to speak to you, My Lord," Sir Kay said.

Britt scratched the back of her neck. "What for?"

"He claims he recently spoke with you, and you instructed him to seek you out in Camelot should he need anything," Sir Kay said. Although he spoke no chiding words, his displeasure of Britt's generosity was made obvious by the slant of his mustache and the rebuke in his eyes.

Britt waved Sir Kay's unspoken concern off. "Oh! Him! Don't

worry, Kay. He's not a nut or a covert killer. He's the fancy-pants knight that gave me the shaving idea."

"Still, one should be cautious when extending hospitality to an unknown knight," Sir Kay grumbled.

"Yes, yes. I'm sorry. I should have let you look him over before I made any invitations. Send him in, please?" Britt said.

Sir Kay bowed and swept out of the room.

Moments later, the handsome, dark-haired, clean-shaven knight entered the hall.

His entrance raised some notice from Britt's knights. Several of the men clustered closest to Britt's throne fell silent as they watched the young knight approach Britt.

"Welcome to Camelot," Britt said as she stood and glided down the stairs of the dais upon which her throne was perched.

"Thank you, My Lord," the knight said, bending over in a perfectly executed bow.

"What brings you here today?" she asked.

"I approach you to ask for living quarters for myself and my two cousins. We grow weary of making our beds under the stars and would like to rest for a time before setting off in search of more adventures."

"There are just three of you? I don't think that will be a problem." Britt glanced to Merlin, who was crouched over an abacus and parchment.

The wizard flapped his hand without looking up. "Go ahead. Adopt any number of vagabond knights. We have enough room."

Britt nodded in satisfaction. "There you have it. You and your cousins may seek refuge in Camelot as long as you like. We can speak to Sir Kay, who will make the proper arrangements."

The young knight smiled. "I thank you for your generosity, My Lord."

"Name," Merlin said.

Britt winced. "I must beg you to forgive my poor manners, for I do not know your name,"

"It is I who must beg your pardon, My Lord, for I never thought to introduce myself. My cousins are Lionel and Bors, the sons of King Bors. I am Lancelot du Lac, the son of King Ban."

All of Britt's good cheer left her. She forced her lips into the shape of a smile that held no warmth. "Lancelot?"

Merlin looked up in alarm, hearing the frigid edge to Britt's inquiry.

"Yes, My Lord," Lancelot said, bowing again.

"If your name is indeed Lancelot, you can go—" Britt was cut off when Merlin hustled to her side.

"Lancelot, welcome to Camelot. You know who Kay is, yes? He's the man with the unfortunate face and the intimidating mustache who showed you in. Talk to him, and he will show you and your cousins to your rooms. If you will excuse us," Merlin said, yanking Britt out of the throne room.

They stumbled past Sir Kay and a squad of guards and nearly ran into a gaggle of servants before Merlin hauled Britt into an unused bedroom.

"I want him *OUT* of Camelot, right now," Britt snarled.

Merlin folded his arms across his chest and stood in front of the door, barring the way. "Why?"

"Because he's a back-stabbing, spineless worm who destroys Camelot and ruins Arthur."

"Is that in the Arthur legends from the future?" Merlin asked.

"Yes."

"What happens?"

"He worms his way into the position of Arthur's best friend and has an affair with Arthur's wife, Guinevere," Britt spat. "The two rip Arthur's kingdom to shreds."

Merlin didn't even blink. "I see. You fail to realize one thing."

"What?"

"That is a legend from the future, Britt, but right now *you* are the legend," Merlin said.

"What do you mean?"

"It is your decision to marry. You decide who your closest knight is. You are in control. It is your decision whether or not you wish to put Lancelot in a position of power."

"Exactly, which is why I'm kicking him out of Camelot," Britt said.

"You can't."

"Why not?"

"Did you hear anything he said after he gave his name?"

"No."

Merlin sighed. "I thought as much. He said his father is King Ban."

"So?"

"King Ban is your ally, and his cousins' father, King Bors, is as well. They were the pair who rode to your rescue when King Lot and his allies attacked you. Don't you remember?"

"I do. So what?"

"We cannot kick out the sons of our closest allies."

Britt groaned and pinched the bridge of her nose. "This is why I didn't want to know his name. Now we have to be afraid about offending all of his relatives. Bother feudalism!"

"It's worse than that, I'm afraid," Merlin said.

"How? How can it possibly be worse?"

"As long as he stays, he and his cousins will have to be seated in positions of honor."

"*What?*"

"They are princes and the offspring of your closest allies. Naturally, they will sup with you at your table," Merlin said.

"You mean I'll have to interact with Lancelot?"

"I do."

"Being a king sucks. You can't do anything you want," Britt sighed.

"Well done. Now you're starting to get it."

2

A QUEST

B ritt tipped back the remaining wine in her goblet before letting a page refill it.

Merlin, seated at her side, leaned in and whispered, "I do hope you're not going to tolerate the young princes' presence by consuming as much alcohol as you did during Queen Morgause's stay?"

Britt spoke through clenched teeth as she smiled at Lancelot when the handsome knight glanced at her from further down her dinner table. "If my methods work, I see no need to correct them."

Normally, Merlin invading her personal space made her squirrely. Today, she was too angry to notice.

Merlin patted her shoulder. "Cheer up. At least these three won't be here long, and they're not trying to kill you."

"Fantastic," Britt said, stabbing a radish with her knife.

Britt's attention was redirected by a dust-covered courier who hurried up the steps. "This is for you, Milord: a correspondence from King Leodegrance," he said, passing over an envelope sealed with wax.

Britt carelessly passed the letter to Merlin—she couldn't read old English writing—and took another slug of her wine as the wizard opened the letter and read it.

"What is it?" Britt asked.

"You're never going to guess," Merlin said, shaking his head in disgust. "King Leodegrance's lands are about to be invaded."

"*Again?*"

"Again."

"By whom?"

"Duke Maleagant."

"Who's that?"

"One of King Ryence's allies."

"We should attack Ryence's lands and be done with it. I thought Lot was annoying, but Ryence is proving to have more perseverance," Britt said, slumping in her chair.

"I'm not much inclined to help him," Merlin said, folding the letter. "We've already bailed him out once. If we lose him as an ally, I suppose it is not the worst thing in the world. You have prince Gawain and prince Ywain in your halls. If they had to, King Urien (and perhaps even King Lot) would ride to your aid, so you are not in any danger."

"Yeah," Britt said. She stared out at her dining knights and watched them eat, drink, and roar in laughter. "Wait a second," Britt said. "If Maleagant and Leodegrance do make an alliance, my chances of getting the Round Table are ruined, aren't they?"

"Undoubtedly."

Britt thought for a moment before she stood and declared, "It is not right to let an ally face an enemy alone. We must help King Leodegrance. My honor is staked on it," Britt said.

"Bravo," Lancelot clapped.

Merlin rolled his eyes at the foreign knight's antics and muttered, "You just want to save your precious table."

Britt ignored the observation and slowly turned to face Lancelot, a stiff smile molded on her face. "Were you listening in on our private conversation, Lancelot?"

"Only a bit. I admire the stoutness of your loyalty, My Lord. You are truly worthy of being the King of Britain," Lancelot said, rubbing his chin.

On either side of him, his hulking cousins shoved food in their mouths like it was their last meal for the week.

"Hmm," Britt said before forcibly turning her body back to Merlin. "It doesn't matter what my motives are. What is clear is that we must ride to King Leodegrance's aid."

Merlin sighed. "It's not that easy. If you save him, he's going to insist you marry his daughter."

"So, we help him without his knowledge," Britt said.

"Go on—I am intrigued," Merlin said.

"A small party of our best knights could easily enter King Leodegrance's borders. They could pillage and plunder Maleagant's forces," Britt said.

"Pillage and plunder? What happened to honor and chivalry?" Merlin asked.

"They flee the moment I sense my table is in danger," Britt said.

"There is some intelligence in what you say. Maleagant will not be able to amass the army Ryence did. At the very least, the knights could scout the land as we prepare the army."

"We. We could scout the land."

Merlin shook his head. "You are not going with them."

"Yes, I am. I want to see the Round Table." She folded her arms across her chest.

"You cannot. Not only would it be asinine to send a *king* on a scouting trip, but looking at the blasted table would mean getting into Camelgrance, King Leodegrance's castle."

Britt leaned into Merlin and whispered. "You just made me welcome the man I hate most on Earth in *any* century *and* his cousins into my castle. I. Am. Going."

Britt sank back into her chair as Merlin raised an eyebrow.

"Very well, I suppose I should let you win occasionally. Besides, I doubt there's much danger if we head out immediately."

"We'll call a meeting after dinner?"

"Yes, of course."

"My Lord," Lancelot said, making Britt stiffen. "My compliments on your bountiful table."

"Yes, it's certainly a good thing that it is bountiful," Britt said. Her gaze did not waver from Lancelot, and his cousins continued to eat with great enthusiasm.

Lancelot laughed. "I must say, My Lord, I find your kingdom both unusual and beautiful. I have never met folk half as clean nor well fed as the subjects of Camelot. 'Tis a charming kingdom, and all can see that you have the blessing of your faerie neighbors. They guard your forests and do mischief on your enemies, leading them astray in the woods and such."

"Perhaps, but I think lately they have failed in that area," Britt said.

Merlin choked on his wine and gave Britt a dirty look, but Lancelot did not catch the implied slight and laughed.

"Careful with your words," Merlin growled.

Britt smiled triumphantly. "Always."

"Ywain and Gawain should come. Gawain has become quite adept in combat, and Ywain will never allow us to bring his cousin and not him," Merlin said, tucking his hands into the sleeves of his robe.

"The three younger Orkney princes will remain behind," Sir Kay said.

"Naturally. This isn't an outing; it's a scouting party," Merlin said.

"You will be the one to tell them they are remaining behind," Sir Kay said.

Merlin grimaced. "Fine," he said.

"When we split into two groups, Gawain and Ywain should travel with My Lord," Sir Bodwain said. "My Lord will be able to keep them safe."

Britt snorted. "I fear you over estimate my abilities, Sir Bodwain."

Sir Bodwain shook his head. "You are the best swordsman in all of Camelot, and your jousting has much improved since last year. You do not give yourself enough credit, My Lord."

Next to Sir Bodwain, Sir Bedivere nodded in agreement.

Britt gave the pair a pained smile before looking to Merlin in a plea for help.

The wizard avoided Britt's gaze.

"If you say so," she said finally.

When Britt first came to England, Sir Bodwain, one of Merlin's star Minions, tolerated Britt. He had no belief in her combat skills or her intelligence. His opinion of her changed greatly during the war with Lot. Now, however, Britt couldn't help but wish he retained some of his disbelief.

Sir Bedivere's reaction was not a surprise as he always beheld Britt in a saint-like light. He was the only knight in an administrative position who did not know the truth of her gender and origins. His estimation of Britt was already undeservedly high, but when she broke off an enchantment Queen Morgause—her one-time enemy and now her pigeon correspondence pen pal—had cast over all her men (Bedivere included), Bedivere's esteem of Britt reached uncomfortably new heights.

"Kay and I will ride with Arthur's party," Sir Ector said, slapping his pot belly.

"No," Britt said. "You will remain behind, Sir Ector."

"What, what?" Sir Ector said, his round face wrinkling with the force of his frown.

"Arthur is right," Merlin said. "Someone needs to stay with Sir

Ulfius and see to the administration of Camelot. As Kay has *insisted* on coming along, you are the natural candidate, Ector."

"I say, that's not fair," Sir Ector grumbled. "Why does Kay get to go?"

"Because he asked first and held a sword to my throat as he did so," Merlin said.

Sir Kay smoothed his mustache to cover his smirk.

"With the addition of Gawain and Ywain, we still should send one more knight with My Lord," Sir Bodwain said.

"Do you have any suggestions?" Merlin asked. "And no, Bedivere, we cannot bring Griflet. We will have enough untrained knights to watch the way it is."

Sir Ector scratched his dry scalp. "Shall you take another one of your men, Merlin?"

Merlin shook his head. "With Bodwain, Bedivere, and Kay out of the castle, you will need all the help you can get. My... associates will remain behind to aid you and Ulfius."

"Who else is gifted in arms and combat?" Merlin asked.

"We don't know. We haven't had any jousts or tournaments since My Lord came to Camelot. We only know My Lord is the most skilled swordsman because no one has beaten him in practice fights," Kay said.

"Perhaps you should take a hunter with you? Not a knight but a forestman skilled in tracking and such. It may be useful," Sir Bedivere said.

"Perhaps," Sir Bodwain agreed.

Britt pressed her lips together. "There is someone I wish to bring."

"Who?" Merlin asked.

Britt briefly closed her eyes, unable to believe what she was about to say. "Lancelot du Lac."

"He is a fair choice. He is certainly gifted in arms," Sir Bodwain said.

"I doubt his cousins would insist on going. They are enjoying their stay here," Sir Bedivere added. "They have been with us for five days and show no signs of wishing to leave."

"He's a good lad," Sir Ector said.

Sir Kay was the only knight who did not look pleased.

Merlin leaned close to Britt and whispered, his breath tickling her neck. "What are you planning? You *hate* Lancelot."

"I do," Britt acknowledged, gritting her teeth. "But as much as I hate him, I would rather die than leave him in Camelot without supervision."

Merlin chuckled and said, "That's my lass," before pulling back with a handsome grin. "It's settled then. Lancelot du Lac will join us, should he be willing. We will leave two days hence. Remember, when recruiting the knights, we must be subtle. All of Camelot must believe we are going on an extended hunting trip."

"Aye," Sir Bodwain said, barely able to conceal a smile as he rubbed his hands together.

Sir Bedivere's grin stretched across his face. "Ready your gear and your weapons in secret. We are setting out on a quest."

Britt was not quite so giddy. She was looking forward to the trip, but she wasn't about to forget that Lancelot would be coming with them. "It will be interesting," she said.

"It's not fair. This is the first adventure since Morgause left last summer. I want to come," Sir Ector objected. "Kay, we should switch. I will go with Arthur; you stay here."

"I respectfully decline, Father. I will accompany My Lord."

"You little urchin. It's not fair, I tell you!"

"Yes, Father."

BRITT STARTED to regret her decision to bring Lancelot immediately after they set out. The young knight, of course, accepted the invitation— "I would never refuse to come to the aid of a king such as you, My Lord!"—and since they set out early in the morning, he had done nothing but grate Britt's nerves.

To begin with, he aligned his horse next to Britt for the day, never straying from her side.

Hourly, he felt the need to share a "rousing story" in which he always had the starring role, usually defeating a blackguard knight, a giant, or a serpent. He filled the day with mindless chatter and observations, remarking on everything from bird songs to tree foliage.

Britt almost wished she had brought Cavall along so she could tell the massive dog to bite him.

In the twilight hours, Kay signaled the party to halt for the night.

"This journey is going to be more painful than I thought," Britt said, loosening Llamrei's girth.

"Are you alright, My Lord?"

Britt turned to find Ywain behind her, his head tilted as he studied her with concern.

Britt blinked. "Yes."

"Your old wound isn't hurting you, is it?" Ywain asked, wringing his hands.

She laughed. "My thigh wound healed last summer, Ywain. It didn't even leave a scar."

"Yes, but I thought it still might twinge. You haven't made a long ride like this in some time," Ywain said.

"I am fine, but I thank you for your concern," Britt smiled.

The young knight nodded. "If you need anything at all, My Lord, do not hesitate to call," he said before seeing to his horse.

She barely had enough time to slip the saddle off Llamrei before she was again interrupted.

"Do you need any help, My Lord? Shall I fetch water for your horse?"

Britt set the saddle down. "I appreciate the offer, Gawain, but I should be the one to care for my mount."

"Can I help you with your armor then? Do you need anything unbuckled?" he offered.

"No," Britt said, swapping Llamrei's bridle for a rope halter. "I think I can manage, but thank you," she said.

Shimmying out of her armor was a tricky thing. She usually didn't bother to wear a full set, but she wore several pieces (the cuirass, pauldrons, faulds, and gorget—which covered her chest, upper legs, and throat.) to bulk up her form. She was tall—for both her century and this one—but too slender for a boy. The armor gave the illusion of broader shoulders, thighs, and chest.

Everyone assumed Britt's new bulk was maturity. If they helped her remove the armor, they would notice she was still as slender as ever. Kay or Merlin could help if she needed it.

"I see," Gawain said.

Britt leaned against her horse and studied the Orkney prince. "Tell me, how goes your lance training? Agravain told me you were seeking to improve your skills."

Gawain placed his saddle packs on the ground and began unpacking. "I have improved some. I have gotten a better feel of where to aim. Previously, I was content just to hit my opponent on the shield with as much force as I could muster, but some parts of the shield make a man yield easier than others. I fear Kay can still unhorse me though," Gawain said.

Britt winced in sympathy. "Kay could unseat a knight tied to his mount. The man is a nightmare as an opponent."

Gawain sat down, his gear spread around him. "You practice with him?"

"From time to time," she said vaguely. In truth, she had been practicing with Kay ever since she pulled the Sword from the Stone. The stony knight was pleased with her swordsmanship skills and was determined to make her a passable knight. He took it upon himself to train her in the use of a lance and spear. (He gave up on her archery skills after a brief stint of practice revealed she had no aptitude for the weapon.)

"If you're looking to beat Kay, I suggest you ask Sir Bodwain for help," Britt said.

"Sir Bodwain? Why?"

She brushed Llamrei's broad back. "Before he took up the position of my constable, he was a particularly fierce knight. He was quite a terror to battle in his younger days, I've been told. I am certain he would be able to help you."

"I never knew," Gawain said.

"I'm not surprised. I don't think much information about any of my knights would travel as far as Orkney. But it was why Merlin advised I select him as my constable," Britt said.

"I shall ask him to train me, in that case," Gawain said.

Britt smiled. "I'm sure the request will please him. I need to water Llamrei. Did you already water your mount?"

Gawain nodded and went back to organizing his gear. "There's a river just a stone's throw north from here."

"Excellent. Thank you, nephew," she said, leading her horse from the camp.

"My pleasure, My Lord," Gawain said.

When Britt turned to acknowledge the comment with a wave, she noticed Lancelot intently watching her.

The handsome knight made no movement to cover up his stare. Instead, he twisted his lips into a thoughtful frown.

Britt was distracted from his odd behavior when Sir Kay joined her. "Good evening, Sir Kay. Watering your horse?"

"Yes. You shouldn't go alone," Sir Kay said.

Britt chuckled. "Of course. Thank you for accompanying me."

"Yes."

"What is that supposed to mean?"

"Yes."

"You remain as enigmatic as ever, brother."

"Thank you."

THE FOLLOWING MORNING, Britt knelt at the riverbed and splashed water on her face in an effort to wake up. Since arriving in ancient Britain, she had been infected by a horrible case of insomnia, making mornings a bear to get through.

Britt rocked back on her heels in a squatting position and considered the riverbed. There were a number of strange tracks on the moist banks. She studied them with a frown, looking up when she heard the pounding of horse hooves.

A knight dressed in black armor and riding a sturdy horse crashed through the underbrush, popping out a few feet away from Britt.

"You there, knight. Have you seen anything—like a strange beast—pass this way?" the knight demanded.

"No," Britt said, stifling a yawn.

"Did you hear anything? Perhaps a noise that is not unlike the baying of hounds?"

She boosted herself into a standing position. "No, we're in the Forest of Arroy, faerie lands. There are no dogs in these parts."

"Oh, I say, Arthur, is that you?" the knight asked.

Britt studied the black armor and ventured a guess. "Pellinore?"

"At your service," King Pellinore said, flipping up the visor of his helm.

"What are you doing here? Your lands are far from this forest."

"Does it displease you to find me near your kingdom?"

"No, I told you before that you could pass through whenever you wish so long as you don't disturb my people," Britt said.

"I thank you for your generosity. I am on a noble adventure, for I am chasing the Questing Beast."

"The Questing Beast? I remember you mentioning that when we argued about your Sable Knight title. What exactly is a Questing Beast?"

King Pellinore removed his helm and patted his horse on the neck. "It is a great creature that has the head and neck of a serpent, the body of a leopard, the haunches of a lion, and the feet of a stag. A great noise emits from its belly, sounding like thirty or so baying hounds."

"Really," Britt said.

"You don't believe me?"

"No, it's more that I suspect we have a miscommunication—like the fact that you wear black armor and call yourself the Sable Knight," Britt said, placing her hands on her hips.

Pellinore frowned. "You are an odd boy."

"Perhaps. How far have you chased this beast?"

"From my castle. I have sought it my entire life, although it often eludes me. It roams Britain like the winds. I lost its trail some days ago."

"But?"

Pellinore laughed as he dismounted. "You are odd but just as sharp as Merlin. I lost its trail, but I am not much enthused by the prospect of returning home. To say my wife was not pleased at my departure would be a vast understatement."

"I see."

"What has dragged you from the paradise of Camelot, King Arthur?" Pellinore asked as he led his horse to the river's edge, letting it drink.

"A small party of knights and I are on our way to Camelgrance."

"King Leodegrance's lands? I received word that Duke Maleagant is approaching his borders. You aim to help him?"

"Partially. We mean to spy on Maleagant's forces so we know what army I must amass. King Leodegrance does not know of our party, for we mean to keep things secret." She hesitated. "Would you care to join us?" she asked on a whim.

"Come with you to Camelgrance, you mean?"

"Yes."

King Pellinore thought for a moment before a smile broke the stoic look on his noble face. "I would be delighted! Does Merlin ride with you?"

"Naturally," Britt said. "Has your horse drunk its fill? I can lead the way to our camp."

Pellinore looked at his mount, who stopped lipping the water and shook like a dog. "She is well. Lead on, Arthur!"

Britt led the way back to camp, calling when she grew close enough, "Merlin, Sir Kay? I have brought us another companion."

Kay looked up from the logbook in which he was writing, and Merlin almost choked on the carrot he was chewing. "King Pellinore, welcome to our camp," Merlin said.

"It is my honor. King Arthur spoke of your mission to scout Maleagant's forces," King Pellinore said.

"If it pleases you, Sir Bodwain, Sir Bedivere, Sir Kay, and I would like to hear your thoughts on our plan," Merlin said.

"It would be my pleasure," King Pellinore said, joining Merlin at the nearly burned out campfire.

Britt watched with a fond smile before she took a squashed, stale piece of bread from Gawain to serve as her breakfast.

"I don't understand, is King Pellinore not your enemy?"

Britt glanced at Lancelot, who joined her at the camp edge. She gave him a false smile. "He was when he joined King Lot and fought against me, but I have since made peace with him. He is noble and quite likeable—something I cannot say of all who are present."

"You are kind to your enemies," Lancelot said. "You include Prince Ywain and Prince Gawain in your company when they are the sons of men who sought to kill you."

Britt tried to act serene instead of snapping at Lancelot that for King Arthur, it was really his *best friend* and *wife* he had to worry about rather than the sons of his onetime enemies. "Both Sir Ywain and Sir Gawain have proven their loyalty to me. I have no reason to question them, for I know *their* allegiance is boundless."

Lancelot frowned. "My father was once forced to flee his kingdom by Claudas. I do not know if I could treat Claudas as you have treated King Pellinore."

Britt fixed a smile as sweet as poison on her lips. "Perhaps that is why the Sword in the Stone chose me," she suggested. "If you'll excuse me, I must prepare for our day."

"Of course, My Lord."

Britt thought nothing more of the conversation, and it would have surprised her to learn that Lancelot, on the other hand, dwelled upon it for a long time.

∼

A FEW MORE DAYS OF riding brought Britt and her knightly escort to King Leodegrance's lands.

"This is where we part," Merlin said, swinging his spindly legged horse to address Sir Bodwain. "You take the main company and scout Maleagant's camp. Sir Kay, Sir Gawain, Sir Ywain, Sir Lancelot, King Pellinore, King Arthur, and I will move ahead to Camelgrance. We will meet at the mill south of here this evening."

"As planned," Sir Bodwain nodded. His horse pranced a few steps until he stood directly in front of Britt. "Good luck, My Lord. God's speed and safety," he wished, bowing from the saddle.

"I look forward to your return, My Lord," Sir Bedivere added. Behind him, the remaining knights of Camelot bowed their heads in reverence.

"Thank you, I wish you luck with your part of the quest," Britt said.

As Sir Bodwain and Sir Bedivere rode off, leading the larger party of knights east, Merlin turned to the remaining group. "Now then, we set out on a ridiculous quest to break into our ally's castle to look upon a nasty table. We must go silently, which means we shall have to leave behind some of our equipment," Merlin said, staring at Britt and Llamrei.

Britt's armor and clothes were liberally embroidered with the image of a red dragon. Even Llamrei had a red dragon with its wings thrown open embroidered on her saddle blanket and burned into her leather tack."What?" Britt blinked.

"You couldn't have chosen less obvious equipment?" Merlin scolded.

"You were the one who declared my symbol would be a red dragon and went crazy decorating all my things with it," Britt said.

Merlin rolled his eyes. "Either way, we will have to part with any equipment that bears a personal symbol. Someone shall have to remain behind with horses and things to make sure they are not plundered by thieves," he said, eyeing Ywain.

The young knight violently shook his head. "Not I, I'm staying with My Lord," he informed the wizard.

Merlin narrowed his eyes. "Would you like to bet on that?"

"I will remain behind," King Pellinore said. "King Leodegrance and I are not on excellent terms. It would be better for the party if I remained away from Camelgrance."

"Are you certain, King Pellinore?" Britt asked. "I did not ask you to come with us so you could serve as a hostler."

King Pellinore dismounted. "Of that I am sure. Do not concern yourself with me, Arthur. I do not desire to see Camelgrance, but I would not mind routing any thieves or recreant knights in the area," he said with a fiendish grin.

"Excellent, we thank you for your cooperation, King Pellinore," Merlin said before he too dismounted. "We shall enter Camelgrance on foot in the plainest clothes we have."

"What?" Sir Ywain squawked. He wore a suit of fancy armor, intricately designed and completed with a large, red plume on his helm.

"Yes, Ywain, you shall have to change out of your odious armor," Merlin said.

"We wish to avoid detection," Gawain said.

"A handful of foreign knights would at the very least raise interest, if not suspicion," Lancelot added.

"Exactly," Merlin said.

"That sounds ideal. We'll be able to slip into the castle keep easier if we are dressed as servants or merchants," Britt said, sliding off Llamrei.

"Sir Ulfius did not know where the Round Table is kept. We will have to inquire further when we enter Camelgrance," Merlin said.

"Is it wise to go as one group? Six strange men wandering in the inner courts of Camelgrance might raise suspicion, regardless of the station we adopt," Sir Kay said, stroking his mustache.

"I am astounded, Kay. For once I find myself agreeing with you," Merlin said.

"Do not take it to heart. I am certain before the hour is over, you shall change your mind," Sir Kay said.

"Perhaps you should enter in pairs," King Pellinore suggested, slipping his horse a shriveled carrot.

"Yes, but the question is who travels with whom?" Merlin asked, narrowing his eyes as he studied the party.

Britt was filled with a sense of dread. "Kay and I should enter together. We can truthfully say we are brothers," Britt said, hoping to cut the wizard off.

Merlin snorted. "Such a statement would be like saying the finest destrier and a pack mule are siblings. No, Sir Kay will go with young Ywain, as he is able to keep the lad on a short lead."

"I beg your pardon," Ywain sputtered.

Britt's stomach plunged. "Merlin, no," she said.

Merlin smiled sweetly. "It would be the polite thing to do."

"*No.*"

3

SCOUTING FUN

Britt sourly stared directly in front of her as she slumped against a stone wall. Her eyes were narrowed, and her mouth was an unbecoming and deeply unpleased slant.

"It is my honor to be paired with you, My Lord. I have heard a great deal about you. I am flattered to be selected as your guard during this expedition," Lancelot said.

Britt slowly turned her neck to stare at Lancelot, her unpleasant expression still in place.

The talkative knight did not notice. "I imagine Merlin selected me as your companion because I am the most experienced knight—having gone on many quests and adventures in my youth."

"He placed me with you because he wants me to suffer," Britt said through gritted teeth.

"I do not understand what you mean, My Lord."

Her features morphed into an insincere smile. "No, I imagine you don't."

"In any case, as we have safely arrived in the inner sanctum of Camelgrance, we should inquire after this table you seek."

"Of course." She pushed off the keep wall, her eyes combing through the bustling castle innards. She did not see Merlin and Gawain, nor Kay and Ywain. They were likely in a different part of the castle, suffering less than her and having a great deal more fun.

Lancelot, dressed like Britt in a tunic of muted colors, waited for a few moments before he sauntered in the direction of a female servant who was struggling to carry a sack of flour.

"If I might take a moment of your time, My Lady?" Lancelot asked with an appealing smile.

"What? Oh, h-hello," the servant said, her eyes widening when she got a good look at the handsome knight.

"Greetings, fair lady. It is great fortune that has brought you, maiden with eyes of morning dew, across my path," Lancelot said.

The young woman grappled with her sack of flour and stared wide-eyed at Lancelot. "Thank you," she said.

Behind Lancelot, Britt rolled her eyes. "I apologize for my companion's lack of decorum. It is entirely rude of us to speak with you while you carry such a burden. Please, allow me." She took the sack from the maid, slung it over her shoulder, and offered the maid a full smile.

The young woman's arms went slack as she stared at Britt, a blush spreading across her cheeks.

"Where shall I carry it?" Britt asked.

"This way," the maid said, tottering off to a side door of the castle keep.

Britt and Lancelot followed in her wake, slipping into the bustling kitchens. The maid led them to a pantry, where Britt placed the flour on a shelf.

"Thank you," she said.

"I am pleased to have been able to help you," Britt said. "I ask that you forgive our ignorance, but my *friend* and I are looking for a storage room. We've been told to fetch a spare table for some outdoor business, but as we are servants for our visiting master, we are not versed with the castle Camelgrance."

"I think the storage rooms are on the second floor. I'm a kitchen girl, so I don't properly know. Sorry," the young woman said.

"There is no need to apologize. You have sent us down the right path. Thank you," Britt said, offering the girl another smile before she bent forward in a slight but stately bow.

"We are in your debt," Lancelot added.

The girl turned bright red and attempted a curtsey.

"Come, *friend*. We should find a table." Britt grabbed Lancelot by the shoulders and steered him from the pantry.

Britt and Lancelot slunk from the kitchens, wandering until they found a servants' stairway to the second floor.

"Great, we'll need to find more detailed instructions. This corridor alone has twenty doors. If someone sees us going through all of them, they're going to notify a guard," Britt said.

"Let us peer beyond the corner and see if there is someone who might be able to help us," Lancelot suggested.

Britt shrugged and followed the younger man. They rounded a corner and found a girl jumping up and down, grabbing at a ledge. A white cat was perched on the ledge, watching the bouncing girl with feline interest and a twitching tail.

"Wyne, come down here, you foolish cat! If My Lady finds out you've run off again, she won't be happy," the girl pleaded with the cat.

"I beg your leave, My Lady, but if we could speak to you for a moment?" Lancelot called.

The girl whirled around. She was young, probably fifteen or sixteen, and wore markedly better clothes than the kitchen girl. She was probably a lady in waiting based on her braided hair and clean face.

"Good afternoon," she said, bobbing in a curtsey as she smiled at Lancelot.

"Good afternoon to you, beautiful maiden," Lancelot said.

"What did you want to discuss?" the girl asked, shyly clasping her arms behind her back.

"I find myself in the gravest need of your sage advice and knowledge, My Lady," Lancelot said, batting his long eyelashes.

The girl held a hand to her mouth to cover her grin. "Oh?"

"Indeed. The stars have aligned to bring us together, so that you may have mercy upon me, your lowly servant, and help me in my time of need."

Britt heaved her eyes to the ceiling as Lancelot beat around the bush. "What he means to say is that we are in need of some direction." She edged around Lancelot to draw closer to the ledge. Britt extended her hand and reached the cat on the ledge. She let it sniff her hand before she picked it off the ledge and held it against her chest. She briefly rubbed under its chin, getting a purr from it, before she offered the cat to the girl.

"We have been sent to gather a table from a storage room for our master, who is visiting. Sadly we are not familiar with Camelgrance and have been woefully unable to find such a room," Britt said as the girl took the cat.

When the maid looked up at her, Britt flashed the girl with her most charming smile.

"Oh," the girl said.

Britt waited patiently for several moments. When a reply was not forthcoming, she ventured, "Do you know, perhaps, where a table may be stored?"

The girl shook herself. "For certain. This way, if you would," she said, holding the cat with one arm as she led the way. She stopped in front of a plain-looking door and opened it. Light from the hallway pierced the darkness of the room, letting Britt see stacks of wooden furniture.

There were roughly cut benches, square tables, chests, wall hangings, and stools. There not one circular or round table.

Feeling the young woman's eyes on her, Britt flashed another smile. "Perfect. We thank you for your assistance."

"It was my pleasure," the girl said, stroking the cat and showing no signs of leaving.

Britt glanced at Lancelot, who was frowning most uselessly.

Britt was saved from trying to nudge the girl away when someone from the hallway called, "Eleanor, have you found Wyne?"

The lady's maid, looking dismayed, curtseyed again. "I am sorry, but I must go."

"We thank you once more for your kindness and mercy," Lancelot said.

The girl darted from the room, her arms clamped around the cat. "I have apprehended Wyne. Will you tell My Lady…" her voice faded as she hurried from hearing.

"It's not here. At least, I don't think it is." Britt folded her arms across her chest.

"The Round Table?"

"Yes. Come on, let's keep looking."

Britt and Lancelot talked to another maid, a minstrel, and a clerk before they found a squire who could show them where the Round Table was stored.

"You say your father served King Uther?" the squire asked, holding a torch as they ventured down a dusty, abandoned hallway.

"He did. He told me stories of King Uther's legendary Round Table. When I heard it is under the custody of King Leodegrance, I knew I would have to look upon it should I ever journey to Camelgrance," Britt said, the lie coming easier since she had changed it and repeated it multiple times.

"It don't look like much. 'Tis awkwardly big," the squire warned before he opened a door and ventured inside.

Britt and Lancelot followed the squire, staring in confusion at the room.

"This is the Round Table?" Lancelot asked.

"Yep."

"I don't understand," Britt said, her forehead wrinkling.

The room was filled with chipped, curved tables. They were covered in dust, and reminded Britt of pieces of a toy train track.

"They fit together. Like a ring, see?" the squire said.

"How many does it seat?" Lancelot asked.

"About a hundred and fifty knights, I think. Depends how fat they are," the squire said.

"A hundred and fifty?" Britt said, pinching the bridge of her nose. "This isn't quite what I thought it would be."

"It's why Ol' King Leodegrance only drags it out for feasts. It's perfect for those occasions when everyone is drunk and don't look closely at the furniture, plus servants can get on the inside of the ring to serve everyone real easy," the squire said.

"Maybe Merlin is right. We should just build our own Round Table," Britt muttered.

"Oh, what a dream come true this is," Lancelot said.

Britt lowered her hand to see if the handsome knight had gone stark, raving mad.

"To think that we're seeing the Round Table. Such great things must have happened at this table, like your father's stories, Art," Lancelot said, turning to face Britt.

Britt stared at the knight until the squire shifted, reminding Britt of her role. "Absolutely. It's not how I imagined it, but to think that Uther Pendragon himself sat here. How noble."

The squire shrugged. "Glad you're not disappointed," he said. "That all you want to see?"

"Indeed, thank you, young squire, for taking the time to show us this great piece of history," Lancelot said, a glittering coin appearing in his fingers. He tossed it to the squire, who caught it with enthusiasm.

"Right, no problem at all. You men need me to lead you out?" the squire asked.

"If you wouldn't mind taking us to the kitchens, we would much appreciate it. Thank you," Britt said as she and Lancelot exited the room, the squire right behind them.

The helpful squire took them to the kitchens where they easily joined the mass of servants and slipped out the supplies door.

"That was a disappointment," Britt said as she and Lancelot passed through the castle gates.

"Camelgrance seems to be a very odd place," Lancelot said.

Feeling protective of her ally, even though she did not particularly like him, Britt asked, "Why do you say that?"

"The females of that castle."

"What of them?"

"They did not react to me how most ladies do."

Britt heaved her eyes to the heavens. "Of course your description of odd would contain preferences to yourself."

"Pardon?"

"Lads, you've made it safe and sound."

Britt, recognizing that voice, craned her neck and spotted Merlin, Kay, Ywain and Gawain standing near a large hay bale.

"As have you," Britt said.

"Did you see the Round Table as you wished to, My Lord?" Gawain asked.

"We did," Britt said.

"How?" Ywain asked, stunned.

"We entered Camelgrance and asked an assortment of servants until we found a squire who could take us to it," Britt said.

"Tis in a shamble and somewhat disgraceful," Lancelot said, earning a look of irritation from Britt.

"How did you get in the keep?" Merlin asked.

"Through the kitchens," Britt said. "Why?"

"We could not even gain entrance to the keep, and thus were unable to see the table," Gawain said.

"Us as well," Kay added.

"Oh," Britt said.

"It is a good thing, then, that My Lord and I were able to see the table," Lancelot said.

"What did you think of it?" Merlin asked.

"It's not what I pictured. It's much bigger than I thought it would be. The squire told us it can seat 150 knights," Britt said.

Merlin nodded. "That would be about right. Although more than 150 knights served Uther, not all of them were at his castle at once. You are surprised?"

"Yes. Based on the stories, I thought it would be much smaller and that it would be one table. It is essentially many tables pieced together," Britt said.

"Well, you've seen it. We can depart for Camelot, and you can judge for yourself what price you're willing to pay to get it. If you still want it," Merlin said.

"I apologize for the intrusion, but the light is dimming. We should return to King Pellinore and meet up with the main company before sunset," Sir Kay said.

"Kay is right. Let us set out, men," Merlin said, leading the way away from Camelgrance.

"Did you get to see King Leodegrance, My Lord?" Ywain asked, moving to walk at Britt's side.

"No. I mostly saw furniture and a multitude of tables. You?" Britt asked.

Ywain nodded. "Sir Kay and I saw him return from a hunt early in the morning. He's a regular player. An actor I mean."

"I agree with you, cousin, for Merlin and I saw him as well," Gawain said, falling in line at Britt's other side.

"Oh?" Britt said. "What is it about him that reminds you of an actor?"

"He's not how he appears to be," Ywain said. "He looks noble, like a king should, but he's not."

"Agreed," Gawain said. "It seems like he tries to imitate a man of high caliber, like King Pellinore, to cover his shortcomings."

"And what are his shortcomings?"

"He was harsh to his mount, which isn't often a sign of an even temper," Gawain carefully said. "And he wore lavish clothes. Of course a king should dress well, but he wore an embroidered, red tunic to go hunting."

"His wife was…quiet," Ywain added. "Mother always has an earful for my father whenever she sees him. Not so with King Leodegrance's wife."

"I see," Britt said. "Thank you for your insight."

"My pleasure, My Lord," Ywain said.

"Please do not take our words seriously. We know little of ruling; our only wish is to serve you, My Lord," Gawain said.

"Aye," Ywain echoed.

Britt smiled and slung her arms around their shoulders. "I am blessed and grateful to have you," she said, getting grins from the cousins.

"So are we, My Lord," they said.

"My Lord," Sir Kay said.

"Yes?" Britt asked, removing her arms from her young friends. She stopped and fell in line with Sir Kay, who was behind her.

Sir Kay was silent for a few moments. "Well done today," he finally said.

Britt grinned. "Thanks. It has certainly given me a lot to think about."

THE HORIZON WAS BARELY PINK with dawn when Britt arose the following day. Few of the knights were up, and those who were spared Britt no second glance as she walked to the edge of their camp, gazing in the direction of Camelgrance.

"What is on your mind, King Arthur?" King Pellinore asked, clamping a giant hand on her shoulder.

"Please, just Arthur," Britt said with a weak smile. "My knights will not budge on calling me 'My Lord,' but you are a fellow king."

King Pellinore nodded. "Very well, but only if you extend the same rule to me. What is it that weighs you down, Arthur? You have been thoughtful since your return yesterday."

"I have never interacted much with King Leodegrance. Ywain and Gawain both gave me unfavorable reports of him yesterday."

"That worries you?"

"It does. I feel foolish saying it, but I always thought of my allies as being...honorable."

"Righteous?"

"I suppose so, yes. I find it discomforting that one of my allies might not be a very good person," Britt said, turning to look at the older king. "You are not allies with King Leodegrance. Why?"

King Pellinore hooked his thumbs on the belt of his tunic. "Anglesey is far north of Leodegrance's lands. There's never been a reason to be allies. But even if he had asked, I would be reluctant to accept an offer of friendship from him."

"Why?"

"As far as kings go, Leodegrance isn't such a bad fellow. He's no fool. He sees that his people are fed and that his army is provided for. But he lacks the courage to push back enemy forces. He bends easily and would rather have an ally help him than stand on his own."

"Like when King Ryence attacked him. King Ban and Bors and a company of my own men saved him," Britt said.

"That sounds like Leodegrance, yes."

Britt sighed, and King Pellinore once again rested a hand on Britt's shoulder. "He's not evil, Arthur. He's just greedy."

"I see."

"Perhaps you should take a look at him and judge his conduct for yourself," King Pellinore suggested. "When again will you have a chance to see him, unguarded and unaware of your presence?"

Britt nodded thoughtfully. "Thank you for your advice, Pellinore."

King Pellinore shrugged. "You're a great king, Arthur. Certainly you are a better king than I. Listen to your gut," he suggested before striding back into the camp.

Britt thoughtfully scratched her cheek. "Judge for myself, huh," she muttered. "I won't stand with a man who may beat his horse—or his wife."

None of the barely conscious knights paid much attention when Britt returned to her bedroll to collect Excalibur. She set off from camp at a walk, and by the time she reached Camelgrance, the sun was a disk on the horizon.

Britt entered the castle and made her way to the keep. The inner courtyard buzzed with activity. Servants swarmed like worker ants, carrying supplies in and out. They moved at an almost frenzied pace. Grooms stacked hay high in the stables and double the guards patrolled the castle walls as the day before.

After kicking up her heels for fifteen minutes, Britt realized how stupid her plan was. *Just because I show up, there is no guarantee that Leodegrance is going to go off on a hunt or something, and I am not venturing into the keep without backup,* Britt muttered as she left the inner courtyard. *I was an idiot for coming here without telling anyone. Merlin is going to kill me, if Kay doesn't throw me into a dungeon first.*

Someone on the castle walls blew a horn, and Britt leapt out of the main road to avoid a heavily loaded wagon pulled by a team of oxen. A farmer and his family scurried at the wagon's side, and Britt realized with unease that a great deal of people and animals from the farm land surrounding Camelgrance were pouring into the castle.

Britt ran the remaining distance to the castle gatehouse,

dodging goats, chickens, and people. Fear curdled her blood when she saw that the gate portcullis—a wooden and metal grille —was down, blocking all traffic. A squad of soldiers was stationed around the portcullis and gatehouse. One of the soldiers blew a horn again.

"No," Britt breathed as she lunged forward, pushing her way through the crowd of people gathered near the entrance.

Through the narrow window the portcullis provided, Britt could see a small squad of mounted knights, bearing a flag with a coat of arms Britt did not recognize.

One knight stood separate from the rest. He rode a red roan horse and carried a heavy-looking lance and a shield.

A racket arose behind Britt.

"Make way for the King!"

"Move. Step aside."

A man Britt vaguely recognized galloped up to the portcullis, pulling his horse to a halt at the last moment. A troop of guards accompanied him, but it wasn't until the knight on the red roan horse outside spoke that Britt recognized him.

"King Leodegrance, you are wise to cower behind your gates," the knight shouted.

"What brings you to my doors so early and dressed for war, oh great Duke Maleagant?" King Leodegrance asked.

"I am here to learn if you are a friend or a foe," the knight on the red roan horse said, who was evidently Duke Maleagant.

"Oh?" King Leodegrance said.

"Indeed. If you are a friend, I shall put aside my weapons, and we will feast together, toasting a blessed companionship," the duke said.

"But certainly we *are* friends," King Leodegrance said, nodding.

"If that is so, you will give me your daughter Guinevere as my wife," Duke Maleagant said.

King Leodegrance didn't even pause to think. "Absolutely, I would be much honored to call you my son-in-law."

"In addition, you will grant me the lands that she will inherit from her mother," Duke Maleagant said.

King Leodegrance hesitated, a fat frown spreading on his face.

"I will give you two days to decide if we are friends or foes. If, at the end of those days, you decide we are friends, we will put this matter aside and prepare a wedding feast. If, at the end of the two days, we are foes, I shall march against Camelgrance with the army I have brought to the borders of your lands."

"My daughter Guinevere has many admirers. What do I tell them?" King Leodegrance asked, squeezing the reins of his horse's bridle.

Duke Maleagant laughed. "If any man so deeply loves Guinevere that he dares to fight on her behalf, he may challenge me at the end of the two days. When he loses, I will kill him."

"And if he wins?" King Leodegrance asked, perking up.

"No man can hope to win against me in combat. But should such a thing come about, I will leave these lands and relinquish all my demands. Now, I will wait the agreed-upon two days. Make your decision, king," Maleagant said before he wheeled his horse around and rode off.

His companion knights did not follow him. Instead, they dismounted and started sliding gear off their horses, settling in and setting up camp.

"The gates remain closed," King Leodegrance said to the soldiers before he, too, turned his horse around and rode back to the castle keep.

The crowd dispersed, and even the soldiers returned to their patrols and their positions. Only Britt remained, staring at the portcullis and knights that separated her from her men.

She was trapped.

4

TRAPPED

Britt sat on the edge of a fountain inside the castle gardens. Excalibur lay balanced on her lap, and she placed her hand upon it, as if stroking a cat or dog.

She was in trouble.

If King Leodegrance agreed to ally himself with Maleagant, the castle would open, and Britt would be free to return to her companions. However, Maleagant (and King Ryence) would likely march upon Camelot as soon as he was married to Guinevere.

If King Leodegrance grew a spine and said no, Britt would be locked in the castle when Maleagant laid siege to it. If she was lucky, Merlin would figure out where she was and bring an army from Camelot. If she was not lucky…

"The best scenarios involve war for my people." Britt clenched her hands into fists. "I don't want that."

Her only hope was for a champion to fight Maleagant on Guinevere's behalf. "Where is that priggish Lancelot when you need him?" Britt grumbled.

"Oh," said a feminine voice.

Britt looked up to find a ladies maid, the same ladies maid

who chased the white cat and helped her look for the Round Table the day before. "Good morning to you, My Lady," Britt said, rallying a smile for the girl's sake.

The young lady's eyes grew large, and she clasped a hand to her chest. Without a word, she turned and ran, her skirts flapping as she disappeared into the castle.

"And now I frighten females. Wonderful." She sighed and leaned back, closing her eyes and listening to the fountain bubble at her back as she considered her options.

Britt was almost dozing—insomnia makes for great morning and mid-day naps—when she was again jarred from her thoughts.

"See!"

"My word, it's true."

Britt opened her eyes to the ladies maid, who stood with a lavishly dressed young maiden. She had reddish-blonde hair that was artfully arranged in a complex braid, wide eyes, and a smile that said she was *exactly* aware how beautiful she was. She was a little older than the ladies maid, but certainly not more than seventeen or eighteen.

Britt instantly recognized her, even though she had seen her only once before with Merlin. This teenage girl was the infamous Guinevere. Britt knew because she had burned her image in her mind as someone to distrust and dislike.

"I thought my luck was bad to bring Lancelot to my courts, but to encounter both of them in the same week? Wretched," Britt grumbled.

"Are you an Elf King?" Guinevere asked.

Merlin would throttle her if he learned she had treated the daughter of a king with disrespect. So Britt flattened her lips and arranged her expression into one of amusement. "Although I am often asked that question, I can tell you with certainty, I am not."

"A faerie lord then?"

"No, I am not that either."

"But surely you must be. I have never before met one so striking as you," Guinevere persisted.

Britt didn't understand why people insisted she was so comely—she was not gorgeous, after all; she wasn't even a man—and shrugged. "That reveals more about the people you have met than it does of me," Britt said, standing and strapping Excalibur to her belt.

Guinevere approached Britt and extended a hand.

Britt caught her by the wrist when she almost touched Britt's face. "What are you doing?"

Guinevere gazed up at Britt. "I am staring into the face of the noblest man in Britain."

Britt smiled again to keep from laughing. Guinevere sounded like a lovesick high school girl. If this was her character, it was no surprise she eventually fell for Lancelot. "I regret to inform you, but you do not," Britt said, dropping Guinevere's arm and backing away.

"How can you say that?" Guinevere said, batting her thick eyelashes at Britt.

Britt was not impressed. "Because I apparently have met more men than you have and know better. If you will excuse me, My Lady."

"You leave?"

"I do."

"How can you?"

"Quite easily, I assure you."

Tears welled up in Guinevere's eyes. "Will you not give me a token to remember you by?"

Britt frowned. "You're nuts, aren't you?" she said before recovering and adopting the proper words. "Forgive me, My Lady, but we have met for but a few moments. What is there to remember?"

"A pure love that began on a spring morn," Guinevere said. Her tears began to flow, and Britt was still unmoved. She was about to tell Guinevere so when another lady's maid scrambled into the gardens.

"My Lady, your father the King calls for you," the lady's maid said.

Guinevere's tears dried. "He what?" Her forehead creased with an emotion Britt couldn't put her finger on.

"He summons you and desires to speak with you and your honorable mother," the lady's maid said.

No one noticed as Britt started to edge away.

Guinevere looked down and stared at the garden path.

"I wish you well, Lady Guinevere," Britt said, safely on the other side of the fountain. She bowed and fled, not taking the chance to look over her shoulder to see the ladies' reaction.

She had a bad feeling she knew why King Leodegrance was calling Guinevere.

"As shallow as she is, I don't think any girl deserves to be stuck with Duke Maleagant," Britt said, ducking into the courtyard.

She walked past the stables and yelped when someone grabbed her and dragged her inside.

Britt grappled for Excalibur as a hand covered her mouth.

"I ought to kill you, you stupid lass," a rough voice hissed into her ear.

Britt looked up, and to her surprise found herself standing eye to eye with Merlin.

"Merlin?" Britt said, her words muffled by his hand.

"Yes," Merlin said, removing his hand.

"Merlin! Finally, something is going right." Britt said, throwing her arms around the wizard and leaning into him.

"No thanks to your hard work," Merlin wryly said, although he fixed an arm around her waist and patted the back of her head.

Britt sagged against Merlin's chest, breathing in the woodsy scent of his robe. He was warm and steady. Even better, with Merlin around, Britt knew she would be safe.

Merlin pressed his cheek to her head, and for a brief moment everything was right in the world. Then Britt felt him stiffen, and he abruptly pushed her back. "See here, now. If someone sees us, there will be questions we cannot answer." He shook out his robe before leading the way down the stable aisle. They ducked out a far door, joining a crowd of farmers who were grimly setting up camps in the castle courtyard.

"How did you know I would be here?" Britt asked.

"King Pellinore. When Kay discovered you were missing this morning, Pellinore told us he might know where you ran off to," Merlin said. "Gawain, Lancelot. I found him."

The two knights were standing in the shadows of a wall. They both looked up when Britt and Merlin approached them.

"My Lord," Gawain bowed.

"I am glad you have been found, My Lord," Lancelot declared.

Britt ignored the foreign knight's greeting. "Hello Gawain. Did the three of you make it into Camelgrance before the portcullis closed for Maleagant?" Britt asked.

"No," Merlin said. "We saw Maleagant issue his warning to King Leodegrance though."

Britt frowned. "If you didn't get in before, how did you make it inside?"

Gawain looked queasy. "Magic," he said.

"Merlin is quite the impressive wizard," Lancelot added, for once somewhat subdued.

"Indeed. I was *going* to bring Sir Kay and Gawain with me, but at the last minute, Lancelot pushed Kay back just before I finished the spell to get us through—King Pellinore was holding back Ywain as he was hotly demanding he come—getting the spell cast on him. So, I had no choice but to bring Lancelot in Kay's place," Merlin said, sounding just the smallest bit disgusted.

"I find myself gladdened by this news," Britt said.

Merlin raised an eyebrow in surprise. "Are you?"

Lancelot beamed. "I am pleased my presence delights you, My Lord."

"It's not that. Since you kept Kay from coming to get me, in all likeliness that means you are now higher on his list of people to maim than I am," Britt said.

Merlin coughed to cover a laugh, but Gawain seriously considered Britt's words. "He has a list?"

"What do you think he's always writing in that logbook of his?"

Gawain nodded. "You must be right, My Lord."

"So what's the plan?" Britt asked.

"For what?" Merlin said.

"To leave Camelgrance?"

"There is no plan."

"Can't we go out the way you came in?" Britt asked.

"No," Merlin said as Gawain shuddered behind him. "It took a lot of magic to get us in. I certainly don't have enough to get four of us out until I recover a bit."

"We could always leave Lancelot behind," Britt mumbled before Merlin elbowed her.

"Sir Bodwain is riding back to Camelot as we speak. He means to muster an army to aid King Leodegrance and free us," Gawain said.

"In the meantime, we will sit tight," Merlin added.

"We shall have to stay on the streets with the rest of these poor outcasts," Lancelot said, benevolently looking at the peasants crowding the courtyard.

"Not on your life. I have several contacts living in Camelgrance. We will stay with one of them." Merlin set off towards another part of the castle. "Follow me."

⁓

MERLIN'S CONTACT WAS A SHORT, skinny merchant who seemed to be scarcely less intelligent than Merlin himself. He agreed to host them and provided beds and food for all four of them. Merlin spent most of the afternoon closeted with the merchant, leaving Britt with Lancelot and Gawain.

Due to a particular member of her company, Britt had a headache by the time night fell. When the midnight watch called, the headache still hadn't left. Rather than wake her companions, Britt told the merchant—who was wide awake and inspecting his wares—she was going to take a walk.

He insisted she wear a short, hooded cloak, which Britt put on before she slipped out of the house and wandered Camelgrance freely. *They have quite lax security here considering it's under siege.* Britt nodded to a patrolling soldier—who didn't even stop to question her reason for being out at such a late hour.

Britt's wanderings eventually brought her to the keep. As she passed near the stables, she thought she heard crying. She followed her ears to the castle garden. Keeping to the shadows, she stopped when she saw the sobbing came from Guinevere.

The younger girl had cast herself face-down on the lip of the fountain. Her normally glossy, braided hair was a wild bush around her, and instead of her beautiful dress, she wore a plain kirtle.

"Probably agonizing over a handsome face," Britt muttered. Her heart softened, though, when she remembered Leodegrance's trouble. In all likelihood, Leodegrance had told Guinevere she was going to marry Maleagant.

Britt sighed and pulled up the hood of her cloak, making sure it covered her golden hair. "What troubles you, My Lady?" Britt asked in the gruffest voice she could muster.

"What? Who is there?" Guinevere said, wiping tears from her red eyes.

"I mean you no harm," Britt said, hoping the princess wouldn't call for guards.

"Who are you?"

"I'm…the gardener," Britt said.

Guinevere wiped her nose on her sleeve. "What would a gardener care about the troubles of a silly girl?" Guinevere harshly laughed.

"I care for the troubles of most people. Silly girls included. Now, what troubles you, My Lady?" Britt patiently asked.

"You must have heard. Father must give me to Duke Maleagant, or the duke will bring war upon us."

"Does he have no allies he can turn to for help?"

A bark of laughter escaped from Guinevere's throat. "He does, but that is hardly any better."

"What do you mean?"

"His only ally that seems even remotely inclined to aid him is King Arthur, and if he does rescue us, my father will see me married to *him*."

Obviously Guinevere hadn't heard the rumors of how handsome and loved 'King Arthur' was. Feeling slightly offended, Britt said, "And marrying King Arthur would be just as bad as marrying Duke Maleagant?"

"No," Guinevere said, shifting until she sat on the brim of the fountain. "He's a great deal younger, and I'm sure he's not as rotten as Maleagant. He's also richer. I would have more jewels and clothes if I were to wed him," Guinevere said.

Just as Britt thought the girl was nothing but a mindless mercenary, Guinevere added, "But the only reason Father wants me to marry Arthur is because of my lands."

"I beg your pardon?"

"How long have you served us? Don't you know that when my mother dies, I shall inherit all the lands my Father gained when he married her?"

"I, um, of course know of this. I fail to see what your inheritance has to do with King Arthur," Britt said.

"Arthur is richer than my father, and he doesn't need more

land holdings. He wants some stupid table, so Father would get to keep my lands," Guinevere bitterly said. "Father doesn't care whom I marry, so long as he profits the most from the union."

"And what do you want?"

"Pardon?"

"What would you like to do?"

It was a long time before Guinevere responded. "I just want everything to stay the same," she whispered. "I want to go on picking flowers, and laugh and talk with my friends, and choose pretty dresses to wear. I don't want to be a wife yet; least of all to a man I do not love."

"You do not get to chose whom you marry?"

"Of course not. I am a bargaining chip for my father to use. I will marry whomever he chooses. The only variable is the beauty of the cage in which I will be locked and the kindness of the gate-keeper." Guinevere laughed. "I don't know why I'm telling you all of this. I suppose it's because you're the first person to ever ask."

"And you have no one to fight on your behalf?" Britt asked. Guinevere was a pretty thing. Surely there was a knight some-where who would fight for her.

"What do you mean?"

"No knight has pledged himself to serve you?"

"No. Why should one? Knights only serve in times of war," Guinevere sniffled.

Britt frowned for a moment. Now that she thought of it, Guinevere was right. In Camelot, all the young knights who were supposed to be off questing and having adventures hung around the courts. The knights who were older and married were at home, seeing to their families and lands.

Lancelot and his piggy cousins, in fact, were the first knights Britt had come across who had gone on quests—if one excluded King Pellinore and his romps after the Questing Beast.

Why was that?

From what Britt could recall, chivalry and questing and doing great deeds for King Arthur or a favored lady was the very foundation of the Round Table.

Guinevere stood, fumbling to push her wild hair over her shoulder. "I thank you for your kindness, gardener, but I must depart. I have much to prepare," she said, her lower lip trembling.

Britt studied the genuinely upset princess. This was not the falsified moroseness she had tried to trick Britt with earlier in the day. Guinevere was struggling. "Have hope, My Lady," Britt said.

Guinevere laughed harshly. "Hope in what?"

"In mankind."

"Mankind is no comfort. Every man only cares for himself. Those of us who are weak, those of us who are powerless will never be saved."

"Then hope for a future where that is not so. Hope that somewhere in Britain there is a person who is willing to fight for the weak and the powerless," Britt said.

Guinevere turned to face the keep, placing her back to Britt. "If such a person, no, if such a *being* existed, whether they be faerie, man, woman, or saint, life would not be like this," she said. "Good night, gardener."

Britt watched the princess leave. "This country needs King Arthur. The real King Arthur, not a fake. They need a hero."

❧

"THERE IS SOMETHING ON YOUR MIND."

Britt stirred at Merlin's words. "It is nothing. I'm just tired."

It was mid-morning. King Leodegrance had a few scant hours to make his decision. Merlin had sent Gawain and Lancelot up the castle walls to see if they could spy any sign of an army—Britt's or Maleagant's. With their merchant host gone to see what kind of profit he could turn in the chaos, Merlin and Britt were alone in the small home.

"No," Merlin said. "When you are tired, you yawn more and shut your eyes. You are thinking."

Britt stared at Merlin in surprise, eliciting a smile from the cunning man. "I know your habits, lass. You can't hide much from me. Now, what is the problem?"

"This is wrong. Guinevere being forced by her father to marry Maleagant or me, Maleagant cornering Leodegrance, it's all wrong."

"The world is filled with evil men, lass. Not everyone is as good of a person as you are. Camelot is blessed that the Sword in the Stone chose you as King," Merlin said.

"I know that. Not about me, about bad people. I know some people are just downright evil. That's not what I'm protesting. Where are the champions? There should be a dozen knights doing good deeds in Guinevere's name. My lands shouldn't be the only ones free of trouble. Why aren't knights *doing* anything?"

"You mentioned something similar to Ywain months ago. What do you mean?" Merlin thoughtfully asked.

"In my time, most of the stories and legends about King Arthur are about his knights. They were always off doing a good deed or following some long-winded quest to bring honor to their name, their lord's name, or their lady's name. They served people."

"Unfortunately, it's not like that, lass," Merlin said.

Britt twirled a lock of hair around her finger and thought. Ywain wasn't the only person she had discussed the role of kings, knights, and courts with. She had a similar talk with his aunt, Queen Morgause. Before the Orkney queen left Camelot after an extended stay, Britt promised that she would try to improve the living conditions for mankind—women in particular.

Since making that promise, she had done very little to make it a reality.

Yes, this was her chance to change history, to kick out Lancelot and avoid Guinevere altogether. But the sound of Guinevere's heartbroken cries and her hopeless laugh echoed in Britt's ears. Britt opened her eyes. "Then I will *make* it be so."

A slow smile spread across Merlin's lips. He leaned in so close Britt could feel his breath on her face. "There's my red dragon. What did you have in mind, oh King?"

"You're not going to like it."

"Try me."

"I'm going to challenge Maleagant."

"*WHAT?*"

"I HAVE a white charger as well. He is well trained and has been used in tournaments by some of the greatest knights. I paid a pretty price for him," the merchant—Merlin's Minion—said as Gawain buckled pauldrons on Britt's shoulders.

"I don't intend to joust. It will be a trial by sword," Britt said, adjusting her gauntlets. The armor she was borrowing from Merlin's merchant friend was lovely—polished to shine and inlaid with gold—although it did not fit her as well as the suit of armor the blacksmiths of Camelot had forged for her over the winter months. What was important, though, was that the armor had no marks of any kind. Britt's personal armor was etched with red dragons. Her borrowed armor was beautiful and provided anonymity with its lack of decoration.

"Even so, you will still need a horse, My Lord," Gawain quietly said, checking the snugness of the pauldrons.

"You will look a great deal more poetic riding a charger up to Duke Maleagant rather than walking, My Lord," Lancelot said.

"All of you hush up. Arthur hardly needs more encouragement," Merlin complained.

"I'm going to be fine, Merlin," Britt said.

Britt had confidence in her sword skills. She was a greatly celebrated swordsman in the twenty-first century, but it had taken some months of living in Camelot before Britt was convinced she was still considered devastatingly skilled even several hundred years earlier.

Merlin approached her, twitching the faulds covering her thighs into place. "I know you have a right to be confident, Arthur, but one day you're going to meet someone who is a better swordsman than you," Merlin said.

"Unlikely," Gawain said.

"I cannot wait to observe your skills, My Lord. I heard much of your prowess with the sword during my stay at Camelot," said Sir Lancelot. "Although I am disappointed it will not be a jousting match. T'would be much more fitting."

"My Lord's skill with Excalibur is more beautiful than a joust," Gawain said, fiddling with armor.

Britt slipped on the gauntlets. "I'll be fine," Britt said to Merlin. "I doubt Maleagant has had the time to practice as I have."

Merlin pressed his lips together but said nothing.

Lancelot filled the silence with no difficulty. "This is exciting. I think one day it shall be made into a song the troubadours will sing of for eons. How often does a king ride off to save his beloved and challenge a blackguard duke to battle for her hand?"

"Wait a moment. I never said Guinevere was my beloved," Britt said.

Lancelot stared at Britt. "She's not?"

"Of course she isn't," Britt said as Gawain checked the last of her armor. "To begin with, she's a silly little thing who is overly concerned with wealth. And I've only seen her three times. That is not enough time to get to know her and fall in love with her."

"But what of love at first sight? Did she not enthrall you with her beauty?" Lancelot persisted.

Britt narrowed her eyes at the vivacious knight. "Why do I suspect you have already thought yourself to have fallen in love numerous times?"

Merlin eyed Britt in warning as the merchant guffawed. Gawain ignored the situation and bent over to check the plate mail covering Britt's feet.

Lancelot blinked. "Women are meant to be admired."

Britt was grateful Lancelot was standing far across the room. If he was any closer, she would be too tempted to smack him.

"So, you will need the charger?" the merchant asked.

Britt looked to Merlin, who nodded almost imperceptibly. "Yes, please. You'll have him prepared?"

The merchant sketched a bow. "I expected My Lord's need of a mount and sent word to the groom when I sought out the armor."

Gawain stood, inspecting the armor one last time. "You are ready, My Lord."

Merlin tilted his head, his eyes directed upwards. "And just in time. If I am not mistaken, I hear horns and drums. King Leodegrance is leaving the keep."

"In that case, we must hurry. This way, please," the merchant said, leading the way to the small lot behind his store.

Outside, a young groom waited with a milk white horse. The charger's equipment was white, unadorned, and startling in its simplicity.

"If this animal throws Arthur, I will have your head," Merlin warned the merchant.

Britt mounted the horse, who was a bit taller than she was used to, before she put her helm on. "No worries, Merlin. All he has to do is carry me up to Maleagant," she said, gathering up the reins.

"Godspeed, my Lord," Gawain said.

"I don't understand the fuss over a horse," Lancelot complained.

"We don't expect you to," Britt said.

"This way, My Lord. You need to hurry. The gates will soon

open," the merchant said, leading the way to the main road that ambled through the castle.

Britt nudged the warhorse forward, joining the rush of gawkers and guards who were traveling to the front gates of Camelgrance.

King Leodegrance, a squad of soldiers, his wife, and Guinevere exited Camelgrance a minute before Britt.

More soldiers and many of Camelgrance's citizens flocked outside, anxious to see what was to become of their home.

Britt followed the crowd outside, but rather than standing with the masses, she directed her horse behind a soldier bearing Leodegrance's flag, intending to hide since she stuck out like a sore thumb as the only armored knight in the entire company.

Merlin, Gawain, and Lancelot joined her. Merlin held the bridle of Britt's mount while Lancelot craned his neck to see.

Maleagant, wearing armor and riding his red roan horse, brandished a lance in the air. "King Leodegrance of Camelgrance. What is your decision? Are you friend or foe?"

"I am your friend," King Leodegrance said.

"Then you will give me your daughter Guinevere as my bride and prove to me your loyalty?" Maleagant demanded. His voice was hoarse and unfriendly.

"What a blackguard," Lancelot said.

Gawain nodded, but Britt hissed, "Quiet."

King Leodegrance's expression grew pinched. "How would you have me prove myself?"

"Break off your alliance with Arthur and march with me to Camelot," Maleagant said.

"Isn't it enough to pledge loyalty to you?" King Leodegrance said. "Gladly, I would give you my daughter."

Guinevere, mounted on a small palfrey, stared at her hands. Her face was red, probably from all the crying, but she wore a beautiful dress, and her hair was carefully arranged.

"If you remain allies with Arthur, you are no friend of mine," Maleagant said.

"Now," Merlin said.

Britt nudged her horse forward, leaving her companions behind. Gawain bowed, and Lancelot beamed as he pumped an arm in encouragement.

"Could I have more time to consider your request?" King Leodegrance asked.

"No."

King Leodegrance's shoulders slumped in defeat. "Then...," he trailed off and fell silent as Britt directed her horse into the gap between Maleagant and King Leodegrance's family.

"Who is this?" Maleagant demanded.

"I know not. Sir Knight, why are you here?" King Leodegrance asked.

Britt slid Excalibur out of its scabbard and brandished it in the air. She waited for a moment, looking quite picturesque, and then swung Excalibur down in an arc and thrust it in Maleagant's direction. While prepping for battle, Merlin told her to keep her mouth shut and say nothing. "Let them draw their own conclusions. If Leodegrance discovers you're King Arthur, we'll never be able to refuse his request to make Guinevere your bride," Merlin had warned.

Although Britt was moved by the girl's plight, in no way was Britt going to welcome the faithless girl into Camelot. She would remain silent to the bitter end.

Maleagant flipped up the visor of his helm so he could peer at Britt. He had beady eyes, and his face looked like someone had taken a mace to it on several different occasions. "You mean to challenge me for the Lady Guinevere."

Britt dismounted her borrowed horse and bowed.

"Very well, champion. I will face you with great eagerness," Maleagant said, an evil grin crawling across his lips as he hefted his lance.

Britt quickly raised Excalibur, pointing it at Maleagant.

"I think he means for it to be a contest of swords," King Leodegrance ventured in the silence.

"Fine," Maleagant said, handing his lance off to one of his men before he too dismounted. "Be it by sword or lance, I shall beat you soundly."

Britt eased into an offensive stance, studying Maleagant through the slits of her helm. She hated fighting in full armor thanks to its added weight. But in spite of what she learned in her history classes, her armor was easy to maneuver in and barely hindered her movements thanks to her height.

Maleagant stiffly strode towards Britt, walking bowlegged. He unsheathed his sword and roared like a bear.

Britt darted forward, striking first to gain the offensive advantage. Fighting and winning with the sword depended on going offensive and *staying* on the offense.

Britt drove Maleagant back, feinting an upper cut before reversing and striking from below. She rained blow after blow on Maleagant, who struggled to block and dodge the strikes.

The crowd from Camelgrance, which had first winced and watched with pain, started rustling with hope as Britt kicked Maleagant in the knee cap when he blocked her thrust to his right shoulder.

The kick hadn't hurt—he was wearing armor after all—but it did make Maleagant take a tottering step backwards.

Exploiting his already tipsy balance, Britt dove forward and stabbed Excalibur at Maleagant's foot, wedging it between the armor covering his foot and his ankle.

She didn't prick skin, but it hurt enough to make Maleagant fumble again. Britt jumped from the crouch she was in, using all her force to slam Maleagant in the helm with Excalibur's pommel.

Maleagant's head snapped backwards, and Britt helped him lie down by pushing on his chest with her forearms.

She kicked Maleagant's sword away, placed her foot on his right wrist, and let the edge of Excalibur rest near a slit in Maleagant's helm.

King Leodegrance, realizing Britt wasn't going to talk, spoke for her. "Do you yield to my daughter's champion, Duke Maleagant?" he eagerly asked, leaning forward off his horse.

Maleagant struggled, roaring with anger instead of replying.

Britt used her foot to kick Maleagant's arm away from his body—still pinning it to the ground, before pressing Excalibur into his unprotected armpit.

Maleagant finally stilled, although Britt could tell he boiled with anger. His armor heaved up and down as he breathed inside his armor like a murderous dragon.

"I yield," Maleagant snarled.

5

A WHITE KNIGHT

Britt prodded him in the arm pit, letting Excalibur's sharp tip poke the padding that leaked out under Maleagant's pauldrons before she stepped back.

Some of Maleagant's knights ran to their lord's side, helping him stand even though he kicked at them.

"Now remember, Duke Maleagant. You said you would leave should a champion best you," King Leodegrance eagerly said, satisfaction lining his voice and face. One could hardly tell a few short minutes ago he was close to sniveling.

Duke Maleagant roared in reply, sounding very much like an angry boar.

Britt retreated to her horse, looking for Merlin and Gawain in the joyful crowd. (Lancelot could rot for all Britt cared.)

Soldiers and subjects alike cheered, clapped, and shouted, making it very difficult to pick anyone out of the crowd.

Britt happened to glance at Guinevere and froze. The princess's gaze was fastened on Britt. She wore a sickly sweet smile, and her eyes were big and dreamy.

Sensing she ought to make a hasty exit—as much to avoid further confrontation from Maleagant as to avoid getting cornered by Guinevere—Britt mounted her white horse, throwing herself on in an ungainly manner.

She turned the horse towards the distant forests—intending to meet up with her knights rather than return to Camelgrance, which was going to be a deathtrap now. She was just barely within shouting distance when she heard Guinevere call, "Wait, Sir Knight!"

Britt heeled her horse and clung to the saddle as the charger jolted into a canter, swiftly carrying her away.

When she reached the forest, Britt checked over her shoulder. No one had followed her. "That's a miracle," Britt muttered, directing her horse into the woods. "Although I suppose Leodegrance would ignore me. He doesn't know I'm Arthur," Britt said as she wove around trees.

In a few minutes, Britt reached the small enclosure where her company previously pitched their camp. There were still signs of their stay, but there weren't any horses or gear in sight.

"Where did they go? Merlin said a few knights returned with Sir Bodwain, but at the very least Kay should be hanging around," Britt said.

Britt's horse pawed the ground. "Maybe Merlin and Gawain have made it to the edge of the forest by now." She turned the horse in a neat circle before nudging him back in the direction from which they came.

Rather than follow the same trail, Britt took her mount through a different part of the forest. After all, who knew if Guinevere would beg Leodegrance to send soldiers after her? Britt was so intent on reaching the edge of the woods that she almost missed it, a glimmer of metal among the trees.

Britt halted her horse. *If I'm careful I can investigate it*, she decided, changing directions.

The glint was sunlight bouncing off a shield that was tied to a post.

There was writing on the shield. Britt couldn't read it, but when she spotted a small pile of shields arranged nearby, she could guess what it said. "PELLINORE," she shouted. "PELLINORE!"

"How do you know my name, mysterious knight?"

Britt whipped around to find Pellinore at her back, dressed in armor and holding his horse's bridle.

"Although, it matters not. If you wish to fight me, I will not attempt to talk you out of it. Be warned, though, for I am a fierce warrior," King Pellinore said.

"What?! Pellinore, it's me," Britt said, briefly fumbling with her armor so she could remove her helm.

"Oh, Arthur. I am glad to see you are back. Whose horse are you riding?" Pellinore asked, relaxing his stance.

"Never mind that, what does the writing on the shield say?" Britt asked.

Pellinore avoided Britt's eyes and tucked his chin against his neck.

"Pellinore, what does it say?"

"Whoso smiteth this shield doeth so—"

"Pellinore," Britt groaned.

"Your foster brother, Sir Kay, has taken your knights and ridden around Camelgrance these past two days. He asked me to remain behind to watch your equipment and mounts. What was I to do? I had to amuse myself *somehow*," Pellinore said.

"I suppose it could have been worse. At least you didn't run off after the Questing Beast," Britt sighed. "Where is Kay now?"

"I'm not certain, but he is likely to return soon. Where are Merlin, Sir Gawain, and Sir Lancelot? Did they not find you in Camelgrance?"

"No, we met up. We were separated in the crowd."

"Crowd?"

"I accepted Maleagant's challenge and championed King Leodegrance and his family," Britt said.

"Congratulations on your victory," Pellinore smiled.

"How did you know I won?"

"You are too skilled to lose," Pellinore shrugged.

"Arthur?"

Britt looked up to see Sir Kay and the remaining knights leading their horses through the trees. "Kay," Britt said, flashing him a sincere smile. "I am glad to see you," she said, sliding off her borrowed horse.

Sir Kay was at her side to steady her when she landed on the ground with a jarring bounce. He traced her armor with narrowed eyes. "You are not hurt?"

"I'm fine," Britt smiled.

"You should have told me your plans before you left for Camelgrance."

"You're right. I should have. It was my mistake, and I am sorry for it," Britt said.

"Next time, please tell me. I will not try to keep you from going, but I would like to accompany you," Sir Kay said.

Britt placed her hand on his shoulder. "I thank you, and I will remember that."

Sir Kay nodded and pitched his voice even quieter than usual. "You are not typically so impetuous. Is everything alright?"

Britt hooked her helm on her horse's tack. "It is. I was conflicted. Leodegrance isn't exactly how I pictured him."

"And it bothers you?"

"More than I would like to admit."

"I say, My Lord. You were the white knight who fought Maleagant, were you not?" Sir Bedivere asked, joining Britt and Kay.

"I was. You saw?" Britt asked.

"*We* saw," Ywain said, joining the group with a smile. "You were wonderful, My Lord."

Sir Bedivere glanced at the younger knight before he added, "We were all posted in various hidden locations surrounding Camelgrance. I was in the forest and was able to see the fight.

Not very well, though. Congratulations. As usual, you were stupendous."

"You fought Maleagant?" Sir Kay said.

"Merlin said I could," Britt quickly said, able to sense the displeasure behind Sir Kay's statement.

"How did you manage to convince him?" Sir Kay suspiciously asked, his eyebrow twitching.

Britt avoided Sir Kay's gaze. "Well, it was for one of our allies so...Lancelot thought it was a terrific idea," Britt blurted out.

Sir Kay narrowed his eyes.

"He spoke of ballads and troubadours and thought I should challenge Maleagant to a joust instead of a sword fight," Britt said.

Sir Kay looked into the forest. "Where is Sir Lancelot now?"

Having managed to redirect Sir Kay's ire, Britt almost sighed in relief. "He's with Merlin and Gawain. I imagine they'll be here soon. They are on foot."

"Humph," Sir Kay said before striding off.

"I suspect the army will no longer be necessary based on the outcome of your battle with Maleagant. Correct, My Lord?" Sir Bedivere asked.

"Perhaps," Britt said. "I'm not convinced Maleagant will stay true to his word. Is there any news from Sir Bodwain?"

"None. He only left for home yesterday morn. It will be a week at the earliest before he would be able to arrive with any men," Sir Bedivere said.

"I was afraid of that," she said. "How many knights remained here?" She tried to count the swirl of armor clad knights.

"Fifteen, including Gawain and Lancelot, My Lord."

"What-ho. Greetings companions!"

Britt ground her teeth and forced her expression into a smile. "Lancelot, so you've returned. Hello, Merlin, Gawain," Britt said as the trio trooped out of the woods and into the camp.

"I must say, My Lord, that was an astounding fight. I never

thought I would live to see someone so skilled as you! You are far better at swordplay than I. Some time—assumedly when we return to Camelot—would you mind watching my form? I would greatly appreciate any advice you could give me. Oh, hello, Sir Kay," Lancelot chattered.

Britt almost wished the chattery knight had claimed to be a better swordsman than her. It would give her another reason to hate him. Instead, she was forced to settle for joyfully watching the stone-faced Kay step in front of Lancelot.

Sir Kay studied the younger knight for a few moments before making a derogatory, "Hm," and walking off.

Lancelot looked to Gawain, who ignored the exchange and bowed to Britt. "You did wonderfully well, My Lord."

"You were lucky, that's what you were," Merlin griped. "One day, you are going to meet someone better than you are, and they will teach you a lesson."

"What? Nonsense," Ywain protested.

"Forgive me for saying so, Merlin, but I cannot agree with you," King Pellinore said. "Arthur isn't just skilled; he's as gifted as one of God's warriors."

"Hear, hear," Sir Bedivere nodded.

Merlin scowled, and it was Gawain who intervened. "Pardon me, Merlin, but you have not faced My Lord with a sword, nor would you understand as we do, for you have your magic arts. When one faces My Lord and he is serious, it makes his family heritage show."

"It makes his *faerie blood* show. I met Uther. He did not have the talent his son possesses. No, our young dragon has no equal when it comes to the sword, Merlin. Do not worry over such a thing," King Pellinore said.

Merlin turned to Britt. "Do not let what they say go to your head. You would still be quite easy to kill," he warned her.

"I know," she sighed. "What happened after I left?"

Merlin snorted. "A chaotic mess. The lady Guinevere was

dreamy-eyed and lovesick, as was every other maiden in the crowd. Maleagant roared more than necessary, and King Leode-grance grew a bit of a backbone since you won. Maleagant is, of course, demanding to know your identity, as is Lady Guinevere."

"Do you think Maleagant will honor his word and leave?" Britt asked.

"Of course, he will," Lancelot said. "He can hardly take back his vow, and you defeated him so soundly!"

Gawain looked unconvinced, and Merlin said, "I do not hold the same conviction as you, Sir Lancelot. I suspect he will try to wiggle out of it."

"So, what do we do now?" Ywain asked.

"We will spend the night here. As we will not have daylight much longer, it hardly makes sense to begin our journey now, and I would feel better knowing what Maleagant is doing," Merlin frowned.

"In the morning, King Arthur and an escort group will set out. A small remnant can remain behind to observe Duke Maleagant's movements," Sir Kay said, his voice as strong as iron.

Merlin nodded, "A wise thought, Sir Kay. I agree with you."

"Someone will need to return the merchant's horse and armor to him," Britt said.

"Trivialities. Do not worry your head over such things," Merlin said.

"Well, I'm starved. Who is up for a bit of hunting for our supper?" Ywain said.

"Ahh, hunting is such a great sport. I would be honored to join, should no one object," Lancelot said.

"Please, by all means," Britt said, eager to get the knight out of sight.

"Shall I help you remove your armor, My Lord?" Gawain asked.

"Yes, if you do not mind. You have my thanks, Gawain."

"Of course, My Lord."

~

I<small>T WASN'T YET DAWN</small> when Britt woke Sir Kay.

"Kay, you said you wanted me to tell you next time," Britt whispered.

Sir Kay rubbed his face, and his voice was rough with sleep. "You just got out of that blasted castle. Are you so eager to return to it?"

Britt chuckled. "No. I don't plan to leave the woods, but I want to see if Maleagant and his men are still camped at Camelgrance's front door."

Sir Kay shut his eyes for a moment before he stood and stretched. "Very well, let us go."

"I'm surprised you are letting me leave the camp," Britt said as the two left the encampment and plunged into the trees.

"I thought of tying you up or refusing, but if I do that, it is unlikely you will ever tell me your movements again," Sir Kay said dryly.

Britt laughed and hopped over a fallen tree.

"Please explain to me, My Lord. If you are unsure of Leodegrance, why does Maleagant offend you so?" Sir Kay asked.

"It's the people of Camelgrance I worry for, as well as Guinevere's plight."

"I did not know you liked her so."

"I don't," Britt darkly said. "She's a silly girl who is emptyheaded and downright worthless."

Sir Kay waited for further explanation in silence.

"But…even so, she doesn't deserve to be married to a man like Maleagant. I knew that before I faced him in combat. Only a greedy jerk would demand from Leodegrance all his lands. Plus, he's in King Ryence's pocket, which isn't a good sign," Britt said, her speech lapsing as she spoke with Sir Kay—the only knight around whom she could relax.

Sir Kay held a branch back so Britt could pass by unhindered. "Camelgrance is not your responsibility, My Lord."

"I know, but letting Ryence get his hands on more land and people doesn't seem right." She sighed. After a few moments of silence she asked, "Did Ywain give you any trouble while I was gone? I doubt he happily stayed behind with you."

"Let me say that you probably enjoyed your time in Camelgrance more than I."

"Ahh, but I had Sir Lancelot the brat with me," Britt said.

"Even so," Sir Kay said, frowning so deeply his mustache could not hide it. "I ask that you would try to keep your distance from him."

"From Ywain?"

"No. Lancelot."

"I have *no* issues with that suggestion," Britt snorted. "But for the sake of my curiosity, why?"

"He is smarter than he acts."

"Are you kidding? He's a flirtatious twerp who needs a good smack."

"I do not understand all of what you say," Sir Kay said. "But he is crafty. Make no mistake, My Lord. You cannot let your guard down with him, even with your distaste."

"What makes you wary of him?"

"He is too well spoken and too well liked. Although he is scant months older than Gawain, he has the presence of a full knight and is not easily cowed. If he was the idiot he appeared to be, he would not last a month adventuring in Britain."

"I don't know about that."

"Think, Britt. Would Ywain or Griflet last long in the wild?" Sir Kay said.

"No," Britt finally said.

"He chatters to cover his observations. Please, be careful, My Lord."

"Alright. You have never steered me wrong. I will watch my

step with the dull Sir Lancelot. Ah, here we go," Britt said as the trees started to thin.

In the dusty, pink glow from the horizon, Britt could see tents were still pitched in front of Camelgrance.

"They are still there," Britt said, not entirely surprised.

"The portcullis of Camelgrance is down again, I think," Kay said, squinting in what little light was available.

Britt sighed. "I didn't think he would take his defeat well."

"What do you mean to do?"

Britt glanced at her supposed foster brother. "What do you mean? I thought I was getting packed up and sent back to Camelot today whether I wanted to leave or not."

"You are king, My Lord," Sir Kay said.

Britt watched smoke rise from a campfire near the tents. "I would like to speak to Merlin and see what he advises. If Sir Bodwain and our reinforcements will not arrive for a while, I don't like the idea of leaving just yet."

"As you wish, My Lord."

"Sir Kay, thank you," Britt said. "I know I put you through a lot, but I am truly thankful for your support."

"It is my honor, My Lord."

"Is it really? I know the way Arthur, the real Arthur, abandoned his duties hurt you. I'm sure you would rather be going through this with him than with me," Britt said. "He was your foster brother."

"And you are my foster sister," Sir Kay said. "Both of you are dear to me. I am truly happy to serve you, Britt."

"Thank you, Kay."

◊

"I DON'T LIKE IT," Merlin declared from the back of his spindly-legged horse.

"What part of it?" Britt asked, patting Llamrei on the neck as

Merlin wove his horse between the trees at the edge of the forest and peered out at Camelgrance.

"All of it," Merlin said, waving his hands at the camp. It was mid-morning, and even from the forest, one could see Maleagant's knights walking through their camp.

"Duke Maleagant is a dishonorable knave," King Pellinore said. "There is not much one can do to correct such a character flaw so late in his life besides beating him soundly and muzzling him like a mongrel."

"You have seen his kind before, have you?" Britt asked.

"They are unfortunately common," King Pellinore said.

"What will you do, My Lord?" Sir Gawain asked.

Britt smiled at the quiet knight. "I'm not certain. What are your thoughts, Merlin?"

"Wash your hands of Leodegrance and be done with it," Merlin said, driving his horse back into the woods. "You gave him an exit. He obviously did not push back against Maleagant hard enough, or that pig would have left last night."

"You are so accepting that we will lose an ally and quite possibly see another war?" Britt asked, following Merlin as he made for their camp.

"King Leodegrance must live with the consequences of his inaction. He survived before you were crowned king, Arthur. Besides, you have other allies now," Merlin said, his eyes briefly falling on King Pellinore and then Gawain.

Britt offered Gawain a tense smile when the prince looked to her.

They returned to camp in silence.

"Hail, My Lord. What have you decided?" Sir Bodwain asked.

Britt dismounted Llamrei as Merlin announced, "We are leaving. King Leodegrance has ruined himself. It is good that Sir Bodwain rallies the army, for we will need to protect our borders when Leodegrance caves and gives his daughter to Maleagant."

Britt started packing with the rest of the knights, listening to Merlin speak.

"You think it will be war, then?" Sir Kay said.

"Perhaps. At the very least, there will be a threat. You can bet as soon as Leodegrance is cowed, King Ryence will muster another army. If we are ready for them, it is likely they will not attack. Maleagant is a cheat, but King Ryence is just as cowardly as King Leodegrance."

"I shall ride home and prepare an army of my own to back you," King Pellinore said.

"This isn't your fight, Pellinore. King Ryence was once your ally; I will not pit you against him," Britt said.

Pellinore shook his head. "My Anglesey is closer to Camelot than Leodegrance's Camelgrance. We are neighbors. If they try to march against you, they will march against me as well."

"I will ride forth and alert my father and uncle to the threat," Lancelot said. "They will aid you, My Lord."

"I can send word to my father, too. I am certain he will send a company of knights," Ywain said.

She placed a hand on Ywain's shoulder. "I thank you, both of you," Britt grudgingly said, acknowledging Lancelot's offer. "But I hope the war is not so big we will require help from all my allies."

"King Pellinore's forces and ours should be enough to crush Maleagant's dreams. Ryence already knows Arthur is strong, and Britain knows he's only grown stronger since he was crowned over a year ago. Ryence will hold back his forces and let Maleagant take the brunt of it if he marches against us at all," Merlin said.

"It is settled then. We prepare for war," Sir Bedivere nodded.

Britt finished tying off her bedroll before attaching it to Llamrei's saddle. She gathered her things and moved to lead Llamrei to the small pond they camped near when she saw her borrowed charger from the merchant.

The milk white horse bobbed his head, making his bridle

jingle. Someone had already tacked him up and tied the unornamented armor to him.

"He will have to come with us, for we cannot return him," Merlin said, shattering Britt's thoughts.

"I know," Britt said.

"Do not fear. My merchant friend will be well compensated," Merlin said, patting Britt on the head.

"Will he survive the siege?"

"Of course, or he wouldn't be a merchant," Merlin snorted before he too led his horse to the pond.

Britt did not follow him. Instead, she stared at the horse and armor, thoughtfully entwining her hand in Llamrei's mane.

It was just like one of the legends: a knight on a white charger fights to save the lady. Too bad it hadn't worked.

Britt closed her eyes and was assaulted by her memory of battle. Everything reeked of blood and bile. The screams were the worst; the shouts of the injured and the dying ate away at Britt's soul. It was horrible. It was a nightmare. And it was going to happen again.

Whom would she lose? Sir Ywain, Sir Kay? Last time, she almost lost Sir Ector.

Britt opened her eyes again and studied the white charger.

"No," she said.

"I beg your pardon, what did you say?" Merlin called from the pond.

"I will not march to war. Nor will I abandon Camelgrance," Britt said, pulling back her shoulders.

"Arthur, Leodegrance must encounter the consequences of his decisions. It will do neither you nor him any good to keep saving him," Merlin said.

"Forget Leodegrance!" Britt shouted, making all of the knights in the camp freeze. "So perhaps I am not allies with him for his sake—I'm allies with him for the sake of his people. They did nothing to deserve such treatment. Nor will I stand to lose a single one of my knights in a war that does not need to occur."

"What would you have us do? The contest against Maleagant failed," Merlin said.

"We are in a world at war, Arthur. You cannot stop a man like Maleagant without force," King Pellinore said, folding his arms across his chest.

"I find your desires refreshing, My Lord," Lancelot piped in. "But saving castles and entire populations is something that requires an army, not a single knight. Doing a few good deeds is the most one man can do. As much as the minstrels sing of it, mankind does not value honor."

"Then I will change that," Britt said, locking her legs and tilting her head up. "I will fight until I cannot stand and talk until I run out of air, but I will see that every maiden I come across has someone willing to fight for her, and that every lesser subject knows that if all else fails, there is someone *good* in this world who would like to see them not only survive, but be happy! I will do everything I can. If I cannot reach all of Britain, so be it—but right now, there is a castle that cries out for a champion, and I will not forsake them."

There was utter silence in the encampment.

The horses snorted and neighed in the sudden stillness, and then Gawain kneeled before Britt. "I will follow you, My Lord, and I will do as you do."

"As will I!" Ywain declared, joining his cousin.

A faint smile was spread on Sir Bedivere's lips. "I doubted you could leave Camelgrance the way it is, My Lord. But that is why I serve you, because you will not abandon anyone," he said, holding Britt's gaze for a few lengthy moments before he too bowed.

"I wish you wouldn't care for chivalry. It makes guarding you a wretched experience, My Lord," Sir Kay said, joining the others.

"You're a good man, Arthur. I have never seen the likes of you as a King. As a ruler, I know what you say is hopeless…but I can't help but think that you will make it happen," King Pellinore said.

Other knights spoke up, speaking vows and assurances of their loyalty to Britt until the only ones left to speak out were Sir Lancelot and Merlin.

Merlin sighed. "You foolish boy. There you go changing more minds with your pretty speeches. Arthur, are you certain that you are not forcing yourself to follow a legend that hasn't yet been made?"

Although the knights around Britt looked confused, Britt understood what Merlin meant. "I am positive. This is what *I* want, Merlin."

"It would be easier to run you if you were a dunce," Merlin grumbled, glancing at Lancelot. "What say you, only son of King Ban?"

Lancelot stared at Britt for several long moments. Britt thought she saw something stir in his eyes, but it disappeared when Lancelot pumped his fist in the air. "I stand with Arthur. Honor and chivalry to all!"

"Then we will stay, and we will drive off Maleagant with just us, a small band," Merlin said, grimacing.

"I will face Maleagant again. Beating him is not the issue; driving him off is another matter," Britt said.

"Of this I am aware," Merlin said. "Thankfully, Maleagant's army might be raised, but it is not too close to Camelgrance. If we can frighten Maleagant enough to make him flee to his army, I don't think he would dare return, not if we convince him that he cannot defeat us."

"And how do you propose to do that?" Sir Kay asked.

Merlin grinned wickedly. "Through trickery."

～

"I still don't see why I couldn't ride Llamrei," Britt complained as she rode her borrowed charger across the open span between Camelgrance and the surrounding forest.

"Llamrei is not a charger. She is trained to flee at the first sign of danger and bring her rider to safety," Sir Kay said.

"So that's why you prefer I ride her when we're around Camelot. She won't attack like Roen; she'll just carry me off," Britt said, looking down at Sir Kay, who was walking shoulder to shoulder with her horse.

Sir Kay grunted and did not respond.

"I'm impressed you managed to bully Merlin into letting you come instead of him," Britt said.

"He is needed to make the second part of the plan work, and he would raise Maleagant's suspicions, as he reeks of magic," Sir Kay said.

"I'm not saying I disagree with you, just that I was surprised it worked," Britt said.

"Merlin knows he would not be as much help to you as I in this case. He knows little of armor and even less of fighting. He would not make a proper squire."

"Kay you are *not* here to act as my squire; you are here to speak so I don't have to," Britt protested.

Sir Kay shrugged. "If that is what you think, My Lord. Prepare yourself, for we draw close."

Britt checked to make sure her helm was in place as she and Sir Kay stopped between Camelgrance and Maleagant's camp.

A knight from Maleagant's forces stood at the edge of the camp while men madly scrambled behind him. "Who goes there?" he called.

"'Tis the White Knight, the champion of Camelgrance. He wishes to know why you have not departed," Sir Kay said.

Britt twisted in the saddle to look at Camelgrance. Based on the amount of noise radiating from the castle, the soldiers standing guard had sent word to Leodegrance.

"Where is he?" a raspy voice roared.

Maleagant stormed out of his camp, wearing his armor but not a helm. "You!" Maleagant snapped, thrusting a finger in Britt's direction.

"The White Knight wishes to say that he was told you promised to leave should a champion beat you, Duke Maleagant," Sir Kay said, his voice steady and reflecting no emotion. "As he trounced you soundly, he desires to know why you are still here."

"I was not beaten," Maleagant said, his nostrils flaring.

"Being that the White Knight knocked you to the ground and held you helpless, he wishes to know what your definition of beaten is, as it does not match common expectations," Sir Kay said.

From behind the veil of her helm, Britt stared at Sir Kay. "Kay, what are you doing?" she hissed.

The ground rumbled as Camelgrance's portcullis was raised. King Leodegrance and a squad of his soldiers left the castle.

"Champion!" King Leodegrance called, his face pinched in the gleefulness of his expression. "Thank Heaven you have returned."

"When I gave my ultimatum, I meant that I must be defeated in a joust, not a mere *swordfight*."

Britt's blood turned cold. *What?*

"The White Knight wishes to know if knocking you off your horse will actually count this time, or if he needs to strip all weapons from your person and tie you up in order for you to admit defeat," Sir Kay said.

"Kay!" Britt hissed, barely audible over Maleagant's roar. Maybe she would have been better off if Merlin had come instead of Sir Kay after all.

"Prepare yourself, for I will run you through," Maleagant promised when he finished shouting. He turned and stalked back into his camp. "Where are my horse and my lance?" he demanded.

"It is to be a joust this time then? Splendid. Is a fence necessary, or will you two be able to run at each other?" King Leodegrance asked, rubbing his hands together.

"The White Knight will need a lance. As it is the *least* you can do, can I assume you will supply one?" Sir Kay asked Leodegrance.

"Absolutely! You there, fetch a lance for our great champion," King Leodegrance said to a soldier.

As the soldier went back into Camelgrance, Guinevere charged out of it on the back of her riding horse. She blushed when she espied Britt. "Champion," she called.

Britt turned her back to the girl. "Kay, what are you doing? It's not like you to run your mouth like this, and you have just gotten us into a mess of trouble. I *can't* beat Maleagant in a joust. What are you thinking?" Britt said, her voice lowered.

"But you can, My Lord," Kay said. "You haven't the passion for jousting as you do for the sword, but you've gotten quite good at it."

"How can you say that? I've never even unseated you!"

"Forgive my pride, My Lord, but as it stands, I am the best knight at jousting in all of Camelot. It would take much for you to defeat me. Trust my judgment, My Lord. You can beat Maleagant."

Britt turned to glance back at the Maleagant's camp. "Do you really believe that?"

"I do. If you do not lose heart, My Lord, you will certainly win."

Britt sighed. "Merlin is going to kill you when we get back to him."

"Of that I am well aware."

"Does this lance suit you, champion?" King Leodegrance's soldier asked, trotting up to the pair, carrying a long, tapered weapon.

Britt recognized it as a jousting lance, so the end was blunted and cupped to prevent a knight from impaling his opponent.

Sir Kay went over it and nodded. "It will do, thank you," he said, handing the weapon up to Britt.

When Maleagant appeared again, fully armored and mounted, Sir Kay asked, "The White Knight wishes to know if you, too, plan to use a jousting lance, or if you intend to take a much-needed advantage and use an actual lance."

Maleagant growled and presented the blunted tip of his jousting lance.

"Very well," Sir Kay said before walking off.

Britt nudged her charger and followed him.

"You're taking this better than I thought you would," Sir Kay said when they were far enough away that their words would be muted to the crowd gathering at the gates of Camelgrance.

"The only thing that is keeping me here is your judgment. I have absolute belief in you. So, if you say I can do this…" Britt trailed off and shivered in her armor.

"Am I one who normally lets you gamble with your life?"

"No."

"Then I promise you. You will win." Sir Kay stopped when they were far enough away from Maleagant for a proper joust. "Sit deep in your saddle, and push from your stirrups," he said, unhooking a plain shield from Britt's charger and passing it up to her.

"Ok," Britt said, her heart pounded in her throat as she slid her left arm through the shield straps. She swiveled her horse to face Maleagant, wishing she could wipe off the sweat that was starting to bead on her face.

Maleagant was on his red roan horse again, and he seemed especially sinister dressed in his armor embellished with blood-red swirls and decorations.

"Don't panic. You will win," Kay said, backing away as one of Leodegrance's men raised a flag.

When the soldier swung it down, Britt and Maleagant cued their horses forward, rushing towards each other in a canter.

Britt pressed her butt deep into the saddle to anchor herself as she rocked with her horse's rolling gait. She steeled herself so she wouldn't flinch, and too quickly Maleagant was upon her.

Britt steadied her joust with her right hand, carefully aiming for Maleagant's shield. She hit it, but Maleagant also hit her.

Numbness followed by a flash of pain hit Britt when Maleagant pushed, trying to toss her from the saddle. Gritting her teeth, Britt managed to keep her seat. So did Maleagant. It was a draw.

Britt raised her lance and trotted back to Kay, flexing her arm to get feeling back into it.

Kay stared at her when Britt stopped her charger in front of him.

"He isn't as strong as you," Britt said. "Getting hit by you in a serious charge hurts enough to make my eyes water and my arm useless for an hour."

Sir Kay nodded as Britt guided her horse back into place. "You didn't push," he said.

"What?" Britt said, tugging her shield back into place, ignoring the tingling in her arm.

"You did not push him with your strength—it was all the force of your mount," Sir Kay said.

"I was guarded and more concerned about staying in the saddle," Britt admitted.

"Staying on isn't going to win this joust. He's bigger and has more stamina than you; he'll wear you down. You must use all your strength to unseat him," Sir Kay said as again Leodegrance's soldier raised the flag.

"Right," Britt said moments before the flag dropped and her horse exploded forward in a canter.

Britt braced herself as her mount charged across the field, again holding her lance aloft as she carefully aimed for Maleagant's shield.

The impact was worse this time. Instead of numbness, Britt's side burned as if she had been hit by a sledgehammer. Maleagant didn't seem to feel Britt's lance, but Britt was almost popped from her saddle. She hit the back of her jousting saddle, its raised rim biting into her lower back.

Britt coughed, feeling significantly more pained as she turned her horse and trotted back to Kay, ignoring Maleagant's sneering laughter.

Sir Kay had his arms folded as he studied Britt.

Even though he couldn't see her eyes, Britt looked away, embarrassed by the knowledge she still hadn't done as Sir Kay said to.

She couldn't help it. She was weighed down by the knowledge of what a loss would mean.

"Britt."

Britt looked to her foster brother. "Yes?"

"That man down there in the armor," Sir Kay said, pointing with a thick finger.

"Yes?"

"That's Lancelot."

"What?"

"You are not riding to trounce a tyrant. You're riding to toss Lancelot from his horse like you have always wanted."

Britt started to protest. "I never wanted to throw Lancelot."

Sir Kay interrupted, "Britt, that is Lancelot," he said before he walked off.

Britt thoughtfully turned her charger, staring at Maleagant at the far end of the field. The soldier raised and lowered his flag, and Britt's mount leaped into a canter.

Britt leaned forward slightly, squeezing her legs and urging the horse to go faster. It complied, and Britt thundered down the field at a crazy speed. She was on Maleagant in an instant, and this time it was different.

When Britt felt her lance hit Maleagant's shield, she pushed. She pushed her feet down in the stirrups to give herself something to strain against as well as the saddle and used that force to lean into Maleagant. The superior velocity of Britt's charger made it more difficult to aim, but it also gave her a great deal of more force when she hit Maleagant.

Every muscle in Britt's body burned as she pushed in spite of the painful blow Maleagant landed on her shield.

A split second, and it was over.

Maleagant was knocked from his saddle and went sprawling over the side of his horse, falling to the ground with a clang.

Britt couldn't feel her left arm anymore, and she had to prop the lance up on her saddle as her right arm trembled from the exertion.

Kay walked back to Britt as men hurried to Maleagant's side. Cheers exploded from Camelgrance, and Guinevere cried and clasped a hand to her chest.

Maleagant's men rolled Maleagant onto his back, removing his helm for him. Slowly, they sat him up. The fallen knight briefly held his head before he narrowed his eyes and snarled at Britt, "Who are you, knight? I demand to know."

Britt couldn't have asked Maleagant to perform any closer to the dialog Merlin had prepared.

As Kay reached her side and held her horse, Britt removed her helm. "I am Arthur, King of Camelot, wielder of Excalibur, and ally of King Leodegrance."

Maleagant roared and struggled to stand.

Britt dropped her lance on the ground and pulled Excalibur from its scabbard, using it to point at Maleagant. "I have beaten you twice now, Duke Maleagant. I thought you to be a man of your word, but if you are not, I will trounce you a third time, this time with the aid of my men," she said, thrusting Excalibur towards the sky.

On cue, three different hunting horns from three different directions were sounded. In three different parts of the forest, knights on horseback emerged from the trees—barely visible in the shadows—and spread like three great companies disappearing deep into the forest. On the forest perimeter, there were glints of metal where sunlight reflected off armor and weapons.

Entirely alone, Merlin walked some feet away from the forest. He waved his staff over his head, and fire exploded from the tip, igniting in orange flames that were at least twenty feet tall.

Maleagant stopped muttering under his breath and stared at the forest with wide eyes.

"Do you understand what I am saying, Duke Maleagant?" Britt asked, cuing her charger closer to the cheater. "Leave, or this third time, I will not be so generous in letting you live," Brit said, swinging her sword down in an arc to again stab it in his direction.

Maleagant scrambled for his horse, his men right behind him. "You shall regret this, beardless youth!" Maleagant promised as he rode off, leaving behind tents and equipment.

Maleagant and his accompanying knights urged their horses faster when the hunting horns were blown again. They disappeared, riding off in the direction of Duke Maleagant's lands, and Britt slumped in her saddle.

"I can't believe they bought that," she said, sliding Excalibur back into its scabbard.

"Merlin is a fox," Sir Kay said in explanation.

"Arthur! I am delighted to have such a close ally protecting Camelgrance. It is good fortune that you brought your army with you," King Leodegrance said, riding up to Britt with a greasy smile.

"Of course," Britt said, lying through her teeth.

There was no army.

While Britt fought Maleagant and distracted everyone, Merlin and the rest of the knights were busy planting shields, swords, and any piece of reflective metal they had in the forest. (There was a small hoard thanks to King Pellinore's obsession with jousting and taking shields from those he defeated.) The small group of fifteen knights then carefully planted themselves in three different groups, spreading out and doing their best to fade into the forest to give the illusion that there were more of them than there really were. Kay's horse, Merlin's horse, and Llamrei were used to bulk up the numbers. The forest was far enough away that when the horses were placed in the back, no one would be able to tell that they were without riders.

Not, of course, that they were going to tell Leodegrance any of this. Who knew how the idiot would run his mouth to Maleagant.

"Will you stay with us for a time? I am sure Camelgrance cannot match the magnificence of Camelot, but I would like to express my gratitude. Have you met my daughter, Guinevere? You must have, or you would not have acted as her champion," King Leodegrance said.

"I and a small group of my knights would take pleasure in remaining at Camelgrance for the night," Britt said as Kay signaled to Merlin and the others that all was well. "And yes, I have met Lady Guinevere, although I must correct you. I acted as Camelgrance's champion," Britt said, politely bowing from the saddle to Guinevere.

Gone was Guinevere's schooled smile. Instead, she looked perplexed as she studied Britt.

"Of course, of course you must claim so. I will not pretend to understand young love. Come inside, we must feast and toast to your win," King Leodegrance said, turning his back to Britt to cut off her objections to his statements.

Britt frowned and looked at Sir Kay.

"You said it was for the people, not their ruler," Sir Kay reminded her.

"I know. I just wish the ruler would leave me out of it," Britt muttered, following Leodegrance into Camelgrance.

6

GOING HOME

"Are you sure you require no more assistance, My Lord?" Gawain asked, setting aside the last of Britt's armor.

"I'm sure. I must apologize; I did not mean to make you act as my squire for this trip," Britt said, wincing as she flexed her left arm.

"I am aware of that, My Lord. But it is my pleasure to serve you any way I can."

"Thank you, Gawain."

"You're welcome, My Lord." Gawain bowed and slipped out of the room.

Britt groaned as she started struggling out of the padding she wore under her armor. Her muscles ached, and getting down to her loose underclothes made them burn again.

Someone knocked on the door. "Arthur," Merlin said, opening the door. He shrieked a little when he saw Britt was still struggling out of the padding and slammed the door shut.

Britt wrenched off the last of the padding. "There's no need to be squeamish, Merlin. I'm still wearing clothes." She winced as she used a leather cord to pull her hair back in a perky ponytail.

Merlin didn't reply, and Britt heaved her eyes to the ceiling and shook her head as she slipped on a doublet and buttoned it up. It wasn't her padded one she normally used to flatten her chest, so her female body showed, but Britt didn't care. Her sides ached horribly, and she wouldn't be expected to join in the festivities for at least half an hour to an hour. She could wear whatever she pleased as long as Merlin and Kay were the only ones who saw her.

There was a knock on the door again. "Merlin, I already told you to come in," Britt said, turning to face the door.

It opened, and Britt was shocked to see Guinevere instead of Merlin staring back at her. When Guinevere's eyes widened as she gaped at Britt, Britt realized her mistake.

Britt swore under her breath, but she was even further shocked when Guinevere stepped into the room and shut the door behind her.

"I thought it was odd that you wouldn't give me your proper attention," Guinevere said, approaching Britt. She placed her hand on Britt's cheek, feeling her smooth, feminine skin. "Now I know why."

"What do you mean?" Britt asked, her mind scrambling. Perhaps she could knock Guinevere out and find Merlin and have him cast some sort of memory spell on her?

"You are a woman. I have never met a man who is not attracted to me, except for you. I thought perhaps you already had some sort of lover—there are rumors about you and the Lady of the Lake, you know—but this makes even more sense," Guinevere said. She smiled. It was the winning one she used whenever she tried to sway a man's mind. "Take me with you, or I shall tell my father what you really are."

Britt's fear disappeared, burning like dry twigs from the fire of her rage. "I beg your pardon?"

"If you do not take me back to Camelot, I will tell my father that you are a woman. Word will spread around Britain in a year, and you'll be ruined," Guinevere said.

Britt could hardly believe it. She had been right to hate Guinevere all along. After she had just saved her from Maleagant, the brat had the audacity to make threats? "Do you *really* think that threat frightens me?" Britt asked. (It did, but it affected the small part of Britt's mind that wasn't completely infuriated and thus was easily forgotten.) "I just defeated a duke not only in swordplay, but jousting as well. I singlehandedly drove off an enemy your *father* was too frightened to confront. I have been through a war, broken off powerful enchantments laid upon my men, and survived an attempt against my life. Do you really think the hissings of one silly girl will move me? Please, I am not your father," Britt scoffed.

Guinevere swallowed. "I'll tell Merlin."

"As if he didn't already know," Britt laughed. "He's a wizard. If you think he doesn't know, you are even more simple-minded than I estimated. No, most of my powerful friends know of my secret, princess. Tell me, have you ever made yourself an enemy out of a faerie enchantress? I'm certain Nymue, the Lady of the Lake to whom you previously referred, would love to take you on. She dislikes stupidity just as much as I do."

"I'm not stupid," Guinevere said, tucking her chin like a mulish pony.

"You are. You are thoughtless, self-centered, and your idiocy is in abundance if you think threats will force me to bow to you," Britt said, taking a step closer to Guinevere.

She towered over the princess, and the distaste in her eyes and the dark tilt of her head made Guinevere stumble backwards.

"Your enemies will care. King Lot, King Urien," Guinevere said, backing up until her back was flush against the door.

"So?" Britt asked. "I have their sons. And just because you tell them does not mean they will believe you. After all, whom will they trust more: the sniveling daughter of a coward or the red dragon who faced them in battle?"

"Please," Guinevere whispered.

"So now you've moved on to begging?"

"Please, don't leave me here," Guinevere said, tears filling her eyes. She wasn't acting anymore; her face was an unbecoming red color and pinched in the same expression she wore the night Britt found her in the garden.

Britt sighed and turned away. "Leave me, and tell no one of this," she said.

"You don't understand. I am the fattened calf my father will use for his ambitions. Can't you have mercy on me?" Guinevere said, grabbing Britt's arm.

Britt studied the broken girl. In the legends, Guinevere ruined Camelot arm-in-arm with Lancelot. All her life Britt hated hearing stories about the faithless queen. As far as Britt was concerned, Guinevere never deserved Arthur, and the legendary King was an idiot for never seeing her fickle ways.

Hours ago she took a vow before her men that she would champion women, and she had. She saved a girl she genuinely disliked. But Britt found she had neither the strength of character nor the smallest drop of mercy that would move her to bring this female disaster into Camelot.

"I saved you from Maleagant, Guinevere. That is the most I will do for you," Britt said, brushing the shorter woman off her arm.

"I'll do anything. Take me as your servant. I could be a lady's maid or work as a seamstress," Guinevere said, her skirts swirling as she cut in front of Britt and grabbed her by the doublet.

"Guinevere, stop your baseless offers. You are not the type to be pleased with working. You don't even know how."

"I could learn—I *will* learn. I would rather be a servant who earns a wage and makes her own decisions than be auctioned off to Father's best offer and forced into slavery."

Britt pinched the bridge of her nose. "Getting married is not like being a slave."

"You don't know. You wouldn't know! Maleagant is not the

worst man father is considering for me. He doesn't care what they are like as long as they are rich and will give him a pretty sum of money for me, or he can call upon them to pull up his breeches when he is in need of saving. I am doomed, Arthur, unless you help me," Guinevere pleaded.

"I already have. Leave me," Britt said pointing to the door.

Guinevere's lower lip trembled. "I see now that I was wrong about you. You might be a woman, but you are just as cruel as a man."

"I repeat, Guinevere. I have saved you once. Remember that, and be grateful. I don't even like you, so there is no way I will sacrifice my subjects' happiness for your own. Your happiness would cost me a kingdom," Britt said.

"How can you say that? Father will not lift a finger against you."

"Guinevere," Britt said, her words quiet but sharp like a dagger. "I know what you are like, and I know what you would do. You will have to find another person to save you."

Guinevere shook her head. A sob tore from her throat as she threw the door open and tripped into the hallway.

Britt rubbed her forehead. "I can't wait to leave this place. Between her and Lancelot, I'll be living not just with insomnia but with a perpetual headache, too."

~

"Is NOT Guinevere beautiful this night, Arthur?" King Leodegrance said, slapping his hand on the table.

"Of course, My Lord," Britt said, privately thinking anything but.

Apparently, the lady in question had gone out and sobbed until the celebration started, for she was puffy-eyed and red-cheeked. She stared at her plate and did not look up, even though

King Leodegrance had made his observation at the sound level of a shout.

"It is such a good thing that you saved her from Maleagant, for I would rather she married for love than fear," King Leodegrance said.

"If that is the case, I wish her luck in finding love," Britt said, sipping her wine.

"But hasn't she already found it in a staunch champion such as you?"

"I cannot speak for the lady, but when I championed Camelgrance, I must confess I did it for the sake of our friendship," Britt said.

King Leodegrance patted Britt on the back. "You are so discreet. I am honored my daughter caught your eye."

Britt sighed and looked for her men—they were the only reason she was suffering through this. After the test of courage in putting together the fake army to trick Maleagant, she owed it to them to eat a feast and sleep indoors for the night before they set out in the morning.

Merlin was nowhere to be seen. Lancelot, Gawain, and Ywain were in the center of a crowd of young ladies. King Pellinore and Sir Kay were seated together, deep in conversation. Sir Bedivere and the rest of the knights were eating merrily with abandon.

Britt sighed and took a bite of the roasted boar sitting on her plate. It was dry and tough.

"I do wish I could call you son, Arthur," King Leodegrance said.

Britt offered the older king a slight smile. "I apologize, but I am already quite happy with the father I have."

"He is nothing but your foster father. That hardly counts."

"Sir Ector has been very kind to me. He is more of a father to me than my real father ever was," Britt truthfully said. Her father had left her family when she was young. It was why she had been wary of Sir Ector in the first few months of her stay in Britain.

But now Britt couldn't imagine Camelot without her jolly foster father.

"Then you have no choice but to marry into my family to become my son," King Leodegrance triumphantly said.

"I beg your pardon, My Lord, but I must refuse."

"Just for now, of course."

Britt stared at her wine cup and wondered how soon she could leave the feasting hall. She was almost knocked to the ground when Merlin shoved a seat between Britt and King Leodegrance, pushing the two of them apart.

"King Leodegrance, I am most eager to ask you about your hay crop. When do you believe you will be able to have the first cut?" Merlin asked, angled so his back was almost entirely facing Britt and acting as a block between the two kings.

"Greetings, Merlin. I cannot say I am entirely certain of the condition of the hay fields. Tomorrow before you leave, would you like to see them?" King Leodegrance asked.

"No, I was merely curious. It was a mild winter, and the peasants at Camelot were hoping for an early first crop of hay. I do not know how likely such a thing is."

"Indeed, I echo their hopes. My cattle have produced more offspring than estimated—which is a good thing to be sure, but I *must* have enough hay to feed them all."

King Leodegrance rambled on, but Britt shut her eyes and filtered it out. Merlin had rescued her. King Leodegrance respected Merlin—probably even more than he respected Britt. He would happily entertain Merlin as long as the wizard appeared interested, leaving Britt alone.

In a rush of exuberance, Britt slipped her arm under the table, sliding her hand into Merlin's. She squeezed his fingers, and he gently squeezed her hand in return—acknowledging her gesture —before disengaging his hand and propping it up on top of the table.

Britt glanced to Guinevere. The princess still stared at her pewter plate, listlessly pushing food across its surface.

Britt took another bite of her roasted boar. Tomorrow they would leave. After tomorrow, King Leodegrance and Guinevere would no longer be her problem. They would be out of sight and out of Britt's mind.

Britt vowed it again as she watched Guinevere wanly smile at her mother. The girl may be heartbroken, but Britt had done what she could. Knowing as she did about Lancelot and Guinevere, Britt would be crazy to take the girl back to Camelot.

∽

"I DO WISH you would stay longer. Can Camelot not spare you?" King Leodegrance wheedled the following morning.

"No, I have been away from home far too long as it is," Britt said, patting Llamrei when the mare tossed her head. Britt's knights were in a formation behind her, standing just outside of Camelgrance.

"We thank you for hosting us, although next time perhaps you should be sharper with your enemies, hm?" Merlin said, as close to a chiding as he would ever give a dignitary. (Not including Britt, of course.)

"I'm growing old, Merlin. I would like to see my line secured through grandchildren," King Leodegrance said, giving Guinevere a significant look. "Although heaven only knows there are but a few men who are worthy of her."

Guinevere stood next to her mother, her arms tucked behind her back. She hadn't so much as looked at Britt since Britt shooed her out of her room the previous night. "Oh," Britt said.

"What?" Merlin asked through a clenched smile as King Leodegrance continued to moan over his daughter's marriage prospects.

"I have to talk to you about something. There was an incident last night," Britt said.

"An incident? You didn't kill Lancelot, so it can't be that bad," Merlin said.

"No, but it might be worse. I suspect you're going to chain me to my throne when we return to Camelot."

"You don't enjoy peace, do you?"

"My Lord, if I may interrupt? We really ought to leave," Sir Kay said.

"Right, thank you again, King Leodegrance, for your hospitality. Take care, my friend," Britt said before wheeling Llamrei around. Merlin did the same with his horse, and the knights of Camelot set out, their mounts moving at a swift walk.

The residents of Camelgrance cheered at their departure. The farmers who had returned to their lands now that the siege was over raised their tools over their heads in bravos.

Britt smiled and waved, ignoring the clenching of her gut as they rode farther and farther away. They had just reached the forest when Britt pulled Llamrei to a halt. "Dang it. Merlin I can't do it."

"Can't do what?" Merlin asked as their companions also stopped.

"I can't leave Guinevere at Camelgrance."

"I thought you hated her?"

"I do. She's a thoughtless, silly brat, but I can't expect my knights to go about saving maidens when I refuse to do the same," Britt sighed. "Plus, I want my Round Table."

"Still? As hideous as it is?"

"Yes."

"Very well, let us go back and tell her father. Do *not* agree to marry her, though," Merlin warned before holding a hand out to King Pellinore.

"Hurrah for King Arthur," Ywain cheered.

"My treatment of the lady is hardly something to be cheered," Britt said.

"Quite the contrary, it is remarkable. Most would be glad to see those they scorn in pain," Gawain said.

"I've said it before, but I suspect I shall be saying this for the rest of my life: you think too highly of me. Merlin, what are you doing?" Britt asked as King Pellinore placed a handful of coins on Merlin's palm.

"Just settling a bit of a bet," Merlin said, jingling the coins with satisfaction.

King Pellinore smiled widely at Britt. "No one could mistake your disdain for the lady. I thought for certain you would leave her behind. But Merlin knows you better, it would seem. You're a good man, Arthur. Lead on."

"All of you, stay here. I don't want Leodegrance dragging us back to his castle in his joy. We won't be but a few moments. Come along, Arthur," Merlin said, already riding back to Camelgrance.

Soldiers were still standing at attention, and the people were still cheering when Britt returned. "Are you staying longer after all?" King Leodegrance eagerly asked.

"No," Britt said, dismounting her mare. "If you will excuse my bluntness, but I ask that you would—sometime soon—send Guinevere to live at Camelot."

King Leodegrance's face lit up, and Britt quickly added, "I do not intend to marry her. Indeed, I will not marry…until I see all of Britain united," Britt said. She paused to smile at Merlin, proud of her quick-thinking.

Merlin nodded in concession and motioned for her to continue.

"Yes, so I will not marry for many years, if at all. But I have several nephews—princes, all of them—who will one day wish to marry. I desire to expose them to women of high birth and noble blood so they may choose carefully," Britt said.

King Leodegrance was thoughtful. "Princes, you say?"

"Yes. Sir Ywain—the heir of King Urien—and Gawain and his brothers—the sons of King Lot," Britt said.

"Lancelot du Lac and his cousins, Lionel and Bors, are also staying at Camelot, and they are the sons of King Ban and King Bors," Merlin added, ignoring the glare Britt shot at him.

"Really?" King Leodegrance asked, rubbing his hands with greed. "And aren't King Ban and King Bors rulers across the sea?"

"They are," Britt reluctantly said.

King Leodegrance nodded several times before he smiled. "Guinevere would be delighted to join your courts, My Lord. I will send her with an escort of men as soon as she is prepared"

"And the Round Table?" Britt asked.

"Will come with her as a token of our alliance," King Leodegrance said.

Everyone, most of all Britt, was shocked when Guinevere released a shriek of joy. "Thank you, Arthur. Thank you," she said, throwing herself at Britt.

The fiery-haired girl wept into Britt's doublet, alarming Merlin but affirming to Britt that she had made the right choice.

Every girl deserved to be saved, not just the ones Britt thought to be worthy.

"There, there," Britt said, patting Guinevere's head. "I would be honored to act as your guardian during your stay at Camelot."

"Should you change your mind and wish to marry her yourself, Arthur..." King Leodegrance started.

"Not until Britain is united," Britt firmly said.

"Yes, I see. Very well, then. Safe travels. Come, Guinevere. Stop crying, and let go of His Majesty," Leodegrance ordered.

Guinevere stepped back but smiled and wildly waved through her tears as Britt remounted Llamrei and once again headed for the woods.

"Arthur," Merlin tightly said.

"Hm?"

"You need to be more careful about whom you allow to be so close to you as to *touch* you," Merlin said, his voice sharp and delicate like thin ice.

"It doesn't matter. Guinevere knows."

"*SHE WHAT?*"

BRITT YAWNED in the afternoon sun. She tilted her back, nestling farther into the large haystack behind which she was hiding. She had returned to Camelot a week before. Merlin had just finally forgiven her for revealing her gender to Guinevere, releasing her from her kingly duties for the first time since her homecoming.

Britt heard her guards shift around her. Cavall, who was splayed out next to her, bumped her legs as he stood. "What is it?" she called.

"Merlin approaches, Milord," the captain of her guard said.

Britt grimaced and opened her eyes. "Can't you detain him?"

"We've seen too much of the magic he can do for me to attempt that, Milord."

"Very well," Britt grumbled. "Merlin, what brings you outside of Camelot's walls?" she asked when the wizard drew near.

Merlin squinted up at the sunlight. "Lancelot is looking for you," he said, patting Cavall on the head.

"I know."

"He intends to pledge his loyalty to you."

"Why do you think I'm hiding out in the farmland?" Britt asked.

Merlin chuckled and plopped down next to Britt, also leaning into the hay. "Scat," he said to Britt's guards.

The soldiers saluted him before walking out of hearing distance—although they still stood at attention with their weapons bared.

"It might not be as bad as you think."

"I seriously doubt that."

Merlin picked up a piece of straw and prodded Cavall with it when the massive dog settled back down on the ground. "Maybe…but both Ywain and Griflet have shaved."

"*What?*"

"'Tis true. They no longer sport those hideous, scraggily patches of facial hair they tried to pass off as beards," Merlin reported.

"But why?"

"It seems the ladies of Camelot coo over Lancelot, and it has spawned some jealousy."

"Merlin, no!" Britt said.

"It is out of my control."

"But it can't be!"

"Too late. It seems your fashion icon has arrived."

She groaned. "No, not Lancelot. Anyone but him."

Merlin laughed in deviant delight. "You must admit, he will make clean-shaven faces all the rage."

"The price is too high," Britt grumbled, nestling farther into the hay bale.

Merlin was silent for several moments before saying, "I've received word from Leodegrance. In two weeks time, Guinevere will set out for Camelot."

"Oh, goodie," Britt said wryly. "Sir Ulfius will arrange a room for her?" Britt asked.

"Yes. You do realize that in spite of your claim that you will not marry until Britain is united, everyone—from your allies to your knights—thinks you mean to marry her?"

"If they do, that is their problem," Britt said.

"You don't mind?"

"Not if it keeps the other ladies of my court from batting their eyes at me," Britt said. "It's not like Guinevere is going to have false expectations."

"No thanks to you," Merlin grunted.

"It will still work out," Britt said.

"Only if she is able to keep her mouth shut. Most ladies are dreadful gossips, you know. They twitter like birds in springtime at all hours of the day. Women are pests."

"Excuse me?"

"Oh, come now, you hardly count."

"*What?*" Britt said, sitting upright.

"Not that I see you as a man—you are too clean for that, especially since you insist on smelling like flowers," Merlin said in disgust.

"Then how exactly do you see me?" Britt demanded.

"Genderless?" Merlin tried.

Britt's elbow to his gut told him he guessed wrong.

"See, you do things like that and wonder why I don't see you as being quite female," Merlin wheezed.

Britt folded her arms across her chest and shut her eyes as she leaned back into the hay, ignoring the wizard.

"Arthur."

Britt did not stir.

"Arthur."

"…"

"Britt?"

Britt turned her head to the side and swatted a bug away from her face. Her eyes flew open when Merlin grasped her chin.

"I will admit defeat. Were you clothed like a lass and kitted up, you would be the most beautiful woman in England," Merlin said, his eyes held Britt's like hypnotic magnets. There was something in his expression that Britt hadn't seen before. It wasn't love—Britt shuddered to picture what love would look like on the young wizard—but there was honesty and truthfulness mixed with some kind of affection in his eyes.

Britt smiled as Merlin's hand slid along her jaw line. "It's not like you to exaggerate," she said.

"You still don't know how powerful your smiles are, do you?"

"My what?"

"Nothing," Merlin said, removing his hand from her face like she was a hot coal. "Enjoy your doze. When you come in for dinner, you will have to accept Lancelot's oath of loyalty."

"Must I?"

"You must."

Britt grumbled as Merlin lurched forward. "Wait, you aren't going to stay with me?"

"I wasn't planning on it."

"Do you have work to do?"

"Nothing dreadfully important. What, did another lass find out your secret?"

"No, we just haven't talked much since, well, I suppose since the plague of Lancelot descended upon us."

"You're right, but I was told you were up all last night pacing. You should sleep while you can," Merlin said.

"That's true," Britt said, muffling a yawn with her hand. "Wait, who gives you those reports?"

Merlin shook his head and settled back into the hay. "I will stay until you sleep," he decided.

"Thank you. I appreciate the company."

"All you appreciate is the fact that it means your guards will stand more than a horse's length from you."

"That, too."

Merlin laughed. "Pleasant dreams, lass."

Britt murmured a reply before she took another deep breath and shut her eyes.

Next to her, Merlin tapped two pieces of straw together as he looked out at the farmland surrounding Camelot.

AT THE MIDNIGHT WATCH, Lancelot stood on a castle wall, staring intently at the bright spot of wall across Camelot. He could see

King Arthur on the castle walkway—his guards standing at attention. The young king was practicing with his famed sword, which glimmered in the moonlight.

Lancelot's green eyes traced King Arthur's movements as he thoughtfully rested his hand on the pommel of his sword. "He does this every night?" Lancelot asked his cousins, never removing his gaze from the king.

"Just about, according to what the servants say," Lionel said.

"He's a popular one," Bors, Lancelot's younger cousin, said as he cleaned his fingernails with a dagger. "Could hardly get anyone to shut up about him whilst you were gone."

Lancelot tapped his sword and narrowed his eyes. "He is unlike anyone I've met before."

"So?"

"I do not think of that as a good thing," Lancelot said, finally dragging his eyes away from the young monarch.

Lionel shrugged. "Mayhap you are over-thinking him. He's a ruddy saint if half the reports of him are correct."

"That may be so, but I've never had much use for saints," Lancelot said.

"So why did you pledge yourself to him then?" Bors asked.

"For the adventure. Things are changing because of him. I would rather be around when there's a good fight to be had than to miss it by being stuffed back in a tower at home," Lancelot said.

"Ah, your father called you back home, then?"

"Yes. But he won't complain if I tell him I am staying at Camelot. Besides, I'm an opportunist. It will be interesting to see what I can make of young Arthur," Lancelot said, his smile slanted mockingly.

"Step carefully, cousin," Bors warned. "He has powerful allies."

"Aren't you just miffed he is even more popular with the ladies than you?" Lionel laughed.

Lancelot gave him a withering glare.

"Just saying," Lionel shrugged.

"Whatever the reason, I will stand with Arthur. For now," Lancelot decided, thoughtfully rubbing his chin.

"We'll stand with you then," Lionel said.

"Bors?" Lancelot asked in the silence.

"He's a good man," Bors finally said.

Lancelot chuckled and looked back at the pacing figure. "We shall see about that."

THE END

EMBITTERED EXTRA SCENES

This scene is supposed to take place on the way to Camelgrance, the day before Britt encounters King Pellinore at the riverbed and invites him to come with. The scene was supposed to show how self centered Lancelot is, and to illustrate how clueless Britt is about the physical shape of the Round Table. I originally planned to include this scene in the book as it has a nice bit of foreshadowing in the last few lines, but by the end of **Embittered** even I would have gladly smashed Lancelot in the head to silence him, so I decided it would be best not to push my readers' patience. Enjoy!

"WHEN I WAS eight I killed my first giant," Lancelot said.

"Oh, I'm sure," Britt muttered.

"It was a miraculous event, stunning and shocking for the grown men present. None had expected me to launch myself at the giant, but that is just what I did," Lancelot continued.

Britt stared hard at Merlin's back, willing him to turn around from his place at the front of the line and call for her. She badly needed a savior, and Sir Kay did not seem inclined to rescue Britt from Lancelot's endless supply of stories as the man was actually a decent knight.

"I was armed with nothing but two daggers. I dispatched the giant in a matter of moments, applying the sharp edges of my daggers to his neck."

Britt narrowed her eyes and stared harder at Merlin.

He didn't budge.

"To be fair, it was a small giant. But my feat has not been bested by another man—or child as I was really."

"How surprising," Britt said when she realized Lancelot was expecting a comment of some sort.

"It is, isn't it? I did kill a much larger giant, though, when I first set out with my cousins Lionel and Bors."

Britt's eyes glazed over as Lancelot launched into another story. She relaxed in the saddle, her shoulders slumping, and let her mind wander.

It was important to remember why she endured Lancelot's presence, and dared to venture forth in to Guinevere's domain. It was all for the Round Table.

She hadn't told Merlin, but she was planning to steal the table.

"It must come apart, or it wouldn't be able to fit through a door unless it is the size of a coffee table. I bet we could reassemble it in the hallway and roll it out," Britt mumbled. "We would have to keep rolling it down the road, though. That would get it very dirty…"

"—net couldn't properly hold back a giant of such size, so Lionel and I set out to wrestle it to the ground."

"Who will I allow to sit at the table?" Britt wondered. "It will have to be a limited amount of people, and it *certainly* won't include chatty, flighty foreign princes," Britt said under her breath. "But how will I able to invite Gawain to the Round Table and not him? Hmm…"

"After we killed that giant we discovered it was naught but a *babe*, and its father found us."

"It won't be a problem. He can't plan on staying long. I'll get rid of him before then. He would have to pledge himself to me, and I can't see *that* happening," Britt decided.

"—and I plunged my sword through his heart, killing him in one blow."

"Yep. I'll see Guinevere in Camelot before I accept an oath of fealty from *him*," Britt decided.

"What do you think of that, My Lord? Was it not an entertaining battle?" Lancelot finished.

"Oh certainly. Not," Britt said.

"What tales have you to tell of your strength and valor in battle?"

"Oh. Um."

"Arthur, come up here for a moment. I need to run over the plan with you," Merlin called right on cue.

Britt smiled in relief. "I apologize," she said to Lancelot before nudging Llamrei ahead. "Thank you, Merlin. You are a hero," Britt said when she reached the handsome wizard.

"Mmhmm. You owe me."

"Absolutely."

"And don't let that young buck fill your head with silly ideas. You **aren't** going to get a chance to ride off and challenge blackguard knights to battle. EVER. Am I clear?"

"Perfectly."

THIS NEXT SCENE depicts how Merlin, Lancelot, and Gawain got into Camelgrance after it was sealed up and prepped for a siege—with an unknowing Britt inside. I knew how Merlin got inside the castle, but I didn't include it because I try to keep the story with Britt, seeing things from her point of view. If I stray from her too many spoilers are to be had. But including this scene in the extras seems harmless enough, and

it lets you feel a little sympathy for Gawain and Lancelot and what they endured to get inside Camelgrance.

"THIS ISN'T FAIR, I want to go too," Ywain complained, straining forward.

"Rescue missions aren't about what's fair, boy. It's about what is *smart*," King Pellinore said, easily holding Ywain back by grabbing the collar of the young man's tunic.

"But why does Gawain get to go?" Ywain said, pursing his lips at his older cousin.

"Don't ask questions you don't want to know the answer to," Merlin said, the tip of his tongue hanging out of the corner of his mouth as stood on his tip toes and planted a hand on a Camelgrance's wall.

"But Merlin," Ywain said.

Sir Kay placed a hand on the younger knight's shoulder. "It is not wise to speak to a wizard when he is working magic," he said, nodding at Merlin.

Merlin ignored the comment and squinted up at the brick he was touching. "You will do what I want you to do," he said to the wall, almost falling into the brush hugging the stone structure.

"Father always said you have to be half mad to work magic," Ywain said.

"Ywain," Gawain scolded.

"Alright, lads. Here is the situation. I will be working two sets of simultaneous, powerful spells to get us inside this sorry excuse of a castle. It will take a great deal more of my power than I thought, so I can't take all three of you like I said I could. One of you will have to remain behind," Merlin said, brushing his clothes off.

"Gawain and I should go, if that is the case," Sir Kay said.

"Oh?" Lancelot asked.

"Arthur is our king and our sovereign. You have taken no

oaths to aid him, it is only natural that Gawain and I would be the ones to accompany Merlin," Sir Kay said, bowing slightly to Lancelot.

"I suppose that is true," Lancelot said with a half smile as he moved to stand with King Pellinore and the still struggling Ywain.

"We thank you for understanding," Gawain said, mimicking Sir Kay's bow.

"Right then, we should set off before the guards on the wall realize we've been standing out here for quite a while. Kay, Gawain, if you would stand here with me."

"How will you get us inside?" Sir Kay asked as he stood on Merlin's left side.

"I did a bit of trickery on the stone wall, so when I activate my spell it will let us walk through it."

"Brilliant," King Pellinore praised.

"Thank you," Merlin smugly said. "The problem is the wretched greenery,"

"Greenery?" Gawain asked.

"Yes. I know how to work a basic transparency spell on rock, live wood is an entirely different dragon to slay. Because I can't get the wood to let us walk through it, I've added a second spell which will shoot us up, letting us hop over the brush and into the wall."

"Hop? That doesn't sound too bad," Gawain said.

"We shall see," Sir Kay said, not as easily convinced.

"Right, hold on to me. At the count of three the spells will activate. You don't need to do anything, just stand there and relax. Try not to tense up when we collide with the wall," Merlin said.

"Collide?" Gawain asked.

"Here we go," Merlin said, ignoring the younger man's uneasy tone. "One, two, *three!*"

Unfortunately all did not go quite as planned.

Between the count of two and three Lancelot—who previously was relaxed and motionless, burst forward and grabbed hold of Sir Kay. He yanked him backwards—wrenching him off Merlin—before elbowing him in the chest and clinging to Merlin in his place.

Merlin, surprised by the sudden change and unable to stop his spells, accidentally poured a little more power than he meant to in the jump spell. Instead of 'hopping' over the bush as Gawain hoped, Merlin, Lancelot, and Gawain rocketed into the air, traveling at least twenty feet up before they zoomed towards the wall.

"Oh dear," Merlin muttered before he wildly gestured.

The wall hurtled closer. It must be confessed that both knights shut their eyes rather than see the looming structure. Passing through the stone was like walking through a particularly thick bit of fog, but both knights scraped or jostled a body part on a piece of the stone wall that did *not* have Merlin's magic coating it.

They were flung through the wall, landing on the (thankfully) steady roof of a cottage built against the wall. Merlin landed stiffly on his feet, but both Lancelot and Gawain crashed to the ground, rolling a bit.

"That was good luck. I sent us too high in the air, for a moment I thought we were going to hit the wall instead of pass through it. It's a good thing I was able to extend the area affected by the spell further up the wall," Merlin said, smoothing his hair.

"M-my head scraped the rock. I could feel my hair streaming against it," Lancelot said.

"That's what you get for upsetting my calculations," Merlin said, jamming his hands into the sleeves of his robe.

"Frightening," was all Gawain could say as he pushed himself up on his knees. He scuttled across the cottage roof, reaching the edge of it.

"It worked out in the end, I suppose. I hadn't thought of what might be on the other side of the wall. If we were any lower we may not have cleared this cottage. That would have been an uncomfortable realization," Merlin said, tapping his foot on the straw covered roof.

Gawain released a shaky breath and fell off the side of the roof while Lancelot stayed where he was—most likely paralyzed with fear.

"Good show, all around. So, shall we search for Arthur?" Merlin asked, hopping off the cottage.

Gawain shook his head and tried to stand. Up on the roof air leaked out of Lancelot in a high pitched whistle.

Merlin rolled his eyes. "Really, even Arthur has a better stomach for magic than you two. I will search alone, then. You weaklings recover," Merlin said before he set off at a brisk walk.

"Uncle Urien is right. Wizards must be h-half mad indeed," Gawain sputtered once Merlin was out of sight.

"Yes," Lancelot agreed. "At least half mad."

*THE FOLLOWING SCENE I actually thought through and planned for while writing **Embittered**, but I didn't include it because Britt isn't in it, and as I mentioned before I try to keep my scenes fixed on her. This scene occurs right before Sir Kay escorts Britt out to Duke Maleagent's camp to challenge him to a joust. It explains why Sir Kay decided Britt's borrowed horse was an acceptable mount. It was a blast to write, I hope you enjoy it.*

"I THOUGHT Arthur would be leaving shortly for his fight with Maleagant," Lancelot said as Sir Kay led him through the woods.

"He is," Sir Kay said.

"How can he ride off to his fight without his horse? And aren't you going with him?" Lancelot asked.

"We will be finished with our task before Gawain is done helping My Lord into his armor."

"I see. In that case, what are we doing?" Lancelot asked as they entered a small meadow.

"I want to see what kind of charger this borrowed mount is," Sir Kay said, hefting a lance in one hand and leading the milk white horse Merlin had bargained for in Camelgrance with the other.

"But why?"

"I need to know how well it can joust. My Lord must have a trustworthy steed."

"But I didn't think Arthur was going joust? And why would it matter how skilled it is? Any halfwit knight can joust," Lancelot said.

Sir Kay narrowed his eyes. "That is *King* Arthur to you, and never mind why."

"I don't understand," Lancelot said with a grieved sigh.

"You don't have to. Just stand right there," Sir Kay said before swinging up on the horse's back.

Lancelot shrugged as Sir Kay rode the horse to the far end of the meadow.

Sir Kay wheeled the horse around, lowered the lance, and the mount burst forward in a canter.

Lancelot shifted as Sir Kay and his mount charged across the meadow, their pace increasing rather than decreasing.

"Sir Kay," Lancelot shouted to his fellow knight. "Sir Kay," he tried again when the horse and rider still bore down on him.

Kay and the horse were maybe three horse lengths from him before Lancelot realized they weren't going to stop. "Sir Kay! KAY! What has gotten into you, man?" Lancelot yelled as he started running.

"Kay, **KAY**!" Lancelot said, his voice started to grow a subtle hint of desperation as Sir Kay and the milk white horse chased him across the meadow. "Stop it, turn off, *turn off*! KAY!"

Lancelot said, changing his strategy and fleeing to the trees when it became apparent that Kay was going to keep on chasing him.

Sir Kay barely avoided hitting him, and slowed the horse down to a trot, a walk, and then halted it altogether when the trees grew thick again. "Yes, this mount shall serve My Lord well," he said with great satisfaction.

"If you wanted to test its jousting skills I could have brought my horse and we could have had a practice match. That was dangerous," Lancelot said, leaning against a tree as he breathed deeply.

"Where would be the fun in that?" Kay asked, cuing the horse forward.

"You weren't really aiming for me, were you?" Lancelot asked, following behind. "Sir Kay?" he said when silence was his answer.

"The safety of My Lord will always be my priority, Lancelot," Sir Kay said, disappearing into the trees. "Always."

OF LANCELOT AND GUINEVERE

T he main problem I faced in *Embittered*, which actually started in *Enchanted*, was figuring out how to introduce Lancelot to Britt and my readers. Lancelot has appeared in every book—he's the knight Britt runs into when she first retrieves the sword and is running back to the tournament (You can go back and read it and see that he is dressed in his colors and his dapple grey horse is with him.) and he and his cousins are the knights Britt encounters in the woods when she is on her way to visit the Lady of the Lake. However, officially introducing him with his name was tricky.

There is very little information in the early Arthur stories about Lancelot's arrival at court. Usually it's never mentioned when he arrives, although his name pops up typically whenever Guinevere makes her entrance. In fact, in many stories Lancelot arrives with Guinevere. His name is first revealed as one of the knights sent to fetch Guinevere when she is brought to Camelot to marry Arthur. This gave me a free rein for my creativity in bringing Lancelot into Britt's life, but the timing had to be right.

On the other hand, there is far more information on Guinevere's arrival at Camelot. In some of the stories she first meets

Arthur when he's on his way to fight the Sable Knight, aka King Pellinore, so I tucked that story in *Enchanted*. However, in most legends the audience doesn't get to see Arthur meet Guinevere. Instead Arthur is pressed to find a wife and he talks about how he admires Guinevere and would like to marry her.

Before he marries her, Arthur always saves her father, King Leodegrance, from various enemies, usually King Ryence. I decided to use Maleagent in order to introduce him to the readers, because in future books he will be returning.

The Story of King Arthur and His Knights by Howard Pyle is one of the few "modern" (I use that term loosely as the book was written a century ago) books that expands on the enemies Arthur saves King Leodegrance from.

The one thing that almost all the stories agree on is that King Leodegrance owned the Round Table, and he gave it to Arthur as a marriage gift, *because then he didn't have to send a dowry with Guinevere*. (Usually her dowry is lands, but sometimes its money.) I was shocked when I read of King Leodegrance's greed in multiple stories. The sad thing is that no one else seems to see how horrible that is. Some stories even say Leodegrance was thrilled to marry Guinevere off to Arthur because he didn't have to lose money over the marriage, *not* because Arthur was a great King and a good man.

When I discovered that it made me rethink my planned character for Guinevere, and it gave emotional tension to *Embittered*. Britt needed to learn that everyone, her allies included, isn't as honorable as her court and her friends.

I'm happy with the way *Embittered* played out. It allowed readers to see why Guinevere is the way she is, and it added realism to a type of story where usually everyone is either excessively good or vile and evil.

But what about Lancelot's character? Why do I make him publically act like a handsome dandy, and then in the last scene reveal that he's actually quite cunning?

I pondered Lancelot's character for a long time. All stories agree that he is Arthur's best knight, and most stories paint him as Arthur's best friend. Typically he's more on the chattery/poetic side, so I wanted to include that in my story. But by looking objectively at his role in Arthurian lore I had to face the facts. It takes a certain kind of ruthlessness to sleep with your best friend's wife. To be able to do that and still face Arthur and act like his best friend means Lancelot had to be capable of being incredibly cruel. Guinevere never hides her admiration for Lancelot, but Lancelot is acknowledged as being a ladies man and a flirt. He covered his romantic attachment to Guinevere, pulling off the worst backstab in the history of fiction.

Make no mistake, Lancelot might pretend to be dashing and gallant, but he is not an idiot. He's even more calculating than Merlin, and twice as willing to hurt people to get what he wants.

ON THE OBSERVATIONS OF SIR KAY

K ay rubbed his eyes and leaned back in the rough wooden chair. He sighed and pushed the two flickering candles arranged on the table back to make room for a logbook. It was new and almost cost him a fortune, but Kay couldn't stomach writing about this new future king, Britt Arthurs, in the book he previously used to record his foster-brother's progress.

Kay mended his quill and removed the lid of his inkwell before he started writing.

Today Merlin cast a spell to summon a proper king from the future. I had my doubts it would work, as the future king would have to touch the sword, but Merlin's magic pulled through. Or so he claims.

The future king is no man at all, but a woman. She is older than me and arrived wearing odd, indecent clothes. She accepted Merlin's explanation without much fuss, and indeed she seems to be an agreeable person. She speaks well, but she uses words and refers to locations and things that I have never heard of, a side effect of being from the future I should think.

Nice as she may be, Merlin is mad to try and place a woman on the throne, even if he is the one that is really ruling.

KAY SIGHED AGAIN and put his writing materials away. "Arthur, you fool," he said with no feeling. His simmering anger with his foster brother had finally burned away to leave only regret.

∾

KAY RUBBED his hands together as he watched Britt scoot closer to the inn fireplace. It was in the evening hours of Christmas Day, and Merlin and his men were celebrating in the inn common room.

Knights toasted to the success, not so much in Britt's ability to pull the sword and prove her worthiness in becoming King of Britain as in Merlin taking the first step towards unifying the country's.

Kay swept crumbs off the table he sat at and set down his logbook and inks.

TODAY WAS the day of the tournament. Merlin insisted on making Britt Arthurs pull the sword as part of an elaborate play which I doubt more than a handful of people noticed and amused only himself.

He wanted me to take the sword from Britt Arthurs and go to my father, claiming I had pulled the sword. A pox on Merlin! What knight who has a healthy respect for the heavens would dare come between the God appointed King and the sign of his worthiness? I know Merlin plans to grace me with the influential title of seneschal, but sometimes I wonder what I did to deserve to be the butt of his jokes.

I must confess that Britt Arthurs is more competent than I gave her credit for. She has not been blinded by Merlin's persuasive statements and admits in wry humor that she's aware she won't be ruling. She is guarded in her meetings with myself and my father. I must get her to be forthcoming somehow, for I greatly need to find out if she has any defensive skills at all.

One of the reasons I was against a woman as a king is because I feared she would be easy to kill. If I could teach Britt Arthurs how to wield a dagger, perhaps it would give her a fighting chance.

As Kay wiped his feather quill clean Britt plopped down on a bench opposite from him. "I can't decide if Merlin is a raving genius, or a lucky idiot," she announced, watching Merlin laugh in good humor as he toasted a knight.

"Wizards are often an unfortunate combination of both," Kay grunted.

Britt started at Kay for a moment before her lips cracked into a rather pleasing grin. "You may be right."

≈

Kay winced as he rolled his shoulders, attempting to relax his bruised, stiff muscles. "I did not think my duties as seneschal would include being beaten senseless," he grumbled, hiding the pleased quirk of his lips behind his mustache as he retrieved his logbook, quill, and ink.

Today Britt Arthurs has surpassed my greatest hopes. My father— being the inquisitive soul he is—asked Britt Arthurs if she knew how to ride.

She does, not very well if one listens to her, but I am certain she must be good based on her modest description of her skills with the sword.

I asked her to fight so I could properly gage her skills—after all I must calculate how many guards will need to be posted around her. How foolish I was!

Britt Arthurs is the best swordsman I have ever encountered. She moves with a swiftness that is unparalleled, and never blocks or parries a blow. She moves forward, constantly pushing with endless attacks. If I moved fast enough I could occasionally attempt a blow, but she would always counter strike or—in a rare case—dodge.

Facing Britt Arthurs with a sword is, I will admit, terrifying. She does not have the bloodlust or the intent to kill as many men have. She is, instead, far worse. When she lashes at you it is like facing a dragon. There is no cruelty in her eyes, only the promise of a swift end.

She has not the strength necessary to wield some of the more brutal weapons, like a mace or spear, and she knows nothing—not even the rules—of jousting. Her utter hopelessness in these various weapons, though, is eclipsed by her skill with the sword.

She does not appear to know her own talent as she claimed I was holding back during our brief skirmishes. (If only that were so.)

It was disheartening to be so soundly beat by a woman, but I am so relieved that Britt Arthurs will not die easily that I am not much repulsed.

I must think of a creative way to guard her, for she jealously protects her privacy. Guards posted to her will not be a popular rule, but what else can I do?

~

KAY STUMBLED into his room in the wee hours of the morning. He stared at his bed for a few moments before shaking his head. "No, it is important to write while the memories are fresh," he said, making his way to the small writing table.

TODAY, the day of Pentecost, my Lord Britt Arthurs was crowned King of Britain. King Lot, King Urien, King Pellinore, and King Ryence all protested as expected, but it was still done.

During the celebration feast my Lord Britt Arthurs granted boons and such. She gave me the post of seneschal. I know Merlin made the decisions of whom to post to what positions, but I am honored by the title all the same.

My Lord Britt Arthurs did buck orders and announced Sir Bedivere as her marshal. Merlin was displeased—likely more over my Lord Britt Arthurs making a decision without his say so—but Sir Bedivere does not seem to be a bad sort of knight. I have already sent out inquires about his character and skills. I have heard back from my London contacts, who speak favorably of him, but I will have to wait until we arrive at my Lord Britt Arthurs' new castle—which is yet unnamed for Merlin gave little thought to it when he ordered construction some 10 years ago —to conduct a more detailed character study.

Preparations for war are underway as King Lot and his sniveling brother King Urien insulted my Lord Britt Arthurs at the celebration feast. Something of a fist fight broke out during the feast. I am sorry I did not get to do more than knock King Urien to the ground. I should have liked to shake him until he was dazed, but my Lord Britt Arthurs and Merlin ended the fight before I had time.

I am taking pains to record the London price of grain and ale and other necessary provisions that an army will need. The prices are somewhat steep, I feel, so I will inquire in other parts of Britain as soon as possible.

In more favorable news the training of Cavall goes well. The kennel master has been training him in protective and battle maneuvers since I sent a letter to him in February. He claims the dog is not overly aggressive, but I shall have to judge for myself before I gift him to my Lord Britt Arthurs.

I am still well pleased with the idea, for a dog will be able to follow my Lord Britt Arthurs everywhere—even into her private quarters, where I dare not send guards. Additionally, my Lord Britt Arthurs will *most likely be less offended by a dog she believes I mean to be a pet than a squad of soldiers.*

Finally, I—and most all of the knights here in London—made the discovery that my Lord Britt Arthurs has another tool with which she can break a man: her smile.

I would be sorely embarrassed to write this, for it sounds like worshipful dribble, but my Lord has a lethal smile. The smile is entirely too feminine, but Merlin's rumor that my Lord has faery blood makes most perceive it as an enchanting smile. I have never seen such straight, white teeth, and my Lord's entire face and countenance seems to change when she smiles. I suspect she is in a state of constant apprehension, for I did not notice how tense she is until she relaxed in her smile.

I suspect she will unknowing swindle many a knight change many a mind with the smile. Merlin is already amusing himself, trying think of the ways he use my Lord's new found charisma.

Kay frowned as he reread the paragraph. "Errors, I'll have to rewrite it," he said, glancing at his bed before he hunched over the logbook. Not five minutes later Sir Kay was sprawled across his desk, clenching the quill in his sleep.

...HOPE we can claim a suitable sword for my Lord. Faery swords are known for being temperamental, but I believe the right one will be instrumental for my Lord's welfare. It grieved her so to give up the sword she pulled from the stone.

Tomorrow I will record the details of my Lord's magical weapon, and my first impressions of the castle Merlin has built for my Lord.

Kay put away his writing materials and waited until the ink dried before he shut the book. He arranged the saddle packs behind him so he could sleep propped up, and settled down to doze as the campfire crackled and his father snored.

He was pulled from sleep some hours later when Britt sat

upright, a strangled gasp exiting her chest. She was wide eyed and mussed, but eventually her posture slumped as she relaxed.

Kay nodded when she met his gaze and he shut his eyes. He was surprised when he heard rustling as Britt went through a pack. His eyes popped open and he watched Britt unearth a thick, strangely covered book.

Britt flipped through the pages, stopping abruptly. She read from it—murmuring softly under her breath.

Kay watched curiously, but his curiosity turned to worry when the book fell from Britt's hand like a stone. Britt was pale, and her eyes were hazy with confusion and terror.

When she picked up the book again Kay stood. He hesitated, intending to take a step towards her, before retreating and approaching his father—who had suspiciously stopped snoring when Britt started paging through her book.

"Father," Kay quietly said.

"I know, what's wrong?" Sir Ector said, putting aside the pretenses of sleep as he stood.

"I don't know," Kay admitted.

Sir Ector patted Kay on the shoulder before he stood and picked his way around the fire. "Britt?"

When the frightened woman looked up Sir Ector crouched down. "Lass, you're crying. What's wrong?"

Britt burst into heart wrenching tears.

Kay hurried to the horses, affectionately patting his hobbled stallion when it blearily blinked at him.

Kay winced as he leaned against his mount. The raw grief of Britt's sobs were like a sword to his gut. He glanced back at the fire.

Merlin was up now, but Sir Ector held Britt in a fatherly embrace, speaking to her in the soothing tones he used with small children and hurt animals.

Kay grimaced again when Britt cried louder. It occurred to him that while he marveled over Britt's hidden skills and talents and busied himself with his new duties he never dwelled on the personal sacrifice she had made by becoming king.

"I won't let this happen again," Kay vowed, his words frosted with Britt's tears in the otherwise quiet darkness.

~

SOME WEEKS later Kay looked up from his calculations—he was trying to estimate the cost of lady's maids with enough discretion to keep their mouths shut—and watched Britt eat.

The tall monarch stared at the ceiling as she slipped Cavall a piece of egg. She yawned and shook her head slightly before she grabbed her wine cup. "Sir Kay, am I holding open court today?"

"I apologize, I do not know, my Lord," Kay said.

Britt leaned back in her chair, slipping her enormous dog another piece of food. "There's no need to apologize, you aren't my secretary, but thank you," she said before she stared at her pewter plate.

Kay pushed away his sheet of calculations and unearthed his logbook. His records on the new King were growing so detailed it was easier to write throughout the day than wait until the evening. Britt was the only one who showed any interest in the logbook, and he didn't have to worry about her ever reading it—she couldn't read his writing.

My Lord Britt Arthurs is troubled. I cannot say for certain, but I suspect she is homesick for her time. The captain of the guard squad that is posted to my Lord during the night has informed me that she does not sleep, but instead roams the castle walls. I followed my Lord and her guards twice at a distance. She appears to be restless and disheartened.

I fear the lack of sleep will weaken her constitution. I must say something to Merlin about it.

At least Britt is well enough to eye me balefully whenever she complains of her guards. I am glad her insomnia does not affect her personality, but I am gladder still she hasn't yet figured out Cavall's purpose as a guard dog.

Note: I must find and train a secretary for my Lord.

❦

KAY SNAPPED awake and rubbed the sleepy haze from his eyes before he blearily looked around his desk. There were lists of soldier enlistment, weapon costs, provisions purchases, and detailed maps of the area Merlin and his men had selected to serve as base camp.

Kay leaned back in his chair and glanced at his Britt Arthurs logbook. He hadn't written in it since Merlin left to magic King Ban and Bors' 10,000 mounted men across the ocean. He hadn't even had a chance to report his impressions of Roen—Britt's new horse. (Who was really becoming more of a pet to her than a warsteed.)

Kay sighed before he leaned back over his sheets of figures and numbers. "Later," he said.

Internally Kay promised himself he was *not* delaying the record keeping because then he would be forced to face the fact that they were going to place Britt Arthurs in the middle of a bloody battle.

❦

KAY WATCHED BRITT THROW A STICK. Cavall dutifully fetched it and brought it back to her, earning himself a pat on the head.

Kay smiled briefly before he returned his attention to his logbook and finished his entry for the day.

My Lord appears to bear no ill marks from the war. She was not physically hurt, but I had feared all the blood and death would affect her. It is good Merlin brought her back early—although I wish he had taken a squad of soldiers with him.

Young Ywain follows my Lord like a puppy. His admiration of her grows on a daily basis. Merlin sees this too and has begun studying Britt more thoughtfully. He asks for her opinion now before making final decisions.

Sir Bodwain's attitude towards my Lord has shifted as well, for he now treats her with a great deal of respect instead of toleration. I do not know what has changed his mind, but I am glad for it.

Writing this down has made me note how my Lord's knights and advisors have changed, but I do not think my Lord has changed at all. She is still easy going and strong both physically and mentally. Perhaps even I do not give her enough credit, for she is but one person and she has changed the fate of an entire country.

Kay looked up from his writing to watch Britt throw the stick again. Cavall retrieved it, eliciting praise and a hug from Britt.

Merlin was circling Britt, speaking to her although the monarch clearly was not paying attention. As if to prove the point Britt turned and called out, "Kay, when are we going to go on our daily ride? I have a carrot I've been holding onto for Roen and it's going to turn to mush soon if I keep sitting on it like I have been."

Kay glanced at his log book and smiled. "Whenever you wish, my Lord."

"Let's go now, then."

"I object, you still haven't learned how to properly bow," Merlin said.

"I'm King, why do I need to know how to bow?"

"There is that," Merlin grudgingly admitted.

"Come on, Sir Kay. Let's go," Britt said, hurrying through the courtyard before Merlin could come up with a rebuff.

"As you wish, my Lord."

ACKNOWLEDGMENTS

I started writing the *King Arthurs* series in 2013—the very first year of my writing career—all because of a poll I posted on my blog. In the poll I asked my Champions which series they would be the most interested in. King Arthurs was one of the options, and won with a whopping eleven votes. (For reference, the last character poll I held had over 250 readers checking in to vote.)

Those eleven voters inspired a series that included six novellas, one full-length novel, and gathered one of the most loyal fanbases I have the pleasure of claiming.

Over the years I've received hundreds of messages about Britt Arthurs and her boys. I'm so humbled to learn how they've inspired others, and I'm always happy to hear how they make readers laugh.

And none of this would exist if it weren't for those eleven voters who were sweet enough to follow me—a new-to-the-scene author with only a few books to her name. Thank you, Champions. When I say you impact my writing, I *really* mean it.

The Elves of Lessa:

Red Rope of Fate

Royal Magic

King Arthur and Her Knights:

Enthroned

Enchanted

Embittered

Embark

Enlighten

Endeavor

Endings

Three pack 1 (Enthroned, Enchanted, Embittered)

Three pack 2 (Embark, Enlighten, Endeavor)

Robyn Hood:

A Girl's Tale

Fight for Freedom

The Magical Beings' Rehabilitation Center:

Vampires Drink Tomato Juice

Goblins Wear Suits

The Lost Files of the MBRC

Other Novels

Life Reader

ABOUT THE AUTHOR

K. M. Shea is a fantasy-romance author who never quite grew out of adventure books or fairy tales, and still searches closets in hopes of stumbling into Narnia. She is addicted to sweet romances, witty characters, and happy endings. She also writes LitRPG and GameLit under the pen name, A. M. Sohma.

Printed in Great Britain
by Amazon